PENGUIN CLASSICS

THE TALE OF GENJI

MURASAKI SHIKIBU was a lady of the Heian court of eleventh-century Japan.

ROYALL TYLER, an American as well as an Australian, recently retired from the Australian National University, where he taught Japanese language and literature for many years. He has a B.A. from Harvard University and a Ph.D. from Columbia University and has also taught at Harvard, Stanford, and the University of Wisconsin.

MURASAKI SHIKIBU

The Tale of Genji

ABRIDGED

Edited and Translated by
ROYALL TYLER

PENGUIN BOOKS

PENGUIN BOOKS

Published by the Penguin Group

Penguin Group (USA) Inc., 375 Hudson Street, New York, New York 10014, U.S.A.
Penguin Group (Canada), 90 Eglinton Avenue East, Suite 700, Toronto,
Ontario, Canada M4P 2Y3 (a division of Pearson Penguin Canada Inc.)
Penguin Books Ltd, 80 Strand, London WC2R 0RL, England
Penguin Ireland, 25 St Stephen's Green, Dublin 2, Ireland (a division of Penguin Books Ltd)
Penguin Group (Australia), 250 Camberwell Road, Camberwell,
Victoria 3124, Australia (a division of Pearson Australia Group Pty Ltd)
Penguin Books India Pvt Ltd, 11 Community Centre, Panchsheel Park,
New Delhi–110 017, India
Penguin Group (NZ), cnr Airborne and Rosedale Roads, Albany,
Auckland 1310, New Zealand (a division of Pearson New Zealand Ltd)
Penguin Books (South Africa) (Pty) Ltd, 24 Sturdee Avenue,
Rosebank, Johannesburg 2196, South Africa

Penguin Books Ltd, Registered Offices:
80 Strand, London WC2R 0RL, England

First published in the United States of America by Viking Penguin,
a member of Penguin Putnam Inc. 2001
Published in Penguin Books 2003
This abridged edition published 2006

1   3   5   7   9   10   8   6   4   2

LIBRARY OF CONGRESS CATALOGING-IN-PUBLICATION DATA
Murasaki Shikibu, b. 978?
[Genji monogatari. Selections]
The tale of Genji : abridged / Murasaki Shikibu; edited and translated by Royall Tyler.
p.   cm.—(Penguin classics)
Includes bibliographical references.
Contents: The paulownia pavilion (Kiritsubo)—The broom tree (Hahakigi)—The twilight beauty
(Yūgao)—Young Murasaki (Wakamurasaki)—Beneath the autumn leaves (Momiji no ga)—
Under the cherry blossoms (Hana no en)—Heart-to-heart (Aoi)—The green branch (Sakaki)—
Suma (Suma)—Akashi (Akashi)—The pilgrimage to Sumiyoshi (Miotsukushi)—
The picture contest (Eawase).
ISBN 0 14 30.3949 0
I. Tyler, Royall. II. Title. III. Series.
PL788.4.G4A6 2006
895.6'314—dc22 2005048742

Printed in the United States of America

Contents

List of Maps and Diagrams   vii
Introduction   ix
Main Characters   xxi

PROLOGUE: Genji on the Art of Fiction   1

1. The Paulownia Pavilion
(Kiritsubo)   Abridged   4

2. The Broom Tree (Hahakigi)   Complete   18

3. *The Cicada Shell*
(Utsusemi)   [Omitted]

4. The Twilight Beauty
(Yūgao)   Slightly abridged   54

5. Young Murasaki
(Wakamurasaki)   Complete   87

6. *The Safflower*
(Suetsumuhana)   [Omitted]

7. Beneath the Autumn
Leaves (Momiji no Ga)   Complete   128

8. Under the Cherry
Blossoms (Hana no En)   Complete   152

9. Heart-to-Heart (Aoi)   Abridged   162

10. The Green Branch (Sakaki)   Complete   186

11. *Falling Flowers*
(Hanachirusato)   [Omitted]

12. Suma (Suma)   Abridged   225

13. Akashi (Akashi)   Slightly abridged   253

14. The Pilgrimage to
    Sumiyoshi (Miotsukushi)   Slightly abridged   283

    15. A Waste of Weeds
        (Yomogiu)   [Omitted]

    16. At the Pass (Sekiya)   [Omitted]

17. The Picture Contest
    (Eawase)   Complete   305

Further Reading   325

Maps and Diagrams

Places Mentioned in the Tale   321
The City   322
The Inner Palace   323
A Ranking Nobleman's House   324
Inside the Main House   324

Introduction

The Tale of Genji is the oldest novel still recognized today as a major masterpiece, and it ranks in Japan as do the Homeric epics, the works of Shakespeare, Proust's *Remembrance of Things Past*, and so on, elsewhere. Being rich, diverse, and very long (fifty-four chapters, well over a thousand pages), it cannot be collapsed successfully into a volume this size. For this abridgment I have therefore selected twelve widely read early chapters, through chapter 17. I have omitted chapters 3, 6, 11, 15, and 16, as well as brief passages elsewhere that allude to them. Many readers feel that the heart of the book is to be found in chapters 34 through 36, but appreciation of this complex part of the work requires knowledge of what precedes it. Others value the last ten chapters, but by that time Genji, whose name gives the work its title, has been dead a decade or so. The early chapters vividly evoke him as a young man and leave him at his first moment of triumph. I have also included, as a sort of prologue, the famous passage from chapter 25 in which Genji, speaking for the author herself, discusses the art of fiction.

Names are rare in the original text of *The Tale of Genji* and likewise in my complete translation, for reasons I have explained in the introduction to it. In this abridgment, however, I have adopted the centuries-old nicknames used by readers to designate the major characters, and have sought in other ways as well to make all identities immediately clear.

THE AUTHOR

Born about 973 into the middle-level aristocracy that supplied provincial governors, Murasaki Shikibu belonged to a minor branch of the powerful Fujiwara family. A daughter's given name usually went unrecorded in the genealogies, and so Murasaki Shikibu is only a nickname. "Shikibu" ("Bureau of Ceremonial") refers to a post once held by her father, while "Murasaki" is the name of her tale's fictional heroine.

Her father, Fujiwara no Tametoki (died 1029), served as governor in the provinces of Harima, Echizen (to which she accompanied him in 996), and Echigo. He was also a scholar of Chinese. She married in 998 or 999 and was widowed in 1001. Her daughter Katako, later known as Daini no Sanmi, was probably born in 999 and may have died about 1080. About 1006, Murasaki Shikibu was called to serve Empress Akiko, no doubt because of her talent for writing fiction. The last record mentioning her is dated 1013, and she may have died the next year. Apart from *The Tale of Genji* she left diary fragments (*Murasaki Shikibu nikki,* much of which describes events at the palace in 1008) and a personal poetry collection (*Murasaki Shikibu shū*), which was probably compiled after her death.

Nothing indicates when Murasaki Shikibu began her tale or when she finished it, but her diary suggests that the work as it existed in 1007 or 1008 was hers, and she has been recognized ever since as the author of all fifty-four chapters. However, internal evidence suggests that these chapters were not all written in their present order. *The Tale of Genji* contains much brilliant writing, but it also leaves an impression of brilliant editing.

Murasaki Shikibu's sole authorship has seldom been questioned, but the evidence for it is not conclusive. The tale her diary mentions was probably not the whole work, and she may have continued writing for years after that. At any rate, something like the present text existed in 1021, when a young girl returned from a distant province to the capital and received a complete copy of it from her aunt. Later on, in an autobiographical memoir entitled *Sarashina nikki,* she described the joy of reading it. Her "over fifty chapters" suggests the present fifty-four, but no manuscript from that time survives. In the early thirteenth century a scholar collected as many copies as he could, and, finding them corrupt, set about compiling a restored text of his own. All modern editions are ultimately based on his version.

A SUMMARY OF THE TALE

A major ambition of any ranking gentleman in the world of *The Tale of Genji*—that of the court in the imperial city that is now Kyoto—was to present a daughter to the Emperor or the Heir Apparent. For this reason the Emperor normally had a range of recognized relationships with women, less because of sexual acquisitiveness on his part than because he was required to make his prestige relatively widely accessible to the members of the upper aristocracy. Below his single Empress he had several Consorts and, lower still, a number of Intimates. His Mistress of Staff, in theory a palace official, could also be in practice a junior wife. These imperial women were not equal. An Empress was normally appointed from among the Consorts, but by no means did all the Consorts have any realistic hope of such success, and the Intimates had none at all. Their birth rank was too low, and they lacked the necessary weight of political support.

Genji, the hero of the tale, is an Emperor's son by an Intimate who has lost her father and so has no support of any kind beyond the Emperor's personal devotion to her. It is not enough. The Emperor longs to appoint Genji Heir Apparent over his firstborn son, but he knows that the court would never stand for it. He therefore decides to remove Genji entirely from the imperial family by giving him a surname (the Japanese Emperors have none) so that he can serve the realm as a commoner and a senior government official.

The surname Minamoto was first conferred on a historical Emperor's son in 814. When the boy receives it from his father (chapter 1) he becomes "a Genji"—that is to say, a bearer of the Minamoto (*gen*, another reading of the same character) name (*ji*). This device allows him to belong to both realms, the imperial and the common, and so gives him maximum scope as a character.

Some readers feel that *The Tale of Genji* is more about the women in it—their feelings, their experiences, their fates—than about Genji himself. Nonetheless it is to Genji that the narrative returns again and again during his life. He is its reference point. That is why this summary will follow his story, passing over in silence along the way a great many characters and scenes. Its purpose is simply to orient a reader of the tale.

At the end of chapter 1, Genji is married to Aoi, the daughter of a particularly powerful courtier. No one consults his feelings on the matter, and he is really too young for the marriage to affect him much. His wife continues to live at her father's, which was normal, while he remains in residence at the palace. His mother died too soon after his birth for him to have known her, but he hears that his father's future Empress (Fujitsubo) resembles her closely, and in his earliest adolescence he comes to adore her. In time he will secretly make love to her, and their son will succeed to the throne.

Still, Fujitsubo is really beyond his reach, and he longs for someone who can be his alone. He finds this special love in a little girl (Fujitsubo's niece) who looks just like her. This is Murasaki, then about ten. He brings her up personally, and when she is old enough he marries her. She is the true, great love of his life, and her death (chapter 40) destroys him. In the meantime, however, he will have known many other women.

As a boy Genji begins to love Fujitsubo because people say she looks like his mother, and he is aware that Murasaki's resemblance to Fujitsubo makes her uncannily attractive to him. Much has been made of these substitutions, some readers having even affirmed that all Genji's women are stand-ins for his mother; but the narrative up to the time of his death does not really encourage that view. Fujitsubo dies in chapter 19, and she vanishes from his reported thoughts after chapter 20.

In chapter 2 the teenage Genji listens while three young men share the secrets of their love lives. This is the famous "rating women on a rainy night" conversation, which opens his eyes to wider possibilities. Later in the same chapter he goes exploring, and in several succeeding ones (not all included in this abridgment) he begins further affairs. As a result he has been called a playboy, a profligate, or worse. However, these chapters are also thoroughly entertaining, presenting as they do a wide range of youthful amorous folly, in a series of episodes ranging from tragic obsession to utter, hilarious disaster. In any case, Genji is generally loyal to his loves, as the narrator repeatedly observes.

Genji the lover is devastatingly handsome, charming, and eloquent, and he seems to enjoy throughout his life unlimited material means. As a very young man he has little weight or responsibility in the world at large, but increasing age and rank, as well as his extraordinary natural gifts, soon begin to make him a political force, hence to stiffen political opposition against him. Being Genji, always out for adventure, he cannot resist making love to one of the daughters (Oborozukiyo) of his chief political enemy, and disaster strikes when the gentleman finds him in bed with her. Unfortunately, the girl's older sister (the Kokiden Consort, the Heir Apparent's mother) is not only powerful but evil-tempered. She sets out immediately to destroy Genji, and he has to retreat into self-exile.

He goes to Suma, a stretch of shore on the Inland Sea that is now included within the city of Kobe, and since he is in disgrace he must leave Murasaki behind. The narrative dwells on the poignancy of his suffering as he languishes in the wilds. Then a great storm threatens his very life. He has strange dreams of his late father and of supernatural beings. As soon as the storm subsides, the eccentric and astonishingly wealthy Akashi Novice arrives by boat to invite him farther along the shore, to a place called Akashi. Genji accepts.

At Akashi, Genji comes to know the Akashi Novice's daughter (the Akashi Lady), who is pregnant when at last he is called back to the City. He already has a son by Aoi, who has died some years ago, and of course there is also the future Emperor Reizei, his secret son by Fujitsubo. This new child, his last, is a girl; in time, after Reizei's long reign, she will become the Empress. It is she who will lift Genji toward the supreme good

fortune of a ranking nonimperial noble: that of being the grandfather of an Emperor.

After his triumphant return from exile (chapter 13), Genji is
above all a man of power. Although still susceptible to the
charms of certain women, he does not actually consummate
any new affairs. He seems concerned mainly with beauty and
prestige.

His only serious courtship between chapters 14 and 33 is
addressed to Princess Asagao, with whom he clearly had some
sort of relationship as a very young man (chapter 2). This
courtship comes early (chapter 20), it does not last long, and it
fails. Wondering why he tries at all, readers have advanced ex-
planations mainly connected with nostalgia for Fujitsubo. Perhaps his rapidly rising stature has reminded him that although
he loves Murasaki deeply, she is not really worthy before the
world (as Princess Asagao would be) of the figure he has become.

By chapter 33 Genji has risen to extraordinary heights. He
has built a magnificent complex of four interconnected man-
sions, each linked with one of the four seasons and housing a
lady important to him, on land that seems to have passed to
him from the late Rokujō Haven, a former lover or his. This is
his incomparable Rokujō ("Sixth Avenue") estate. Still more remarkably, Emperor Reizei has appointed him Honorary Retired Emperor. Genji now towers over his world.

Then, in chapter 34, Genji responds to an appeal from his
half brother, Retired Emperor Suzaku. As an ineffectual young
Emperor, Suzaku was forced by his mother to persecute Genji
and his allies. Now he means to renounce the world. His favorite daughter, the Third Princess, is still young and immature,
and he therefore wants Genji to marry her. Genji agrees. Perhaps Genji hopes for a new, younger Murasaki, since this girl,
too, is Fujitsubo's niece. However, she is also a prize sought
by the most ambitious young men of the court, and she has the
one thing Murasaki lacks: the rank to be a fitting wife even for
an Honorary Retired Emperor.

Alas, she offers nothing else, since personally she is a nonen-
tity. Too late, Genji realizes he has made a bad mistake. Even he

cannot afford to slight Suzaku's daughter, but when Murasaki becomes ill, he abandons the Third Princess for weeks on end to look after Murasaki. In time this causes a new disaster. One of the Third Princess's disappointed suitors (Kashiwagi) makes love to her while Genji is away (chapter 35).

Genji soon finds out, and he is furious. To make matters worse, the Third Princess is pregnant. In time she bears Kaoru, a boy wrongly assumed by the world to be Genji's son. Kashiwagi soon dies of guilt and shame, and the Third Princess becomes a nun. Meanwhile Murasaki is still ill. Genji's new marriage has been a catastrophe.

Murasaki dies two or three years later, in her early forties. Genji, then in his early fifties, survives her as a mere shell of his former self. After the reader sees him for the last time (chapter 41) he apparently leaves the world, retires to a temple, and dies a year or two later.

The last thirteen chapters pick up the tale again after a gap of about eight years. Several major characters have disappeared from the scene. Chapter 42 reintroduces, as young men, Kaoru and Genji's grandson Prince Niou, a son of the daughter (now Empress) born long ago at Akashi. Niou and Kaoru are fast friends, and from chapter 45 on they are rivals in love.

After experiencing bitter failure at court, the Eighth Prince, a widower, has retired with his two daughters to Uji, a few hours' ride south of the City. There, beside the Uji River, he has sought refuge in religion, and the rumor of his noble piety reaches Kaoru, who also feels vaguely out of place in the world. In chapter 45 Kaoru begins visiting the Eighth Prince and hears at last, from an old woman, the secret of his own birth. He also catches a glimpse of the Prince's daughters and longs for the elder (Ōigimi). The Eighth Prince then dies. When Kaoru tells his friend Niou about the sisters, Niou begins courting the younger one (Naka no Kimi) and soon manages to make love to her.

This should commit Niou to Naka no Kimi, but he can seldom make the trip to Uji, and his prolonged absences convince both sisters that he has only been toying with her. Ōigimi becomes certain that if she ever accepts Kaoru she will suffer the same fate, and she decides not to live any longer. At the end of chapter 47 she starves herself to death. Kaoru is heartbroken.

In chapter 48 Niou moves Naka no Kimi to the City, but in chapter 49 intense political and parental pressure forces him to accept as his main wife a daughter of Genji's son Yūgiri, now the most powerful official at court. Kaoru remains in touch with Naka no Kimi, and his attentions arouse Niou's jealousy. To deflect Kaoru, Naka no Kimi tells him about a half sister of hers: Ukifune, a third, unrecognized, daughter of the Eighth Prince. She assures Kaoru that Ukifune looks extraordinarily like Ōigimi, and the resemblance indeed stuns Kaoru when he sees her. Henceforth, he pursues Ukifune.

Unfortunately, Niou then discovers Ukifune too. Kaoru consummates his union with her and moves her secretly to the now empty house at Uji, but Niou still manages to track her down and to make love to her himself (chapter 51).

Ukifune is now caught between Kaoru and Niou. Kaoru is a far greater lord than she could normally expect to marry even as a junior wife, and her mother favors him, but Niou excites her more. Kaoru, who has been building a house for her in the City, announces the date when he will come to fetch her, and the tension mounts as Niou plots to spirit her away first. Unable to choose between them, Ukifune decides to drown herself in the Uji River.

As chapter 52 begins, she has disappeared. Her body is not found, and to keep up appearances the household arranges a quick, false funeral. Kaoru and Niou mourn her. However, she has not drowned. Near the beginning of chapter 53 a senior cleric (Yokawa no Sōzu) finds her, speechless and weeping, under a tree. The cleric's sister, a nun, nurses her tenderly and then takes her home to a place called Ono, where Ukifune remains in a sort of trance for two months. At last the cleric exorcises her, and she recovers some of her memory, although she keeps what she remembers to herself. Soon she convinces the cleric to make her a nun.

By the end of chapter 53, a year after Ukifune's supposed death, Kaoru has caught wind of her existence. In chapter 54 he sends her a letter by her young half brother, but she refuses either to recognize the boy or to acknowledge that the letter is for her. In the book's closing lines, the disappointed Kaoru wonders whether someone else (he may be thinking of Niou) has been keeping her hidden for himself. This inconclusive ending may mean that the author left the tale incomplete, but it may just as well be intentional.

READERS AND READING IN THE AUTHOR'S TIME

In Murasaki Shikibu's social world, the men (apart from clerics) were all officials great or small. They studied philosophy, history, law, and so on in Chinese, learned to write the Chinese language, and also composed Chinese poetry. They of course composed poetry in Japanese as well, but fiction was in principle beneath their dignity, since it was classified as worthless fantasy—an idea hardly unique to early Japan. Still, some clearly knew about tales anyway, and once *Genji* came to be widely admired, it was men who most visibly championed its worth.

Women were not supposed to study Chinese, but some did. Murasaki Shikibu wrote in her diary that she taught the Empress to read Chinese poetry, but that she did it in secret. Chinese was considered unladylike. Chapter 2 describes a scholar's daughter who taught her lover to write Chinese poetry and gentlewomen who liked to fill their letters with Chinese characters, but such things were not encouraged. A ranking lady who could read Chinese advertised her knowledge at her peril.

Prose fiction in phonetically written Japanese, with few Chinese characters, was therefore especially for women. In *Genji* only women openly read or listen to tales (*monogatari*). Caught in strange or painful circumstances, a woman might comb tales for examples like her own, just as a troubled Emperor might review the formal histories of China and Japan in search of a precedent for his plight, but of course a tale's usual purpose was to entertain. A new tale in the possession of an imperial wife might even make her company more attractive to a young

Emperor or an Heir Apparent and so give her (hence her family) an advantage over her rivals. Paintings play just that role in chapter 17, the last included in this abridgment. *The Tale of Genji* does not mention anyone writing tales, but in chapter 17 gentlewomen, as well as professional artists, paint illustrations for tales.

A great lady like an Empress seems not to have read a tale on her own. Instead she listened while a gentlewoman read the story aloud and she herself looked at the pictures. However, others lucky enough to have access to a copy clearly read silently, by themselves, as people do now.

THE PATTERN OF HIERARCHY

In an ideal image that Japan adopted from China, the Emperor faces south to survey his realm, flanked by his two main Ministers: the Minister of the Left (the Emperor's left, the east) and the Minister of the Right. This pattern explains the government's bilateral symmetry. Many official organs had Left and Right components, and in *The Tale of Genji* this division appears in the titles borne by their officers. In the early chapters included here, the same symmetry appears in the power struggle between the factions represented by the Minister of the Left and Genji, and the Minister of the Right and his daughter, the Kokiden Consort. Even the Capital was divided administratively into Left and Right.

All offices were associated with a numbered rank, from one down to nine. Numbered ranks are not prominent in the text, but the characters are acutely aware of them. Of course, the Emperor stood above this numbered hierarchy. He was not obliged to recognize all his children, particularly those from socially or politically insignificant mothers, but most of the imperial children prominent in the tale are recognized. Except for Genji himself, they are Princes and Princesses. In this book, a Prince (His Highness) is therefore an Emperor's son whom that Emperor has formally acknowledged and appointed to a suitable rank. The same can be said of a Princess (Her Highness).

However, "Princess" also covers an imperial granddaughter in the male (*not* the female) line. For example Aoi, Genji's wife, is not a Princess because, although her mother is one, her father (the Minister of the Left) is a commoner.

An Emperor who does not appoint a son a Prince, but who nonetheless prefers not to consign him to oblivion, can give him a surname. This is what Genji's father does for Genji. In English, Genji is often and quite understandably called "Prince Genji," but my usage forbids that. "Prince" is a title formally conferred by an Emperor on a son whom he wishes to recognize fully and to retain in the imperial family. Before Genji receives his surname he is an imperial son whose station in life remains to be determined, and afterward he is a commoner.

THE POEMS

In the world of *The Tale of Genji,* poetry (in Japanese) was considered the noblest of all the arts. All of Japan's early prose literature includes poems, and *Genji* contains 795 of them. Some readers over the centuries have valued them even above the prose.

Composing poetry was first of all a matter of social necessity. Courting required exchanges of poems, as did many other occasions, and someone distinctly inept at poetry was socially disadvantaged. People learned to write by copying poems; they acquired the language of poetry by memorizing many examples; and they confirmed what they knew by composing more themselves. Although many poems in the tale are spoken or written spontaneously, their spontaneity springs in practice not only from simple feeling but also from mastery of complex rules of diction, vocabulary, form, and so on. Most poems were of course more or less conventional, but some rose to great heights of poignancy, passion, elegance, or wit. Among the characters in *The Tale of Genji,* the "best poet" is said to be the Akashi Lady.

The poems in question are known as *tanka* ("short song"). Each consists of five subunits of 5-7-5-7-7 syllables, for a total of thirty-one. They have no rhyme, which would be too easy and monotonous to be interesting, and no meter, since the language does not lend itself to that, either. Their character as poetry arises from a range of sophisticated devices, including wordplay, that make most of them extremely difficult to translate.

My translations of the poems follow the syllabic form described, and they are divided into two centered lines: one of 5-7-5 syllables and the other of 7-7. Observing the original syllable count sometimes requires more words in translation than the polysyllabic original readily supplies, but the result is not unsuitable for poems integrated into a prose narrative. (The poems quoted in the notes are translated for narrative meaning only.)

TIME AND AGE

The text of *The Tale of Genji* often identifies the numbered month in which an event takes place, but these are lunar months, not solar, so they differ from the months of the modern calendar. A lunar month is roughly six weeks later than the solar month with the same number. For example, the first day of the first lunar month is not the first of January, in the middle of winter, but the first day of spring (mid-February).

By the fifteenth century scholars had worked out for each chapter the ages of most of the characters. I have indicated these ages, wherever possible, according to the Japanese method of counting. In Japan, a child's first year is the calendar year of birth, and the child enters his or her "second year" with the New Year. For example, a child born in the twelfth month becomes "two" in the first month of the next year, with the result that age leaps one ahead of the Western count. Genji's age of seventeen in chapter 2 therefore means that he is in his seventeenth year and that his age in English would usually be counted as sixteen.

Main Characters

*Numbers in regular type are ages; parenthetical numbers in **boldface** designate chapters. Where no age is indicated, the text does not provide enough information to calculate it.*

AKASHI LADY
Daughter of the Akashi Novice; bears Genji a daughter.
Former Governor of Harima's daughter, age 9 (**chapter 5**);
Akashi Novice's daughter, 17–18 (**12, 13, 14**)

AKASHI NOVICE
Former Governor of Harima, father of the Akashi Lady.
59–62 (**12, 13, 14**)

AKIKONOMU, PRINCESS
Rokujō Haven's daughter; serves as High Priestess of Ise.
13–22 (**9, 10, 14, 17**)

AOI
Daughter of the Minister of the Left, married to Genji.
16 when Genji is 12 (**1**); 21–26 (**2, 5, 7, 9**)

DAME OF STAFF
Genji's aged admirer.
Late 50s when Genji is 19 (**7**); early 60s (**9**)

EMPEROR
Genji's father.
Emperor, His Majesty (**1, 5, 7, 8**); Retired Emperor, His
Eminence (**9**); the Late Retired Emperor (**10, 12, 13, 14**)

EMPEROR (SUZAKU)
Genji's elder half brother, son of the Kokiden Consort; succeeds
his father as Emperor.
Appointed Heir Apparent at 7 when Genji is 4 (**1**); Heir

Apparent, 21–23 (7, 8); Emperor, 27–30 (10, 12, 13); abdicates, becomes Retired Emperor, 30–33 (14, 17)

EMPEROR (REIZEI, *though name does not appear in this abridged edition*)
Son of Genji and Fujitsubo, but believed to be the son of Genji's father; succeeds Suzaku as Emperor.
Born (7); Heir Apparent, 3–10 (9, 10, 12, 13); Heir Apparent, Emperor, 10–11 (14); Emperor, 13 (17)

EMPRESS MOTHER (*see* Kokiden Consort)

FUJITSUBO
Daughter of an earlier Emperor; becomes Genji's father's Empress.
Marries Emperor at 16 when Genji is 11 (1); 23–36 (5, 7, 8, 9, 10, 12, 13, 14, 17)

GENJI
Son of the Emperor by the Kiritsubo Intimate; younger half brother of the Heir Apparent (the future Emperor Suzaku).
Birth through 12 (1); Captain of the Palace Guards, 17–18 (2, 3, 4); Captain of the Palace Guards, then Consultant, 18–19 (5); Consultant, 20 (7); Commander of the Right, 22–25 (9, 10); stripped of rank, 26–27 (12); Acting Grand Counselor, 27–28 (13); Palace Minister, 28–31 (14, 17)

GOVERNOR OF KII
A retainer of the Minister of the Left.
(2)

HEIR APPARENT (1)
Son of Genji's father and the Kokiden Consort; becomes Emperor Suzaku.
(1, 7, 8, 10, 12, 13, 14)

HEIR APPARENT (2)
Son of Genji and Fujitsubo; succeeds Suzaku as Emperor.
(7, 9, 10, 12, 13, 14, 17)

HOTARU, PRINCE
Genji's half brother.
(12, 17)

HYŌBU, PRINCE
Fujitsubo's elder brother, Murasaki's father; Lord of the Bureau
of War.
33–46 (5, 7, 10, 14, 17)

IYO DEPUTY
Utsusemi's husband.
(2)

KOKIDEN CONSORT
Daughter of the Minister of the Right; mother of the Heir
Apparent (the future Emperor Suzaku); becomes Empress
Mother.
Kokiden Consort (1, 7, 8); Empress Mother (9, 10, 13, 14)

KOREMITSU
Genji's foster brother and confidant.
(4, 5, 8, 9, 14)

MINISTER OF THE LEFT
Father of Aoi and Tō no Chūjō; Genji's father-in-law.
Becomes Genji's father-in-law at 46 (1); 51–57 (2, 5, 7, 8, 9);
resigns, 59 (10); former Minister of the Left, 60–61 (12);
Chancellor, 62–63 (14)

MINISTER OF THE RIGHT
Father of the Kokiden Consort and Oborozukiyo; grandfather
of the Heir Apparent (the future Emperor Suzaku).
Minister of the Right (1, 8, 10, 12, 13); Chancellor (13)

MURASAKI
Unrecognized daughter of Prince Hyōbu; niece of Fujitsubo.
10–23 (5, 7, 8, 9, 10, 12, 13, 14, 17)

OBOROZUKIYO
Sixth daughter of the Minister of the Right.
(8, 9, 10, 12, 14)

PRELATE
Murasaki's great-uncle, a distinguished Buddhist cleric.
(5)

ROKUJŌ HAVEN
Daughter of a Minister; widow of a deceased Heir Apparent;
mother of Akikonomu.
29–36 (4, 9, 10, 12, 14)

TŌ NO CHŪJŌ
Son of the Minister of the Left; brother of Aoi; friend of Genji;
his "name" designates the dual civil-military post (Secretary
Captain) that he occupies throughout most of these chapters.
(1, 2, 4, 5, 7, 8, 9, 10, 12, 14, 17)

UTSUSEMI
Iyo Deputy's wife, pursued by Genji.
(2)

YOSHIKIYO
Genji's retainer, son of current Governor of Harima.
(5, 8, 12, 13)

YŪGAO
A young woman loved by Genji; mother of Tamakazura (Tō no
Chūjō's daughter).
19 (4)

PROLOGUE

Genji on the Art of Fiction

In this excerpt from chapter 25, Genji finds Tamakazura (Yūgao's daughter, mentioned as a little girl in chapter 4) copying out a tale. Genji accuses her of believing glib falsehoods, but she retorts that it takes a liar like Genji to find lies everywhere. In response, Genji explains the value of fiction (made-up tales), as distinguished from "true" history. He presumably speaks for the author herself. At this point in the book Genji is thirty-six, Tamakazura twenty-two.

[. . .]

The long rains were worse this year than most, and to get through the endless wet the ladies amused themselves day and night with illustrated tales. The Akashi Lady made up some very nicely and sent them to her daughter. This sort of thing particularly intrigued Tamakazura, who therefore gave herself all day long to copying and reading. She had several young gentlewomen suitably gifted to satisfy this interest. Among her assemblage of tales she found accounts, whether fact or fiction, of many extraordinary fates, but none, alas, of any like her own.

[. . .]

Finding her enthralled by works like these, which lay scattered about everywhere, Genji exclaimed, "Oh, no, this will never do! Women are obviously born to be fooled without a murmur of protest. There is hardly a word of truth in all this, as you know perfectly well, but there you are caught up in fables, taking them quite seriously and writing away without a thought for your tangled hair in this stiflingly warm rain!" He laughed but then went on, "Without stories like these about the old days, though, how would we ever pass the time when there is nothing else to do? Besides, among these lies there certainly are some plausibly touching scenes, convincingly told; and yes, we know they are fictions, but even so we are moved and half drawn for no real reason to the pretty, suffering heroine. We may disbelieve the blatantly impossible but still be amazed by magnificently contrived wonders, and although these pall on quiet, second hearing, some are still fascinating. Lately, when my little girl has someone read to her and I stand there listening, I think to myself what good talkers there are in this world, and how this story, too, must come straight from someone's persuasively glib imagination—but perhaps not."

"Yes, of course, for various reasons someone accustomed to telling lies will no doubt take tales that way, but it seems impossible to me that they should be anything other than simply true." She pushed her inkstone away.

"I have been very rude to speak so ill to you of tales! They record what has gone on ever since the Age of the Gods. The *Chronicles of Japan*[1] and so on give only a part of the story. It is tales that contain the truly rewarding particulars!" He laughed. "Not that tales accurately describe any particular person; rather, the telling begins when all those things the teller longs to have pass on to future generations—whatever there is about the way people live their lives, for better or worse, that is a sight to see or a wonder to hear—overflow the teller's heart. To put someone in a good light one brings out the good only, and to please other people one favors the oddly wicked, but none of this, good or bad, is removed from life as we know it. Tales are not told the same way in China, and even in Japan the old and new ways are of course not the same; but although one may distinguish between the deep and the shallow, it is wrong always to dismiss what one finds in tales as false. There is talk of 'expedient means'[2] also in

1. *Nihongi,* an official history of Japan written in Chinese and completed in A.D. 720.
2. *Hōben,* a device adopted by an enlightened being in order to guide the unenlightened. The term may cover what could be conventionally called a lie.

the teaching that the Buddha in his great goodness left us, and many passages of the scriptures are all too likely to seem inconsistent and so to raise doubts in the minds of those who lack understanding, but in the end they have only a single message, and the gap between enlightenment and the passions[3] is, after all, no wider than the one that in tales sets off the good from the bad. To put it nicely, there is nothing that does not have its own value." He mounted a very fine defense of tales.

[. . .]

3. A paradox of Japanese Buddhism is that "the passions are enlightenment"— the passions aroused by desire and the senses being far removed from enlightenment as commonly conceived.

I
(ABRIDGED)

KIRITSUBO
THE PAULOWNIA PAVILION

Kiri means "paulownia tree" and *tsubo* "a small garden between palace buildings." Kiritsubo is therefore the name for the palace pavilion that has a paulownia in its garden. Genji's mother lives there.

In a certain reign (whose can it have been?) someone of no great rank among the Emperor's Consorts and Intimates[1] enjoyed exceptional favor. Those others who had always assumed that pride of place was properly theirs despised her as a dreadful woman, while the lesser Intimates were unhappier still. The way she waited on him day after day only stirred up feeling against her, and perhaps this growing burden of resentment was what affected her health and obliged her often to withdraw in misery to her home; but His Majesty, who could less and less do without her, ignored his critics until his behavior seemed bound to be the talk of all.

From this sad spectacle the senior nobles and privy gentlemen[2] could only avert their eyes. Such things had led to disorder and

---

1. A Consort (*nyōgo*) is an imperial wife whose father is at least a Minister or a Prince. An Intimate (*kōi*) is an imperial wife whose father is at most a Grand Counselor. The word *kōi* refers literally to someone who dresses the Emperor.
2. Senior nobles (*kandachime*) are nobles of at least the third rank who hold a post at least at the level of Consultant. Privy gentlemen are gentlemen of the fourth and fifth ranks, together with certain Chamberlains of the sixth rank, authorized to enter the privy chamber (*tenjō no ma*), the room frequented by courtiers on duty to wait upon the Emperor.

ruin even in China, they said, and as discontent spread through the realm, the example of Yōkihi³ came more and more to mind, with many a painful consequence for the lady herself; yet she trusted in his gracious and unexampled affection and remained at court.

The Grand Counselor, her father, was gone, and it was her mother, a lady from an old family, who saw to it that she should give no less to court events than others whose parents were both alive and who enjoyed general esteem; but lacking anyone influential to support her, she often had reason when the time came to lament the weakness of her position.⁴

His Majesty must have had a deep bond with her in past lives as well, for she gave him a wonderfully handsome son. He had the child brought in straightaway,⁵ for he was desperate to see him, and he was astonished by his beauty. His elder son, born to his Kokiden Consort,⁶ the daughter of the Minister of the Right, enjoyed powerful backing and was feted by all as the undoubted future Heir Apparent, but he could not rival his brother in looks, and His Majesty, who still accorded him all due respect, therefore lavished his private affection on the new arrival.

The rank of the boy's mother had never permitted her to enter the Emperor's common service.⁷ His insistence on keeping her with him despite her fine reputation and her noble bearing meant that whenever there was to be music or any other sort of occasion, his first thought was to send for her. Sometimes, after

3. The beauty Yōkihi (Chinese Yang Guifei) so infatuated the Chinese Emperor Xuanzong (685–762) that his neglect of the state provoked a rebellion, and his army forced him to have her executed. Bai Juyi (772–846) told the story in a long poem, "The Song of Unending Sorrow" (Chinese "Changhenge," Japanese "Chōgonka"), which was extremely popular in Heian Japan.
4. She had no influential male relative on her mother's side and was often pushed aside when an event took place.
5. Such a birth took place not in the palace but at the mother's home.
6. Kokiden (a Chinese-style name that means "Hall of Great Light") is the name of her residence within the palace compound.
7. Her standing was too high to allow her to wait on the Emperor routinely, like a servant. She should have come to him only when summoned and for a limited time.

oversleeping a little, he would command her to stay on with him, and this refusal to let her go made her seem to deserve contempt;[8] but after the birth he was so attentive that the Kokiden Consort feared he might appoint his new son Heir Apparent over her own. This Consort, for whom he had high regard, had been the first to come to him, and it was she whose reproaches most troubled him and whom he could least bear to hurt, for she had given him other children as well.

Despite the lady's faith in his sovereign protection, so many belittled her and sought to find fault with her that, far from flourishing, she began in her distress to waste away. She lived in the Kiritsubo. His Majesty had to pass many others on his constant visits to her, and no wonder they took offense. On the far too frequent occasions when she went to him, there might be a nasty surprise awaiting her along the crossbridges and bridgeways, one that horribly fouled the skirts of the gentlewomen who accompanied her or who came forward to receive her; or, the victim of a conspiracy between those on either side, she might find herself locked in a passageway between two doors that she could not avoid, and be unable to go either forward or back. Seeing how she suffered from such humiliations, endlessly multiplied as circumstances favored her enemies' designs, His Majesty had the Intimate long resident in the nearby Kōrōden move elsewhere and gave it to her instead, for when he wanted her close to him.[9] The one evicted nursed a particularly implacable grudge.

In the child's third year his father gave him a donning of the trousers just as impressive as his firstborn's, marshaling for the purpose all the treasures in the Court Repository and the Imperial Stores. This only provoked more complaints, but as the boy grew, he revealed such marvels of beauty and character that no one could resent him. The discerning could hardly believe their eyes, and they wondered that such a child should have ever been born.

8. Because the Emperor himself seems to treat her like a servant.
9. The Kōrōden (*den* means approximately "hall") was very near the Emperor's residence. He gives it to her not to replace the Kiritsubo but as a nearby apartment to stay in when he requires her company often.

In the summer of that year Genji's mother became unwell, but the Emperor refused her leave to withdraw. He felt no alarm, since her health had long been fragile, and he only urged her to be patient a little longer. However, she worsened daily, until just five or six days later she was so weak that her mother's tearful entreaties at last persuaded him to release her. In fear of suffering some cruel humiliation even now, she left the child behind and stole away.

Unable any longer to keep her by him, he suffered acutely to think that he could not even see her off.[10] There she lay, lovely and ever so dear, but terribly thin now and unable to tell him of her deep trouble and sorrow because she lingered in a state of semiconsciousness—a sight that drove from his mind all notion of time past or to come and reduced him simply to assuring her tearfully, in every way he knew, how much he loved her.

When she still failed to respond but only lay limp and apparently fainting, with the light dying from her eyes, he had no idea what to do. Even after issuing a decree to allow her the privilege of a hand carriage, he went in to her again and could not bring himself to let her go. "You promised never to leave me, not even at the end," he said, "and you cannot abandon me now! I will not let you!"

She was so touched that she managed to breathe:

"Now the end has come, and I am filled with sorrow that our ways must part:
the path I would rather take is the one that leads to life.

If only I had known . . ."

She seemed to have more to say but to be too exhausted to go on, which only decided him, despite her condition, to see her through to whatever might follow. He consented only unwillingly to her departure when urgently reminded that excellent healers were to start prayers for her that evening at her own home.

10. She was too ill to stay in the palace, lest it be polluted by death, and imperial etiquette forbade the Emperor to see her off.

With his heart too full for sleep, he anxiously awaited dawn. He expressed deep concern even before his messenger had time to come back from her house. Meanwhile, the messenger heard lamenting and learned that just past midnight she had breathed her last, and he therefore returned in sorrow. This news put His Majesty in such a state that he shut himself away, wholly lost to all around him.

He still longed to see his son, but the child was soon to withdraw, for no precedent authorized one in mourning to wait upon the Emperor.[11] The boy did not understand what the matter was, and he gazed in wonder at the sobbing gentlewomen who had served his mother and at His Majesty's streaming tears. Such partings[12] are sad at the best of times, and his very innocence made this one moving beyond words.

[. . .]

As the dreary days slipped by, the Emperor saw carefully to each succeeding memorial service.[13] The passage of time did so little to relieve his sorrow that he called none of his ladies to wait on him after dark but instead passed day and night in weeping, and even those who merely witnessed his state found the autumn very dewy indeed.

"She meant so much to him that even dead she is a blight on one's existence" summed up the sentiments of the Kokiden Consort, as merciless as ever, on the subject. The mere sight of his elder son would only remind His Majesty how much he preferred the younger, and he would then send a trusted gentlewoman or nurse[14] to find out how he was getting on.

[. . .]

The sound of the wind and the calling of crickets only

---

11. After the year 905, children not yet in their seventh year no longer went into mourning for a parent, and the present of the story therefore seems to be earlier.

12. The death of a parent.

13. A rite was performed every seven days for the first forty-nine days after the death, in order to guide the spirit of the deceased toward peace. The Emperor probably sent a representative to each and provided for it generously.

14. A woman who had nursed the Emperor in place of his natural mother. The relationship with a nurse was normally intimate and lasting.

deepened his melancholy, and meanwhile he heard the Kokiden Consort, who had not come for so long now to wait on him after dark, making the best of a beautiful moon by playing music far into the night. He did not like it and wished it would stop. Those gentlewomen and privy gentlemen who knew his mood found that it grated upon their ears. The offender, willful and abrasive, seemed determined to behave as though nothing had happened.

[. . .]

In time the little boy went to join his father in the palace. He was turning out to be so handsome that he hardly seemed of this world at all, and for the Emperor this aroused a certain dread.[15] The next spring, when he was to designate the Heir Apparent, he longed to pass over his elder son in favor of his younger, but since the younger lacked support,[16] and since in any case the world at large would never accept such a choice, he desisted for the boy's sake and kept his desire to himself. "He could hardly go that far," people assured one another, "no matter how devoted to him he may be." The Kokiden Consort was relieved.

[. . .]

Now the boy was permanently in attendance at the palace. When he reached his seventh year, His Majesty had him perform his first reading, which he carried off with such unheard-of brilliance that his father was frankly alarmed. "Surely none of you can dislike him now," he said; "after all, he no longer has a mother. Please be nice to him." When he took him to visit the Kokiden Consort, she let him straight through her blinds and would not release him, for the sight of him would have brought smiles to the fiercest warrior, even an enemy one. She had given His Majesty two daughters, but by no stretch of the imagination could either be compared with him. Nor did any other imperial lady hide from him, because he was already so charmingly distinguished in manner that they found him a delightful and challenging playmate. Naturally he applied himself

15. People believed that supernatural powers coveted unusually beautiful people and stole them. The tale often alludes to this fear.
16. He had no influential male relative on his mother's side to support him.

to formal scholarship,[17] but he also set the heavens ringing with the music of strings and flute. In fact, if I were to list all the things at which he excelled, I would only succeed in making him sound absurd.

During this time His Majesty learned that a delegation from Koma[18] included an expert physiognomist, and since it would have contravened Emperor Uda's solemn admonition to call him to the palace, he instead sent his son secretly to the Kōrokan.[19] The senior official charged with taking him there presented him as his own.

The astonished physiognomist nodded his head again and again in perplexity. "He has the signs of one destined to become the father of his people and to achieve the Sovereign's supreme eminence," he said, "and yet when I see him so, I fear disorder and suffering. But when I see him as the future pillar of the court and the support of all the realm, there again appears to be a mismatch."

The official himself was a man of deep learning, and his conversation with the visitor was most interesting. They exchanged poems, and when the physiognomist, who was soon to leave, made a very fine one expressing joy at having met so extraordinary a boy, together with sorrow upon parting from him, the boy composed some moving lines of his own, which the visitor admired extravagantly before presenting him with handsome gifts. The visitor, too, received many gifts, conveyed to him from the Emperor. News of this encounter got about, as such news will, and although His Majesty never mentioned it, the Minister of the Right, the Heir Apparent's grandfather, wondered suspiciously what it might mean.

17. Chinese studies, mainly in political philosophy, law, history, poetry, and court usage.
18. The ancient Korean kingdom of Koguryŏ.
19. When Uda (reigned 887–97) abdicated, he wrote down articles of advice for his successor, Daigo (reigned 897–930), and one of these advised against admitting any outsider to the palace. Judging from this passage, the Emperor in the tale corresponds to Daigo. The Kōrokan was the building where foreign ambassadors and other visitors were received, near the crossing of Suzaku Avenue and Shichijō ("Seventh Avenue").

His Majesty was greatly impressed to find that the visitor's reading tallied with one that he had obtained in his wisdom through the art of physiognomy as practiced in Japan, and on the strength of which he had refrained from naming his son a Prince. He therefore decided that rather than set the boy adrift as an unranked Prince,[20] unsupported by any maternal relative, he would assure him a more promising future (since, after all, his own reign might be brief) by having him serve the realm as a commoner; and in this spirit he had him apply himself more diligently than ever to his studies. It was a shame to make a subject of him, considering his gifts, but he was bound to draw suspicion as a Prince, and when consultation with an eminent astrologer only confirmed this prediction, His Majesty resolved to make him a Genji.[21]

Month after month, year after year, His Majesty never forgot his lost love. After summoning several likely prospects, he sorrowfully concluded that he would never find her like again in this world, but then he heard from a woman of the palace about another possibility: the fourth child of a former Emperor, a girl known for her beauty and brought up by her mother, the Empress, with the greatest care. Owing that Emperor her office as she did, the woman had served the young lady's mother intimately as well, and so she had known her, too, from infancy; in fact, she saw her from time to time even now. "In all my three reigns of service at court,[22] I have seen no one like Your Majesty's Kiritsubo Intimate," she said, "but the Princess I refer to has grown to be very like her. She is a pleasure to look at."

20. An imperial son was not a Prince until appointed by his father. The appointment was to one of four ranks, and the appointee received a corresponding stipend. One not so appointed but still retained in the imperial family was "unranked" (*muhon*).

21. Members of the imperial family had no surname, but after the early ninth century some excess imperial sons were made commoners (*tadabito*) with the surname Minamoto. "Genji" means simply "a Minamoto."

22. Since the present Emperor's reign is her third, she must have been appointed by his grandfather. The word *sendai* ("previous Emperor") means an Emperor who did not abdicate but died in office, and Kōkō (reigned 884–87), who preceded Uda (Daigo's predecessor), did just this.

His Majesty approached the mother with great circumspection, eager to discover the truth of this report. She received his proposal with alarm, because she knew how unpleasant the Heir Apparent's mother could be, and she shrank from exposing her daughter to the blatant contempt with which the Kokiden Consort had treated her Kiritsubo rival. So it was that she passed away before she could bring herself to consent. Once the daughter was alone, His Majesty pressed his suit earnestly, assuring her that she would be to him as a daughter of his own.[23] Her gentlewomen, those properly concerned with her interests,[24] and her elder brother, Prince Hyōbu,[25] all agreed that she would be far better off at the palace than forlorn at home, and they therefore insisted that she should go.

She was called Fujitsubo. She resembled that other lady to a truly astonishing degree, but since she was of far higher standing, commanded willing respect, and could not possibly be treated lightly, she had no need to defer to anyone on any matter. His Majesty had clung all too fondly to his old love, despite universal disapproval, and he did not forget her now, but in a touching way his affection turned to this new arrival, who was a great consolation to him.

None of the Emperor's ladies could remain shy with the young Genji, especially the one he now saw so often, because he hardly ever left his father's side. All of them took pride in their looks, no doubt with good reason, but they were no longer in the first blush of youth, whereas Princess Fujitsubo was both young and charming, and Genji naturally caught glimpses of her, although she did what she could to keep out of his sight. He had no memory of his mother, but his youthful interest was aroused when that palace woman told him how much the

23. That he would provide for her himself and not count on her mother's family.
24. The principal men in her mother's family.
25. He is the head of the Bureau of War (*Hyōbu*), an honorary post held by a ranking Prince.

Princess resembled her, and he wanted always to be with her so as to contemplate her to his heart's content.

The Emperor, who cared so deeply for both of them, asked her not to maintain her reserve. "I am not sure why," he said, "but it seems right to me that he should take you for his mother. Do not think him uncivil. Just be kind to him. His face and eyes are so like hers that your own resemblance to her makes it look quite natural." Genji therefore lost no chance offered by the least flower or autumn leaf to let her know in his childish way how much he liked her. The Emperor's fondness for her prompted the Kokiden Consort to fall out with her as she had done with Genji's mother, until her old animosity returned and she took an aversion to Genji as well.

Genji's looks had an indescribably fresh sweetness, one beyond even Fujitsubo's celebrated and, to the Emperor, peerless beauty, and this moved people to call him the Shining Lord. Since Fujitsubo made a pair with him, and His Majesty loved them both, they called her the Sunlight Princess.

His Majesty was reluctant to spoil Genji's boyish charm, but in Genji's twelfth year he gave him his coming of age, busying himself personally with the preparations and adding new embellishments to the ceremony. Lest the event seem less imposing than the one for the Heir Apparent, done some years ago in the Shishinden, and lest anything go amiss, he issued minute instructions for the banquets to be offered by the various government offices and for the things normally provided by the Court Repository and Imperial Granary, eliciting from them perfection in all they supplied.

He had his throne face east from the outer, eastern chamber of his residence, with the seats for the young man and his sponsor, the Minister, before him.[26] Genji appeared at the hour of the Monkey.[27] The Emperor appeared to regret that Genji

26. He sits on a chair in the aisle room (*hisashi*)—his day room (*hiru no omashi*)—on the east side of his residence, the Seiryōden; Genji and the Minister of the Left are a beam width below him in the second aisle (*magobisashi*), an open, floored space not found in ordinary dwellings.
27. Roughly 4:00 P.M.

would never look again as he did now, with his hair tied in twin tresses[28] and his face radiant with the freshness of youth. The Lord of the Treasury and the Chamberlain[29] did their duty. The Lord of the Treasury was plainly sorry to cut off such beautiful hair, and the Emperor, who wished desperately that his love might have been there to see it, needed the greatest self-mastery not to weep.

All present shed tears when, after donning the headdress and withdrawing to the anteroom, Genji then reappeared in the robes of a man and stepped down into the garden to salute his Sovereign. His Majesty, of course, was still more deeply moved, and in his mind he sadly reviewed the past, when the boy's mother had been such a comfort to him. He had feared that Genji's looks might suffer once his hair was put up, at least while he remained so young, but not at all: he only looked more devastatingly handsome than ever.

By his wife, a Princess,[30] the sponsoring Minister of the Left had a beloved only daughter, Aoi, in whom the Heir Apparent had expressed interest, but whom after long hesitation he felt more inclined to offer to Genji instead. When he had sounded out the Emperor's own feelings on the matter, His Majesty replied, "Very well, she may be just the companion for him,[31] now that he seems no longer to have anyone looking after him"; and this had encouraged him to proceed.

Genji withdrew to the anteroom and then took the very last seat among the Princes,[32] while the assembled company enjoyed their wine. The Minister dropped hints to him about this marriage, but Genji was at a bashful age and gave him no real response. Then a woman official sent His Excellency a message

28. *Mizura*, hair bunches that divided the hair evenly on either side of the head. Boys wore *mizura* until they came of age.

29. The Emperor's hair was normally cut by a Chamberlain.

30. Genji's aunt and the Emperor's sister. Genji is about to marry a first cousin.

31. After coming of age, Genji would normally receive material support from his wife's family. The wife to so young a man was called a "companion in bed" (*soibushi*).

32. The imperial sons, who were seated in order of rank. Genji sat next to his future father-in-law, for the Minister of the Left occupied the highest seat among the nonimperial nobles.

from His Majesty, requiring his presence, and His Excellency obeyed forthwith.[33]

One of His Majesty's gentlewomen took the gifts from his own hands to bestow them on the Minister. They included, according to custom, a white, oversize woman's gown[34] and a set of women's robes. On handing him the wine cup, His Majesty gave pointed expression to his feelings:

> "Into that first knot to bind up his boyish hair did you tie the wish
> that enduring happiness be theirs through ages to come?"[35]

> "In that very mood I tied his hair with great prayers bound henceforth to last,
> just as long as the dark hue of the purple does not fade,"

His Excellency replied before stepping down to perform his obeisance. There he received a horse from the Left Imperial Stables and a perched falcon from the Chamberlains' Office. The Princes and senior nobles then lined up below the steps,[36] each to receive his gift.

The delicacies in cypress boxes and the fruit baskets had been prepared for the Emperor that day by a senior official, at the Emperor's own command. There were so many rice dumplings and so many chests of cloth,[37] certainly more than when the Heir Apparent came of age, that there was hardly any room for them all. It was in fact Genji's ceremony that displayed truly magnificent liberality.

That evening His Majesty sent Genji to the Minister of the Left's residence, where His Excellency welcomed him and gave

33. The Minister is to receive the gifts customarily awarded to the "sponsor."
34. This garment, made for presentation, would have been reduced in size for actual use.
35. This poem, like the Minister's reply, plays on the verb *musubu*, "bind up" the hair and "make" a vow (of conjugal fidelity). The cord used was purple (*murasaki*), the color of close relationship.
36. *Mihashi*, the steps down from the Seiryōden to the garden just east of it.
37. Gifts for the lower servants.

the ensuing rite[38] a dazzling brilliance. The family found Genji preternaturally attractive, despite his still being such a child, but Aoi, being somewhat older, thought him much too young and was ashamed that he should suit her so poorly.

The Minister of the Left enjoyed His Majesty's highest regard, and the Princess, his wife, was moreover His Majesty's full sister. Both were of supreme distinction, and the Minister of the Right cut a poor figure now that Genji had joined them, too, despite being destined one day to rule the realm as the grandfather of the Heir Apparent. His Excellency had many children by various ladies. By the Princess herself he had, apart from his daughter, Aoi, the very young and promising Tō no Chūjō, whom the Minister of the Right had wished to secure as a son-in-law, even though he was hardly on good terms with the young man's father, and whom he had therefore matched with his beloved fourth daughter. He treated the young man just as well as Genji's father-in-law treated Genji, and the two sons-in-law got on perfectly together.

Genji was not free to live at home,[39] for the Emperor summoned him too often. In his heart he saw only Fujitsubo's peerless beauty. Ah, he thought, she is the kind of woman I want to marry; there is no one like her! Aoi was no doubt very pretty and well brought up, but he felt little for her because he had lost his boyish heart to someone else; indeed, he had done so to the point of pain.

Now that Genji was an adult, His Majesty no longer allowed him through Fujitsubo's curtains to be with her as before. Whenever there was music, he would accompany her koto on his flute; this and the faint sound of her voice through the blinds[40] were his consolations, and he wanted never to live anywhere but in the palace. Only after waiting upon the Emperor for five or six days might he now and again put in two or three at his father-in-law's, but he was so young that the Minister did not really mind. The Minister treated his son-in-law generously

38. The wedding rite for Genji and Aoi.
39. At his father-in-law's residence.
40. Fujitsubo joined in the music (*asobi*) but remained invisible.

and chose the least ordinary among the available gentlewomen for Genji's service. These entered with him into his favorite pastimes and looked after him very well.

His residence at the palace was the Kiritsubo, as before, and His Majesty kept his mother's gentlewomen together so as to have them serve him in turn. He also decreed that the Office of Upkeep and the Office of Artisans should rebuild his mother's home, which they did beautifully. The layout of the trees and garden hills was already very pleasant, but with much bustle and noise they handsomely enlarged the lake. Genji kept wishing with many sighs that he had a true love to come and live with him there.

They say that his nickname, the Shining Lord, was given him in praise by the man from Koma.

2

(COMPLETE)

HAHAKIGI
THE BROOM TREE

Hahakigi ("broom tree") is a plant from which brooms were indeed made and that had the poetic reputation of being visible from afar and of disappearing as one approached. As the chapter title, it alludes to the closing exchange of poems between Genji and Utsusemi, who has frustrated him by making herself inaccessible.

Genji is twelve when he marries Aoi in chapter 1. Chapter 2 starts when he is seventeen. The tale says nothing about the intervening years.

Shining Genji: the name was imposing, but not so its bearer's many deplorable lapses; and considering how quiet he kept his wanton ways, lest in reaching the ears of posterity they earn him unwelcome fame, whoever broadcast his secrets to all the world was a terrible gossip. At any rate, opinion mattered to him, and he put on such a show of seriousness that he started not one racy rumor. The Katano Lieutenant[1] would have laughed at him!

While Genji was still a Captain in the Palace Guards, he felt at home nowhere but in the palace, and he went to the Minister of the Left's only now and then. The household sometimes suspected his thoughts of being "all in a hopeless tangle"[2] over

1. Katano no Shōshō, an amorous hero whose story has not survived.
2. From *Ise monogatari* 1 (*Tales of Ise,* tenth century), an episode in which the young hero is swept away by a glimpse of two pretty sisters: "Robe dye-patterned with young *murasaki* of the Kasuga meadows, all in a hopeless tangle is my heart as well."

another woman, but actually he had no taste for frivolous, trite, or impromptu affairs. No, his way was the rare amour fraught with difficulty and heartache, for he did sometimes do things he ought not to have done.

The early summer rains were falling and falling, while at the palace seclusion[3] went on and on, so that he was there even longer than usual; but although at his father-in-law's there was concern and annoyance, they still sent him clothing of every kind and in the height of fashion, and his brothers-in-law spent all their time at the palace in his rooms.

One, Tō no Chūjō, was Aoi's full brother and, like Genji, a Guards Captain. He was a particularly close friend with whom Genji shared music and other amusements more willingly than with anyone else. The residence of the Minister of the Right,[4] where the young man was looked after so gladly, thoroughly depressed him, and he had a marked taste for romantic forays elsewhere. Even at home he had his room done up in style, and in Genji's comings and goings he kept him such constant company that the two were together day and night for both study and music, at which he was nearly as quick as Genji himself, until he naturally dropped all reserve with Genji, told him whatever was on his mind, and treated him as a bosom friend.

It had been raining all the dull day long and on into an equally wet evening. There was hardly anyone in the privy chamber, and Genji's own room seemed unusually quiet as the two of them read beside the lamp. When Tō no Chūjō took some letters on paper of various colors from a nearby cabinet shelf and betrayed curiosity about them, Genji demurred. "You may look at the ones that do not matter. Some could be embarrassing, though."

"But it is just the ones you think so personal and compromising that interest me," Tō no Chūjō complained. "Even I get perfectly ordinary letters from ladies of one rank or another, in the course of my correspondence with them. The letters worth

3. *Monoimi*, a time of confinement indoors to avoid evil influences.
4. Tō no Chūjō's father-in-law.

reading are those sent when the writer was angry, or when dusk was falling and she anxiously awaited her lover's coming."

Of course, as he well knew, Genji would hardly leave the important ones, the ones that must be kept secret, lying about on a shelf in plain view; he would have them put away somewhere, out of sight, which meant that these must be of only minor interest. "What a variety!" he exclaimed as he glanced over each, guessing at the sender and getting her now right, now quite wrong. Genji was amused, but with laconic replies he managed in one way or another to put his friend off the track and to hide what he wished to hide.

"You are the one who must have a collection," Genji said. "I should like to see it. Then I would gladly open this whole cabinet to you."

"I cannot imagine that I have any you would wish to read." Tō no Chūjō then took this occasion to observe, "I have finally realized how rarely you will find a flawless woman, one who is simply perfect. No doubt there are many who seem quite promising, write a flowing hand, give you back a perfectly acceptable poem, and all in all do credit enough to the rank they have to uphold, but you know, if you insist on any particular quality, you seldom find one who will do. Each one is all too pleased with her own accomplishments, runs others down, and so on. While a girl is under the eye of her adoring parents and living a sheltered life bright with future promise, it seems men have only to hear of some little talent of hers to be attracted. As long as she is pretty and innocent, and young enough to have nothing else on her mind, she may well put her heart into learning a pastime she has seen others enjoy, and in fact she may become quite good at it. And when those who know her[5] disguise her weaknesses and advertise whatever passable qualities she may have so as to present them in the best light, how could anyone think ill of her, having no reason to suspect her of being other than she seems? But when you look further to see whether it is all true, I am sure you can only end up disappointed."

5. Her gentlewomen.

He sighed portentously, whereupon Genji, who seemed to have reached on his own at least some of the same conclusions, asked with a smile, "But do you suppose any girl could have *nothing* to recommend her?"

"Who would be fool enough to be taken in by one as hopeless as that? I am sure the utter failure with nothing to commend her and the one so superior as to be a wonder are equally rare. When a girl is highborn,[6] everyone[7] pampers her and a lot about her remains hidden, so that she naturally seems a paragon. Those of middle birth[8] are the ones among whom you can see what a girl really has to offer and find ways to distinguish one from another. As for the lowborn,[9] they hardly matter."

His apparent familiarity with his subject aroused Genji's curiosity. "I wonder about these levels of yours, though—the high, the middle, and the low. How can you tell who belongs to which? Some are born high and yet fall and sink to become nobodies, while common gentlemen[10] rise to become senior nobles, pride themselves on the way they do up their houses, and insist on conceding nothing to anyone. How can you draw the line between these two?"

Just then the Chief Left Equerry and the Fujiwara Aide of Ceremonial came in to join the seclusion. Tō no Chūjō welcomed both as enterprising lovers as well as great talkers, and they went straight into a heated discussion of how to tell women of one level from those of another. They told some astonishing stories.

Tō no Chūjō declared, "On the subject of those who rise high

6. *Shina takaku,* "born to a high standing in society." The notion of *shina* includes both formal rank and the family's general social distinction.
7. As before, the gentlewomen around her: talented gentlewomen devote themselves to developing whatever capacity she may have.
8. *Naka no shina,* including particularly the daughters of privy gentlemen or of provincial Governors, i.e., of gentlemen of the fourth or fifth rank.
9. *Shimo no kizami to iū kiwa,* presumably daughters of men in the lower ranks of the official bureaucracy. Such women were beneath the notice of young men like these.
10. *Naobito,* gentlemen of the fourth or fifth rank.

without being born to it, society does not actually feel quite the same about them, despite their rank, while as for those who once stood high but now lack means, times turn bad, and they decline until they have nothing left but their pride and suffer endless misfortune. Either group, I think, belongs to the middle grade.

"Even among the provincial Governors, whose function it is to administer the provinces and whose grade is certainly fixed, there are actually different levels, and these days you can find considerable figures among them. What is a pleasure to see, more so than any mediocre senior noble, is a man of the fourth rank, qualified for Consultant,[11] with a solid reputation, from no unworthy stock, and with an easy and confident manner. His house boasts every luxury, and all those daughters of his, showered with love and dazzling wealth, grow up in grand style. Girls like that often do better in palace service than you might imagine."

"I suppose the thing is to keep an eye out for a father with means," Genji said, smiling, and Tō no Chūjō grumbled, "I do not know how you can say that. It does not sound like you at all!"

"When a girl's rank at birth and her reputation agree," the Chief Equerry observed, "when she commands general respect but is still disappointing in her person and her behavior, you obviously cannot help wondering sadly why she turned out like that. Of course, when her personal qualities match her rank, you take them for granted and are not surprised. The highest of the high, though, are beyond my ken, and I had better say nothing about them.

"Anyway, the really fascinating girl is the one of whom no one has ever heard, the strangely appealing one who lives by herself, hidden away in some ruinous, overgrown old house; because, never having expected anyone like her, you wonder what she is doing there and cannot help wanting to know her better. Her father is a miserable, fat old man, her brother's face is none

11. *Hisangi,* a man of the fourth rank, either a past Consultant (Sangi) or qualified for this office. Consultant (there were eight) was a distinguished appointment, below only Counselor and Minister.

too prepossessing either, and there she is in the women's quarters, far at the back, where you expect nothing unusual: proud, spirited, and giving a touch of distinction to everything she does. Even if she has her limits after all, how could a surprise like that fail to delight anyone? Compared to someone truly flawless, she of course falls short, but for what she is, she is hard to let go." He glanced at the Aide of Ceremonial, who seemed to take this as a reference to his own well-regarded sisters, since he kept his peace.

Oh, come now, Genji thought, it is rare enough to find anyone like that among the highborn! Over soft, layered white gowns he had on only a dress cloak, unlaced at the neck,[12] and, lying there in the lamplight, against a pillar, he looked so beautiful that one could have wished him a woman. For him, the highest of the high seemed hardly good enough.

They talked on about one woman and another until the Chief Equerry remarked, "Many do very well for an affair, but when you are choosing your own for good, you may not easily find what you want. It is probably just as difficult to find a truly capable man to uphold the realm in His Majesty's service, but however demanding that sort of post may be, it takes more than one or two to govern, and that is why those above are assisted by those below and why inferiors obey their superiors and defer willingly to them. Think of the one and only who is to run your little household, and you realize how many important things there are to be done right. Even granting that having this she is bound to lack that, and that you have to take the good with the bad, very few can manage honorably, and so even if I do not recommend pursuing women forever in order to compare them all, I can hardly blame the man who is starting out to make his choice and who, to help himself make up his mind, looks around a little to find one he really likes—one who does not need him to tell her how to do every little thing. Things may not always work out perfectly, but the man who cannot bring himself

12. His white, unstarched gowns are probably two, and his summer dress cloak (*nōshi*) is probably thin enough to be nearly transparent. He seems not to have on its normal complement, gathered trousers (*sashinuki*).

to abandon a woman once he has made her his own deserves respect, and his constancy is also a credit to the woman with whom he keeps faith. It is true, though, that my own experience of couples has shown me no especially admirable or inspiring examples. And you young lords[13] who pick and choose among the most exalted, what height of perfection does it take to gain your approval?

"As long as a girl has looks and youth enough, she avoids anything that might soil her name. Even when composing a letter, she takes her time to choose her words and writes in ink faint enough to leave you bemused and longing for something clearer; then, when at last you get near enough to catch her faint voice, she speaks under her breath, says next to nothing, and proves to be an expert at keeping herself hidden away. Take this for sweetly feminine wiles, and passion will lure you into playing up to her, at which point she turns coy. This, I think, is the worst flaw a girl can have.

"A wife's main duty is to look after her husband, so it seems to me that one can do quite well without her being too sensitive, ever so delicate about the least thing, and all too fond of being amused. On the other hand, with a dutiful, frumpish housewife who keeps her sidelocks tucked behind her ears and does nothing but housework, the husband who leaves in the morning and comes home at night, and who can hardly turn to strangers to chat about how so-and-so is getting on in public or private or about whatever, good or bad, may have happened to strike him and is entitled to expect some understanding from the woman who shares his life, finds instead, when he feels like discussing with her the things that have made him laugh or cry, or perhaps have inflamed him with righteous indignation and are now demanding an outlet, that all he can do is avert his eyes, and that when he then betrays private mirth or heaves a sad sigh, she just looks up at him blankly and asks, 'What is it, dear?' How could he not wish himself elsewhere? It is probably not a bad idea to take a wholly childlike, tractable wife and form her yourself as well as you can. She may not have your full confidence, but you

13. Genji and Tō no Chūjō.

will know your training has made a difference. Certainly, as long as you actually have her with you, you can let her pretty ways persuade you to overlook her lapses; but you will still regret her incompetence if, when you are away, you send her word about something practical or amusing that needs doing, and her response shows that she knows nothing about it and understands nothing either. Sometimes a wife who is not especially sweet or friendly does very well when you actually need her." The Chief Equerry's far-ranging discussion of his topic yielded no conclusion but a deep sigh.

"In the end, I suppose," he went on, "one should settle on someone wholly dependable, quiet, and steady, as long as there is nothing especially wrong with her, and never mind rank or looks. If beyond that she has any wit or accomplishment, simply be grateful, and if she lacks anything in particular, by no means seek to have her acquire it. Provided she is distinctly trustworthy and forgiving, you know, she will gain a more superficially feminine appeal all on her own.

"A woman may behave with comely modesty, put up with things that deserve reproof as though she did not even notice them and, in a word, affect prim detachment, until something is too much for her after all, and off she goes to hide herself away in a mountain village or on a deserted stretch of shore, leaving behind a shattering letter, a heartrending poem, and a token to remember her by. The gentlewomen used to read me stories like that when I was a boy. They upset me a lot—in fact, they seemed so tragic that I cried—but now that sort of thing strikes me as foolish and a bit of an act. Say our heroine *has* a legitimate grievance; she is still abandoning a husband who no doubt is very fond of her and running off as though she knew nothing of his feelings, and all she gains from upsetting him and testing his affection is lifelong regret. It is simply stupid.

"People keep telling her admiringly how right she was to act, until she is swept away, and all at once there she is, a nun. When she makes up her mind to do it, she is perfectly calm and cannot imagine looking back on her old life. 'Oh dear, I am so sorry,' all those who know her say when they come to call, 'I had no idea you felt so deeply about it.' Meanwhile, the husband

she never really disliked bursts into tears when he learns of all
this, prompting her staff and her old women to say, 'There,
your husband cares for you after all, and now look what you
have done!' She puts her hand to the hair at her forehead and
despairs to find it so short. Self-control fails, she begins to cry,
and she breaks down again and again each time she has reason
to feel a new pang of regret, until the Buddha himself can only
be disappointed with her. As far as I can see, halfhearted refuge
in religion is more likely to get you lost in an evil rebirth than
staying on in the mire of this world.

"Suppose this couple have strong enough karma between
them that the husband finds and claims his wife before she has
made herself into a nun: even so, once they are together again
each is bound to worry about what the other may be up to next,
despite the renewed affection that may come from their having
lived through so much. Besides, it is silly for a wife to quarrel
with a husband who is inclined to look elsewhere. Even if he is,
she can always trust him to remain her husband as long as his
first feeling for her still means anything to him, whereas an out-
burst like that may alienate him for good. She should always be
tactful, hinting when she has cause to be angry with him that,
yes, she knows, and bringing the issue up gently when she
might well quarrel with him instead, because that will only
make him like her better. Most of the time it is the wife's attitude that helps her husband's fancies to pass. It might seem en-
dearingly sweet of her to be wholly permissive and to let him
get away with everything, but that will only make her seem not
to deserve his respect. It is too bad when, as they say, an un-
moored boat just drifts away.[14] Do you not agree?"

Tō no Chūjō nodded. "It is bound to be particularly difficult
when one of a couple suspects the other, someone otherwise
loved and cherished, of infidelity; but although the injured
party, being blameless, may well then be quite prepared to overlook the matter, things may not go so easily. At any rate, the
best remedy when something comes between a couple is surely

14. An image from a poem on marriage by Bai Juyi.

patience." This remark, he felt, applied particularly well to his own sister, Aoi, and he was therefore both annoyed and disappointed that Genji was dozing and had nothing to add.

Having appointed himself the arbiter in these matters, the Chief Equerry continued his exposition of them while Tō no Chūjō, who was eager to hear him out, chimed in earnestly.

"Think of all this in terms of the arts," the Chief Equerry intoned. "Take, for example, the joiner who makes what he pleases from wood. He may turn out briefly amusing things, according to no set pattern and for only passing, minor uses—strikingly ingenious pieces that he keeps nicely attuned to fashion so that they pleasantly catch the eye; and yet one still distinguishes him easily from the true master who works with success in recognized forms, producing furnishings prized for being exactly right.

"Or take another example. By the time a skilled artist in the Office of Painting is deemed qualified to design a whole work, it is not easy to tell at a glance whether he is better or worse than another. Startling renderings of what no eye can see—things like Mount Hōrai, raging leviathans amid stormy seas, the fierce beasts of China, or the faces of invisible demons[15]—do indeed amaze the viewer, because they are convincing even though they resemble nothing real. Yet quite commonplace mountains and streams, the everyday shapes of houses, all looking just as one knows them to be and rendered as peaceful, welcoming forms mingling in harmony with gently sloping hills, thickly wooded, folded range upon wild range, and, in the foreground, a fenced garden: with such subjects as these, and there are many, the greater artist succeeds brilliantly in conception and technique, while the lesser one fails.

"In the same way, handwriting without depth may display a lengthened stroke here and there and generally claim one's attention until at first glance it appears impressively skilled, but although truly fine writing may lack superficial appeal, a second

15. Motifs from Chinese-style painting. Hōrai (Chinese Penglai) is a fabulous island inhabited by immortal beings.

look at the two together will show how much closer it is to what writing should be. That is the way it is in every field of endeavor, however minor. So you see, I have no faith in the obvious show of affection that a woman may sometimes put on. And I shall tell you how I learned this, though I am afraid the story is a little risqué."

He moved closer to Genji, who woke up, while Tō no Chūjō sat reverently facing him, chin in hand. The Chief Equerry might have been a preacher preparing to reveal the truth of existence, which was certainly amusing; but by now these young men were eager to share the most intimate moments of their lives.

"Long ago," he began, "when I was still very young, there was someone who meant a great deal to me. She was no great beauty, as I told you, and I, being young and inclined to explore, had no intention of staying with her forever, because although she was home to me, I felt I could do better, and so now and again I amused myself elsewhere. This drove her to a pitch of jealousy that I did not like at all, and I only wished she would stop and be more patient; but instead her violent suspicions became such a nuisance that I often found myself wondering why she was so intent on keeping me, since I was really no great prize. I felt sorry for her, though, and I began to mend my ways after all.

"It was like her to pour all her limited talent into accomplishing somehow for her husband things that really were beyond her and to be so cautious about betraying her shortcomings to her own disadvantage that she looked after me very well indeed, so as to give me no reason for ever being dissatisfied with her. I had thought her headstrong, but she did as I asked and humored me quite well; and lest her lack of looks offend me, she made herself as presentable as she could and hid shyly from strangers for fear of embarrassing me, meanwhile remaining so attentive that, as we went on living together, I found myself well pleased, except for this one detestable failing of hers, which she could not control.

"Then I thought to myself, She seems desperately eager to please: well, I must teach her a lesson. I shall threaten her, cure her a little of this failing, and curb her tongue. I assumed that as long as she really was that devoted, she would mend her ways if I put on a show of being fed up and eager to let her go. I purposely acted cold and distant, and when she grew angry and accusing, as she always did, I said, 'If you must carry on this way, never mind the strength of the bond between us, I shall leave and never come back. If you want to get rid of me, by all means keep up these absurd suspicions of yours. If you want me to stay with you forever, you will have to be patient and put up with things that may offend you, and if you change your attitude, I will like you very well. Once I am properly established and carry some weight in the world, you will have no rival.'[16]

"I was pleased with my sermon, but when I boldly began to elaborate, she gave me a thin smile and had the effrontery to say, 'I do not in the least mind seeing you through these years when you have little credit or standing, or waiting until you matter. No, that does not bother me at all. But I do hate the thought of spending year after year putting up with your cruelty in the vain hope that you will reform, and so I suppose it is time for us to part.'

"Now I was really angry, and I began saying awful things that she could hardly accept. Instead, she pulled one of my fingers to her and bit it, at which I flew into a rage. 'I can't go out in society wounded like this!' I roared. 'My office, my rank, of which you seem to think so little—just how, my fine lady, do you expect me now to hold my head up at all? As far as I can see, all that is left for me is to leave the world!' and so on.

" 'Very well,' I went on, 'as of today you and I are finished,' and I started to leave, hurt finger crooked. I said,

> 'Fingers crooked to count the many times you and I have been together
> show that this outrage of yours is certainly not the first.'[17]

You can hardly hold it against me!'

16. "I shall acknowledge you as my wife."
17. In Japan one crooks the fingers to count. This poem and the reply rely on several wordplays.

"Sure enough, she burst into tears and retorted,

'Talk of outrages: when in my most private thoughts I count up your own,
I believe this time at last I must take my hand from yours.'

"She and I had had a good fight, and although I still did not actually mean to leave her, I wandered here and there for several days without sending her a line. It was not until late one miserably sleety night, after the rehearsal for the Special Kamo Festival,[18] as we were all leaving the palace, that I realized I had no other home to go to than hers. The thought of spending the night at the palace did not appeal to me at all, and I knew how cold the company of some coy woman might be; so off I went, by way of just looking in on her to sound out her feelings, brushing away the snow and biting my nails with embarrassment, but still assuming that on a night like this she would welcome me after all.

"Her dimmed lamp was turned to the wall; a thick, comfortable robe was warming over a large censer frame;[19] all the curtains you would expect to find raised were up; and everything looked as though this was the night when she was expecting me back. Well, well! I thought, very pleased, until I noticed that she herself was not there. I saw only her usual women, who answered that at dark she had moved to her parents' house. She had left no touching poem, no encouraging note, nor any evidence whatever of thoughtfulness or consideration. I felt betrayed, and although I could not really believe that her merciless complaining had been meant only to make me hate her, I was annoyed enough to entertain the idea. Still, what she had left for me to wear was even more beautifully made than before, and its colors were even more pleasing. Even after I stormed out of the house, she had still been looking out for my every need.

18. *Kamo no rinji matsuri,* on the last day of the Bird in the eleventh month. Music was performed for the deity by the palace musicians, and the rehearsal was held in the palace.
19. *Fusego,* a cagelike structure placed over a censer. Clothes could be draped over it to be warmed and scented.

"Nonetheless, I could not imagine her to be serious about giving me up, and I did my best to mend things with her, but while she did not exactly reject me, did not pester me by going into hiding, and sent me tactfully worded answers, her attitude amounted to saying, 'I cannot go on with you as you have been. I will not have you back unless you reform.' I still did not believe she would let me go, though, and to teach her a lesson I said nothing about wanting to change. Instead, I put on a show of headstrong independence. She was so hurt that she died. That taught me that these things are no joke.

"I remember her as the model of a dependable wife. It was well worth discussing anything with her, whether a passing fancy or something important. At dyeing cloth she could have been called a Tatsuta Lady, at sewing she ranked with Tanabata,[20] and her skill at both made her a wonder." The Chief Equerry remembered her with feeling.

"I would have taken her faithfulness over her wonderful sewing," Tō no Chūjō remarked to lighten the conversation. "I have no doubt her marvelous dyeing was a real prize, though. The simplest blossoms or autumn leaves are dull and dreary when their colors fail to suit the season. That is why choosing a wife is so very hard."

"Anyway," the Chief Equerry went on, "I was visiting at the same time a very gifted woman who made poems with genuine wit and grace, wrote a beautiful running hand, had a lovely touch on the koto, and had a way with everything she did. And since there was nothing wrong with her looks either, I kept my scold to feel at home with and secretly went on seeing this other woman until I was quite attached to her. After the one I told you about had died, I was of course very sorry, but now that was behind me, and I saw the other one often until I noticed, as I had not before, that she was inclined to be vain and flirtatious, and so, to my mind, not to be trusted. After that I visited her

20. Tatsuta Hime, the "Tatsuta Lady," was associated with the beauty of colored autumn leaves and was therefore the patron goddess of dyeing. Tanabata, the Weaver Star who meets the Herdboy Star, her celestial lover, once a year on the night of the Tanabata Festival (the seventh day of the seventh month), was a patron of sewing, among other things.

less often, and meanwhile I discovered that secretly she had another lover.

"One beautifully moonlit night in the tenth month I was withdrawing from the palace when one of the privy gentlemen joined me in my carriage. I myself meant to spend the night at my father's, but the fellow insisted he was concerned about a house where someone was expecting him that very evening, and the place was just on the way to where *she* lived. You could see the lake through a break in the garden wall, and it seemed a shame to go straight past a house favored even by the moon,[21] so I got out as well.

"He must have arranged it all with her beforehand, because he was excited when he sat down on the veranda, I suppose it was, of the gallery near the gate. For some time he watched the moon. The chrysanthemums had all turned very nicely,[22] and the autumn leaves flitting by on the wind were really very pretty. Taking a flute from the fold of his robe, he began to play and to sing snatches of 'You will have shade,'[23] and so on, while she accompanied him expertly on a fine-toned *wagon* that she had all ready and tuned. The two of them were not at all bad. The *richi* mode, softly played by a woman from behind blinds,[24] sounded like the height of style, and in the brilliant moonlight the effect was very pleasant indeed.

"The delighted fellow moved right up to her blinds. 'No footsteps seem to have disturbed the fallen leaves in your garden,' he teased her,[25] and then, picking a chrysanthemum,

'With all the beauty of a house filled with music and a lovely moon,
have you yet successfully played to catch that cruel man?

21. The moon is reflected in the garden lake.
22. Frost-withered chrysanthemums were prized.
23. A *saibara* folk song: "You must stop at the Asukai spring, for you will have shade, the water is cool, the grazing is of the best . . ." The singer hints that he hopes to spend the night.
24. The blinds hang between her room and the veranda. The *wagon* ("Japanese koto") has six strings, and the *richi* mode was rather "minor" in feeling.
25. "Dear me, you seem to be all alone this evening."

I would never have thought it of you! Do play on, though. You must not be bashful, now that you have an audience eager for more!'

"To all this shameless banter she replied archly,

'Why, I have no words to play to keep by my side music of a flute
that joins in such harmonies with the wild and wandering wind.'[26]

"Little knowing how distasteful a show she was putting on, she next tuned a *sō no koto*[27] to the *banshiki* mode and played away in the best modern style, and very nicely, too, but I was thoroughly put off. The come-hither ways of a gentlewoman you meet now and again may have their charm for as long as you continue to see her, but when you are calling on someone you do not mean to forget, even if you do not do so all that often, anything silly or loose about her can put you off, and that is why I made that night my excuse to end it.

"Looking back on those two experiences, I note that even then, young as I was, I found that sort of uncalled-for forwardness strange and upsetting. In the future I will no doubt feel that way even more. Perhaps your lordships take pleasure only in the tender, willing fragility of the dewdrop fated to fall from the plucked flower or in the hail that melts when gathered from the gleaming leaf,[28] but I know you will understand me once you have seen seven more years pass by.[29] Please take my humble advice and beware of the pliant, easy woman. Any slip of hers can make her husband look a fool."

26. The wind refers with coquettish modesty to her own playing.
27. A thirteen-stringed instrument of the zither-like koto family.
28. Both similes evoke a young woman ready at a touch to swoon into a suitor's arms. The "flower" is the poetic *hagi,* whose long, drooping fronds bloom deep pink, violet, or white in autumn; while the "gleaming leaf" is *tamazasa,* a species of "dwarf bamboo." The mention of *hagi* refers to *Kokinshū* 223.
29. He is apparently seven years older than Genji. Although he started out talking to Tō no Chūjō, he must have begun addressing the higher-ranking Genji when Genji woke up.

Tō no Chūjō nodded as usual, while Genji smiled wryly in seeming agreement. "From what you say, you made a fine spectacle of yourself both times!" he remarked. They all laughed.

"I will tell you a fool's tale," Tō no Chūjō said.[30] "I had secretly begun seeing a woman who struck me as well worth the trouble, and although I assumed the affair would not last, the more I knew her, the more attached to her I became. Not that I necessarily visited her often, but I never forgot her, and things went on long enough that I saw she trusted me. There were of course times when even I supposed she might be jealous, but she seemed to notice nothing. She never complained about how seldom I came, even when it had been ages; instead she acted just as though I were setting out from her house every morning and coming home every evening. This touched me so much that I promised never to leave her. She had no parents, which made her life difficult, and it was quite endearing, the way she showed me now and again that for her I was indeed the one.

"Once, when I had not seen her for a long time (she was so quiet that I rather took her for granted), my wife, as I found out only later, managed to send her some veiled but extremely unpleasant threats. I had never imagined anything like that, and at heart I had not forgotten her, but she took it hard because she had had only silence from me so long; and what with her painful circumstances and, you see, the child she had as well, she finally resorted to sending me a pink—" He was almost in tears.

"But what did her letter say?" Genji asked.

"Oh, you know, nothing very much, really:

> 'Yes, ruin has come to the mountain rustic's hedge, but now and again
>   O let your compassion touch this little pink with fresh dew!'[31]

---

30. Commentators disagree over whether the "fool" (*shiremono*) is Tō no Chūjō or the woman.
31. "Rustic boor that I am, I know that I hardly deserve your favor, but do at least sometimes remember our dear child." The "little pink" (*Yamato nadeshiko*) is the future Tamakazura. *Kokinshū* 695: "Ah, how I miss her, and how I long to see her, the Yamato pink blooming in the rustic hedge!"

"That reminder brought me straight to her. She was as open and trusting with me as ever, but her expression was very sad, and as she sat in her poor house, gazing out over the dewy garden and crying in concert with the crickets' lament, I felt as though I must be living in some old tale. I answered,

'I could never choose one from the many colors blooming so gaily,
yet the gillyflower I feel is the fairest of them all.'[32]

I set aside the 'pink' for the time being, so as first to soothe her mother's feelings with 'No speck of dust' and so on. She replied mildly,

'To a gillyflower brushing a deserted bed with her dewy sleeves,
autumn has come all too soon, and the sorrows of its storms.'[33]

"I saw no sign that she was seriously angry with me, because even when she cried, she shyly hid her tears from me as well as she could, and her keen reluctance to let me see she knew I had neglected her made me so sure all was well that I again stayed away for a long time, during which she vanished without a trace. Life can hardly be treating her kindly if she is still alive. If she had just clung to me in any obvious way, while I loved her, I would never have allowed her to disappear as she did. Instead of neglecting her, I would have looked after her well and gone on seeing her indefinitely. The 'little pink' was very sweet, and I

32. "You are the only one I really care for." The *tokonatsu* ("gillyflower") and the *nadeshiko* ("pink") are the same flower, but the words have different associations. *Nadeshiko* refers to the child, *tokonatsu* to the mother. This is partly because of a play on *toko* (the "sleeping place" of lovers) in *Kokinshū* 167, by Ōshikōchi no Mitsune, to which Tō no Chūjō alludes a line or two later: "No speck of dust will I allow to soil this bed / gillyflower, abloom since you and I first lay down together."

33. The gillyflower's (lady's) sleeves are wet with tears; "brushing a deserted bed" refers to "No speck of dust will I allow . . ." in *Kokinshū* 167, Tō no Chūjō's source poem. The autumn storms are probably Tō no Chūjō's indifference and his wife's threats.

wish I could somehow find her, but so far I have not come across a single clue.

"This is a small illustration of just what you were talking about. She seemed so serene that I never knew she was hurt, and my lasting feeling for her went completely to waste. Even now, when I am beginning to forget her, she probably still thinks of me and has evenings when she burns with regret, although she has no one but herself to blame. She is a perfect example of the woman you cannot keep long and cannot actually depend on.

"All in all, the scold, though not easily forgotten, was so demanding to live with that anyone would probably have tired of her; the ever-so-clever woman with her koto music was guilty of sheer wantonness; and there is every reason, too, to doubt the fragile one I just told you about.[34] And so, in the end, it is simply impossible to choose one woman over another. That is how it is with them: each is bound to be trying, one way or another. Where will you find the one who has all the qualities we have been talking about and none of the faults? Set your heart on Kichijōten[35] herself, and you will find her so pious and stuffy, you will still be sorry!" They all laughed.

"Come," Tō no Chūjō urged the Aide of Ceremonial, "you must have a good story. Let us hear it!"

"How could your lordships take an interest in anything that a nobody like me might have to say?" But Tō no Chūjō only muttered, "Come, come," and kept at him until after due thought he began. "I was still a student at the Academy[36] when I knew a brilliant woman. Like the one the Chief Equerry wanted, you could talk over public affairs with her, her grasp of how to live life was penetrating, and on any topic her daunting learning simply left nothing further to add.

"It all started when I was visiting a certain scholar's home to

34. He surmises that her disappearance might have involved another man.
35. A seductively ample goddess of good fortune, probably Indian in origin. Her image was common in Buddhist temples, where tales were told about monks falling in love with her.
36. *Daigaku,* largely a school for training lower-ranking officials. The students studied Chinese poetry, philosophy, and history.

pursue my studies. Having gathered that he had several daughters, I seized a chance to make this one's acquaintance, which he had no sooner discovered than in he came, bearing wine cups and declaiming insinuatingly, 'Hark while I sing of two roads in life . . .'[37] I had no such wish, but I still managed somehow to go on seeing her, in order not to offend him.

"She was very good to me. Even while we lay awake at night, she would pursue my edification or instruct me in matters beneficial to a man in government service, and no note from her was ever marred by a single one of those *kana* letters, being couched in language of exemplary formality.[38] What with all this I could not have left her, because it was she who taught me how to piece together broken-backed Chinese poems and such,[39] and for that I remain eternally grateful. As to making her my dear wife, however, a dunce like me could only have been embarrassed to have her witness his bumbling efforts. Your lordships undoubtedly need that sort of conjugal tutelage even less than I did.[40] All this was foolish of me, I agree, and I should have forgone my involvement with her, but sometimes destiny just draws you on. I suppose the men are really the foolish ones."

"But what an extraordinary woman!" Tō no Chūjō wanted to get him to finish. The Aide of Ceremonial knew he would have to, but he still wrinkled up his nose before complying.

"Well, I had not been to see her for a long time when for some reason I went again. She was not in her usual room; instead she spoke to me through an absurd screen. Is she jealous, then? I wondered, at once amused by this nonsense and perfectly conscious that this might be just the chance I was looking for. But no, my paragon of learning was not one to

37. A homily on marriage from a poem by Bai Juyi. The wine cups, too, are in the poem, which stresses the wisdom of taking a bride from a poor home.
38. Women wrote mainly in the phonetic *kana* script, men in more or less accomplished Chinese. This avoidance of *kana* (her letters are entirely in Chinese characters) creates a strangely formal, masculine effect.
39. "Broken-backed" (*koshi ore*) is a term of poetic criticism.
40. Genji and Tō no Chūjō rank so high that they need no accomplishment to get ahead.

indulge in frivolous complaints. She knew the world and its ways too well to be upset with me. Instead she briskly announced, 'Having lately been prostrate with a most vexing indisposition, I have for medicinal purposes been ingesting *Allium sativum*,[41] and my breath, I fear, is too noxious to allow me to entertain you in my normal fashion. However, while I cannot address you face-to-face, I hope that you will communicate to me any services you may wish me to perform on your behalf.'

"It was an imposing oration. What could I possibly answer? I just said, 'Very well,' got up, and started out. I suppose she had been hoping for something better, because she called after me, 'Do return when the odor has abated!' I hated to pretend I had not heard her, but this was no time to waver, and besides, the smell really was rather overpowering, so in desperation I glanced back at her and replied,

'When the spider's ways this evening gave fair warning I would soon arrive,
    how strange of you to tell me, Come after my garlic days![42]

What kind of excuse is that?'
"I fled once the words were out, only to hear behind me,

'If I meant to you enough that you came to me each and every night,
    why should my garlic days so offend your daintiness?'

Oh, yes, she was very quick with her tongue," the Aide calmly concluded.

The appalled young gentlemen assumed that he must have made up his story, and they burst into laughter. "There cannot be any such woman!" cried Tō no Chūjō. "You might as well

41. Garlic.
42. His sally and her retort both play on *hiru* ("garlic") and *hiruma* ("daytime"). Poetic lore had it that a woman could tell whether her lover was coming by watching a spider's behavior.

have made friends with a demon. It is too weird!" He snapped his fingers[43] and glared at the Aide in mute outrage. "Come," he finally insisted, "you will have to do better!"

However, the Aide stood fast. "How do you expect me to improve on that?" he said.

"I cannot stand the way mediocrities, men or women, so long to show off all the tiny knowledge they may possess," the Chief Equerry put in. "There is nothing at all attractive about having absorbed weighty stuff like the Three Histories and the Five Classics, and besides, why should anyone, just because she is a woman, be completely ignorant of what matters in this world, public or private? A woman with any mind at all is bound to retain many things, even if she does not actually study. So she writes cursive Chinese characters after all and crams her letters more than half full of them, even ones to other women, where they are hopelessly out of place, and you think, Oh no! If only she could be more feminine! She may not have meant it that way, but the letter still ends up being read to her correspondent in a stiff, formal tone, and it sounds as though that was what she had meant all along. A lot of senior gentlewomen do that sort of thing, you know.

"The woman out to make poetry becomes so keen on it that she stuffs her very first line with allusions to great works from the past, until it is a real nuisance to get a poem from her when you have other things on your mind. You cannot very well not reply, and you look bad if circumstances at the moment prevent you from doing so.

"Take the festivals, for example. Say it is the morning of the Sweet Flag Festival. You are off to the palace in such a rush that everything is a blur, and she presents you with one of her efforts, quivering with incredible wordplays;[44] or it is time for the Chrysanthemum Festival, you are racking your brains to work out a tricky Chinese poem, and here comes a lament from her,

43. A gesture of censure or irritation.
44. Poems for this occasion are full of plays on *ayame* ("sweet flag") and other words associated with the event, and so at this point is the Chief Equerry's own speech.

full of 'chrysanthemum dew'[45] and, as usual, quite out of place.
At other times, too, her way of sending you out of season a
poem that afterward you might admit is not actually at all bad,
without pausing to think that you may be unable even to give it
a glance, can hardly be called very bright. She would do better
to refrain from showing off her wit and taste whenever her failure to grasp your circumstances leaves you wondering why she
had to do it, or cursing the fix she has put you in. A woman
should feign ignorance of what she knows and, when she wants
to speak on a subject, leave some things out."

Meanwhile Genji was absorbed in meditation on one lady
alone.[46] By the standard of this evening's discussion she had neither too little nor too much of any quality at all, and this
thought filled him with wonder and a desperate longing.

The debate reached no conclusion and lapsed at last into dis-
jointed gossip that the young men kept up until dawn.

The weather today was clear at last. Genji went straight to
the Minister of the Left's, fearing that so long a seclusion at the
palace might have displeased his father-in-law. Both the look of
the place and Aoi's own manner were admirably distinguished,
for neither could be faulted in any way, and it seemed to Genji
that she should be the ideal wife singled out as a treasure by his
friends the evening before, but in fact he found such perfection
too oppressive and intimidating for comfort.

He amused himself chatting with such particularly worth-
while young gentlewomen as Chūnagon and Nakatsukasa, who
were delighted to see him, loosely clothed as he was in the heat.
His father-in-law then appeared and talked with him through a
standing curtain, since Genji was not presentable, while Genji
reclined on an armrest, making wry faces and muttering, "Isn't
it hot enough for him?" "Hush!" he added when the women
laughed. He was the picture of carefree ease.

45. Ladies moistened a bit of chrysanthemum-patterned brocade with dew
from chrysanthemum flowers, rubbed their cheeks with it to smooth the wrinkles of age (since chrysanthemum dew conferred immortal youth), and composed poems lamenting the sorrows of growing old.
46. Fujitsubo.

At dark a woman remarked to him, "Tonight the Mid-God has closed this direction from the palace."

"That is right, my lord, this is a direction you would normally shun."[47]

"But Nijō[48] is in the same direction! How am I to avoid it? Besides, I am exhausted." Genji lay down to sleep.

"Oh, no, my lord, you must not!"

"The Governor of Kii, who serves the Minister of the Left, lives in a house by the Nakagawa,[49] and the place is nice and cool—he recently diverted the stream through his property."

"That should do very well," Genji answered. "I am so tired, I do not care where it is, as long as they will let my ox in through the gate."[50]

There must have been many other houses where he could have gone discreetly to avoid that direction, but having only just arrived at his father-in-law's after a long absence, he did not wish to seek another lady's company in order to do so.

Kii bowed to Genji's command, but he groaned as he withdrew. "A difficulty at the Iyo Deputy's house has obliged all his women to move in with me," he said, "and my little place is so crowded that I am afraid he may suffer some affront to his dignity."

Genji heard him. "I shall be much happier to have them near me. I would be afraid to spend the night away from home without women. Just put me behind their standing curtains."

"That is right. I expect his house will do beautifully," a gentlewoman chimed in, and a runner was sent to announce Genji's

47. The Mid-God (Nakagami), one of the deities of yin-yang lore, moved in a sixty-day cycle. Having spent the first sixteen days in the heavens, the deity descended to earth and circled the compass, spending five or six days in each of the eight directions. One shunned (*imu*) travel in a direction "blocked" (*futagaru*) by this deity. Genji's planned destination violates this taboo, and he must now "evade" (*tagau*) the "blocked" direction by taking refuge elsewhere, in another direction from his point of departure (the palace).

48. Genji's residence, on "Second Avenue."

49. A stream, now gone, in the northeastern part of the city.

50. Only a great lord could have had his ox carriage driven in through someone's gate.

arrival. Genji hurried off so secretly, to so purposely discreet a destination, that he kept his departure from his father-in-law and took with him only his closest companions.

"This is so sudden!" Kii's household complained, but Genji's entourage ignored them. His men had the eastern aisle of the main house swept, aired, and made ready as well as they could.

The stream was very prettily done in its way.[51] There was a brushwood fence, as in the country, and the garden was carefully planted. The breeze was cool, insects were singing here and there, and fireflies were flitting in all directions. The place was delightful. Genji's companions sat drinking wine and peering down at the stream that emerged from beneath the bridgeway.[52] While his host went darting about in search of refreshments,[53] Genji relaxed and gazed out into the night, remembering what he had heard the evening before about the middle class of women and reflecting that this must be the kind of place where such women lived.

He had noted a rumor that the young woman here, Utsusemi, was proud, and he was sufficiently curious about her to listen until he detected telltale sounds to the west: the rustling of silks and the pleasant voices of young women. Yes, he caught stifled laughter that sounded somehow self-conscious.

Their lattice shutters had been up, but when Kii disapprovingly lowered them, Genji stole to where lamplight streamed through a crack over the sliding panel, to see what he could see. There was no gap to give him a view, but he went on listening and realized that they must be gathered nearby in the chamber, because he could hear them whispering to each other, apparently about him.

"He is still so young. It is a shame he is so serious and already so well settled."

"Still, I hear he often calls secretly on suitably promising ladies."

51. It would have run north-south between the main dwelling and its east wing, hence next to where Genji was staying.
52. *Watadono,* between the main dwelling and the east wing.
53. A reference to a folk song in which a host leaves his guests the wine jar and "goes darting about" to fetch edible seaweed from the shore.

Genji, whose every thought was of *her*, was appalled to imagine them next discussing that in the same way, but he heard nothing more of interest and gave up his eavesdropping. They were talking about a poem that he had sent with some bluebells to Princess Asagao,[54] although they had it slightly wrong. Well, he thought, she simply has time on her hands and a taste for poetry. I do not suppose she is worth looking at anyway.

The Governor of Kii returned with more lanterns, raised the lamp wick, and offered him refreshments.

"What about the curtains, then?" Genji asked. "It is a poor host who does not think of that!"[55]

"My lord, I have been told nothing about what might please you," Kii protested deferentially. Genji lay down as though for a nap near the veranda, and his companions settled down as well.

Genji's host had delightful children, one of whom Genji had already seen as a page in the privy chamber. The Iyo Deputy's children were there, too. One of the boys, a child of twelve or thirteen, had something special about him. While answering Genji's questions about which child was whose, Kii told him that this one was the youngest son of the late Intendant of the Gate Watch. "His father, who was very fond of him, passed away when he was small," Kii explained, "and he is here now under his elder sister's care. I hope to have him serve in the privy chamber, since he shows aptitude for scholarship and is generally bright, but things seem not to be going well."[56]

"I am sorry to hear that: This sister of his—is she your stepmother?"

"Yes, my lord."

"Then you have a most unlikely one! Even His Majesty has heard of her. He was saying some time ago, 'Her father hinted

---

54. These bluebells (*asagao*) have supplied the lady's traditional name (Asagao). She is Genji's first cousin, since her father is the Emperor's younger brother.

55. "It is a poor host who does not have a woman ready for his guest." Genji alludes to a *saibara* song: "In my house the curtains are all hung; come, my lord, come: my daughter shall be yours . . ." The song then mentions sea urchin (*kase*), a shell felt to resemble the female genitals.

56. Without his father the boy has no one well placed to back him.

that he was thinking of sending her into palace service—I wonder what became of her.' Ah," he sighed with grown-up gravity, "you never know what life will bring."

"It is a surprise to have her here. No, when it comes to love and marriage, it has always been impossible to divine the future, and unfortunately a woman's fate is especially hard to foresee."

"Does the Iyo Deputy pamper her? He must think the world of her."

"He certainly does, my lord. He seems to adore her, in fact, although, like the others,[57] I dislike his being so engrossed."

"He is not going to leave her to any of you, though, just because you are up on the latest fashions. There is nothing drab about the Iyo Deputy—he rather fancies a certain chic himself. Where is she anyway?"

"I sent them all off to the servants' hall, my lord, although perhaps not all of them managed actually to go."

Genji's companions, by now quite drunk, were asleep on the veranda. Genji, too, lay down, but in vain. Dislike for sleeping alone kept him awake, listening to the sounds from beyond the sliding panel to the north and fascinated that this must be where the lady they had talked about was now hiding. Silently he arose and stood by the panel to listen.

"Excuse me, where are you?" It was the appealingly husky voice of the boy who had caught his attention earlier.

"Lying over here. Is our guest asleep? I thought I would be next to him, but he is actually quite far away." The speaker's sleepy voice had a languid quality very like the boy's, and Genji realized that she must be his elder sister.

"He's gone to sleep in the aisle," the boy whispered. "Everyone is talking about how he looks, and I actually saw him! It's true, he is ever so handsome!"

"I'd have a peep at him myself if it were daytime," she answered drowsily, her voice sounding as though it came from under the covers.

57. The Iyo Deputy's other children.

Oh, come, he thought impatiently, do ask him a bit more about me than that!

"I'll sleep over here. It's so dark, though!" He seemed to be raising the lamp wick.

Utsusemi must be lying diagonally across from Genji's door. "Where is Chūjō?"[58] he heard her say. "I am afraid when there is no one nearby."

"She went to the bath in the servants' hall—she said she would be back very soon." The answer came from the women lying a step below her.[59]

When all seemed quiet, he tried the latch. It was not locked from the other side. In the entrance stood a curtain, and by the lamp's dim glow he saw what seemed to be chests scattered about the room. Threading his way among them to where he guessed her to be, he came upon a slight figure lying all alone. The approaching footsteps startled her a little, but until he actually tugged at her bedclothes she took him for the gentlewoman she had wanted.

"You called for a Chūjō, you see,[60] and I knew my secret yearning for you had inspired its reward."

Utterly confused, she thought she was having a nightmare and cried out, but the covers over her face stifled the sound.

"This is so sudden that you will surely take it for a mere whim of mine, which I quite understand, but actually I only want you to know that my thoughts have been with you for years. Please note how eagerly I have made the best of this chance, and so judge how far I am from failing to be in earnest."

He spoke so gently that she could not very well cry out rudely, "There is a man in here!" because not even a demon would have wished to resist him; but shock and dismay at his

58. One of her women.
59. They are in the aisle room, diagonally across the chamber from Genji. The aisle was a beam width lower.
60. He pretends to take the woman's name to mean himself. Chūjō means "Captain" (she may be the daughter or the wife of a Captain), and Genji is a Chūjō in the Palace Guards.

behavior drew from her, in an anguished whisper, "Surely you mean someone else!"

Nearly fainting, she roused him to pity and tenderness, and he decided that he liked her very much. "If only you would not doubt the unerring desire that has brought me to you!" he said. "I will take no liberties with you, I promise, but I must tell you something of my feelings."

He picked her up, since she was very small, and he had carried her to the sliding door when he came on someone else, presumably the Chūjō she had called for. Chūjō, startled by his exclamation, was groping her way toward him when a breath of his pervasive fragrance enveloped her, and she understood. Although shocked and appalled, she found nothing to say. If he had been anyone ordinary, she would have wrested her mistress bodily from him, but even that would have been a risk, since everyone else would then have known what was going on; so she simply followed with beating heart while he proceeded, unruffled, into the inner room.[61]

"Come for your mistress at dawn." He slid the door shut.

The lady could have died to imagine what Chūjō might be thinking. Dripping with perspiration, she was so clearly miserable that Genji felt sorry for her, but he managed as always to draw from some hidden source a flood of tender eloquence to win her over.

"This is not to be believed!" She was indignant. "I may be insignificant, but even I could never mistake your contemptuous conduct toward me for anything more than a passing whim. You have your place in the world and I have mine, and we have nothing in common."

It upset him to find that his forwardness really did repel her, and he saw how justly she was outraged. "I know nothing of your place and mine in the world," he protested earnestly, "because I have never done anything like this before! It is cruel of you to take me for a common adventurer. You must have heard

61. It is not clear which room is meant, but the most plausible possibility is a divided-off section of the chamber itself—perhaps a fully walled-in "retreat" (*nurigome*).

enough about me to know that I do not force my attentions on anyone. I myself am surprised by this madness, which has earned me your wholly understandable disapproval. I can only think that destiny has brought us together."

He gravely tried every approach, but his very peerlessness only stiffened her resistance, and she remained obdurate, resolved that no risk of seeming cold and cruel should discourage her from refusing to respond. Although pliant by nature, she had called up such strength of character that she resembled the supple bamboo, which does not break.

Her genuine horror and revulsion at Genji's willfulness shocked him, and her tears touched him. It pained him to be the culprit, but he knew that he would have been sorry not to have had her. "Why must you dislike me so?" he said accusingly when she refused to be placated. "Do see that the very strangeness of all this confirms the bond we share. I cannot bear your remaining so withdrawn, as though you knew nothing of the ways of the world!"

"If you had shown me such favor when I was as I used to be, before I settled into my present, unhappy condition, I might have entertained giddy hopes and consoled myself with visions of the day when you would think well of me after all, but the very idea of a night with you, when there can be no more, troubles me greatly. No, you must forget that this ever happened."[62]

No wonder she felt as she did. He undoubtedly did his best to comfort her and to convince her that her fears were misplaced.

A cock crowed, and the household began to stir. "How long we have slept!" a voice exclaimed from among Genji's men, and another, "Advance his lordship's carriage!" The Governor of Kii appeared, too, and one of the women protested, "He is only here to avoid a taboo! There is no reason why he should hurry off again in the middle of the night!"[63] Genji suffered to think that such a chance might never come again, that he could

62. "You must not imagine that the liberties you have taken constitute any kind of precedent for the future. What you have done has not established a relationship between you and me."
63. As there would be if he had come for a secret rendezvous.

hardly visit the house on purpose, and that even correspondence with her was probably out of the question.

She was so upset when Genji came in that he let her go, but then he drew her to him again. "How can I keep in touch with you? Both your unheard-of hostility and my feeling for you will leave vivid memories and be a wonder forever." His tears only gave him a new grace.

Cocks were crowing insistently. He said in despair,

"Dawn may well have come, but when I could still complain of your cruelty,
must the cock crow me awake before I have all I wish?"[64]

Mortified by the gulf between them, since she was who she was, she remained unmoved by his attentions. Instead her thoughts went to the far province of Iyo and to the husband whom she usually dismissed with such loathing and contempt, and she trembled lest he glimpse this scene in a dream. She answered,

"Now that dawn at last has broken on the misery that I still bewail,
the cock himself lifts his voice to spread my lament abroad."

It was quite light by now, and Genji saw her to the door of the room. He kept it shut as he said good-bye, because the house was alive with movement within and without, and he grieved that it should be about to part them, as he supposed, forever. Then he slipped on his dress cloak and gazed out south across the railing. To the west, shutters went up with a clatter: women must have been stealing a look at him. No doubt the more susceptible were thrilled by his dim form, visible over the low screen that divided their stretch of veranda from his. The moon still lingered on high, clear despite the pallor of its light, turning

64. Genji's poem plays on *tori* ("cock") and *tori aenu* ("before I grasp [what I seek]"); hers similarly exploits *tori kasanete* ("again and again [I / the cock lament . . .]").

dull shadows to a lovely dawn. To one viewer the vacant sky intimated romance, while to the other it suggested aloof indifference. He was heartsick to think that he could not even get a note to her, and as he left, he looked back again and again.

At home once more he still could not sleep. What tormented him even more than being unable to see her again was the thought of her own feelings. Not that there was anything remarkable about her, but, as he knew, she nicely represented the middle grade they had discussed, with all its appeal, and he understood how truly the man of broad experience had spoken.

These days he spent all his time at the Minister of the Left's. Forever anxious about her feelings in the absence of any message from him, he called the Governor of Kii and said, "Would you give me that boy I saw the other day—the late Intendant's son? He appealed to me, and I should like to take him into my personal service. I shall present him to His Majesty myself."

"You do him and us too great an honor, my lord. I shall convey your request to his elder sister."

"Has she given you any brothers or sisters?" Genji managed to ask with beating heart.

"No, my lord. It is two years now since she joined our family, but I gather that she regrets not having done as her father wished and that she dislikes her present condition."

"What a shame! People speak well of her. Is it true that she is pretty?"

"I expect so, my lord. She keeps me at such a distance that I am no closer to her than a stepson should be."

Five or six days later Kii brought Genji his young brother-in-law. The boy was not strikingly handsome, but he had grace, and his distinction was plain. Genji called him in for a very friendly talk. The boy was thoroughly pleased and impressed in his childish way. He answered pointed questions about his sister as well as he could, until his daunting composure made it difficult for Genji to go on. Still, Genji managed cleverly to convey his desire.[65]

The boy was surprised when Genji's point dawned on him at

65. That the boy should carry messages for him.

last, but he was too young to understand very well what it implied, and his arrival with Genji's letter brought tears of vexation to Utsusemi's eyes. It horrified her to imagine what he might be thinking, and she opened the letter so that it hid her face. It was very long.

> *"Even as I mourn not knowing whether that dream[66] means another night,*
> *endless time seems to go by while my eyelids never close.*

At night I cannot sleep . . ."[67] His writing was so extraordinarily beautiful that her eyes misted over, and she lay down to ponder the strange destiny that had broken in upon her otherwise dreary life.

When Genji's summons reached her little brother the next day, he let her know he was going and asked for her answer.

"Tell him there was no one here to receive such a letter."

He only laughed. "How can I say that? He made himself perfectly clear."

She gathered that Genji had told him everything, and she recoiled. "I'll thank you not to be impertinent. Then just don't go."

He went anyway, though, saying, "He wants me—I can't just ignore him."

Kii liked women too much not to think his stepmother's marriage a great shame, and he was always eager to please her, which is why he made much of her little brother and took him about everywhere.

Genji called the boy in. "I waited for you all day yesterday. Getting on with me seems to mean nothing to you." The boy reddened.

"Well, where is it?"

The boy explained what had happened. "It is really hopeless, isn't it," Genji said. "She is impossible." He handed him yet another letter.

66. *Yume*, a lovers' meeting.
67. *Shūishū* 735, by Minamoto no Shitagō: "What comfort have I from my longing for you, when at night I cannot sleep and so never dream?"

"You may not realize this," he went on, "but I was seeing her long before that old man the Iyo Deputy. She probably thought me too spindly then to lean on, so she found herself a man of real substance to look after her, and now she is making a fool of me. Be a son to me, though. That fine husband of hers will not last much longer." It amused him to see the boy so gravely credulous and impressed.

He kept her brother with him all the time and took him even to the palace. He had those in charge of his wardrobe make clothes for him, and the boy really did treat him like a father. There was always a note for him to deliver. However, she worried that he was much too young, and that if unfortunately he lost one, she might find added to her present woes a light reputation unbecoming to someone in her position, and she therefore kept her answers formal, reflecting that what constitutes good fortune depends after all on where one stands in the world. Not that she failed to recall his figure and manner, extraordinary as these had been that one time when she had made him out through the gloom, but she concluded that nothing could come of her seeking to please him.

Genji thought of her endlessly, with mingled consternation and longing. He could not keep from dwelling on how much her distress had affected him. He might risk slipping in to see her, but with so many people in the house his misbehavior would be discovered, and that, he saw with alarm, would be disastrous for her.

While he was spending day after day at the palace, as always, a directional taboo favored him once more. Feigning an impromptu departure for His Excellency's, he turned off on the way there toward the house of the Governor of Kii. The surprised Kii took his visit for a gratifying tribute to the stream that he had diverted through his garden.

Genji had brought her little brother into the plot that afternoon. In the evening he immediately called for him again, since he had him at his beck and call day and night. Utsusemi had heard from him as well. She did not underestimate the interest that his scheme revealed, but she still had no wish recklessly to yield him her whole, modest person or to add new troubles to those already heaped upon her by their first, dreamlike encounter. No, decidedly, she would not fall in with his machinations and receive him; and so, as soon as Genji called her little brother away, she announced that she disliked being so near where he was staying and that anyway she was feeling unwell. "I shall move farther off for a quiet massage," she said, and she went to hide in Chūjō's room along the bridgeway.

Genji, whose plans were laid, had his entourage retire early and sent her a note, but her brother could not find her. Only after hunting high and low did he go down the bridgeway and come across her at last. "He'll think I'm no use at all!" the boy cried, nearly weeping with anger and frustration.

"I will not have you take this awful attitude!" she scolded him. "They say a child should never carry such messages. Tell him that I am not feeling well and that I have kept my women with me for a massage. Everyone will be wondering what you are doing here."

In her heart of hearts, though, she felt that she might receive Genji gladly, however seldom, if only she were not now settled for life but were still at home, where the memory of her late parents and of their ambitions for her lived on. Despite her resolve, she suffered acutely to think that he must find her adamant rejection outrageously impertinent. However, it was too late now for such thoughts, and she made up her mind to remain stubbornly unresponsive to the end.

Genji lay waiting, eager to find out what her little brother might devise and at the same time nervous about his being so young. When he learned that there was no hope, her astonishing obduracy made him so detest his own existence that his distress was painfully obvious. For some time he was silent and only heaved great sighs. He was very hurt.

> "I who never knew what it was the broom tree meant now wonder to find
> the road to Sonohara led me so far from my way.[68]

68. Sonohara (in Shinano Province) is associated with a bush called *hahakigi* ("broom tree"), similar to broom. *Kokin rokujō* 3019 (slightly modified as *Shinkokinshū* 997), by Sakanoue no Korenori, describes *hahakigi* as visible from a distance and yet invisible as one comes nearer.

I have nothing to say," he wrote at last.

She, too, was still awake, and she answered,

> *"Stricken with regret to have it known she was born in a humble home,*
> *the broom tree you briefly glimpsed fades and is soon lost to view."*[69]

She did not like to have her brother roaming about like this, too upset over Genji's annoyance to sleep, because she was afraid that he might arouse suspicion.

Genji's men slept soundly, as usual, while he alone gave himself over to vain, outraged ruminations. It infuriated him that her amazing resistance, far from disappearing, had instead risen to this pitch, and he was beside himself with outrage and injury, although he also knew perfectly well that strength of character was what had attracted him to her in the first place.

So be it, he told himself, but he remained so unconvinced that he was soon saying, "All right, then take me to where she is hiding."

"She has shut herself up in a little room and has several women with her—I wouldn't dare," her brother replied, desperately wishing he could do better.

"Very well, then you, at least, shall not leave me." Genji had the boy lie down with him. The boy so appreciated his master's youth and gentleness that they say Genji found him much nicer than his cruel sister.

---

69. *Fuseya,* associated with the name Sonohara, may be a place name or a word for a low, humble dwelling.

4
(SLIGHTLY ABRIDGED)

YŪGAO
THE TWILIGHT BEAUTY

The *yūgao* ("twilight beauty"; more literally, "evening face")
is a vine that the chapter introduces this way: "A bright
green vine, its white flowers smiling to themselves, was clambering merrily over what looked like a board fence." Near
the start of the chapter, these flowers figure in an exchange of
poems between Genji and the young woman known ever
since as Yūgao.

Chapter 4 begins in the summer when Genji is seventeen
and continues up to the tenth month.

In the days when Genji was calling secretly on the Rokujō
Haven,[1] he decided to visit his old nurse on the way there, since
she was seriously ill and had become a nun. Her house was on
Gojō.[2]

When he found the gate that should have admitted his carriage locked, he sent for Koremitsu,[3] and while he waited he examined the unprepossessing spectacle of the avenue. Next door
stood a house with new walls of woven cypress, surmounted by
a line of half-panel shutters. Four or five of these were open,
and through very pale, cool-looking blinds he saw the pretty

1. Rokujō ("Sixth Avenue") is where this lady lives. The title "Haven" (*Miya-sudokoro*) means that she has borne an imperial child. In the original of chapter 1, Genji's mother, too, is called *Miyasudokoro* after his birth.
2. "Fifth Avenue," between the palace and Rokujō.
3. This use of his personal name suggests his intimate, subordinate relationship
with Genji.

foreheads of several young women who were peering out at him.[4] They seemed oddly tall, judging from where the floor they were standing on ought to be. He wondered who they were, to be gathered there like that.

Having kept his carriage very modest and sent no escort ahead, he was confident of remaining unrecognized, and he therefore peered out a little.[5] The gate, propped open like a shutter panel,[6] gave onto a very small space. It was a poor little place, really. Touched, he recalled "What home is ours forever?"[7] and saw that the house might just as well be a palace.[8]

A bright green vine, its white flowers smiling to themselves, was clambering merrily over what looked like a board fence. "A word I would have with you, O you from afar,"[9] he murmured absently, at which a man of his went down on one knee and declared, "My lord, they call that white flower 'twilight beauty.'[10] The name makes it sound like a lord or lady, but here it is blooming on this pitiful fence!"

---

4. The house is an *itaya,* a modest dwelling roofed with boards rather than cypress bark thatch or tiles. To about chest height it has *higaki*—walls faced with thin, crisscrossed slats of cypress (*hinoki*) wood; these are then extended upward by half-panel shutters (*hajitomi*) that can be swung up and secured open in a horizontal position. Each panel covers the full space (*ken*) between two structural pillars. The "four or five" panels probably cover the full width of the house. The paleness of the blinds (*sudare*) shows them to be new.

5. Presumably through his carriage's side window (*monomi*) or past the edge of the blind that covered the carriage's rear entrance.

6. The gate was attached to a horizontal crosspiece and swung open vertically. It was propped open with a pole.

7. *Kokinshū* 987: "In all this world, what home is ours forever? Mine shall be the lodging I come upon tonight."

8. *Kokin rokujō* 3874: "What need have I for a palace? Rather to lie with you where the weeds grow thick."

9. *Kokinshū* 1007: "A word I would have with you, O you from afar who gaze into the distance: that white flower blooming yonder—what is its name?"

10. *Yūgao* (more literally, "evening face"). Genji's attendant observes that this name makes the flower sound like a "person" (*hito*), meaning someone who "is someone," that is, socially distinguished. In this context *yūgao* refers either to Genji himself or to the woman for whom the chapter is named, and "beauty" is therefore meant as an allusion to both.

The neighborhood houses were certainly cramped and shabby, leaning miserably in every direction and fringed with snaggle-toothed eaves, but the vine was climbing all over them. "Poor flowers!" Genji said. "Go and pick me some."

His man went in the open gate and did so, whereupon a pretty little servant girl in long trousers of sheer yellow raw silk stepped out through a plain but handsome sliding door and beckoned to him. "Here," she said, "give them to him on this—their stems are so hopeless." She handed him a white, intensely perfumed fan.

The other gate opened just then, and out came Lord Kore-mitsu. The man had him give Genji the flowers. "My lord," Koremitsu apologized, "we had unfortunately mislaid the key, and so we have caused you a great deal of trouble. No one in this neighborhood could possibly know you, but still, the way your carriage is standing out here in this grubby avenue . . ." He brought the carriage in, and Genji alighted.[11]

Koremitsu's elder brother the Adept,[12] his brother-in-law the Governor of Mikawa, and his sister were all gathered in the house. Genji's arrival pleased them and made them very grateful.

The nun sat up. "For me it no longer matters," she said tear-fully, "but what made it difficult to renounce the world was the thought that you would then have to see me in so strange a guise.[13] I feel much better, though, now that I have received the Precepts and have had the joy of this visit from you, and I can look forward in peace to the light of Lord Amida."[14]

"It has worried and saddened me that your illness has contin-ued so long unrelieved, but I deeply regret that you have now vis-ibly renounced the world. Please live on to see me rise higher still.

---

11. Genji enters this gate in his carriage, as he did at the Governor of Kii's, be-cause the people are below him in rank.

12. *Ajari*, a Buddhist ecclesiastical title.

13. As a nun.

14. She has vowed to uphold the Buddhist rules of conduct (the Precepts) and looks forward to going to the paradise of the Buddha Amida. There were nine possible grades of birth into this paradise. The lowest of these required a more or less long wait before the soul could fully witness Amida's glory.

Once I have done so, you may achieve as swiftly as you wish the loftiest of the nine births in Paradise. They say one should retain no attachment to the world." Genji, too, spoke in tears.

The eyes of one as fond as a nurse will see implausible perfection even in the least gifted child; no wonder, then, that she felt honored to have been in his intimate service and wished to avoid causing him the pain of her loss. This was why she could not keep from weeping. Her acutely embarrassed children darted each other sidelong glances before so unbecoming a show of emotion in Genji's presence, as though their mother could not after all give up the world that she was supposed to have renounced.

He was very moved. "When I was little, everyone who should have loved me left me.[15] Of course I had people to look after me, but you were then the one to whom I felt especially close. Now that I am grown up and can no longer always be with you or visit you as I please, I still miss you when I have been away from you too long. How I wish that there were no final parting!"[16] He talked on tenderly, and the scent of the sleeves with which he wiped his eyes meanwhile perfumed the whole room, until the children, who just now had deplored their mother's behavior, willingly granted that she had indeed enjoyed great good fortune in her life, and they all dissolved in tears.

After ordering further rites for her, he had Koremitsu bring in a hand torch in preparation for leaving. On inspecting the fan presented to him earlier, he found it to be deeply impregnated with the scent favored by its owner and delightfully inscribed with this poem:

> "At a guess I see that you may indeed be he: the light silver dew
> brings to clothe in loveliness a twilight beauty flower."[17]

15. Probably his mother, who died in his third year, and his grandmother, who died in his sixth.
16. *Kokinshū* 901 (also *Ise monogatari* 154, section 84), by Ariwara no Narihira: "Would that in this world there were no final parting, for a son who wishes his mother a thousand years!"
17. "You *are* Genji, are you not?" He is the dew, she the flower.

The writing was disguised, but its grace and distinction pleasantly surprised him.

"Who lives in that house to the west?" he asked Koremitsu. "Have you inquired?"

Here he goes again! thought Koremitsu, but he kept his peace and only answered a little curtly, "My lord, I have been here five or six days, it is true, but I have been too occupied caring for my mother to learn anything about next door."

"You dislike my asking, don't you. Still, I believe I have reason to look further into this fan, and I want you to call in someone acquainted with the neighborhood and find out."

Koremitsu went inside and questioned the caretaker. "The place apparently belongs to a provincial official," he eventually reported. "He says the husband has gone to the country and that the wife, who is young and likes pretty things, often has her sister visiting her, since the sister is in service elsewhere. That is probably all a servant like him can be expected to know."

I see, Genji thought, it must be the young woman in service. She certainly gave me that poem of hers as though she knew her way about! She cannot be anyone in particular, though.

Still, he rather liked the way she had accosted him, and he had no wish to miss this chance, since in such matters it was clearly his way to be impulsive. On a piece of folding paper he wrote in a hand unlike his own,

"Let me then draw near and see whether you are she, whom glimmering dusk
gave me faintly to discern in twilight beauty flowers."

He had it delivered by the man who had received the fan.

Yūgao had known his profile instantly, despite never having seen him before, and she had not let pass this chance to approach him, but his prolonged silence upset her, and she was thrilled when his reply arrived. She then took so long discussing her answer with her women that Genji's messenger was offended and returned to his lord.

Genji set off very discreetly. His escort carried only weak

torches. The house next door had its half-panel shutters down. The lamplight filtering through the cracks was more muted by far, and more moving, than the glow of fireflies.

There was nothing common about the groves or the garden at the residence where Genji was bound, and the lady there lived a life of supreme elegance and ease. Her distant manner, never more marked than now, obliterated for him all memory of the vine-covered fence he had just left. He slept quite late the next morning and left at sunrise, his looks in the early light making it clear why everyone sang his praises.

Today again he passed those shutters. No doubt he had come that way before, but now, with that little encounter lingering in his mind, he wondered whenever he went by just who it was who lived there.

Koremitsu appeared a few days later and came straight up to Genji. "My mother is weaker than ever, and I have been doing what I can for her. After you last spoke to me, I called in someone who knows the house next door and questioned him, but he told me nothing clear. Someone seems to have come in the fifth month to live there incognito, but he said the household has been told nothing about her. Now and again I have a look through the fence, and I have indeed seen young women wearing a sort of apron, which suggests they are serving a lady. Yesterday the late-afternoon sun was shining into the house, and I clearly saw a pretty woman sitting down to write a letter. She looked sad, and the others around her were quietly weeping." Genji smiled and thought how much he would like to know who she was.

Koremitsu felt that despite the weight of Genji's exalted station it would be a shame if he did not take some liberties, considering his age and the admiring response he received from women; after all, those too low to be granted such freedom by the world at large fancied attractive women nonetheless. "I thought up a little pretext and sent over a note in case I might discover anything," he continued. "I got an answer straight back, written in a practiced hand. As far as I can tell, there are some quite nice young women there."

"Keep at it, then. It would be very disappointing not to find out who she is." This was the sort of house Genji had heard dismissed as inhabited by "the lowborn," but it excited him to imagine himself finding an unexpected treasure of a woman there.

[. . .]

Autumn came. Troubles for which he had only himself to blame weighed upon him and discouraged all but the most sporadic visits to the Minister of the Left's, inviting further resentment from Aoi.

Meanwhile, after successfully overcoming the Rokujō Haven's reserve, he had changed and taken most unfortunately to treating her like any other woman. One wonders why there lived on in him nothing of the reckless passion that had possessed him when he first began courting her. She herself, who suffered excessively from melancholy, feared at the same time that rumors of an affair already embarrassing because of their difference in age would soon be in circulation, and she spent many a bitter night, when he failed to come, despairing over her troubles.

One very misty morning when the still-sleepy Genji was at last taking his leave in response to insistent urging, though with many sighs, the gentlewoman Chūjō raised a lattice shutter and moved her mistress's curtain aside as though to say, "My lady, do see him off!" She lifted her head and looked out: there he was, standing before all the colors of the garden as though he did not wish to miss their beauty. No, there was no one like him.

Chūjō accompanied him toward the gallery.[18] Silk gauze train neatly tied at her waist, over an aster layering[19] perfect for the season, she carried herself with delicious grace. He glanced back and sat her down by the railing at the corner of the building. Her comely deference toward him, the length of her sidelocks[20]—all seemed to him a miracle.

18. Probably the gallery leading to the middle gate where Genji will enter his carriage.
19. The aster (*shion*) layering presumably achieved the blue-violet of the simple *shion* color, close to that of the bluebell.
20. *Kami no sagariba,* locks cut short above the ears to frame the face.

> *"I would not be known for flitting lightheartedly to every flower,*
> *but this bluebell this morning I would be sad not to pick.*

What do you suggest?" he said, taking her hand; but she replied
with practiced wit,

> *"Your haste to be off before morning mists are gone makes it all too plain,*
> *so I should say, that your heart cares little for your flower,"*

so turning his poem to refer to her mistress. A pretty page boy,
handsome in trousers that might have been made for this very
moment and that now were wet with dew, wandered out among
the flowers and brought him a bluebell. One would have liked
to paint the scene.

Whoever chanced to lay eyes on Genji was smitten by him.
After one glimpse of the radiance that attended him, men of
every degree (for the crudest woodcutter may yet aspire to pause
in his labors beneath a blossoming tree)[21] wished to offer him a
beloved daughter, while the least menial with a sister he thought
worthy entertained the ambition to place her in Genji's service.
It was therefore all but impossible for a cultivated woman like
Chūjō, one who had had occasion to receive poems from him
and to bask in the warmth of his beauty, not to be drawn to
him. She, too, must have regretted that he did not come more
often.

Oh, yes, it must also be said that Koremitsu gave Genji a fine
account of what he had learned from spying as ordered through
the neighbors' fence. "I have no idea who she is," he reported.
"As far as I can tell, she is hiding from everyone. Her women
have little to keep them occupied. They seem now and again to
cross over to the southern part of the house—the one with the
half-panel shutters—and the younger ones go to look whenever
they hear a carriage. The one I take to be their mistress is brave

21. The Japanese preface to the *Kokinshū* criticizes the "uncouthness" of
Ōtomo no Kuronushi's poetry: "It is, so to speak, like a woodcutter pausing
with his load of firewood beneath a blossoming tree."

enough to do the same.[22] What I have seen of her face suggests that she is lovely. The other day a carriage passed with an escort, and a little page girl who was watching it cried, 'Look, Ukon, look! It's Lord Tō no Chūjō going by!' A rather older grown-up then came out, calling 'Hush, hush' and motioning her to be quiet. 'How do you know?' she asked, and she added, 'Come, I'll look myself.' She was hurrying across what I suppose was the crossbridge when her skirts caught, and she stumbled and almost fell. 'Goodness,' she exclaimed, 'the God of Kazuraki certainly didn't make *that* one very well!'[23] I think they gave up watching after that. The girl said the gentleman in the carriage had been in a dress cloak, and to prove it had been Tō no Chūjō she named several of the attendants and pages she had seen with him."

"I wish I had seen his carriage myself." Genji wondered whether she might be the one Tō no Chūjō could not forget.

"I am doing well at courting one of the women there," Koremitsu went on, smiling at Genji's obvious eagerness to learn more, "and I know the house by now, but the young women still talk to each other as though they were there by themselves, and I go about pretending to believe them. They think their secret is safe, and whenever a child threatens to blurt out something,[24] they talk their way past the difficulty and keep up their show of being alone."

"Give me a look through that fence next time I call on your mother." Judging from where she was living, at least for now, she must belong to that lower grade that his friend had so curtly dismissed. Yes, Genji thought, what if there really were a surprisingly pleasant discovery to be made there?

22. The bridge between the buildings seems to consist only of planks, and the word in the original, *haiwataru* ("crawl across"), suggests that she crosses it in trepidation.

23. The God of the Kazuraki Mountains, ordered by a wizard to build a stone bridge from one mountain range to another, refused to work in daylight and so never quite finished.

24. They talk to their mistress as equals, but the children sometimes begin to address her in honorific language.

Koremitsu, who could not bear to disappoint his lord, marshaled his own wide experience of courtship to devise a way at last to introduce him into the house. All that makes a long story, though, so as usual I have left it out.

Having failed to discover who she was, Genji withheld his identity from her and pursued her in deep disguise,[25] with such patient ardor that Koremitsu let him have his own horse and walked beside his lord. "I should be sorry to have the great lover seen approaching the house on foot, like a menial," he complained; but Genji, who trusted no one else with his secret, had himself accompanied otherwise only by the man who had passed him the twilight beauty flowers and by a single page whose face no one in the house would know. He even avoided calling at the house next door, lest they guess after all who he was.

In her bewilderment Yūgao had Genji's letter-bearer followed and tried to discover where Genji himself went after he left her at dawn, all in the hope of finding out where he lived, but he and his men always managed to evade hers, even as the thought of her so filled his mind that he could not be without her and was constantly appearing at her side, tormented by his unseemly folly.

An affair of this kind may lead the most staid man astray, but so far Genji had always managed to control himself, and he had done nothing to merit censure. It was extraordinary, though, how leaving her in the morning or being away from her only for the day made him miserable enough to wonder whether he had lost his senses, and to struggle to remind himself that nothing about her required this degree of passion. In manner she seemed very young, for she was remarkably sweet and yielding, and hardly given to deep reflection; yet she knew something of worldly ways, and she could not be of very high birth. Again and again he asked himself what it was that he saw in her.

He made a show of dressing modestly in a hunting cloak, of changing his costume, and of giving her no look at his face, and he never came to her until everyone in the house was asleep. He

25. Dressed so as to conceal his rank, and in this case apparently also his face.

was so like a shape-changing creature of old[26] that he caused her acute anguish, although his manner with her, and her own sense of touch, made her wonder how great a lord he might be. It must be that great lover I have to thank for this, she reflected, her suspicion falling on Koremitsu; but Koremitsu only feigned ignorance and went on lightheartedly visiting the house as though he knew nothing, until confusion overcame her and she sank into a strange melancholy.

Genji assumed that she was in hiding only for the time being, and he wondered where he would seek her if she were to vanish after snaring him so artlessly. It worried him that he would never know on what day she might go, or where. She would have been just a passing distraction if he then failed to find her and accepted her loss, but he did not believe for a moment that he could forget her that easily. Every night when discretion kept him from her was such a trial that he thought of bringing her to Nijō, whoever she might be, and if the resulting gossip embarrassed him, so be it. Despite himself he wondered what bond from the past could have aroused a passion so consuming and so unfamiliar.

"Come," he said, "I want to talk quietly somewhere where we can be alone."

"But that would be so strange," she protested naively. "I understand your feeling, but that sort of thing is not done. The idea upsets me."

No doubt it does, Genji reflected with a smile. "Yes," he said gently, "one or the other of us must be a fox: so just let *me* bewitch *you*."

She let him have his way and yielded completely. Her utter submissiveness, however curious, was extremely engaging. She *must* be the "gillyflower" described, as he now remembered, by Tō no Chūjō, but if she was in hiding she must have her reasons, and he refrained from pressing her. He saw no sign that

26. In the myth of Mount Miwa, for example, a young woman is visited every night by an invisible lover. At last she ties a thread to his clothing, follows it, and finds that he is the serpent deity of the mountain.

she might suddenly flare up at him and vanish—he foresaw no such change unless he neglected her badly—and he even fancied despite himself that a little coolness from him might add to her appeal.

On the fifteenth night of the eighth month,[27] bright moonlight poured through every crack into the board-roofed house, to his astonishment, since he had never seen a dwelling like this before. Dawn must have been near, because he heard uncouth men in the neighboring houses hailing one another as they awoke.

"Goodness, it's cold!"

"Not much hope for business this year—I'll never get out to the country![28] What a life! Say, neighbor, you on the north, d'you hear me?"

She was deeply embarrassed by this chatter and clatter all around them of people rising and preparing to go about their pitiful tasks. The place would have made anyone with any pretensions want to sink through the floor, but she remained serene and betrayed no response to any sound, however painful, offensive, or distressing, and her manner retained so naive a grace that the dismal commotion might just as well have meant nothing to her at all. Genji therefore forgave her more readily than if she had been openly ashamed. Thud, thud, a treadle mortar thundered almost at their pillow,[29] until he understood at last what "detestable racket" means. Having no idea what was making it, he only was aware that it was new and that it was awful. The assortment of noises was no more than a jumble to him.

The sound of snowy robes being pounded on the fulling block reached him faintly from all sides, and wild geese were crying in the heavens. These and many other sounds roused him to

27. The great full moon night of the year. In the lunar calendar this date is in autumn.
28. Perhaps the speaker would normally be buying rice in the country to sell in town.
29. It is probably polishing rice.

painfully keen emotion.[30] He slid the nearby door open, and together they looked outside. The tiny garden boasted a pretty
clump of bamboo on which dew gleamed as brightly as elsewhere. Insects of all kinds were singing, and to Genji, who seldom heard even a cricket in the wall, this concert of cries almost
in his ears was a bizarre novelty, although his love for her must
have inclined him to be forgiving. She was engagingly frail in
the modesty of her soft, pale gray-violet gown over layers of
white, and although she had nothing striking about her, her
slender grace and her manner of speaking moved him deeply.
She could perhaps do with a touch of pride, but he still wanted
very much to be with her in less constricting surroundings.

"Come, let us spend the rest of the night comfortably in a
place nearby. It has been so difficult, meeting nowhere but
here."

"But I do not see how . . . This is so sudden . . ." she protested
innocently. Never mind his promises that their love would out-
last this life; her meek trust was inexplicably gone, and he could
hardly believe that she knew worldly ways. He therefore threw
caution to the winds, had her nurse Ukon call his man, and got
his carriage brought up. This demonstration of ardor gave her
anxious gentlewomen faith in him after all.

It would soon be dawn. No cocks were crowing. All they
heard was an old man's voice as he prostrated himself full-
length, no doubt for a pilgrimage to the Holy Mountain.[31] The
labor of throwing himself down and rising again sounded
painful. Genji wondered what in this dewlike world he so desired that he insisted on such strenuous prayers.

---

30. These sounds, unlike the earlier noises, are poetically evocative. *Shirotae
no* ("snowy") is a noble epithet for *koromo* ("robe"). The sound of a robe being beaten on a fulling block (*kinuta*), to clean it and restore its luster, meant
autumn and the waning of the year, and perhaps a woman under the moon
calling to her lost love; the motif is originally Chinese. The cries of migrating
geese, too, told of autumn and farewell.
31. He is "touching his forehead to the ground," that is, doing repeated, full-
length prostrations. The pilgrimage to Mitake (now Sanjō-ga-take, 5,676 feet,
in the Ōmine range) required strict purification and attracted both nobles and
commoners. The mountain was then particularly sacred to Miroku, the future
Buddha.

"Hail to the Guide who is to come!"[32] the old man chanted. Genji was moved. "Listen to him: he, too, is thinking beyond just this life.

Let your own steps take the path this good man follows so devotedly
and in that age yet to come still uphold the bond we share."

He had avoided the old lines about the "Hall of Long Life" and turned "sharing a wing"[33] into a prayer that they should greet the Age of Miroku together. It was a grand leap into the future.

"Such are the sorrows that make plain what fate past lives require me to bear
that I have no faith at all in better from times to come."

Her reply, such as it was, was forlorn.

While he sought to persuade her, since she could not make up her mind to launch forth so boldly under the slowly sinking moon, the moon suddenly slid behind clouds and the dawn sky took on great beauty. He hurried out as always, lest day betray his doings to the world, and lifted her easily into the carriage. Ukon got in, too.

They soon reached a certain estate,[34] and while waiting for the steward they gazed at the ferns along the old gate's ruinous eaves. All was darkness under the trees. The fog hung wet and heavy, and Genji's sleeves were soaked merely because he had put up the carriage's blinds. "I have never done anything like this," he said. "It is nerve-racking, isn't it?

---

32. *Namo tōrai dōshi*, the invocation to Miroku, who will descend into a transfigured world many eons from now. The pilgrim prayed to be born into his age and to hear his teaching.
33. Allusions to "The Song of Unending Sorrow," where, in the Hall of Long Life, the lovers swear that in the hereafter they will be like trees with shared branches or birds that share a wing.
34. Reminiscent of Kawara no In ("Riverside"), built by Minamoto no Tōru (822–895) and later imperial property. Kawara no In was the scene of a famous ghost story, and its location matches the tale's description.

Once upon a time could it be that others, too, lost their way like this?
I myself have never known such strange wanderings at dawn.

Have you ever done this before?"
    She answered shyly,

"The wayfaring moon uncertain what to expect from the mountains' rim,
may easily fade away and disappear in mid-sky.[35]

I am afraid."
    It amused him to see her so tremulous and fearful. He assumed
that she just missed the crowd always around her at home.
    He had the carriage brought in and its shafts propped on the
railing[36] while their room was made ready in the west wing.
The excited Ukon thought back over the past, because the way
the steward rushed officiously about showed what sort of man
her mistress's lover was.
    They left the carriage as day was beginning to restore shape
and color to the world. The place was nicely arranged for them,
despite their sudden arrival.
    "I see you have no one else with you, my lord," said the stew-
ard, a close lower-level retainer also in the service of the Minister
of the Left. "This makes things rather difficult." He approached
and asked through Ukon whether he should summon a suitable
entourage.[37]
    Genji quickly silenced him. "I came here purposely to hide.
Say not a word about this to anyone." The man hastened to provide a morning meal, although he did indeed lack staff to serve it.
    Genji had never slept away from home quite like this before,
and he assured Yūgao over and over that he would love her even

35. The "mountains' rim" (where the moon sets) is Genji; the moon is the
woman, who does not know how far Genji's intentions toward her go.
36. Around the veranda: a makeshift arrangement, since carriage shafts normally rested on a "shaft bench" (*shiji*).
37. The steward ranks too low to address Genji directly; his earlier speech, too,
must be indirect.

longer than the Okinaga River would flow.[38] The sun was high when they rose, and he lifted the shutters himself. The unkempt and deserted garden stretched into the distance, its ancient groves towering in massive gloom. The near garden and shrubbery lacked any charm, the wider expanse resembled an autumn moor, and the lake was choked with water weeds. The place was strangely disturbing and quite isolated, although there seemed to be an inhabited outbuilding some distance off.

"The place *is* eerie," he said, "but never mind: the demons will not trouble *me*."

She was thoroughly offended that he still had his face covered, and he agreed that this was unnatural by now.

> *"The flower you see disclosing now its secrets in the evening dew*
> *glimmered first before your eyes in a letter long ago,"*

he said. "Does the gleam of the dew please you?"

With a sidelong glance she murmured,

> *"The light I saw fill the dewdrops adorning then a twilight beauty*
> *was nothing more than a trick of the day's last fading gleam!"*

He was delighted. When at his ease he really was extraordinarily beautiful—in this setting, in fact, alarmingly so. "The way you kept your distance hurt me so much that I meant never to show you my face. Do tell me your name now. You frighten me, you know."[39]

"But you see, I am only a diver's daughter,"[40] she answered mildly, as always refusing to tell him more.

38. In *Man'yōshū* 4482, by Umanofuhito Kunihito, the poet assures his lady that he will love her even if the Okinaga River stops flowing. This name, which can be taken to mean "long breath," is linked in the poem to the grebe (*nio*), which holds its breath to feed underwater.

39. Genji plays at being afraid that she is a fox.

40. *Wakan rōei shū* 722 (also *Shinkokinshū* 1703), a reply to a gentleman's advances: "No home have I of my own, for I, a diver's daughter, live beside white-breaking waves upon the ocean shore."

"All right, I suppose the fault is mine."[41] He spent the rest of the day now reproving her, now whispering sweet nothings in her ear.

Koremitsu managed to find them, and he brought refreshments. He avoided waiting on Genji in person because he did not want to hear what Ukon would say to him. It amused him that Genji had resorted to bringing her here, and, assuming that her looks deserved this much trouble, he congratulated himself rather bitterly (since he could quite well have had her himself) on his generosity in ceding her to his lord.

While gazing at the ineffably peaceful sunset sky, Genji remembered that she disliked the gloom inside the house. He raised the outer blinds[42] and lay down beside her. They looked at each other in the twilight glow, and despite her anxiety she forgot her cares and charmingly yielded to him a little. She had now lain by him all day, piercingly young and sweet in her shy terror.

He lowered the lattice shutters early and had the lamp lit. "Here we are," he complained, "as close as we could possibly be, but at heart you are still keeping yourself from me. I cannot bear it."

He knew how anxiously His Majesty now must be seeking him, though he could not imagine where his men might be looking. How strange a love this is! And what a state the Rokujō Haven must be in! She above all stirred his guilt, and he understood her anger, however painful it might be. The more fondly he dwelled on the artless innocence before him, the more he longed to rid *her* a little of the pride that so unsettled him.

Late in the evening he dozed off to see a beautiful woman seated by his pillow. She said, "You are a wonder to me, but you do not care to visit me: no, you bring a tedious creature here and lavish yourself upon her. It is hateful of you and very wrong." She began shaking the woman beside him awake.

41. Genji's reply acknowledges "I am a diver's daughter" with a wordplay on *warekara:* "my fault" but also the name of a creature alleged to live in seaweed.
42. Those between the aisle and the veranda.

He woke up, aware of a heavy, menacing presence. The lamp was out. In alarm he drew his sword and laid it beside her, then roused Ukon. She came to him, clearly frightened, too.

"Go," he commanded, "wake the guard on the bridgeway and have him bring a hand torch."

"But how can I, my lord, in the dark?"

"Don't be silly!" Genji laughed and clapped his hands. Weird echoes answered.

No one could hear him, no one was coming. She was shivering violently, helplessly. Soaked with perspiration, she seemed to be unconscious.

"She is always so timid anyway," Ukon said. "What she must be going through now!"

Genji pitied her, frail as she was and so given to spending her days gazing up at the sky. "I shall wake him myself. Tiresome echoes are all I get for my clapping. Wait here, stay with her."

He dragged Ukon to her, then went to the western double doors and pushed them open. The light on the bridgeway was out, too. A breeze had sprung up, and the few men at his service—just the steward's son (a young man he used on private errands), the privy chamber page,[43] and his usual man—were asleep. The steward's son answered his call.

"Bring a hand torch. Have my man twang his bowstring[44] and keep crying warnings. What do you mean by going to sleep in a lonely place like this? I thought Lord Koremitsu was here. Where is he?"

"He was at your service, my lord, but he left when you had no orders for him. He said he would be back for you at dawn." The young man disappeared toward the steward's quarters, expertly twanging his bowstring (he belonged to the Palace Guards) and crying over and over again, "Beware of fire!"[45]

Genji thought of the palace, where the privy gentlemen must

43. A youth described earlier as "a single page whose face those in the house could not know."
44. To repel the baleful spirit.
45. An all-purpose warning cry.

have reported for duty and where the watch must even now be being announced.[46] It was not yet really so very late.

He went back in and felt his way to her. She still lay with Ukon prostrate beside her. "What is this? Fear like yours is folly!" he scolded Ukon. "In empty houses, foxes and whatnot shock people by giving them a good fright—yes, that is it. We will not have the likes of them threatening us as long as I am here." He made her sit up.

"My lord, I was only lying that way because I feel so ill. My poor lady must be quite terrified."

"Yes, but why should she . . . ?" He felt her: she was not breathing. He shook her, but she was limp and obviously unconscious, and he saw helplessly that, childlike as she was, a spirit had taken her.

The hand torch came. Ukon was in no condition to move, and Genji drew up the curtain that stood nearby.[47]

"Bring it closer!" he ordered. Reluctant to approach his lord further in this crisis, the man had stopped short of entering the room. "Bring it here, I tell you! Have some sense!"

Now in the torchlight Genji saw at her pillow, before the apparition vanished, the woman in his dream. Despite surprise and terror, for he had heard of such things at least in old tales, he was frantic to know what had become of her, until he shed all dignity and lay down beside her, calling on her to wake up; but she was growing cold and was no longer breathing.

He was speechless. There was no one to tell him what to do. He should have recalled that at such times one particularly needs a monk,[48] but despite his wish to be strong he was too young, and seeing her lost completely undid him. "Oh, my love," he cried, throwing his arms around her, "come back to life! Don't do this terrible thing to me!" But she was quite cold by now and unpleasant to touch. Ukon's earlier terror yielded to a pathetic storm of weeping.

46. At the hour of the Boar (circa 9 P.M.), the privy gentlemen, reporting for duty in the privy chamber, announced their names to the official in charge. Then the guards reporting for the watch likewise announced their names.
47. To conceal himself and the lady from the man with the light.
48. As an exorcist.

He gathered his courage, remembering how a demon had threatened a Minister in the Shishinden.[49] "No, no," he scolded Ukon, "she cannot really be gone! How loud a voice sounds at night! Quiet, quiet!" The sudden calamity had him completely confused.

He called for the steward's son. "Someone here has been strangely attacked by a spirit and appears to be gravely ill. Send my man straight for Lord Koremitsu and have him come immediately. If the Adept happens to be there, tell him privately to come, too. He is to be discreet and keep this from their mother. She disapproves of such escapades."

He got this out well enough, but he was in torment, and the awful thought that he might cause her death[50] gave the place terrors beyond words. Midnight must have passed, and the wind had picked up. The pines were roaring like a whole forest, and an eerie bird uttered raucous cries; he wondered whether it was an owl. The house was so dreary, so lonely, so silent. Oh, why, he bitterly asked himself in vain regret, why had he chosen to spend the night in this dreadful place? The frantic Ukon clung to him, shaking as though she would die. He held her and wondered miserably what was to become of her. He alone had remained lucid, and now he, too, was at his wits' end.

The lamp guttered, while from shadowy recesses over the screen between him and the chamber[51] came the thump and scuff of *things* walking; he felt them coming up behind him. If only Koremitsu would come soon! But Koremitsu was hard to track down,[52] and the eternities that passed while Genji's man hunted for him made that one night seem a thousand.

At last a distant cockcrow set thoughts whirling through his head. What could really have led him here to risk his life in such

49. In legend the Chancellor Tadahira was passing the Emperor's seat in the Shishinden late one night when a demon seized the tip of his scabbard and threatened him. Tadahira drew his sword and cried, "How dare you interfere with His Majesty's emissary?" The demon fled.
50. He still seems to believe that she is somehow alive.
51. Genji, Ukon, and the lady seem to be in the aisle with a folding screen between them and the chamber.
52. Having many mistresses, he spent his nights in different places.

a catastrophe? His recklessness in these affairs now seemed to have made him an example forever. Never mind trying to hush this up—the truth will always out. His Majesty would hear of it, it would be on everyone's lips, and the riffraff of the town would be hawking it everywhere. All and sundry would know him only as a fool.

At last Koremitsu arrived. He had always been at Genji's service, midnight or dawn, yet tonight of all nights he had been delinquent and failed to answer his lord's call. Genji had him come in, despite his displeasure, and he had so much to tell that words failed him at first. Ukon gathered that Koremitsu was there, and she wept to remember all that had happened. Genji, too, broke down. While alone he had borne up as well as he could and held his love in his arms, but Koremitsu's arrival had brought him the respite to know his grief, and for some time he could only weep and weep.

At length his tears let up. "Something very, very strange has happened here, something horrible beyond words. In a moment so dire I believe one chants the scriptures, so I have sent for your brother to do that and to offer prayers."

"He returned to Mount Hiei yesterday," Koremitsu replied. "But all this is quite extraordinary. Could it be that my lady was feeling unwell?"

"No, no, not at all."

Genji, weeping once more, looked so perfectly beautiful that Koremitsu, too, was overcome and dissolved in tears. After all, in this crisis their need was for someone mature, someone with rich experience of the world. They were too young really to know what to do.

"The steward here must not find out; that would be a disaster," Koremitsu said. "He can perhaps be trusted himself, but the retainers around him will spread the story. My lord, you must leave this house immediately."

"But how could there be fewer people anywhere else?"

"Yes, that is true. At her house the grieving women would weep and wail, and there are so many houses around that the neighbors would all notice. Everyone would soon know. At a mountain temple, though, this sort of thing is not unknown, and in a place like that it might be possible to evade attention."

Koremitsu then had an idea. "I will take her to the Eastern Hills, to where a gentlewoman I once knew is living as a nun. She was my father's nurse, and she is very old. The neighborhood looks crowded, but the place is actually very quiet and sheltered." He had Genji's carriage brought up, now that full day had returned the people on the estate to their occupations.

Genji did not have the strength to lift her in his arms, and it was Koremitsu who wrapped her in a padded mat and laid her in the carriage. She was so slight that he was more drawn than repelled. He had not wrapped her securely, and her hair came tumbling out. The sight blinded Genji with tears and drove him to such a pitch of grief that he resolved to stay with her to the end.

However, Koremitsu would not have it. "My lord, you must ride back to Nijō before too many people are out." He had Ukon get in the carriage as well, then gave Genji his horse and set off on foot with his gathered trousers hitched up.[53] It was a strange cortège, but Genji's desperate condition had driven from Koremitsu's mind any thought of himself.[54] Genji reached home oblivious to his surroundings and barely conscious.

"Where have you been, my lord?" his women wanted to know. "You do not look at all well." But he went straight into his curtained bed, pressed his hand to his heart, and gave himself up to his anguish.

How can I not have gone in the carriage with her? he asked himself in agony. How will she feel if she revives? She will probably assume that I just took this chance to abscond, and she will hate me. He felt sick. His head ached, he seemed to have a fever, and all in all he felt so very ill that he thought he might soon be done for himself.

His gentlewomen wondered why he did not rise even though

53. The legs of the gathered trousers were usually tied at the ankles with a cord, but for ease of movement Koremitsu brings the cord up to just below his knees.

54. He has accepted the inconvenience of contact with death and the embarrassment of being seen to walk when a man of his standing should ride.

the sun was high. Despite their offer of a morning meal he just lay there, suffering and sick at heart. Meanwhile, messengers— the young gentlemen from the Minister of the Left's—came from His Majesty, whose failure to find Genji yesterday had worried him greatly. From within his blinds Genji invited Tō no Chūjō alone to "Come in, but remain standing.[55]

"In the fifth month a former nurse of mine became so ill that she cut off her hair and took the Precepts," he explained, "and that seemed to make her better, but recently her illness flared up again, and in her weakened condition she asked to see me a last time. I went to her because, after all, she has been close to me since I was a baby, and I thought she would be hurt if I did not. Unfortunately, a servant of hers, one already unwell, died before they could remove her from the house. In fear of what this would mean for me, they let the day go by before they took her away, but I found out, and so now, in a month filled with holy rites, this tiresome difficulty means that I cannot in good conscience go to the palace.[56] I apologize for talking to you like this, but I have had a headache ever since daybreak. I must have a cold."

"I shall report this to His Majesty," Tō no Chūjō answered. "There was music last night, and he looked for you everywhere. He did not seem at all pleased."

He spoke now for himself. "What really is this defilement you have incurred? I am afraid I find your story difficult to believe."

Genji felt a twinge of alarm. "Spare His Majesty the details. Just tell him I have been affected by an unforeseen defilement. It is all very unpleasant." His reply sounded casual, but at heart

55. Genji is in the chamber, where the blinds are still down. Tō no Chūjō, if Genji had allowed him to sit, would have incurred the same pollution (from contact with death) as Genji, and he would have passed it on to his family, the palace, and so on.
56. This (fictitious) death means that both Genji and the household are defiled. Genji must stay at home in a sort of quarantine for thirty days until halfway through the ninth month, one particularly busy with Shinto rites. Moreover, the imperial envoy to an important rite at Ise (the Kanname-sai) left on the eleventh of the month, and for the occasion Buddhist priests and persons in mourning were banned from the palace.

he was desperate with grief. In his distress he refused to see anyone. Summoning one of Tō no Chūjō's younger brothers, he
had him convey formally to His Majesty a report on his condition. To the Minister of the Left's he wrote that, for the reason
he mentioned, he could not present himself at court.

Koremitsu came at dark. There were few people about because all Genji's visitors had left without sitting down once he
warned them that he was defiled. Genji called him in. "Tell me,
did you make quite sure there was no hope?" He pressed his
sleeves to his eyes and wept.

"Yes, my lord, I believe that it is all over." Koremitsu, too, was
in tears. "I could not stay long. I have arranged with a saintly old
monk I know to see tomorrow to what needs to be done, since
that is a suitable day."[57]

"What about her gentlewoman?"

"I doubt she will survive this. This morning she looked ready
to throw herself from a cliff in her longing to join her mistress.
She wanted to let her mistress's household know, but I managed
to persuade her to be patient and to think things over first."

Genji was overwhelmed. "I feel very ill myself, and I wonder
what is to become of me."

"My lord, you need not brood this way. All things turn out as
they must. I will not let anyone know, and I plan to look after
everything myself."

"I suppose you are right. I have been trying to convince myself of that, too, but it is so painful to be guilty of having foolishly caused someone's death. Say nothing to Shōshō[58] or to
anyone else," he went on, to make sure Koremitsu's lips were
sealed. "Your mother, especially, disapproves strongly of this sort
of thing, and I could never face her if she knew." Koremitsu assured him to his immense relief that he had told even the monks
of the temple a quite different story.

"How strange! What can be going on?" the women murmured as they caught scraps of this conversation. "He says he is

57. For a funeral, according to the almanac.
58. A gentlewoman, probably Koremitsu's sister. "Shōshō" (Lieutenant) asso-
ciates her with a man, probably her husband, who bore that title.

defiled and cannot go to the palace? But why are the two of them whispering and groaning that way?"

"Keep up the good work, then." Genji gave Koremitsu directions for the coming rite.[59]

"But, my lord," Koremitsu answered, rising, "this is no time for ostentation."

Genji could not bear to see him go. "You will not like this, I know, but there will be no peace for me until I see her body again. I shall ride there myself."

Koremitsu thought this risky, but he replied, "So be it, my lord, if that is your wish. You must start immediately, then, and be back before the night is over."

Genji changed into the hunting cloak that he had worn lately on his secret outings and set forth. Oppressed as he was and burdened by sorrow, he wondered after that encounter with danger whether he really should undertake so perilous a journey, but the merciless torments of grief drove him to persevere, for if he did not see her body now, when in all eons to come would he look upon her again as she had once been?

As always he took his man and Koremitsu with him. The way seemed endless. The moon of the seventeenth night[60] shone so brightly that along the bank of the Kamo River his escort's lights[61] barely showed, and such was his despair that the view toward Toribeno troubled him not at all.[62] At last he arrived.

The neighborhood had something disturbing about it, and the nun's board-roofed house, beside the chapel where she did her devotions, was desolate. Lamplight glowed faintly through the cracks, and he heard a woman weeping within. Outside, two or three monks chatted between spells of silently calling Amida's Name.[63] The early night office in the nearby temples

59. The funeral.
60. A moon two days past the full.
61. The runners who go before him with torches.
62. Genji is riding south down the Kamo River, bound for the southern end of the Eastern Hills. In the distance, to his left (eastward), he sees the burning ground of Toribeno, where Yūgao will be cremated.
63. The *nenbutsu*, the formula for calling the name of Amida, was usually voiced, but not for a funeral. The Buddha Amida welcomes souls into his paradise.

was over, and deep quiet reigned, while toward Kiyomizu there were lights and signs of dense habitation. A venerable monk, the nun's own son, was chanting scripture in such tones as to arouse holy awe. Genji felt as though he would weep until his tears ran dry.

He went in to find the lamp turned to the wall[64] and Ukon lying behind a screen, and he understood her piercing sorrow. No fear troubled him. *She* was as lovely as ever; as yet she betrayed no change. He took her hand. "Oh, let me hear your voice again!" he implored, sobbing. "What timeless bond between us can have made me love you so briefly with all my heart, only to have you cruelly abandon me to grief?" The monks, who did not know who he was, wondered at his tears and wept with him.

Genji invited Ukon to come to Nijō, but she only replied, "What home could I have, my lord, now that I have so suddenly lost the lady I have never left in all the years since she and I were children together? But I want to let the others know what has become of her. However dreadful this may be, I could not bear to have them accuse me of having failed to tell them." She went on amid bitter tears, "I only wish I could join her smoke and rise with her into the sky!"

"Of course you do," he said consolingly, "but that is life, you know. There has never been a parting without pain. The time comes for all of us, sooner or later. Cheer up and trust me. Even as I speak, though," he added disconcertingly, "I doubt that I myself have much longer to live."

"My lord," Koremitsu broke in, "it will soon be dawn. You should be starting home."

Sick at heart, Genji looked back again and again as he rode away.

The journey was a very dewy one,[65] and it seemed to him that he was wandering blindly through the dense morning fog. She had lain there looking as she did in life, under that scarlet robe of his, the one he had put over her the night before in

64. Away from the body, which has been laid out for the wake.
65. "Dew" means tears.

exchange for one of her own. What had the tie between them really been? All along the way he tried to work it out. Koremitsu was beside him once more to assist him, because in his present condition his seat was none too secure, but even so he slid to the ground as they reached the Kamo embankment.

"You may have to leave me here by the roadside," he said from the depths of his agony. "I do not see how I am to get home."

The worried Koremitsu realized that if he had had his wits about him he would never have let Genji insist on taking this journey. He washed his hands in the river and called in the extremity of his trouble on the Kannon of Kiyomizu,[66] but this left him no wiser about what to do. Genji took himself resolutely in hand, called in his heart on the buddhas,[67] and with whatever help Koremitsu could give him managed somehow to return to Nijō.

His gentlewomen deplored this mysterious gadding about in the depths of the night. "This sort of thing does not look well," they complained among themselves. "Lately he has been setting out more restlessly than ever on these secret errands, and yesterday he really looked very ill. Why do you suppose he goes roaming about like this?"

As he lay there, he did indeed seem extremely unwell, and two or three days later he was very weak. His Majesty was deeply disturbed to learn of his condition. Soon the clamor of healers was to be heard everywhere, while rites, litanies, and purifications went forward in numbers beyond counting. The entire realm lamented that Genji, whose perfection of beauty already aroused apprehension, now seemed unlikely to live.

Through his suffering he called Ukon to his side, granted her a nearby room, and took her into his service. Koremitsu managed to calm his fears, despite the anxiety that gripped him, and he

66. Koremitsu can probably still see Kiyomizudera to the east. The temple is dedicated to a form of Kannon, the bodhisattva of compassion and a savior from peril.
67. The buddhas (*hotoke*) invoked by Genji could be one or many. He, too, may have the Kannon of Kiyomizu in mind.

helped Ukon to make herself useful, reflecting that she had after all no other refuge. He called her whenever he felt a little
better and gave her things to do, and she was soon acquainted
with all his staff. Although no beauty, in her dark mourning[68]
she made a perfectly presentable young woman.

"It is strange how the little time that she and I had together
seems in the end to have shortened my life as well," he said to
her privately. "If it had been given me to live long, I would have
wanted to do all I could for you, so as to heal the pain of losing
the mistress you trusted for all those years, but as it is, I shall
soon be going to join her. How I wish it were not so!" The sight
of his feeble tears made her forget her own woes and long only
for him to live.

His household was distraught, while more messengers came
from the palace than raindrops from the sky. He was very sorry
to know that he was causing His Majesty such concern, and he
did his best to rally his own strength. The Minister his father-
in-law visited him daily, and thanks perhaps to his attentive
ministrations, Genji's indisposition all but vanished after twenty
days and more of grave illness, and he seemed bound for re-
covery.

That night the seclusion imposed on Genji by his defilement[69]
came to an end, and he repaired to his apartment at the palace
out of consideration for His Majesty, who had felt such anxiety
on his behalf. His father-in-law came for him there in his carriage
and inquired solicitously about his period of seclusion. Genji felt
for a time as though all this were unreal and he had returned to
life in an unknown world.

By the twentieth of the ninth month he was quite well. He
was extremely thin, it is true, but for that very reason his
beauty had acquired a new and special grace. He was also
prone to spells of vacant melancholy and of tears, which inspired curiosity and gave rise to the rumor that he must be possessed by a spirit.

68. She would normally have worn light gray, but her intimacy with Yūgao
called for a darker shade.
69. Defilement due to contact with death.

Early one quiet evening he had Ukon come to him for a chat. "I still do not understand," he said. "Why did she keep me from knowing who she was? It would have been cruel even of 'a diver's daughter,' if she had really been one, to ignore my obvious love and to keep me so much at a distance."

"Why should she ever have wished to hide who she was from you, my lord? When might she have seen fit to tell you her own, wholly insignificant name? You came to her from the start in a guise so strange that, as she herself said, she could not quite believe you were real. Your very insistence on keeping your identity from her made it clear enough who you were, but it hurt her that you seemed so obviously to be seeking only your own amusement."

"What an unfortunate contest of wills! I had no wish to remain distant from her. But, you see, I still have very little experience of the kind of affair that others might criticize. In my position I must be cautious about a great many things, for fear above all of reproof from His Majesty, and I simply do not have the latitude to go courting any woman I please, because whatever I do could so easily open me to reproach. Still, I was so strangely drawn to her after that first evening's chance exchange that I risked visiting her after all, which I suppose was proof enough that the bond between us was foreordained. How sad it all is, and how bitter! Why did she take such complete possession of my heart, if she and I really were destined to be with each other so briefly? Do tell me more about her. Why withhold anything now? I am having images made every seven days for her memorial services: to whom should I silently dedicate them?"[70]

"Very well, my lord, I see no reason not to give you the answers you seek. I had only wished to avoid gossiping after my lady's death about things that she herself had kept hidden while she lived. Her parents died when she was still young. Her father,

---

70. Rites to guide the soul toward a fortunate rebirth were held every seven days during the first forty-nine days after death and at widening intervals thereafter. New paintings of the Buddhist divinities involved were made for each service during the initial forty-nine-day period.

known as the Third Rank Captain,[71] was devoted to her, but he seems to have suffered greatly from his failure to advance, and in the end he became too discouraged to live on. After his death it happened that his lordship Tō no Chūjō, then a Lieutenant, began coming to see her, and he continued to do so quite faithfully for three years. Last autumn, though, she received terrifying threats from the residence of the Minister of the Right,[72] and these so frightened her, for she was very timid, that she fled to hide at her nurse's house in the western part of the City. Life there was very trying, and she wanted to move to the hills, but this year that direction became closed for her,[73] and she avoided it by making do instead with the poor place where to her dismay, my lord, you at last came upon her. She was so exceptionally shy that she felt embarrassed to be seen looking unhappy, and she pretended to be untroubled whenever she was with you."

So that was it! Genji now understood, and her memory touched him more deeply than ever. "I have heard Tō no Chūjō lament losing a child. Was there one?"

"Yes, my lord, born in the spring the year before last: a lovely little girl."

"Where is she? You must not tell anyone else about her—just give her to me. It would be such joy to have her in memory of her mother, who meant so much to me." And he continued, "I should really tell Tō no Chūjō, but then I would only have to put up with his pointless reproaches. I see no reason why I should not bring her up. Please make up a story for the nurse who must have her now, and bring her here."

71. Sanmi no Chūjō. He had held the third court rank (*sanmi*) and the office of Captain in the Palace Guards. This combination was unusual because a Captain normally held only the fourth rank. Still, since a man of the third rank was a senior noble, Yūgao had in theory been born into the upper class discussed by the young men on that rainy night.

72. Tō no Chūjō explains in "The Broom Tree" that these were sent to her by his wife (Shi no Kimi), the Fourth Daughter of the Minister of the Right, who still lives in her father's residence.

73. Probably a "great obstacle" (*ōfutagari*) resulting from the movements of a deity known as Taishōgun Maō Tennō.

"I shall do so gladly, my lord. I do not like to think of her growing up so far out in the west of the City. My lady left her there only because she had no one else to look after her properly."

While peaceful twilight dimmed to evening beneath a lovely sky, a cricket sang falteringly from the fading garden, and here and there the autumn colors glowed. Surveying the pleasures of this scene, so like a painting, Ukon wondered to find herself in such delightful surroundings and blushed to recall the house of the twilight beauties.

A dove's throaty call from amid the bamboo brought back to Genji, with an affectionate pang, her look of terror when one had called that night at the old mansion. "How old was she? I suppose it was clear enough from her extraordinary frailty that she was not to live long."

"I believe my lady was nineteen. Her nurse's death left me an orphan, and when I remember now how kind my lady's father was, and how he brought me up with his own daughter, I hardly know how I shall go on living. By now I wish I had not been so close to her. I spent such long years depending on a mistress who was after all so very fragile!"

"It is frailty that gives a woman her charm, though. I do not care for a woman who insists on valuing her own wits. I prefer someone compliant, perhaps because I myself am none too quick or self-assured—someone easy for a man to take advantage of if she is not careful, but still circumspect and happy enough to do as her husband wishes. I know I would like such a woman more, the more I lived with her and formed her to my will."

"I am very, very sorry, my lord," said the weeping Ukon, "when I think how perfectly my mistress matched your ideal."

The sky had clouded over, and the breeze had turned cold. Genji murmured in blank despair,

"When the clouds to me seem always to be the smoke that rose from her pyre,
how fondly I rest my gaze even on the evening sky!"

Ukon could give him no answer, and she thought with an aching heart, If only my lady were still alive!

In memory Genji treasured even the noise of the fulling blocks, which he had found so intolerable at the time. "The nights are very long now,"[74] he sang to himself as he lay down to sleep.

[. . .]

On the forty-ninth day[75] he secretly had the Sutra read for her in the Lotus Hall on Mount Hiei, providing the vestments and every other accessory that a generous performance of the rite might require. Even the text and altar ornaments were of the finest quality, and Koremitsu's elder brother the Adept, a very saintly man, did it all beautifully.

Genji asked a Doctor, a former teacher he knew well, to come and compose the dedicatory prayer.[76] When he wrote out what he wished to have in it, not naming the deceased but stating that since one dear to him had passed away he now commended her to Amida's mercy, the Doctor said, "It is perfect as it is, my lord; I see nothing to add." Genji's tears flowed despite his effort to control himself, and sorrow overcame him.

"Who can she have been?" the Doctor asked. "Lacking any clue to who she was, I can only wonder at the loftiness of the destiny that led her to inspire such grief in so great a lord."

Genji called for the trousers that he had secretly had made as an offering,[77] and he murmured,

> "Amid streaming tears today a last time I knot this, her trouser cord—
> ah, in what age yet to come will I undo it again?"

74. From a poem by Bai Juyi on the grief of a wife who beats a fulling block while longing for her absent husband.
75. After Yūgao's death.
76. *Ganmon,* a formal document in Chinese, normally composed by a specialist.
77. It was customary to offer clothing and other belongings of the deceased to the temple, but since at her death she had nothing but what she wore, Genji had had a new set of clothes made as an offering.

He understood that until now she had been wandering restlessly, and as he called passionately for her on Amida, he wondered what path she might at last have taken.[78]

His heart beat fast whenever he saw Tō no Chūjō, and he wanted to tell him that the "little pink" was growing up, but fear of his friend's reproaches kept him silent. At the house of the twilight beauties the women longed to know where their mistress had gone, but they could discover nothing; they could only lament the strangeness of what had happened, since no word reached them even from Ukon. Among themselves they whispered that judging from his deportment the gentleman must have been you-know-who, though of course no one could be sure, and so they presented their complaint to Koremitsu; but Koremitsu ignored them, claimed complete ignorance, and pursued his affair as before, leaving them more confused than ever. They decided that he had been the amorous son of a provincial Governor who had whisked her off to the provinces for fear of Tō no Chūjō.

[. . .]

Genji always hoped to dream of his lost love, but instead, on the night after the forty-ninth-day rite, he glimpsed the woman who had appeared beside her in the deserted mansion, just as she had been then, and with a shiver of horror he realized that the tragedy must have occurred because she haunted the ruinous old place and had taken a fancy to him.

[. . .]

I had passed over Genji's trials and tribulations in silence, out of respect for his determined efforts to conceal them, and I have written of them now only because certain lords and ladies criticized my story for resembling fiction, wishing to know why even those who knew Genji best should have thought him perfect, just because he was an Emperor's son. No doubt I must now beg everyone's indulgence for my effrontery in painting so wicked a portrait of him.

---

78. For the first forty-nine days the spirit wandered in a "transitional state" (*chūu*), then went to rebirth according to its karma. "What path" means which of the six realms of transmigration: the realms of celestial beings, humans, warring demons, beasts, starving ghosts, or hell.

5
(COMPLETE)

WAKAMURASAKI
YOUNG MURASAKI

Waka means "young," while *murasaki,* a plant whose roots yield a purple dye, means also the dye and its color. In poetry *murasaki* purple stands for close relationship and lasting passion. In this chapter Genji comes across a little girl very like Fujitsubo and seeks to make her his own. In a poem he refers to her as *murasaki.* The word *wakamurasaki* ("young *murasaki*") appears only as the chapter title.

Chapter 5 begins in the spring when Genji is eighteen, while chapter 4 ends late in the previous year. There is hardly any narrative link between them.

Genji was suffering from a recurrent fever and had all sorts of spells cast and healing rites done, but to no avail; the fever kept returning. Someone then said, "My lord, there is a remarkable ascetic at a temple in the Northern Hills. Last summer, when the fever was widespread and spells failed to help, he healed many people immediately. Please try him soon. It would be dangerous to allow your fever to become any worse." Genji sent for him, but the ascetic answered that, being now old and bent, he never left his cave.

"Then I shall have to go very quietly to see him." He set off before daybreak with only four or five especially close retainers.

The place was a little way into the mountains. The blossoms in the City were gone now, since it was late in the third month,[1] but in the mountains the cherry trees were in full bloom, and

1. Roughly early May in the solar calendar.

the farther he went, the lovelier the veils of mist became, until for him, whose rank so restricted travel that all this was new, the landscape became a source of wonder.

The temple impressed him as well. The holy man lived near a high peak amid forbidding rocks. Genji climbed there without announcing who he was and quite plainly dressed, but there was no mistaking him.

"Ah, this is too great an honor!" the holy man exclaimed in great agitation. "You must be the gentleman who desired my presence the other day. I have lost all interest in this world by now, and I have given up my healing practices altogether. What has brought you all this way, my lord?" He smiled as his eyes rested upon Genji.

He proved to be a most saintly man. The sun rose high in the sky while he made the necessary talismans,[2] had Genji swallow them, and proceeded with the rite.

When Genji went outside a moment and examined his surroundings, he found himself on a height directly overlooking the monks' lodges. At the foot of a steeply twisting path and surrounded, like the lodges but more neatly, by a brushwood fence, there stood a pretty house, set with its galleries in a handsome grove.

"Who lives there?" he asked.

"That, my lord, is where I gather a certain distinguished Prelate[3] has been secluded these last two years."

"It certainly is the place for someone of a retiring nature. What a pity I am so inadequately dressed. He is certain to find out I am here."

Genji clearly saw several nice-looking page girls come out to offer holy water, gather flowers, and so on.[4]

2. Slips of paper inscribed with the Sanskrit seed syllables of the appropriate deities.

3. An ecclesiastic of high rank and a nobleman himself, hence not someone by whom Genji would wish to be seen improperly dressed.

4. They seem to be placing holy water (*aka*) on a simple offering shelf (*akadana*), which would normally have stood just beyond the veranda of the house. The "flowers" are probably the customary star anise (*shikimi*).

"Why, there is a woman living there!" his companions exclaimed to one another.

"Surely the Prelate would not have one with him!"

"Who can she be?"

Some went down to peer at the house. They reported having
seen some nice-looking little girls, young gentlewomen, and page
girls.

Genji was wondering, as the sun rose toward noon and he continued the rite, how his fever would now behave, when one of
his men remarked, "Instead of just worrying, my lord, you
should somehow get your mind off the matter"; and so Genji
went onto the mountain behind the temple and looked out toward the City.

Mist veiled the landscape into the distance, and the budding
trees everywhere were as though swathed in smoke. "It all looks
just like a painting," he said. "No one living here could wish for
more!"

"But, my lord, this is nothing yet. How much more beautiful
your painting would be if only you had before your eyes the
mountains and seas of other provinces!" Someone else extolled
Mount Fuji and another peak.[5] Then they went on to divert him
further by describing the lovely seaside villages and rocky
shores of the provinces to the west.

"Among places less far away, I think the coast at Akashi in
Harima deserves special mention. Not that any single feature of
it is so extraordinary, but the view over the sea there is somehow more peaceful than elsewhere. A former Governor of the
province—a gentleman who has now taken up the religious
life[6] and who is looking very carefully after his daughter—has
an impressive establishment there. He ought to have done well
in the world, because he is descended from a Minister, but being eccentric he never mixed with society, resigned his post as a
Captain of the Palace Guards, and requested his posting as

5. Probably Mount Asama, also in central Honshu.
6. He is a Novice (Nyūdō): someone who has taken preliminary vows, wears
Buddhist robes, and leads a life of religious devotion at home.

Governor himself.[7] He became a bit of a laughingstock in his province even so, and he was too embarrassed to return to the City, so he shaved his head instead. Not that he retired to any sheltered spot in the hills, because he put himself right on the sea, which is rather strange. It is certainly true, though, that while the province offers many places suitable for retirement, a village deep in the mountains would have been miserably lonely for his wife and his young daughter; and besides, I expect he feels more comfortable there himself. When I was down in the province some time ago, I went for a look at his residence. He may never have made a place for himself in the City, but the sheer scale of the tract he has claimed makes it obvious that he has arranged things—he *was* the Governor, after all—so as to spend the rest of his life in luxury. He does all his devotions to prepare for the life to come,[8] and in fact he makes a better monk than he ever did a gentleman."

"Yes," said Genji, "but what about his daughter?"

"My lord, I gather she has her share both of looks and of character. I hear one Governor after another has respectfully shown interest in her, but her father rejects each one. 'It is all very well for me to have sunk this low,' he says, 'but she is all I have, and I have other things in mind for her.' 'If you outlive me,' he tells her, 'if my hopes for you fail and the future I want for you is not to be, then you are to drown yourself in the sea.' That, they say, is the solemn injunction he repeats to her."

Genji was indeed amused.

"She must be a rare treasure then," someone said, laughing, "if her father means the Dragon King of the Sea to have her as his Queen!"

"Spare me such high ambition!"

The young man who had been telling about her, a son of the present Governor, had risen this year to the rank above Chamberlain.[9] "You're enterprising enough in love," one of them

7. He had resigned a lower-fourth-rank post to take up one rated at upper fifth.
8. For rebirth in the paradise of the Buddha Amida.
9. The fifth rank, lower grade. In chapter 12 he appears as Yoshikiyo.

said. "You'd like to break her father's solemn injunction your-self, wouldn't you!"

"Oh, yes, I'm sure he's always lurking around her house!"

"Get on with you! She must be a country girl, whatever you say. Look at where she grew up, after all, and with no one but her ancient parents to teach her anything!"

"No, no, her mother seems to be of excellent birth. Thanks to her relations she manages to get pretty young gentlewomen and page girls from the best families in the City, and she is bringing up her daughter in grand style."

"He would not feel so safe about having her there if the Gov-ernor assigned to the province happened to be unscrupulous."

"I wonder what it means that his ambitions for her reach all the way to the bottom of the sea," Genji mused. "It cannot be much fun down there, with all that seaweed."[10] He was keenly intrigued. His marked taste for the unusual ensured that he would remember her story, as his companions clearly noted.

"Your fever seems not to have flared up today, my lord, even though the sun will soon be setting. You should start back."

But the venerable monk demurred. "My lord, you seem also to have come under the influence of a spirit, and I prefer that we quietly continue our rites tonight before you return."

All approved. Genji was pleased, too, since he had never spent the night away like this before. "Very well, I shall start at dawn."

For want of better to do during what remained of the long day, he melted into the heavy twilight mists toward the brush-wood fence that had caught his eye. He then sent the others back and peered through the fence with Lord Koremitsu.

There she was, straight before him on the west side of the house, engaged in practice before her personal buddha:[11] a nun. The blinds were a little way up, and she seemed to be making a

10. Genji's remark plays, as do many poems, on the syllables *mirume,* which refer both to seaweed and to a lovers' meeting. The girl's fate will be gloomy if she ends up drowned among the seaweed, and she must be gloomy if that is what she thinks about.

11. *Jibutsu,* a buddha image that is the focus of a person's private devotions.

flower offering. She was leaning against a pillar, with her scripture text on an armrest[12] before her and chanting with obvious difficulty, and she was plainly of no common distinction. Past forty and very thin, with elegantly white skin, she nonetheless still had a roundness to her cheeks, fine eyes, and hair so neatly cut[13] that to Genji it seemed much more pleasingly modern in style than if it had been long.

Two handsome, grown-up women and some page girls were wandering in and out of the room. In among them came running a girl of ten or so, wearing a softly rumpled kerria rose layering[14] over a white gown and, unlike the other children, an obvious future beauty. Her hair cascaded like a spread fan behind her as she stood there, her face all red from crying.

"What is the matter?" The nun glanced up at her. "Have you quarreled with one of the girls?" They looked so alike that Genji took them for mother and daughter.

"Inuki let my baby sparrow go! And I had him in his cage[15] and everything!" declared the indignant little girl.

"So that silly creature has managed to earn herself another scolding! She is hopeless!" a grown-up said. "And where did he go? He had grown to be such a dear little thing. Oh," she went on, rising to leave, "I hope the crows do not get him!" She was a fine-looking woman with very nice long hair. Apparently she was in charge of the girl, since the others seemed to call her Nurse Shōnagon.

"Oh, come, you are such a baby!" the nun protested. "You understand nothing, do you! Here I am, wondering whether I will last out this day or the next, but that means nothing to you, does it! All you do is chase sparrows. Oh, dear, and I keep telling you it is a sin![16] Come here!"

12. *Kyōsoku*, a common item of furniture used here as a reading desk.
13. Her hair is probably cut not far below her shoulders (*ama-sogi*), as was the custom for a nun who remained at home.
14. *Yamabuki*, of which the top layer is ocher (*usu kuchiba*) and the lining yellow.
15. A makeshift cage, since it is actually a *fusego*, a sort of frame that went over an incense burner and on which a robe could then be laid to be perfumed.
16. The Buddhist sin of capturing and imprisoning a living being.

The little girl sat down. She had a very dear face, and the faint arc of her eyebrows, the forehead from which she had childishly swept back her hair, and the hairline itself were extremely pretty. *She* is one I would like to see when she grows up! Genji thought, fascinated. Indeed, he wept when he realized that it was her close resemblance to the lady who claimed all his heart that made it impossible for him to take his eyes off her.

"You hate even to have it combed," the nun said, stroking the girl's hair, "but what beautiful hair it is! Your childishness really worries me, you know. Not everyone is like this at your age, I assure you. Your late mother was ten when she lost her father, and she perfectly understood what had happened. How would you manage if I were suddenly to leave you?" She wept so bitterly that the watching Genji felt a wave of sorrow, too. Child though she was, the little girl observed the nun gravely, then looked down and hung her head. Her hair spilled forward as she did so, glinting with the loveliest sheen.

> "When no one can say where it is the little plant will grow up at last,
> the dewdrop soon to leave her does not see how she can go,"

the nun said. With tears and a cry of sympathy, a woman replied,

> "Alas, does the dew really mean to melt away before she can know
> where her tender little plant will at last grow to be tall?"[17]

The Prelate appeared from elsewhere in the house. "This side seems to be open for anyone to look in. Today is not the day for you to be sitting so near the veranda. I have just learned that Captain Genji is now with the holy man higher up the mountain, seeking a cure for a recurrent fever. He came so quietly

17. "How could you die before you know what will become of your granddaughter?" The "little plant" (*wakakusa*) image recalls *Ise monogatari*, section 49.

that I knew nothing about it, and despite being here I have not even been to call on him yet."

"How dreadful! Here we all are in disarray, and someone may actually have seen us!" Down came the blinds.

"This is a chance, if you like, to see the Shining Genji whose praises all the world is singing. His looks are enough to make even a renunciate monk forget his cares and feel young again. Well, I shall go and greet him." Genji heard him and returned to where he was staying.

What an enchanting girl he had found! Those companions of his, so keen on women and always exploring, might indeed come across their rare finds, but he had found a treasure just on a chance outing! He was delighted. What a dear child! Who could she be? He now longed for the pleasure of having her with him day and night, to make up for the absence of the lady he loved.

He was lying down when one of the Prelate's disciples came inquiring for Koremitsu. The place was so small that he heard everything.

The disciple said on behalf of his master, "I have just learned that his lordship is favoring us with a visit, and despite the suddenness of the news I should be waiting upon his pleasure, but, you see, it pains me that his lordship, who knows I am on retreat at the temple here, should have chosen nonetheless to keep his arrival a secret. I should really have offered him a poor mat in my own lodging. It is all quite upsetting."

Genji replied,[18] "A little before the middle of this month I began to suffer from a recurrent fever, and the severity of its repeated attacks prompted me to accept advice to come here in all haste. I have kept my visit quiet, however, because it seemed to me that it would be a shame if the intervention of so saintly a man were to fail, and that consideration for him enjoined special caution on someone like myself. I shall gladly accept, if that is your wish."

To Genji's embarrassment the Prelate quickly appeared. Monk though he was, his birth entitled him to society's highest

18. Through Koremitsu.

esteem, and Genji's present casual dress made its wearer uncomfortable.

The Prelate first told Genji about his life on retreat and then pressed his invitation. "It is only a common brushwood hut,[19] my lord, but I would gladly show you its pleasantly cool stream." Genji blushed to think of the extravagant terms in which his host had described him to those of the household who had not yet seen him themselves, but interest in the little girl who had so caught his fancy encouraged him to go.

The place, which really was very well done, boasted the usual plants and trees. Cressets were lit along the brook, and there were lights in the lanterns,[20] too, because at this time of the month there was no moon. The room on the south side[21] had been nicely prepared for him. A delicious fragrance of rare incense filled the air, and Genji's own scent as he passed by was so unlike any other that those in the house must have been overawed.

The Prelate talked of mutability and of the life to come while Genji pondered the fearfulness of his own transgression,[22] the way in which this sinful preoccupation had driven all else from his mind, the likelihood that it would torment him all his days, and, worse still, the agonies that awaited him in the hereafter. How he wished that he himself might live as did his host! But the figure he had seen by daylight still called out to him.

"May I ask Your Reverence what lady lives here? I had a dream on which I wished to consult you, you see, and I have only just remembered it."

His host smiled. "How unexpectedly your dream has entered our conversation, my lord! I am afraid that my answer will dis-

---

19. A stock description of a humble dwelling, hence a stock expression of modesty.
20. A cresset (*kagaribi*) is a wood fire contained in an iron cage, used for illuminating a garden at night; a lantern (*tōrō*), containing an oil lamp, was made of wood, bamboo, or metal and hung from the eaves.
21. The "front" of the house, normally used for guests.
22. His love for Fujitsubo.

appoint you. You probably do not know about the late Inspector Grand Counselor,[23] because it is a long time now since he died. His widow is my sister, you see. She renounced the world after he was gone, and when recently her health began to fail, she sought refuge with me, since I myself no longer visit the City. She has secluded herself here."

"I had heard that the Grand Counselor's daughter was still living, though," Genji ventured. "Of course I mean nothing frivolous; my inquiry is quite serious."

"Yes, he had a daughter. It must be ten years and more since she died. He brought her up very carefully in the hope of offering her to the Emperor, but he passed away before he could do so, leaving the present nun to look after her as well as she could, all alone. Meanwhile, someone[24] allowed Prince Hyōbu to take up with her in secret. However, the Prince's wife is a very great lady, and the resulting unpleasantness made my niece so continually miserable that in the end she died. Oh, yes, I have seen with my own eyes how someone can sicken from sheer disappointment and sorrow."

Ah, Genji thought, then the girl is her daughter. I suppose it is being Prince Hyōbu's, too, that makes her look so much like *her.*[25] He was now more eager than ever to have her for his own. She was of distinguished parentage, she was delightful, and she showed no distressing tendency to talk back. How he would love to have her with him and bring her up as he pleased!

"All this is sad news," he said, still keen to be certain who she was. "Did the daughter leave no child to preserve her memory?"

"Yes, she did, not long before she died—another girl. I am afraid she is a great worry to her grandmother, who seems extremely anxious about her as her own life draws to a close."

So I was right! Genji said to himself.

"Please forgive me for being so forward, but would you be

23. Azechi no Dainagon, a dual appointment as Inspector (a mainly honorary post) and Grand Counselor (the office just below Minister in the Council of State).
24. Probably a gentlewoman in the service of the girl and her mother.
25. Fujitsubo.

good enough to advise the child's grandmother to entrust her granddaughter's future to me? I have certain ideas of my own, and although there are of course ladies upon whom I call, they seem not to suit me as well as they might, since I live alone. You may attribute the most common intentions to me and therefore feel that she is hardly yet of a suitable age, but if so, you do me an injustice."

"My lord, your proposal should be very welcome, but she is still so young and innocent that I do not see how you could propose even in jest to favor her that way. At any rate, I myself can make no decision, since it is not for me to rear a girl into adulthood. I shall give you an answer after discussing the matter with her grandmother." He spoke curtly, and his young guest found the formality of his manner so forbidding that he was at a loss to reply. "It is time for me to busy myself in the hall where Amida dwells," the Prelate continued. "I have not yet done the evening service.[26] I shall be at your disposal once more when it is over." He went up to the hall.

Genji felt quite unwell, and besides, it was now raining a little, a cold mountain wind had set in to blow, and the pool beneath the waterfall had risen until the roar was louder than before. The eerie swelling and dying of somnolent voices chanting the scriptures could hardly fail in such a setting to move the most casual visitor. No wonder Genji, who had so much to ponder, could not sleep.

The Prelate had mentioned the evening service, but the night was in fact well advanced. Obviously the nun and her gentlewomen in the chamber were not asleep yet, because despite their efforts to be quiet he could hear the click of rosary beads against an armrest, as well as a rustling of silks most pleasing to his ears. Since they were so close, he opened a gap in the line of screens that bounded his aisle room and rapped his fan on his palm. Though surprised, they seemed to see no point in pretending not to have heard him, for he caught the sound of a gentlewoman slipping toward him. "How odd!" she murmured, flustered, after retreating a little. "I must be hearing things!"

26. *Soya,* a regular service that lasted from about 6:00 to 10:00 P.M.

"I have heard it said that even in darkness the Lord Buddha is an unerring guide," Genji began, overwhelming her with the youthful grace of his voice.

"A guide to what? I do not understand."

"So sudden an approach on my part naturally perplexes you, but I hope that you will convey this message for me:

> Ever since that time I first spied the tender leaves of the little plant,
> the traveler's sleeves I wear are endlessly wet with dew."

"But, my lord, no one here could possibly make anything of such a message, as you must surely know. To whom, then, do you wish me . . . ?"

"Please grant me reasons of my own for expressing myself this way."

The gentlewoman went back to speak to her mistress, the nun, who was both puzzled and shocked. Oh, dear, she thought, he certainly is modern in his ways! He must have got it into his head that our girl is old enough for this sort of thing! But how did he manage to hear what we were saying about the "little plant"? In her confusion she failed to answer him for so long that she feared she was being uncivil.

> "O never compare dews that gather for a night on your own pillow
> to those that in these mountains wet many a mossy robe![27]

Here, the dew never dries."

"I am afraid I am a novice at conversing this way, through somebody else," Genji replied. "I have something to discuss with you seriously, if you will forgive my presumption."

"Surely he has been misled," the nun said to her women. "It

27. "Do not compare the tears of a brief visitor to these mountains with those shed by one whose whole life is spent among them." She ignores the romantic connotations of the dew (the pining lovers' tears) in Genji's own poem.

is so intimidating to have him here that I do not know how to answer."

"But, my lady, you are making him uncomfortable."

"Well, yes, I suppose it would be one thing if I were a young woman myself, but as it is, I really cannot ignore him when he is so much in earnest." She came to Genji herself.

"You may imagine after my abrupt approach that I am only seeking my own amusement," he began, "but as the Lord Buddha surely knows, I find no such feelings in my heart." Restrained by the quiet circumspection in her manner, he could not at first get out what he had to say.

"Why, no, my lord, how could you assume that I make light of your feelings, now that you and I are so unexpectedly conversing with each other?"

"I have been pained to learn of the difficulties that your granddaughter faces, and I hope that you will kindly allow me to take the place of the mother whom I believe she has lost. I myself was very young when those who would have brought me up were taken from me, and the life I have led ever since has been a strangely rootless one. Her situation and mine are so alike that I have longed to beg you to recognize how much she and I share, and so I have seized this rare opportunity, even at the risk of offending you, to address you frankly."

"Your words should make me glad, my lord, but caution restrains me, for I fear that in some things you may be misinformed. There is indeed here one for whom only I am responsible, however little I may deserve it, but she is still extremely young, and since I cannot imagine how you could overlook this difficulty, I see no way to take your proposition seriously."

"I understand you perfectly, but I still urge you to take no narrow view of what I ask. Please consider instead the exceptional nature of my most sincere desire."

However, she remained convinced that he simply did not understand the incongruity of his proposal, and her answers conceded nothing. Meanwhile, the Prelate had returned. Very well, Genji reflected as he once more closed the gap between the screens, it is a relief at least to have broached the subject.

Dawn was near, and the awesome voices chanting the Confession in the Lotus Meditation Hall came to them on the wind down the mountain, mingled with the noise of the waterfall.

"The wandering wind blowing down the mountain slopes sweeps away the dream,[28]
and then tears begin to flow at the clamor of the falls,"

Genji said, and the Prelate,

"The swift mountain stream that so much to your surprise has moistened your sleeves
stirs no trouble in a heart its waters have long washed clean.

I am just so used to it, I suppose."

The lightening sky was thick with mist, and mountain birds were singing everywhere. Flowers Genji could not even name carpeted the ground with a many-colored brocade of petals, on which deer now stood or wandered past—a sight so wonderful that all thought of his fever melted away. The holy man managed to perform a protective rite for him, despite his difficulty in moving about. His hoarse voice was quite indistinct, but his chanting of the *darani*[29] conveyed an impressive sanctity.

Those who had come from the City to escort Genji home now presented themselves before him, expressed their pleasure that his fever had abated, and conveyed as well His Majesty's wishes for Genji's health. The Prelate scoured the depths of the valley to entertain Genji with all sorts of fruits and nuts unknown to the world at large.

"Alas, my lord," he remarked, offering Genji wine, "my solemn vow to remain on the mountain through this year pre-

28. "The dream of the passions that obscures insight into the truth." Genji is paying a compliment to his host.
29. The protective rite was centered, like many others, on the chanting of a *darani,* a mystically powerful utterance voiced in the Japanese pronunciation of a Chinese transliteration from Sanskrit.

vents me from accompanying you as I should otherwise wish
to do."

"While my heart remains in these mountains, His Majesty's
kind expressions of concern leave me no choice but to return,"
Genji replied. "This year's blossoms shall not pass before I
come again.

> I shall go forth now and describe to all at court these mountain cherries,
>   that before the winds arrive they themselves should come and see."

His manner of speaking and the sound of his voice were both
utterly captivating.

> "At last I have seen the udumbara flower: that is how I feel,
>   till I have no eyes at all for mountain cherry blossoms,"[30]

the Prelate courteously replied.

Genji smiled. "What you have before you cannot be the
flower of which you speak, for surely that one blooms only
once, and at its proper time."[31]

The holy man took up the wine cup in his turn.

> "Having just for once opened deep in these mountains my lowly pine door,
>   I see the face of a flower I have never seen before!"[32]

he said, contemplating Genji with tears in his eyes. He gave
Genji a single-pointed vajra[33] to protect him.

---

30. The udumbara flower blooms once in three thousand years, when a per-
fected ruler appears and unites all the world in the Buddha's truth.
31. According to a passage in the Lotus Sutra.
32. The modest "pine" door contrasts evergreen constancy with the flower's
passing beauty.
33. Toko, an esoteric Buddhist ritual implement and a symbol of supreme insight. Other variants of it have three, five, or more points or prongs.

The Prelate then gave Genji his own most appropriately selected gifts: a rosary of embellished bo tree seeds, obtained by
Prince Shōtoku from Kudara, still in its original Chinese-style
box and presented in a gauze bag attached to a branch of five-
needled pine; and dark blue lapis lazuli jars containing diverse
medicines and tied to sprays of wisteria or cherry blossoms.[34]
Genji had already sent for the varied gifts, formal and informal, with which to reward the holy man and the other monks
who had chanted the scriptures for him, and he now distrib-
uted suitable presents to all, even the local woodcutters. At last
he took his leave, after providing for further chanting of the
scriptures.

The Prelate went into the house and repeated to the nun all
that Genji had told him, but her only comment was "At any
rate, we cannot answer him now. If in four or five years his
wish remains unchanged, then perhaps . . ."

The reply Genji received therefore only confirmed the nun's
opposition. Through a small boy in His Reverence's service,
he sent,

> *"Now that I have seen faintly the flower's color through the gathering dusk,*
> *I can hardly bear to leave while morning mists still rise";*[35]

to which the nun answered in a casual hand remarkable for its
character and distinction,

> *"Whether it is true you would never wish to leave the flower you prize,*
> *that we shall look to discern in the mists of future skies."*

34. The Buddha reached enlightenment under a bo tree, the seeds of which
were valued as rosary beads. Prince Shōtoku (574–622) established Buddhism
in Japan after its official introduction from Kudara (an ancient Korean kingdom). The medicine jars (associated with Yakushi, the Buddha of Healing) are
made of *ruri*, in theory lapis lazuli (a blue stone) but in practice, at least in
Japan, more often glass.
35. "Now that I have seen the little girl, I do not wish to be parted from her by
her guardians' objections."

Genji was entering his carriage when a crowd of young gentlemen from the Minister of the Left's arrived to see him home, complaining that he had simply vanished from among them. Tō no Chūjō and his other brothers-in-law had insisted on coming after him.

"We would have gladly accompanied you on a trip like this," Tō no Chūjō said reproachfully, "and it really was not very nice of you to leave us behind. Anyway, it would be a great shame if we were to turn round and start back again without a moment to rest beneath these magnificent blossoms."

They all sat together on the moss, in the lee of a rock, and the wine cup went round. The tumbling stream beside them made a beautiful cascade. Tō no Chūjō took a flute from the fold of his robe and played, while one of his brothers sang, "Westward from the Toyora Temple . . . ,"[36] lightly tapping out the rhythm with his fan. These young gentlemen were all certainly splendid, but Genji's peerless, indeed disturbing beauty as he sat leaning against a rock, quite unwell, made it impossible to have eyes for anyone else.

One of Tō no Chūjō's company was as usual a *hichiriki* player, while another young man of taste had been entrusted with a *shō*.[37] The Prelate brought Genji his own *kin*.[38] "Do play a little, my lord," he said. "If it please you, I should like to give the birds of these mountains a pleasant surprise." Genji protested that he was not feeling himself, but he played enough not to be disobliging. Everyone then set out.

The very least of the monks and young servants wept to see him go, while of course the old nuns in the house, who had never seen his like before, assured each other that he could not

36. From a felicitous *saibara* song entitled "Kazuraki."
37. Tō no Chūjō, known for his mastery of the transverse flute (*fue*), presumably made sure that he traveled with suitable accompanists. The *hichiriki* is a small reed instrument made of bamboo; the *shō* is a cluster of fine bamboo pipes rising from a single air chest into which the player blows.
38. A seven-stringed instrument of the koto family. Highly respected in China, it was prized in Japan, too, in the early tenth century, and Genji's taste for it figures prominently in such chapters as "Suma" and "Akashi." However, it seems not to have been played much in the author's own time.

possibly be of this world at all. The Prelate himself exclaimed, wiping tears from his eyes, "Ah, it is sad to think what karma can have got him born with such looks into these latter days, and into this poor land of ours!"

To the little girl's childish eye, Genji was so splendid that she declared, "He is much better-looking than Father!"

"Then why not be his little girl instead?" a gentlewoman suggested. She nodded and seemed very pleased with the idea. Whenever she played with a doll or painted a picture, she pretended that the figure was Lord Genji, dressed it up nicely, and made a great fuss over it.

Genji first went to the palace and gave His Majesty an account of all that had happened. His Majesty was dismayed to see him so thin. He inquired about the quality of the holy man and was sufficiently impressed by Genji's long description to remark, "I believe he deserves elevation to Adept. How strange that he should have lived a life of practice for all these years without ever coming to his Sovereign's attention!"

Just then the Minister of the Left arrived. "I had thought I should at least come out to meet you, but then I reflected that since you had gone so discreetly, I might do better to refrain. Do come and spend a few quiet days with us. I shall accompany you there straightaway." Genji had little enthusiasm for this, but he let himself be dragged off. The Minister invited him into his own carriage and modestly got in behind him. Genji was touched after all by his attentions.

The household was eagerly awaiting his arrival. His Excellency had had all sorts of things done since Genji's last visit, some time ago, to make the place grander than ever. Aoi slipped off as always to hide and refused to appear until her father persuaded her at last to come forth; and there she sat, precisely where her gentlewomen placed her, as still and as perfect as a lady in a painting.

I could try talking to her about whatever I have on my mind, or tell her about my trip to the mountains, and it would be so nice if only she would then give me some sort of decent response! Genji reflected; but no, she would not unbend, and she remained cold and forbidding. The gulf between them had widened over the years, until he felt provoked to say, "I do wish I might occasionally see you treat me in a normal way. For example, there I was, deathly ill, and you did not even ask after my health—not that this is anything new, I know, but I cannot help feeling hurt."

At last she spoke. "Was it really 'so painful to be ignored'?"[39] She threw him sidelong a chilly glance that accented the stern character of her beauty.

"You so seldom speak, but when you do, you say the most extraordinary things! That is hardly our relationship to each other. What a way to talk! I keep trying this and that in the hope that you may change your mind and give up rejecting me all the time, but as far as I can tell, you only dislike me the more! Well, one day perhaps . . ."

He went into their curtained bed, but she did not immediately follow. At a loss for what else to say, he lay down unhappily and proceeded—for he was no doubt feeling thoroughly out of humor—to feign drowsiness, the better to turn over in his mind all the troubles that love had brought him.

He was still keen to watch the "little plant" grow up, but there was a good deal to be said for the nun's opinion that she was far too young. This is such a tricky business on which to approach anyone! he said to himself. What will I have to do to be able to take her home and enjoy her company always? Prince Hyōbu is a decent enough gentleman, but he has nothing in particular to recommend him, so why is she so like *her*? Because they were both born to the same Empress, I suppose.[40] This intimate tie to her made up his mind that he must have her for his own.

The next day he sent off letters to the Northern Hills. The one to the Prelate no doubt hinted at his wish. He wrote to the nun, "I felt constrained by your distant manner and unfortunately never

39. The poem Aoi quotes has not been identified. Perhaps Genji responds with disapproval because the poem had to do with illicit lovers, not a married couple.
40. "Why does the girl look so much like Fujitsubo? Probably because His Highness of War and Fujitsubo are the children of the same Empress." The girl is Fujitsubo's niece.

managed to say all I wished. I should be glad if a note such as this were to convince you that there is nothing mild about my hopes . . . ," and so on. Inside the letter he placed a little knotted one:[41]

> *"That vision of you never, never leaves me now, O mountain cherry,*
> *even though I left behind in your care all of my heart.*

I worry so about you when the night winds blow!"[42] His writing, of course, but even the casual way he had done up the letter dazzled the eyes of the aging nuns.[43]

How very difficult all this is! What reply can I possibly give him? She wrote, "I confess that I gave little weight to the kind words that I was privileged to have from you, and now that it has pleased you to return to the matter, I find it difficult to frame a reply. Surely there is no point in pursuing it, since she cannot even write her *kana* letters[44] properly yet. After all,

> *Just that little while the blossoms cling to the bough on a windswept hill:*
> *so long you have left your heart, and such times are quickly gone.*

I worry about her more and more." The Prelate answered in the same vein.

The disappointed Genji sent Koremitsu there two or three days later. "The woman they call Nurse Shōnagon should be in the house," he said. "Find her and have a good talk with her."

He never misses a single one, does he! Koremitsu remembered

41. A playful courting note for the girl. This sort of letter (*musubi bumi*) was written on a piece of paper, then folded up very thin and knotted.
42. *Shūishū* 29, by Prince Motoyoshi: "Before dawn I rose to see my plum blossoms, worried about what the night winds might have done." Genji fears that "night winds" may scatter the blossoms' petals, that is, take the girl away somewhere beyond his reach.
43. There seem to be several older nuns, presumably former gentlewomen, around the little girl's grandmother.
44. The letters of the phonetic syllabary, with which writing lessons began.

with amusement his own inadequate glimpse of the girl, and
how very young she had been.

The Prelate professed deep gratification upon receiving yet
another letter. Koremitsu asked to see Shōnagon and spent some
time with her, telling her what Genji had to say and describing
something of Genji's life. He was a great talker, and he made it
all sound very convincing, but the little girl was so impossibly
young that her guardians remained troubled about what Genji
might have in mind.

Genji's letter itself was sincerely felt, and as before it contained a little note: "I should still like to see this broken writing[45] of yours.

> Ah, Mount Asaka! Shallow all my love for you cannot ever be—
> but why does the face in the spring melt away when I draw near?"[46]

The nun replied,

> "They tell of a spring such that one who draws from it knows only regret;
> shallow as your waters are, how could they reveal her face?"[47]

Koremitsu conveyed the same message to Genji.

Nurse Shōnagon wrote in her own reply, "We are soon to
move back to my lady's residence in the City, as long as her condition improves, and I expect that she will wish to communicate

45. She is still writing the *kana* letters separately instead of running them together.
46. The little girl must know the poem to which Genji's alludes, since any
child learning to write had to copy it out. Both play on the place-name Asaka-
yama ("Mount Asaka") and on *asashi* ("shallow"). The original poem
(*Man'yōshū* 3829, also cited in the Japanese preface to the *Kokinshū*) was
spoken in ancient times by a pretty court lady to an ill-humored lord from the
north: "Mount Asaka, shallow the spring that now mirrors your face, but not
this heart of mine in desire." Her declaration brightened the visitor's mood.
47. "I cannot believe you are serious, and I cannot give you my granddaughter." *Kokin rokujō* 987: "Alas that I should have begun to draw water from a
mountain spring so shallow that it only wets my sleeves."

with you further from there." Genji did not find this encouraging.

Princess Fujitsubo was not well and had withdrawn from the palace. Genji felt deep sympathy for His Majesty, whose anxious distress was evident, but he also anticipated feverishly now, at last, a chance for himself, and he no longer went out at all. At the palace or at home he spent the daylight hours daydreaming and those after dark hounding Ōmyōbu.[48] How Ōmyōbu brought off their meeting is impossible to say; but to poor Genji even these stolen moments[49] with her seemed quite unreal. To Fujitsubo the memory of that last, most unfortunate incident was a source of enduring suffering, and she had resolved that nothing of the kind should ever happen again; yet despite her obvious consternation she remained thoughtful and kind, even while she continued to resist him with a profound dignity so far beyond the reach of any other woman that Genji could not help wondering in anguish why it was never possible to find in her the slightest flaw.

How could he have told her all he had to say? He must have wished himself where darkness never ends, but alas, the nights were short now, and their time together had yielded after all nothing but pain.

> *"This much we have shared, but nights when we meet again will be very rare,*
> *and now that we live this dream, O that it might swallow me!"*

he said, sobbing; to which Fujitsubo compassionately replied,

> *"People soon enough will be passing on our tale, though I let our dream*
> *sweep me on till I forget what misfortune now is mine."*

48. The regular intermediary between Genji and Fujitsubo. The initial Ō element shows that she was of imperial blood. *Myōbu* was a title borne by middle-ranking women in palace service.
49. The original expression contains the verb *miru* ("see"), which implies sexual intimacy. The passage is studiously understated because of Fujitsubo's exalted position. The "last, most unfortunate incident" mentioned just below does not otherwise appear in the tale.

Genji could not blame her for being in such torment, and he deeply regretted having caused it. Ōmyōbu gathered up his dress cloak and so on and brought it to him.

At home again, he lay down and wept all day. He gathered that she was refusing as usual to read any letter from him, and although this was indeed her normal practice, the pain of it now all but destroyed him. For two or three days he remained shut up without even calling at the palace, until the Emperor was moved yet again to a concern about what might be wrong that only filled Genji with terror.

Fujitsubo continued to lament the misery of her lot, and meanwhile she began feeling more and more unwell, so that she could not make up her mind to go straight back to the palace, despite a stream of messengers from there urging her to do so. No, she really did not feel herself, and her silent guesses at what this might mean reduced her to despair over what was to become of her.

She rose less and less during the summer heat. By the third month her condition was obvious enough that her women noticed it, and the horror of her fate overwhelmed her. Not knowing what had actually happened, they expressed surprise that she had not yet told the Emperor. She alone understood just what the matter was. Women like Ōmyōbu or her own foster sister, Ben, who attended her intimately when she bathed and therefore had before their eyes every clue to her condition, did not doubt that something was seriously wrong, but they could not very well discuss the matter, and Ōmyōbu was left to reflect in anguish that her mistress's fate had struck after all. To His Majesty, Ōmyōbu presumably reported that a malevolent spirit had obscured Princess Fujitsubo's condition,[50] so that at first it had gone unnoticed. This was at any rate what Fujitsubo's own

50. By causing an illness that diverted attention from the symptoms of pregnancy. In the roughly contemporary historical work *Eiga monogatari* (*A Tale of Flowering Fortunes*), a gentlewoman may watch her mistress's periods, count days, and report to the man concerned. The Emperor would normally have had a clear idea of when Fujitsubo got pregnant and of when to expect the child.

women believed. His Majesty was deeply concerned about her, and the unbroken procession of messengers from him inspired mingled dread and despair.

Genji himself had a dream so strange that he summoned a dream reader. In answer to his questions he received an interpretation beyond the bounds of all plausibility.

"I see, too, my lord, that you are to suffer a reverse and that something will require the most urgent caution."

Genji was troubled. "It is not my own dream. I have only described someone else's. Say not a word about it until it comes true."

He was wondering what it all meant when he heard about Fujitsubo and realized that he probably knew what the matter was. But despite his pleas, now more passionate than ever, Ōmyōbu was too cowed by fear and guilt to contrive anything for him. His love's rare, one-line replies to his letters now stopped altogether.

She did not return to the palace until the seventh month. The Emperor, whose love was extraordinary, showed her renewed affection. A new roundness of figure and a face wasted by suffering gave her now a truly peerless beauty. As usual His Majesty spent all his time in her rooms, and since it was the season for music, he was always summoning Genji to attend him and perform on the *kin* or the flute. Genji struggled to conceal his feelings, but whenever he failed and betrayed a hint of his torment, Her Highness was overcome, despite her best efforts, by a host of disturbing thoughts.

The nun at the mountain temple had recovered well enough to come down to the City. Genji discovered where she lived and sent her frequent messages. Not unnaturally, her position remained unchanged, and what with the more absorbing sorrows that had overtaken him during the last few months, he had no latitude to think of anything else.

Late that autumn he was feeling very reduced and disheartened. One beautifully moonlit night he had at last made up his mind to visit a lady he had been seeing in secret when the weather turned and a cold rain began to fall. He was bound for the vicinity of Rokujō and Kyōgoku—rather far, to his mind, since he was coming from the palace—when he caught sight of an unkempt house amid the darkness of ancient trees.

"That is the house of the late Inspector Grand Counselor," explained Koremitsu, who was with him as always. "I happened to call there the other day, and they told me that my lady the nun is very weak now, and they hardly know what to do."

"What sad news! I should really have called on her before. Why did they not let me know? Do go in and convey my greetings."

Koremitsu sent a man to tell the household of Genji's arrival, instructing him to say that Genji had come purposely to call. The man therefore announced when he entered that His Lordship had been pleased to pay them a visit.

"This is most unfortunate!" The women were startled. "For days now my lady's health has been a great worry, and she is in no condition to receive him." They could not just send him away, though, so they tidied up the south aisle room and invited him in. "This is most unworthy accommodation, my lord, but my lady wishes at least to thank you. It is unfortunately a very dreary room in which to receive you on so unexpected a visit."[51] Genji agreed that the room was indeed unusual for such an occasion.

"I have often thought of calling on you," he began, "but you have always given me so little hope that in the end I refrained. Your illness, of which I had not heard, troubles me very much."

The nun replied, "It is very good indeed of you to look in upon me now that I, who have never been a stranger to failing health, am at last nearing my end, and I apologize for not speaking to you myself. Do by all means approach her once she is no longer a child, if it happens that you remain disposed as you are now. I am afraid that leaving her this way without a protector may well hinder my progress on the path I so long to take."[52]

She was so near that Genji now and then caught her feeble voice. "There is every reason to be grateful for his interest, you

51. Genji seems to have been received not in the main house but in one of the wings, but the precise meaning of the passage is uncertain.
52. The path to rebirth in paradise.

know," she was saying. "If only our little girl were just old enough to thank him properly!"[53]

He was moved to answer, "But why would I exhibit my immodesty this way if I had taken only a passing fancy to her? There is an unfathomable bond between her and me, and my heart went out to her the moment I saw her—indeed, with such uncanny speed that I cannot believe this tie to be from this life alone." And he continued, "I understand that any further pleading would be wasted, but if I might possibly just hear the sound of her voice . . ."

"But, my lord, she does not know you are here, and she is in bed!"

Just then footsteps approached from the depths of the house, and a little girl's voice called, "Grandma, they say Lord Genji is here, the gentleman at the mountain temple! Why are you not looking at him?"[54]

"Hush!" said the shocked women.

"But she said seeing him made her feel so much better!"

This was welcome news, but in consideration for the women's embarrassment Genji pretended despite his pleasure not to have heard, and he brought his visit to a correct conclusion before leaving. Yes, he thought, she really is just a little girl, but I will teach her properly.

The next day he sent the nun a courteous note with as usual a smaller one, tightly folded, inside it:

> *"Ever since these ears listened to that single cry from the little crane,*
>   *I have despaired that my boat should be caught among the reeds.*

'And ever to that same love . . .' "[55] He had purposely written in

---

53. She is speaking to her women, including the one through whom she is talking to Genji.

54. If she had received him in person, she could have seen him through her curtains.

55. Genji's progress is impeded by the nun's resistance. In *Kokinshū* 732 the lover protests that his "little boat" will always return to the same love.

a youthful hand so appealing that all the gentlewomen urged the little girl to put it straight into her copybook.

Shōnagon composed the reply: "The lady you visited seems unlikely to live many days longer, and she will therefore move presently to the temple in the mountains. She will wish to thank you for your kind letter even if she can no longer do so in this life." Genji was deeply moved.

His thoughts would turn of an autumn evening to the one who so constantly stirred his heart, and he surely thirsted more than ever for any relation of hers. He remembered that evening when the nun spoke of being unable to let the little plant go, and he yearned for her, although he also felt a pang of apprehension that if he did have her she might disappoint him; and he murmured,

"How glad I would be to pick and soon to make mine that little wild plant
sprung up from the very root shared by the murasaki."[56]

In the tenth month His Majesty was to make a progress to the Suzaku Palace.[57] He had chosen as dancers those sons of the greatest houses, senior nobles or privy gentlemen, who showed any aptitude for such things, and everyone from the Princes and Ministers on down was busy rehearsing his part.

Genji remembered how long it had been since his last correspondence with the lady in the mountains, and he sent a messenger there. The only answer he received was from the Prelate, who wrote, "She breathed her last on the twentieth of last month, in my presence, and although death comes to us all, hers is a very great loss," and so on. Genji felt the frailty of life sharply

56. *Murasaki,* later the girl's name, refers to Fujitsubo. A common meadow plant, *murasaki* was associated with love because of the purple dye extracted from its roots. The *fuji* ("wisteria") in Fujitsubo's name links her to the same color. *Kokinshū* 867: "Because of a single stem of *murasaki,* I love all the plants and grasses on Musashi Plain."
57. A residence built by Emperor Saga (reigned 809–23) and occupied by Retired Emperors.

as he read it, and he wondered anxiously how the little girl whose future had so worried her was now getting on. Young as she was, did she miss her grandmother? He remembered losing his own mother, if only dimly, and he took care to keep in touch with her. The replies he had from Shōnagon were not unsympathetic.

Once he heard that the mourning confinement[58] was over and the household was back in the City, he let some time go by and then went in person one quiet night to call. It was a depressing, ruinous place, all but deserted, and he could easily imagine how it might frighten a child. He was shown into the same room as before, and there the weeping Shōnagon described to him how the end had come for her mistress, until his own sleeves were wet with tears.

"I gather that she is to go to Prince Hyōbu's," Shōnagon went on, "but her mother always hated the cruelty she suffered there, and my mistress herself believed that although the child is certainly not a baby, at her awkward age, among all her father's other children, she might well be treated more as a nuisance than anything else, since she does not yet understand very well what is expected of her. There is good reason, in fact, to believe that my mistress was right, and at a time like this we should therefore welcome the interest you have been kind enough to express, however casual it may be, and not insist too much on gauging your future feelings toward her. Even so, my lord, we are perplexed about what to do, because she is hopelessly unsuited to you and is actually even more of a child than she should be at her age."

"But why must you be so reluctant to accept the assurances that I have already given you repeatedly? That her very childishness should so attract me suggests—for I can make no other sense of it—that the tie between her and me really is unusual. I should like to tell her so, not indirectly but in person.

58. *Imi,* probably thirty days, though perhaps twenty (starting in this case on the twentieth of the ninth month), during which the mourner remained at home. Mourning gray was worn much longer.

Perhaps the young reed, where she grows on Waka Shore, is for no one yet,
but, say, now the wave is high, can it slip back to the sea?

That would not do at all."[59]
"Nor would I presume to ask it of you, my lord.

Should the gleaming reed on Waka Shore lean to meet the approaching wave,
never knowing what he means, hers no doubt would be light ways.

How difficult this is!"

Genji partly forgave her for thwarting him, since she spoke with a thoughtfulness born of experience. "Why does that day never come?"[60] he sang to himself, dazzling the younger gentlewomen.

The little girl was lying down, crying for her grandmother, when her playmates exclaimed, "A gentleman is here in a dress cloak! It must be His Highness!"

She got up and called, "Shōnagon! Where is the gentleman in the dress cloak? Is Father here?" Her voice as she approached was very sweet.

"No," Genji said, "I am not Prince Hyōbu, but that does not mean you should not like me, too. Come here!"[61]

She recognized the voice of the gentleman who had overawed her, and she regretted having spoken. Instead, she went straight to her nurse. "Come," she said, "I am sleepy!"

"Why are you still hiding from me? Sleep on my lap, then! Do come a little closer!"

59. "You may not wish me [the wave] to see her, but I do not mean to make it easy for you by giving up." The main motif of this and the next poem, with all their wordplay, is that of an impetuous wave surging in toward an object of desire on the shore.
60. From *Gosenshū* 731, by Koremasa: "Secretly I am impatient, but why, for years and years, does that day never come when I meet her at last?"
61. Genji seems to be seated in the aisle, with a blind between him and the women in the chamber. The only light, an oil lamp, is on the women's side.

"You see how little she understands yet at her age, my lord."
Shōnagon propelled her toward him.

The little girl sat down innocently, and he reached under the
blind to touch her. He felt a delicious abundance when his hand
came to the end of her tresses, which spilled richly over her soft
clothing, and he imagined the beauty of her hair. Next he took
her hand, at which she bridled to have a stranger so close and
drew back, complaining to Shōnagon, "But I want to go to
sleep!"

He slipped straight in after her. "But I am the one who is going to love you now. Be nice to me!"

"My lord, what are you doing?" Shōnagon was appalled.
"Oh, dear me! I assure you, it does not matter how you talk to
her, you will get nothing from her at all!"

"What do I care if she is still only a little girl? Just wait and
see how much I love her: more than anyone, ever!"

Hail was coming down hard, and it promised to be a bad
night. "How can you live all by yourselves like this, when there
are so few of you?" Genji began to weep. He could not possibly
leave them. "Lower the lattice shutters! This looks to be an unpleasant night, and I mean to protect you. Gather near me, all
of you!"

With this he strode into the little girl's curtained bed as though
it were the most natural thing in the world,[62] leaving the shocked
and astonished gentlewomen rooted to the spot. Shōnagon could
not very well intervene with a sharp reproof, despite her anxiety, and she only sat there, sighing. The girl began to shiver
with fright, and Genji, his heart melting to find her lovely skin
so chilly, wrapped her in another shift.

He knew perfectly well how outrageously he was behaving,
but he began nonetheless to talk to her gently about things he
thought might catch her fancy. "Come with me, and I will
take you to where there are lots of pretty pictures and you
can play with dolls!" He spoke so kindly that in her childish
way she stopped being quite so afraid, but she never relaxed

62. He seems to carry her in with him, though the text does not say so.

enough to sink into a sound sleep, and she continued to toss and turn.

The wind roared all night long, while the gentlewomen whispered among themselves, "It's true, you know, we would have been miserable without him. Oh, if only she were old enough for him!" The anxious Shōnagon stayed very close to her charge.

Genji left before daybreak, once the wind had dropped a little, looking quite pleased with himself. "She was already constantly on my mind," he said, "and now I shall worry more than ever. I want to take her to where I myself spend my dreary nights and days. She cannot go on this way. It is a wonder she was not frightened half to death!"

"Prince Hyōbu seems to be talking about having her come to live with him as well," Shōnagon answered. "I suppose he means to do it after my lady's forty-nine days are over."

"I am sure he will look after her, but he must be as much of a stranger to her as I am. She has never lived with him, after all. I myself have only just come to know her, but even so, I have no doubt that I am more attached to her than he." He stroked her hair, and he looked back at her many times as he left the house.

The sky, thick with fog, was unusually lovely, and all was white with frost: a scene to please the replete lover, but for Genji not quite enough. He remembered that someone he had been visiting secretly lived on his way, and he had a man of his knock at her gate. No one heard. He was reduced to having an attendant with a good voice sing twice over,

> "By the dawn's first light, while rising mists shroud the skies and confuse the gaze,
> I just cannot bring myself to pass by my darling's gate!"[63]

At this, a nice-looking servant woman came out and replied,[64]

63. Genji's poem weaves in expressions from a *saibara* song known as "My Darling's Gate" ("Imo ga yado").
64. For her mistress.

"If it is so hard to pass straight on by a gate just glimpsed through the mist,
surely its flimsy portal need not really bar your way!"[65]

Then she went back in. No one came out again. He had no wish to retreat, but he felt exposed under the lightening sky, and he went his way.

He lay smiling to himself in fond recollection of that delightful little girl. The sun was high by the time he arose to write the customary letter,[66] and what he had to say was so unusual that he often laid down his brush and simply dreamed. With the letter he sent some pretty pictures.

As it happened, this was the day when Prince Hyōbu came to see his daughter. The house had deteriorated remarkably in recent years, and its being so big and old made it even more forbiddingly lonely. "How could a child spend a moment living in a place like this?" He contemplated the scene before him. "I *must* bring her home with me. There is no reason why you should be uncomfortable there. You will have your nurse, who will have a room of her own, and there are children for you to play with. You should be perfectly happy."

He had her come to him, and he caught the delicious scent her clothing had picked up from Genji's. "What a lovely smell!" he exclaimed, only to add ruefully, "Your clothes are all limp, though!"[67] He went on, "What a pity she spent all those years with an old and ailing lady! I have urged her to come and get to know my household, but for some reason she has resisted the idea, and actually there has been some reluctance at my house as well.[68] I am sorry she must move there at a time like this."

65. The shut "flimsy portal" (*kusa no tozashi*) is from *Gosenshū* 899 and 900, an analogous exchange between Fujiwara no Kanesuke and an unnamed woman.
66. The letter (*kinuginu no fumi*) that a lover sent his mistress after returning home from her house in the early morning.
67. They lack the starched look of new ones, which the household presumably cannot afford.
68. His wife did not want to see his mistress's daughter.

"But must she really, Your Highness? This house is certainly lonely for her, but she ought to stay a while longer. Surely it would be better for her to move after she has grown up a little more. She always misses her grandmother, and she will not eat." It was true, too: the little girl was painfully thin, although this only gave her looks a more enchanting grace.

"But why are you so upset?" The Prince hoped to make her feel better. "Your grandmother is gone, and no mourning will bring her back. You have me, after all."

When evening came and the Prince prepared to leave, the little girl was so unhappy that she cried. Tears sprang to his eyes as well. "Now, now, you must not be so sad," he said comfortingly, over and over again. "I shall have you come to me very soon."

When he was gone, she wept inconsolably. What life might hold in store for her concerned her not at all; she knew only that the lady she had been with every moment through the years was now no more, and, child though she was, the pain of her loss consumed her. She no longer played as she used to, and if she forgot during the day, night returned her to her misery. Her women wondered how she could go on living this way, and they did all they could to comfort her, only to fail and burst into tears themselves.

Toward evening Genji sent Koremitsu to the house with the message "I should come myself, but unfortunately His Majesty has summoned me. I was distressed to see her situation, and now it worries me very much." Koremitsu was to guard the house.

"This is too awful of him!" Shōnagon said. "It is a game to him, I am sure, but what a thing to do at the very start![69] If His Highness were to hear of it, he would accuse us in her service of sheer folly. Do not forget, you must never be foolish enough to give him any hint of what has happened!" Alas, to the little girl none of this meant anything at all.

69. She is incensed that Genji, having slept once (though chastely) with the girl, will not do so again on the two following nights so as to seal their relationship in the manner of a marriage. Genji recognizes this obligation, but the girl is so young that, despite his future intentions, he seems not to take it very seriously for the present.

Shōnagon remarked while recounting their woes to Koremitsu, "When she is older, I doubt that she will escape the destiny
he intends for her, but for the moment his proposition seems to
me hopelessly unsuitable; in fact, I cannot even imagine what he
means by all the extraordinary things he says. I do not know what
to do. Just today His Highness was here, warning us to make
sure that he need not worry about her and to keep a proper eye
on her at all times. I hardly know which way to turn, and now I
worry far more than before about the liberties someone might
take with her." Shōnagon refrained from complaining too pointedly, because she did not wish to give Koremitsu ideas. Koremitsu himself could not make out what she was talking about.

Genji felt Shōnagon's predicament keenly when Koremitsu
returned and told him what he had heard, but the thought of
visiting her regularly still upset him, because if people learned
what he was up to, they would certainly condemn his dubious
eccentricity, and that idea did not appeal to him at all. No, he
decided, he would take her home. He sent repeated notes and
dispatched Koremitsu there after sundown, as before, to say
that he hoped they would not take it amiss if certain difficulties
prevented him from coming in person.

"We are very busy now because we have just heard from His
Highness that he suddenly plans to take her to his residence tomorrow," Shōnagon explained. "I hate after all to leave this
tumbledown old place where I have lived so long, and the others are upset, too." She had little more to say and seemed preoccupied only with her sewing.[70] Koremitsu returned to Genji.

Genji was at his father-in-law's, but Aoi refused as usual to
receive him. He toyed in frustration with a *wagon*[71] and sang to
himself in a pleasant voice, "In Hitachi here I've my field to
hoe . . ."[72] Then Koremitsu arrived. Genji called him in and
asked for his news.

70. She is probably making new clothes for the girl to wear at her father's.
71. *Azuma (goto)*, that is, the *wagon*, the six-stringed "Japanese koto."
72. A folk song in which a peasant woman rejects her lover: "In Hitachi here
I've my field to hoe—who have you come for this rainy night, all the way over
moor and mountain?" He is thinking of Aoi.

Koremitsu's report alarmed him. If she went to her father's, any attempt to remove her from there would appear indecent, and he would be accused of having abducted an innocent child. No, he would have to silence her women for the time being and take her before that could happen.

"I shall go there before daybreak," he announced. "The carriage will do very well as it is, and I shall want you to bring one or two men." Koremitsu left to do as he asked.

Genji now wavered, reflecting anxiously that if anyone found out, he would be considered debauched; that a man would look normal in comparison if people assumed that the woman involved had been old enough to know what was what and had acted in concert with him; and that he would have no excuse for himself when Prince Hyōbu discovered the truth. But despite this whirl of misgivings he could not let the opportunity pass, and he therefore prepared to leave while the night was still dark. Aoi was displeased as always, and she had no forgiveness for him.

"You see, I just remembered something urgent I must go back and look after. I shall not be gone long." Not even her women knew it when he left. In his own room he donned a dress cloak, and then he drove off with only Koremitsu riding beside him.

He had a man of his knock at the gate, and a servant who knew nothing opened it. He ordered his carriage quietly brought inside. Koremitsu then rapped at the double doors and cleared his throat. Shōnagon came out when she recognized his voice. "His lordship is here," he announced.

"But she is asleep! He seems to be out very late." She took it for granted that Genji was on his way home from elsewhere.

"I hear she is to move to her father's, and I have something to tell her before she goes," Genji explained.

"What in the world could it be?" Shōnagon smiled. "And how could she possibly give you a proper answer?"

To her dismay he came straight in. "But there are unsightly old women just lying about in here!"

"I suppose she is still asleep. Come, I shall get her up. There is no excuse for sleeping through such a beautifully misty dawn." He went in through her curtains. There was no time even for them to cry out.

Murasaki was lying there, oblivious to everything. Genji put his arms around her to wake her, and when she woke up she was still so sleepy that she took him for her father, come to fetch her. She did not realize her mistake until Genji tidied her hair and said, "Come! Up! I am here from His Highness!" and in her surprise she took fright. "Now, now, I might just as well be your father," he said, reemerging with her in his arms.

"My lord, what are you doing?" Taifu, Shōnagon, and the others cried.

"I have already told her I want to take her where I can be more comfortable with her, because I do not like being unable to come here often; and now, you see, I learn to my consternation that she is to move to her father's, which will make it even harder for me to keep in touch with her. I want one of you to come with me."

"My lord," the distraught Shōnagon answered, "today is just not the day for this! What would you have us tell His Highness when he comes? Everything will surely work in the fullness of time, if you are to have what you wish, but as it is, you have not left us a moment to think, and you are putting us all in an impossible position."

"Very well, someone may come and join her later." With this, to their utter amazement, he had his carriage brought up. She was alarmed and crying. Shōnagon, who could do nothing to stop him, changed into better clothes and got into the carriage, carrying the things she had been sewing the evening before.

Nijō was not far away, and the carriage reached it before daylight. Genji had it drawn up to the west wing and alighted. He easily lifted Murasaki down in his arms.

Shōnagon hesitated. "I still feel as though I am dreaming. What would you like me to do?"

"Whatever you please. Now I have brought your young mistress here, I will see you home again if you want."

With a wry smile Shōnagon stepped out of the carriage, too. The suddenness of it all had dazed her, and her heart was pounding. She wept to think of Prince Hyōbu's displeasure, of her charge's perilous future, and, above all, of the child's pathetic plight now that she had lost all those who could claim her trust; but she mastered her feelings as well as she could, despite her tears, so as not to blight this moment[73] with ill-omened grief.

The wing lacked a curtained bed and other such furnishings, since Genji did not live in it. He summoned Koremitsu and had him put one up, together with screens and so on. Apart from that, there was no need to do more than let down the standing curtains and tidy the place up a little. He sent to the east wing for nightclothes and lay down.

Murasaki wondered fearfully what he might have in mind for her, but she managed to keep from sobbing aloud. "I want to sleep with Shōnagon!" she declared in a childish tone.

"No." Genji was firm. "That is not the way you are to sleep anymore." She lay down, weeping with unhappiness. Her nurse, who could not sleep at all, sat up in a daze.

Looking around as day came on, Shōnagon was overwhelmed not only by the opulence of the building and its furnishings but even by the sand in the garden, which resembled a bed of jewels and seemed to give off light; and she began to feel like an intruder, even though no other women were actually present. Only household guards were stationed outside the blinds, since Genji lodged no more than the occasional guest here. One of them had heard that Genji had just brought a lady home. "Who can she be?" he whispered. "He must be extremely keen on her!"

Washing water and breakfast[74] were brought in. The sun was high when Genji arose. "She will need her gentlewomen," he said to Shōnagon. "This evening she must call for the ones she prefers." He sent off to the east wing for some children. "I especially want little ones," he added. So it was that four very pretty little girls appeared.

Murasaki was lying wrapped in a shift, and he insisted that she get up. "You must not be so unfriendly," he said. "Would I be looking after you this way if you did not mean a great deal to

73. The moment when her charge begins a new life with Genji.
74. *Ōnkayu*, cooked rice.

me? A woman should be sweet and obedient." And so began her education.

She looked prettier than ever here. Genji chatted disarmingly with her, showing her all sorts of nice paintings and toys that he had had brought from the east wing and doing all he could to please her. At last she got up and looked properly at what he was showing her. She made such an engaging picture in her layering of soft, dark gray,[75] wreathed in innocent smiles, that Genji found himself smiling, too, as he watched her.

With Genji off to the east wing, she went for a look[76] at the park's lake and trees. The near garden, now touched by frost, was as pretty as a painting, and the unfamiliar whirl of fourth- and fifth-rank gentlemen, bustling in and out,[77] convinced her that she had come to a very nice place. In no time she was happily distracted by the fascinating pictures on the screens.

Genji did not go to court for two or three days; he devoted himself instead to making Murasaki feel at home. He wrote or painted all sorts of things to show her, no doubt with the thought of making them up for her straightaway into a book,[78] and he turned them into an extremely attractive collection.

She took out an exceptionally beautiful "Talk of Musashi Plain arouses my complaint . . ."[79] that he had written on *murasaki*-colored paper; and he had added in smaller writing,

75. Mourning for her grandmother. The mourning period in this case was three months.
76. Through blinds.
77. The fourth rank wore black, the fifth red.
78. As calligraphy models.
79. *Kokin rokujō* 3507, which Genji had written out: "I have never been there, but speak of Musashi Plain, and I will complain; yet ah, there is no remedy— the fault is the *murasaki*'s." The poem alludes to *Kokinshū* 867 and many others about *murasaki* on the great plain of Musashi. The *murasaki* refers to the woman whom the poet desires: in Genji's case, Fujitsubo, whose name (because *fuji* means "wisteria") also recalls the color of the *murasaki* dye.

"Her root is unseen, and yet I do love her so, the kin to that plant
the dews of Musashi Plain put so far beyond my reach!"[80]

"Come now," he said, "you write one."

"But I do not know how to write very well yet." She looked up at him with the most engaging artlessness.

He smiled. "Still, you cannot write nothing at all. I shall teach you." Her manner of turning away to write and the childish way she held her brush so entranced him that he wondered at himself.

"Oh, I made a mistake!" She tried in embarrassment to hide what she had written, but he insisted on having a look.

"Why you should complain I have not the least idea, and that troubles me:
who, then, is the kin you mean, and what plant have you in mind?"

The generous lines of her letters were certainly immature, but they showed great promise.[81] Her hand closely resembled the late nun's. It seemed to him that she would soon write beautifully, as long as she had an up-to-date copybook. As far as dolls went, he made her one dollhouse after another, and he found his games with her the perfect distraction from his cares.

For the women who had not come with her, it was acutely embarrassing to have nothing to say when Prince Hyōbu arrived and wanted to know what had become of his daughter. Genji had warned them to keep the secret for the time being, and Shōnagon, who agreed, had insisted that they remain

80. The start of the poem can also be read to suggest "She is too young to sleep with." It comments on the poem just mentioned and alludes to another, earlier in this chapter: "How glad I would be to pick and soon to make mine that little wild plant sprung up from the very root shared by the *murasaki*." The inaccessible plant is Fujitsubo.

81. Her lines are broad (*fukuyoka ni*), in a manner said in old commentaries to be characteristic of a child's writing.

silent. They told him only that Shōnagon had taken his daughter off to hide her; they did not know where. He was obliged to assume that since the late nun had never approved of sending him her granddaughter, Murasaki's nurse had taken it upon herself in an excess of zeal to jeopardize her charge's whole future by spiriting her away instead of objecting openly, and he returned to his residence in tears. "Please let me know if you ever have any news of her!" he said, to their intense discomfort. He also made fruitless inquiries at the Prelate's residence. He was sorry to have lost so remarkably attractive a daughter, and he continued to miss her. Even his wife was disappointed, since her antipathy toward the girl's mother had faded by now, and she had been looking forward to making the most of her authority.

By and by the gentlewomen gathered around their young mistress. Her playmates—young girls in service as pages or even smaller ones[82]—gladly lost themselves in games with so striking and stylish a pair. The young lady might still cry for her grandmother on evenings when her friend was away and she was lonely,[83] but she retained no special memory of her father. Never having been used to living with him anyway, she now cared only for this second father, to whom she became deeply attached. She would always go straight to greet him when he came home, chatting prettily and snuggling into his arms, and she was never in the least reserved or bashful with him. As far as that sort of thing went, she was as sweet with him as she could possibly be.

A woman may be so querulous and so quick to make an issue of the smallest lapse that the man takes a dislike to her, fearing that whatever he does may unleash bitter reproaches, until an estrangement that neither had wished for becomes a reality; but

82. Her playmates are *warawabe* (page girls of her age or older) and *chigo* (smaller girls who perform no services yet).
83. She is called *kimi* ("the young lady") for the first time, rather than *wakagimi* ("the little miss"); while Genji is called *otokogimi* ("the young gentleman"). This pairing of *kimi* and *otokogimi* acknowledges the two as a couple.

not so for Genji with his delightful companion. No daughter by the time she reaches this age can be as free with her father, sleep so intimately beside him, or rise so blithely with him in the morning as this young lady did with Genji, until Genji himself must have wondered at being able to lavish his affection on so rare a treasure.

7

(COMPLETE)

MOMIJI NO GA

BENEATH THE
AUTUMN LEAVES

Ga means a celebration (a jubilee) for a great personage on
the occasion of his attaining a felicitously advanced age. The
personage here is a former Emperor (the father or perhaps
the elder brother of Genji's father); the occasion is probably
his entering his fortieth or fiftieth year; and the celebration
takes place under bright autumn leaves (*momiji*). The chapter title is simply descriptive.

   Chapter 7 begins in the autumn of the year in which Genji
is eighteen and overlaps somewhat with the latter part of
chapter 5. It continues to the autumn of the following year,
when Genji is nineteen.

His Majesty's progress to the Suzaku Palace took place after
the tenth of the tenth month. The excursion was to be exceptionally brilliant, and his ladies were disappointed that they
would not see it. Not wishing Fujitsubo to miss it, he arranged
a full rehearsal in her presence.

   Captain Genji danced "Blue Sea Waves."[1] His partner, Tō no
Chūjō, certainly stood out in looks and skill, but beside Genji he
was only a common mountain tree next to a blossoming cherry.
As the music swelled and the piece reached its climax in the

---

1. *Seigaiha,* a "Chinese" *bugaku* piece for two dancers. The tossing of the
dancers' sleeves is said to evoke the waves of the sea. *Bugaku* is a repertoire of
dances from the continent. The repertoire has two divisions: dances from
China and dances from Korea.

clear light of the late-afternoon sun, the cast of Genji's features
and his dancing gave the familiar steps an unearthly quality. His
singing of the verse could have been the Lord Buddha's
kalavinka voice in paradise.[2] His Majesty was sufficiently transported with delight to wipe his eyes, and all the senior nobles
and Princes wept. When the verse was over, when Genji tossed
his sleeves again to straighten them[3] and the music rose once
more in response, his face glowed with a still-greater beauty.

Even in his moment of triumph the Kokiden Consort remarked bitterly, "With those looks of his, the gods above must
covet him. How unpleasant!" The young gentlewomen listening
thought her hateful.

Fujitsubo knew that she would have liked his dance still better if he were not so importunate in his desires, and she felt as
though she had dreamed this vision of him. She went straight to
attend His Majesty for the night.

" 'Blue Sea Waves' made the rehearsal today, did it not?" he
remarked. "How did it strike you?"

"It was very nice." She was too flustered to answer him better.

"His partner did not do at all badly either. In dancing and
gesture, breeding will tell. One admires the renowned professional dancers,[4] but they lack that easy grace. The performance
under the autumn trees may be an anticlimax now that the rehearsal day has gone so well, but I had them do their best so
that you should see it all."

Genji wrote to her the next morning, "How did you find it?
All the time I was more troubled than one could ever imagine.

> *My unhappiness made of me hardly the man to stand up and dance;*
> *did you divine what I meant when I waved those sleeves of mine?*

2. The "verse" (*ei*) of the dance is a poem in Chinese attributed to Ono no
Takamura (802–852); the music stopped while the lead dancer sang it. The Buddha's voice was often compared to that of the *kalavinka,* the bird that sings in
paradise.
3. The dancer had marked the climactic moment of the "verse" by flipping his
sleeves so they wrapped themselves around his arms.
4. Dancers from hereditary lineages specialized in *bugaku* dancing.

But I must say no more."

She replied, for no doubt she could not banish that beauty and that dazzling grace from her mind,

> *"That man of Cathay who waved his sleeves long ago did so far away,*[5]
> *but every measure you danced to my eyes seemed wonderful.*

Oh, yes, very much."

Overjoyed by the miracle of an answer from her, he smiled to see that with her knowledge even of dance, and with her way of then bringing in the realm across the sea, she already wrote like an Empress. He spread the letter out and contemplated it as though it were holy writ.

The entire court accompanied His Majesty on the progress itself, as did the Heir Apparent. The musicians' barges rowed around the lake, as always, and there were all sorts of dances from Koma and Cathay.[6] The music of the instruments and the beat of the drums set the heavens ringing. His Majesty had been disturbed enough by the magic of Genji's figure at sundown that other day to have scriptures read for him at temples here and there, and everyone who heard of it wholly sympathized, save the mother of the Heir Apparent, who thought the gesture absurdly overdone. His Majesty had pressed into the circle of musicians[7] every officeholder of recognized talent from among the privy gentlemen or the lesser ranks. Two Consultants—one the Intendant of the Left Gate Watch, the other that of the Right—were put in charge of the music of Left and Right.[8] Every

5. "Blue Sea Waves" came from Tang China. The poem alludes to a story about a magic moment in a Chinese dancer's performance.
6. Ancient Korea and China. There was an elaborately decorated barge for the "Korean" music and another for the "Chinese."
7. *Kaishiro.* The dancers emerged after donning their costumes inside the circle.
8. Chinese music was "music of the Left"; Korean, of the "Right." Such high-ranking officials seldom assumed responsibility for the music. "Intendant" translates *kami,* the title borne by the chief officers of these two corps of guards.

gentleman had chosen a first-rate teacher and practiced assiduously at home.

Under the tall autumn trees breath from a circle forty strong roused from the instruments an indescribable music that mingled with the wind's roaring and sighing as it swept, galelike, down the mountain, while through the flutter of bright falling leaves "Blue Sea Waves" shone forth with an awesome beauty. When most of the leaves were gone from Genji's headdress, leaving it shamed by the brilliance of his face, the Intendant of the Left Gate Watch picked chrysanthemums to replace them from among those before His Majesty. In the waning light the very sky seemed inclined to weep, shedding a hint of rain while Genji in his glory, decked with chrysanthemums now faded to the loveliest of shades, again displayed the marvels of his skill. His closing steps sent a shiver through the gathering, who could not imagine what they saw to be of this world. Among the undiscerning multitude sheltered beneath the trees, hidden among the rocks, or buried among fallen leaves on the mountainside, those with eyes to see shed tears.

The greatest treat after "Blue Sea Waves" was "Autumn Wind," danced by the Fourth Prince (then still a boy), the Shōkyōden Consort's son.[9] Attention wandered now that the best of the dances was over, and what followed may even have spoiled things a little.

That evening Captain Genji assumed the third rank, upper grade, while Tō no Chūjō rose to the fourth rank, lower grade.[10] If every senior noble had reason to rejoice,[11] each in the measure due him, it was because Genji's own ascent had drawn him upward. How gladly one would know what merit from lives past allowed him to dazzle all eyes and bring such joy to every heart!

Princess Fujitsubo had withdrawn from court, and Genji gave himself up as always to watching for a chance to see her,

9. The Shōkyōden Consort to Genji's father is mentioned nowhere else.
10. Tō no Chūjō's new rank is high for a Captain in the Palace Guards, and Genji's is very unusual.
11. Over his promotion.

subjecting himself to further complaints from his father-in-law's. Nor was this all, for a gentlewoman there reported his abduction of the "young plant" as his having taken a woman to live with him at Nijō, and Aoi was not at all pleased. He quite understood that she should feel as she did, since she knew nothing of the circumstances; but if only she had unburdened herself frankly to him like any ordinary woman, he might have explained things to her and calmed her fears, whereas in fact she was so intent on misinterpreting all he did that he could hardly be blamed for seeking refuge in dubious diversions. In her person he found nothing lacking or amiss. She was the first woman he had known, and he trusted that even if she failed for the present to appreciate his high regard, she would change her mind in time. He displayed his exceptional quality in the unswerving steadfastness of this faith.

The more Genji's Murasaki grew accustomed to him, the more she improved in manner and looks, and she snuggled up to him now as though it were the most natural thing in the world. He still kept her in the same distant wing, because he did not wish his household staff to know yet who she was; and there he had her room done up beautifully, visited her day and night, and gave her all sorts of lessons. He wrote out calligraphy models for her and had her practice, he felt, just as though he had taken in a daughter from elsewhere. He assigned her a household office and a staff of her own so as to have her properly looked after.

No one but Koremitsu could make out what he was up to. Prince Hyōbu, her father, still knew nothing. When she remembered the past, as she often did, her grandmother was usually the one she missed. Genji's company took her mind off her sorrows, but although he sometimes stayed with her at night, he was more often taken up with calls here and there and would leave at dark, and then she would arouse all his tenderness by making it quite clear how much she wished he would not go. It so upset him to see her in low spirits, after he had spent two or three days at the palace or at the Minister of the Left's, that he felt as though he were responsible for a motherless child and hesitated to go out at all. Reports of all this greatly pleased the

Prelate, despite the irregularity of the girl's situation. Whenever the Prelate performed a memorial service for her grandmother, Genji provided the finest offerings.

Genji was anxious for news of Fujitsubo and called at her Sanjō residence, to which she had withdrawn. He was entertained by such gentlewomen as Ōmyōbu, Chūnagon, and Nakatsukasa. It vexed him to be treated so obviously as a guest, but he swallowed his feelings and was chatting idly with them when Prince Hyōbu arrived.

His Highness received Genji when he learned that he was there. Elegant and romantically languorous as His Highness was, Genji speculated privately about the pleasures of his company if he were a woman and, having a double reason to feel close to him, engaged him in intent conversation. Prince Hyōbu for his part noted how much more open and easy Genji was than usual, liked his looks a great deal, and, being unaware that Genji was his son-in-law, indulged his roving fancy in the pleasure of imagining him, too, as a woman.

Genji was envious when at dark His Highness went in to his sister through her blinds. Long ago Genji's father had allowed him to talk with her in person rather than through go-betweens, and now he could only feel hurt that she kept him at such a distance.

"I have been remiss in failing to call upon you more often," he said with stiff formality, "but unfortunately I am inclined to be neglectful in the absence of any pressing errand. Should you need me for any reason, I shall be pleased to place myself at your service." He then left. Ōmyōbu could devise nothing better for him, since plainly Her Highness was far less warmly disposed toward him than in the past, and her evident displeasure so shamed and distressed Ōmyōbu that all Genji's subsequent entreaties to her went for naught. How soon it was over! each lover cried silently, in an anguish that had no end.

Shōnagon, on the other hand, was astonished to see so happy a pair before her, and for this she felt that she must thank the blessings of the buddha to whom her late mistress had addressed so many prayers of concern for her granddaughter. The Minister of the Left's daughter was no doubt very grand indeed, and the many others whom Genji favored might easily cause trouble when the child was grown, but his special consideration for her charge was deeply reassuring.

On the last day of the month[12] Genji had Murasaki doff her mourning ("Now, now," he said, "for your mother's mother three months will do"); but she had grown up without any other parent, and after that she wore not bright, showy colors but dress gowns of unfigured scarlet, purple, or golden yellow; and very smart she looked in them, too.

Genji came around on his way to the morning salutation.[13] "You are looking ever so grown-up this morning!"[14] he said, with the most winning smile.

She was already busy setting up her dolls, laying out her collection of accessories on a pair of three-foot cabinets, and filling the room with an assemblage of little houses that Genji had made her. "Inuki broke this chasing out devils,[15] and I am mending it," she announced solemnly.

"How careless of her! I shall have it repaired for you straightaway. We are not supposed to say anything sad today,[16] so you must not cry."

As he left, his imposing presence amid his large retinue brought her and her gentlewomen out near the veranda to watch him go, after which she dressed up her "Genji" doll and had him set off for the palace.

"Do grow up a bit this year, at least." Shōnagon wanted to chasten her for thinking only of her games. "A girl over ten should not be playing with dolls. Now you have a husband, you

12. Also the last of the year. Mourning for a maternal grandparent lasted three months, for a paternal one five. Murasaki's grandmother had died about the twentieth of the ninth month.
13. *Chōhai*, when the assembled courtiers saluted the Emperor on the morning of the first day of the year. Genji looks in on Murasaki the day after she has stopped wearing mourning.
14. Because she is a year older than she was yesterday.
15. During the devil-expelling rite (*tsuina no gi*) held on the last night of the year.
16. "Today we must practice *kotoimi*": abstention from ill-omened language, including the sound of weeping.

must be sweet and gentle with him, like a proper wife. You do not even like having me do your hair!"

So I have a husband, do I! The men all these women call their husbands are nothing to look at, but *mine* is a handsome young man! The idea was a revelation. Still, the addition of one more to the count of her years did seem to have made a difference. The household staff were taken aback whenever she turned out still to be a child, but they never imagined how innocently the two were sleeping together.

Genji as usual found Aoi dauntingly perfect when he withdrew to her father's from the palace, and her lack of warmth prompted him to remark, "How happy I would be if this year you were at last to consent to engage with me a little!" But now that she knew he had brought a woman to live with him, she was convinced that he had lofty plans for the newcomer and undoubtedly thought him a sorrier embarrassment than ever.

With an effort she feigned ignorance and responded to his joviality after all in her own distinctive way. Four years older than he, she had a more composed dignity and a mature beauty that put his youth to shame. How could *she* be wanting? Obviously, Genji reflected, it is my own, dissolute behavior that has earned me her rejection. Her lofty pride at being the only daughter not just of any Minister but of the greatest of them all, and of no less than a Princess, moved her to condemn his every lapse, while he on his side kept wondering why he must defer to her so and keep trying to bring her round. Such were the distances that kept them apart.

His Excellency meanwhile deplored Genji's misconduct, but he still forgot his displeasure every time he saw his son-in-law and did all he could to please him. Early the next morning he looked in as Genji was preparing to leave, and when he found him dressed, he personally brought him a famous stone belt,[17] went round behind him to straighten his robe, and all but held his shoes for him to step into. It was very touching.

17. *Sekitai*, worn with the full-dress cloak (*hō*): a black leather belt with a double row of squares or circles made of stone, jade, or horn set in it so as to show at the wearer's back. (A fold of the *hō* covered the front.) The color and material varied with rank. Genji's new rank required white jade.

"I look forward to wearing this at the privy banquet[18] and other such occasions," Genji said.

"Oh, I have better. I just thought this one a little unusual." He insisted that Genji put it on. In fact, looking after Genji in every way was his pleasure in life, and he asked only to welcome such a man and see him off, no matter how rarely.

Genji set out on his round of New Year's calls, although it was not really long: the Emperor, the Heir Apparent, the Retired Emperor, and then, of course, Fujitsubo at her Sanjō residence.

"Today again he is a wonder to behold," Fujitsubo's gentlewomen observed to their mistress. "The more he matures, the more frighteningly beautiful he becomes!" Just a glimpse of him through her curtains threw her feelings into turmoil.

It was worrying that the twelfth month had passed without any sign of the anticipated event.[19] Her Highness's women all looked forward to it this month, at least, and His Majesty pursued his preparations on the same assumption. However, the month went by uneventfully. The rumor went round that a spirit was to blame, and meanwhile Her Highness despaired, because she knew that this might ruin her forever.[20] She also felt very unwell. Genji, who had less and less doubt what the matter was, had rites done in several temples[21] without saying why. Life being uncertain at best, he was tormented by the prospect that their love might end in tragedy, until a little past the tenth of the second month she gave birth to a boy, and for His Majesty as well as for her own women anxiety gave way to happiness. She personally dreaded the life that lay before her, but reports that the Kokiden Consort was muttering imprecations against her reminded her that news of her death might only provoke laughter, and this gave her the strength gradually to recover. His Majesty was impatient to see the child.

18. *Naien,* a banquet given by the Emperor on the day of the Rat that fell on the twenty-first, twenty-second, or twenty-third of the first month. The guests composed poetry in Chinese.
19. The birth of Fujitsubo's child.
20. Or perhaps "that she might die [in childbirth]."
21. To ensure safe childbirth.

Genji, who had his own private reasons for apprehension, called on the new mother at a moment when no other visitor claimed her. "His Majesty is very keen to see him," he said, "and I thought I might do so and report"; but she understandably pleaded that it would be awkward just now and would not allow it. Actually, the boy was astonishingly, frighteningly like Genji himself. The resemblance was impossible to miss. Fujitsubo, conscience-stricken, wondered how anyone could fail after a single look at him to perceive and to censure a misdeed that she herself found repellent. What would they call her when the truth dawned on a world eager to spy out the slightest flaw? Pondering these things led her to despair.

When Genji managed to talk to Ōmyōbu, he filled her ears with passionate entreaties,[22] but without any prospect of success. He pleaded so desperately to see the little boy that Ōmyōbu protested, "Why must you insist against all reason, my lord? You will naturally do so in due course"; but her own manner betrayed equal distress.

On so grave a matter Genji could hardly speak plainly. "Will I never be allowed to talk to her in person?" He wept piteously.

"*What can be the tie that bound us two together a long time ago,*
that in this life she and I should be kept so far apart?

I just do not understand."

Knowing her mistress's suffering as she did, Ōmyōbu could not dismiss him without a reply.

"*Heartsick thoughts for her when beside him and, for you, sorrow not to be;*
ah, this, then, is what they mean by the darkness of the heart!"[23]

22. Entreaties addressed through her to Fujitsubo.
23. "Beside him" means beside the newborn child. Ōmyōbu alludes to *Gosenshū* 1102, by Fujiwara no Kanesuke, about the darkness in the heart of a parent troubled about a child.

she whispered. "It is such a shame that neither of you should ever be happy!"

Thus barred from communication, Genji went away again, but Her Highness, who feared the perils of gossip and warned against them, retreated from her once affectionate familiarity with Ōmyōbu. She continued to treat her equably, so as not to arouse comment, but to Ōmyōbu's sorrow and surprise she must sometimes have betrayed her displeasure.

In the fourth month the young Prince went to the palace. He had developed faster than most children and by now could sit up on his own. His Majesty completely missed the extraordinary, indeed unmistakable likeness between him and his father and assumed instead that it was only natural for supremely beautiful people to resemble one another. He was completely devoted to the child. He had felt the same way about Genji, but in the end, when it became clear that those around him would not tolerate such a move, he had refrained from appointing Genji Heir Apparent, and this had been an enduring disappointment, for it pained him to see all the beauty and distinction of the maturing Genji wasted on a commoner. His new son, on the other hand, had a mother of the highest rank and shone with a light equal to Genji's, and so he loved him as a flawless gem—which for Her Highness only made one more reason for continual sorrow and anguish.

When Genji visited Her Highness's residence as usual, to join in music making, His Majesty appeared with the child in his arms. "I have many children," he said, "but you are the only one I have seen day and night since you were this small. I expect it is the way he reminds me of those days that makes him look so very like you. Perhaps all babies are like that." He simply doted on his little son.

Genji felt himself go pale. Terror, humility, joy, and pity coursed through him until he nearly wept. So eerily adorable was the burbling, smiling child that there came to Genji, despite himself, the immodest thought that if *this* was what he looked like, he must indeed be a treasure. Her Highness was perspiring in torment, and Genji's own pleasure in the boy turned to such anguish that he withdrew.

At home again he lay down, and after allowing the worst of
his agitation to pass, he decided to go on to His Excellency's.
Gillyflowers stood out brightly there in the garden's green expanse. He had one picked and sent it to Ōmyōbu with what
must have been a long letter, in which he said,

> "I see him in this, and yet even so at heart I am not consoled;
>   on the lovely little pink there settles only heavier dew.[24]

I had so wished the flower to bloom, but everything in this world
is hopeless."[25] It must have come at just the right time, because
when Ōmyōbu showed it to her mistress, urging her to give him
back "just a word or two, my lady, here on the petals,"[26] Her
Highness herself was very deeply moved. In faint ink, as though
her writing had given out in midline, she simply wrote,

> "Oh, I know full well he only calls forth further dews that moisten my sleeves,
>   yet I have no heart to scorn so lovely a little pink."

Ōmyōbu happily conveyed this to Genji, who was lying gazing
disconsolately into space, convinced that as always his letter
would go unanswered. His heart pounded, and a rush of joy
started tears from his eyes.

When it gave him no relief to lie there in gloom, he went for
comfort as so often to the west wing. He peeped in with a robe
thrown casually over his shoulders, his sidelocks rumpled and
wispy, and blowing a sweet air on his flute. There was Murasaki,

24. *Shinkokinshū* 1494, by Keishi Joō: "I see the resemblance yet am not a
whit consoled—what am I to do with this little pink?"
25. "Gillyflower" (*tokonatsu*) and "pink" (*nadeshiko*) are the same flower, but
the two words have different associations. "I had so wished the flower to
bloom" is from *Gosenshū* 199, which Genji quotes also in his own verse. The
poem is about planting *nadeshiko* so as to have them stand consolingly for
someone much loved—in this case, the little boy.
26. *Kokinshū* 167, a romantic poem about *nadeshiko* by Ōshikōchi no Mitsune: "I shall let no speck of dust [translated here as "a word or two"] settle
on these pinks where my love and I have lain."

leaning on an armrest, as sweet and pretty as could be and, he felt, moist with the same dew as that other flower.[27] Irresistible or not, she still had a mind to make him smart for not having come straight to see her when he got home, and so for once she was pouting.

"Come here!" He sat down near the veranda.

She hummed "when the tide is high" and put her sleeve bewitchingly to her mouth.[28]

"Dear me, when did you start quoting poems like that? It is not good for people to see each other *all* the time."[29]

He had a koto brought in for her to play. "The *sō no koto* is awkward because the highest treble string breaks so easily," he remarked, tuning the instrument down to the *hyōjō* mode. She could not maintain her ill humor once he had tested the tuning with a few notes and pushed the instrument from him, and she played very nicely indeed. She was still quite small, and the way she had to lean over to put in a vibrato[30] was extremely engaging.

Entranced, he taught her more music by playing his flute. She was very quick and knew the most difficult pieces after a single hearing. He was satisfied that the liveliness of her intelligence met all his hopes. When he amused himself by giving a very nice performance of "Hosoroguseri," despite the piece's peculiar name, she accompanied him in a manner still youthful but very pretty and true to the rhythm.

The lamps were lit, and the two had started to look at pictures when Genji's men, who had been told he would be going out, began clearing their throats to remind him, and someone observed that it looked like rain. Then as always she became

27. The "gillyflower" or "little pink" of his exchange with Fujitsubo.
28. *Shūishū* 967 (also *Man'yōshū* 1398), by Sakanoue no Iratsume: "Is the seaweed on the shore, covered when the tide is high? I see him so little and miss him so much!" Murasaki's gesture is one of embarrassment.
29. Thanks to double meanings from *Kokinshū* 683, Genji's words prolong the seashore imagery of the poem quoted by Murasaki: "Would that I might have enough of the seaweed [*mirume,* also "meeting" with a lover] for which the seafolk dive, they say, morning and evening at Ise."
30. The left hand depresses and relaxes the string plucked by the right, to make the pitch undulate.

sad and dejected. She stopped looking at pictures and only lay facedown, which to Genji was so enchanting that he stroked the rich cascade of her hair and said, "Do you miss me when I am gone?"

She nodded.

"I miss you, too. I hate to spend a whole day without seeing you. As long as you are still a child, though, I must trust in your patience and try not to offend other people who are easily hurt. It is all very awkward, you see, and that is why for the time being I keep going off on these visits. Once you are grown, I will never go anywhere. The reason why I do not want them angry with me is that I hope to live a long and happy life with *you*!"

His earnest reassurances only embarrassed her, and instead of answering, she just put her head in his lap and went to sleep. His heart melted, and he announced that he would not go out after all. The women rose and brought him his evening meal in place.

"I am not going out anymore," he said after he roused her. She felt better then and sat up, and they ate together.

"Then sleep here," she said, hardly touching her food, since she still suspected that he might go away. He did not see how he could ever leave such a companion, even on the last and most solemn journey of all.

He ended up being detained this way time after time, until word of it reached His Excellency's. "Who is she?" the gentlewomen asked each other.

"How can he treat my lady this way?"

"So far no one has suggested who she could be."

"No one at all nice or well brought up would keep the pleasure of his company all to herself this way."

"She must be someone he happened to meet at the palace, and now he is so keen on her, he is keeping her out of sight for fear of criticism."

"They say she is childish and immature."

The Emperor, too, had heard there was such a woman. "It has pained me very much to learn that the Minister of the Left is so displeased," he said to Genji, "and I entirely sympathize, because he is the one who did everything to turn the mere boy you once were into the man you are now, and I hardly think that you are too young to appreciate his kindness. Why, then, are you treating him so thoughtlessly?"

Genji assumed an attitude of contrite deference and did not reply.

I suppose he does not like Aoi, His Majesty reflected commiseratingly.

"Still," as he remarked later, "he shows no sign of tossing caution to the winds and losing his head over any gentlewoman of mine, or indeed over anyone else. What nooks and crannies can he have been poking about in, to have earned himself this degree of resentment?"

Despite the passing years His Majesty himself had not managed so far to give up his interest in the same sort of thing, and he had a particular taste for pretty and clever waiting women,[31] hence the presence of many on his staff. Genji's most casual approach to any of them was seldom rebuffed, but perhaps he found them simply too easy, because he seemed strangely uninterested, and even when now and then one did try her wiles on him, he would answer her tactfully but never really misbehave, with the result that some thought him a perfect bore.

There was an aging Dame of Staff,[32] a lady of impeccable birth, witty, distinguished, and well respected by all, who nevertheless was intensely coquettish; and Genji was curious to know why, when a woman might of course be light in her ways, she should be so thoroughly dissolute even in her declining years. On jokingly testing the waters he was shocked to find that she did not think his proposition at all incongruous, but the adventure still amused him enough to pursue it, although to her great chagrin he kept his distance for fear of starting gossip about his liaison with an old woman.

Once, when she had finished combing His Majesty's hair, he called for a maid of the wardrobe and went out, leaving her and

31. *Unebe* and *nyokurōdo*, two types of junior servants on the Emperor's staff. *Unebe* (or *uneme*) assisted with his meals, *nyokurōdo* with his wardrobe.
32. *Naishi no suke*, one of four women officials (junior fourth rank) under the Mistress of Staff, in the Office of Staff, a palace office staffed by women and concerned above all with matters pertaining to the imperial ladies.

Genji alone in the room. She was more prettily got up than usual, with a graceful bearing and lovely hair, and her costume was assertively brilliant—all of which to Genji's distaste betrayed her refusal to show her age; but he could not resist tugging at the end of her train to see how she would respond. From behind a heavily decorated fan she shot back a languid glance from dark-rimmed, sunken eyes set amid nests of wrinkles.

No one her age should carry that fan, he thought. Offering his in exchange,[33] he took the fan and examined it. On paper red enough to set his face aglow he saw painted in gold a picture of tall trees. On one side, in a style now passé but not undistinguished, were casually written the words "Old is the grass beneath the trees."[34]

This is all very well, but what a horrid idea! "What we have here, I see, is 'the wood in summer,' "[35] he remarked with a smile. He felt strange enough just talking to her to fear being seen, but no such worry crossed her mind.

"*Whenever you come, I shall cut for your fine steed a feast of fresh grass,*
be it only lower leaves, now the best season is past,"

she said with shameless archness.

He answered,

"*If I made my way through the brush I might be seen, for it seems to me*
many steeds must like it there, underneath the forest trees.

It is a bit risky." He rose to go.

She caught his sleeve and cried out through dramatic tears,

33. So that she could still hide her face from him, as manners required.
34. *Kokinshū* 892: "Old is the grass beneath the trees at Ōaraki; no steed grazes there, no one comes to mow it." Genji recognizes the poem as a declaration that she is hungry for a man.
35. *Saneakira shū* 28, by Fujiwara no Saneakira: "I hear the cuckoo calling, for the wood of Ōaraki must be its summer lodging."

"Never in my life have I been made to feel so wretched! Oh, the shame of it, after all these years!"

"I shall be in touch later. There are other things, you see . . ." He broke free and continued on, but she clung to him, angrily bewailing the treachery of time.[36]

Meanwhile His Majesty had finished changing and was now watching this scene through the doorway. What a very odd pair! he thought, greatly amused, and he remarked with a chuckle, "I hear constant complaints about your lack of interest in women, but you did not let this one escape you, did you!" She made no real effort to defend herself, despite a degree of embarrassment, perhaps because she was one of those who are glad enough to have a liaison known as long as the lover is worth it.

Well, Tō no Chūjō said to himself when he heard how all were agog over this incident, I pride myself on leaving no cranny unexplored, but I certainly had never thought of *her*! He then struck up an affair, wishing to taste her undying randiness himself. He was a promising catch who might (she thought) make up for Genji's unkindness, but apparently it was only Genji she wanted—an extravagant choice! Tō no Chūjō kept his doings so quiet that Genji never found out about them.

The Dame of Staff would start straight in on her grievance whenever she came across Genji, and her age so aroused his pity that he wished to console her, but the idea was too depressing in practice, and for a long time he did nothing. Then once, when he was roaming around the Unmeiden under cover of dusk, after a cooling shower of rain, there she was, playing her *biwa* very nicely. No one was better at it than she, for she joined the men in concerts before His Majesty, and her wounded feelings now made her music especially poignant. "Shall I cast my lot with the melon grower?" she was singing in

36. "There are other things, you see" (*omoinagara zo ya*) contains syllables that form the name of the Nagara (Bridge), often mentioned in poems that lament old age. Her answer, *hashibashira* ("bridge pillar"), here rendered for narrative meaning as "bewail[ing] the treachery of time," is taken from such a poem, probably *Shūishū* 864.

a voice of great quality. Genji was not entirely pleased.[37] He wondered as he listened whether his feelings might resemble that other's, long ago at Gakushū.[38] Then she stopped, apparently in the grip of emotion.

He approached her, softly singing "The Eastern Cottage," and in song she supplied him the line "Open the door and come in."[39] He thought her a most extraordinary woman. Next came, with a sigh,

> *"Nobody is there, surely, standing all wet through—ah, how cruelly*
> *my humble eastern cottage suffers in the soaking rain!"*

He objected to taking all the blame for her troubles and wondered what he had done to deserve this.

> *"Someone else's wife is more trouble than she's worth; what with this and that,*
> *in her poor eastern cottage I give up making her mine."*

He meant to pass on by, but it felt so unkind to do so that he changed his mind and humored her by engaging in a bantering exchange from which he did derive a certain enjoyment.

Considering that Genji seemed to be calling secretly on all sorts of women, despite his innocent airs, Tō no Chūjō resented his show of sober seriousness and his constant sermons, and he was forever plotting to catch him in the act. Now he was

37. In her *saibara* song a girl, courted by a melon grower, wonders whether to say yes. Genji takes her to mean, "Shall I give up that man [Genji] who rejects me and make do with someone else?"
38. In "On Hearing a Girl Sing at Night," Bai Juyi described being on a journey at Ezhou (Gakushū) and hearing a woman on a nearby boat sing a heartbreaking song that turned to piteous weeping.
39. In the *saibara* song "Azumaya" ("The Eastern Cottage"), a man arrives at the woman's door in the pouring rain and demands to be admitted. The woman, inside, answers that the door is unlocked and urges him to come in. An *azumaya* was a form of thatched house characteristic of eastern Japan. This song inspired the poem that gave the "Azumaya" chapter its title.

delighted to have found his chance. He bided his time in the hope of frightening and upsetting Genji just enough to teach him a lesson.

A chilly wind was blowing rather late one night when Tō no Chūjō gathered that the two must have dropped off to sleep, and he stole into the room. Genji heard him, since he had not meant to sleep soundly, but he did not recognize him, and he assumed that the intruder was a certain Director of Upkeep who apparently had never been able to forget her.

"Well, I do not like this at all. I am leaving," he declared, humiliated to be found by a man of mature years in so incongruously compromising a situation. "You undoubtedly knew quite well that this gentleman was coming,[40] and I will not put up with being made out to be a fool." With this he gathered up his dress cloak and retired behind a screen.

Smothering his mirth, Tō no Chūjō strode up to the screen that Genji had just opened and with a great clatter folded it up again, producing a spectacularly menacing din. Meanwhile the lady, who played the proud beauty despite her age and who knew something of crises like this one, having been through several before, was not too panic-stricken to restrain the intruder firmly, trembling with apprehension over what he might do to Genji. Genji would gladly have escaped unrecognized, but a vision of himself from the rear in full flight, clothing flapping around him and headdress askew, gave him pause, for he saw how silly he would look.

To keep Genji from recognizing him, Tō no Chūjō next put on a dumb show of maddened rage and drew his sword, at which the lady cried out, "Oh, no, my darling, no!" and wrung her hands entreatingly before him. It was all he could do not to burst out laughing. Her veneer of comely youthfulness was all very well, but the spectacle of a distraught woman of fifty-seven or -eight, caught in the throes of terror between two superb youths of twenty, was absolutely absurd.

40. Literally, "I am sure the spider's behavior was perfectly clear." In the proverbial *Kokinshū* 1110, by Princess Sotōri, "the spider's behavior" clearly foretells a lover's visit.

Tō no Chūjō's ostentatious disguise and the very fierceness of his pantomime now betrayed him to Genji, who felt an utter idiot when he understood that the entire performance had been for his own benefit. Highly amused, now that he knew his opponent, he seized Tō no Chūjō's sword arm and gave it a hard pinch. Tō no Chūjō got angry, but he nevertheless broke down and laughed.

"Seriously, though," Genji said, "are you sure you are in your right mind? What a joke to play on me! Anyway, I shall put on my cloak"; but Tō no Chūjō got a grip on it and refused to let go.

"All right, you, too, then!" Genji undid Tō no Chūjō's sash to strip the cloak off him. They wrestled back and forth while Tō no Chūjō struggled to keep him from succeeding, until a seam gave way and Genji's cloak came apart.

> *"The misdeeds you hide may well soon be known to all, now our tug-of-war*
> *has torn a rent in the cloak that covered so many sins!"*

Tō no Chūjō said. "Wear it now, and everyone will know!"[41]

> *"Such a summer cloak may hardly hide anything, that I know full well,*
> *but what a poor friend you are to uncover me that way!"*[42]

Genji retorted; and the two of them went off together, their garments trailing about them, the best of friends.

Genji lay down to nurse his vexation at having been found out. As for the outraged Dame of Staff, the following morning she sent back a pair of trousers and a sash they had left behind, with the message

41. This exchange of poems bristles with wordplays. Tō no Chūjō's remark after his poem alludes to *Kokin rokujō* 3261, which evokes a red robe that when worn on the outside displays the wearer's amorous preoccupation to all.
42. "If you did not want everyone to know about *your* affair with this lady, you should have thought twice before barging in on me like this."

> *"No complaint of mine could relieve my misery, now the double wave*
> *that dashed itself on my shore has again slipped out to sea.*[43]

The river is dry . . ."[44]

She has no shame! Genji's thought was unkind, but he was still sorry to have upset her, and he therefore answered simply,

> *"Never mind that wave and its boisterous assault—that I can let pass;*
> *but I would lodge a complaint against the welcoming shore."*

The sash was Tō no Chūjō's. He observed that it was darker than his own dress cloak, and he noted also that his cloak was missing the outer band of one sleeve.[45] What a ridiculous business! he said to himself. He was beginning to feel better. I suppose you are bound to play the fool when you let yourself in for this sort of thing.

From his room at the palace Tō no Chūjō now sent Genji the missing piece of sleeve, wrapped in paper, with the advice to have it sewn back on. How did he manage to make off with that? Genji grumbled to himself. If I had not got his sash . . . He wrapped the sash in matching paper and sent it to him with the verse

> *"In fear of your blame, lest the sash should tear in two, and so you and she,*
> *I have not once looked upon the bright color of its blue."*[46]

43. "It is no use my complaining (although I would like to), now that the two of you have gone, never to return." The image of waves breaking on a beach suggests erotic desire.
44. The river of my tears.
45. *Hatasode*, an extra width of cloth that further lengthened the sleeve.
46. "Lest you blame me if that woman wants no more of you, I have not even touched this blue sash of yours." The poem plays on "tearing" the sash (the liaison) and borrows twice (for example, *hanada no obi*, "blue sash") from the *saibara* song that Tō no Chūjō, too, quotes in his reply.

"Now that none but you has made off as you have done with that sash of mine,
I shall not spare you my blame for having torn us two apart.

My wrath will strike you in the end!" Tō no Chūjō retorted.

Both set off when the sun was high to wait upon the Emperor. Genji cultivated a bland innocence that greatly amused his friend, but the day was crowded with memorials and decrees, and the sight of each other behaving with such punctilious gravity allowed them no more than an exchange of grins.

Tō no Chūjō came up to Genji during a lull in the proceedings and said with a detestable leer, "I trust you have now learned not to keep secrets."

"Why should I have? The fellow I pity is the one who got nothing for all his long wait. Seriously, though, rumor is rife!" The two of them swore each other to silence.[47]

Thereafter Tō no Chūjō brought up the incident whenever he had a chance, thus impressing Genji ever more vividly with what he owed to that tiresome woman. Meanwhile Genji stayed out of her way, lest she subject him again to her tragic complaint that he had done her a grievous wrong.

Tō no Chūjō kept all this from his sister Aoi, but he reserved the idea of telling her as a threat to hold over Genji when the occasion might warrant it. Even Genji's half brothers, born to the greatest of their father's ladies, held Genji in awe and deferred to him as His Majesty's favorite, but not so Tō no Chūjō, who rose bravely to Genji's every challenge and clearly remained determined never to be outdone. Tō no Chūjō was Aoi's only full brother. Yes, Genji was an Emperor's son, but he himself was the preferred son of His Majesty's foremost Minister and of a Princess, and for that reason he did not feel at all Genji's inferior. His person combined all desirable qualities, and there was no attribute of excellence that he lacked.

47. "Rumor is rife!" is from *Kokin rokujō* 2108 ("Though rumor be as rife as seaweed the seafolk gather, as long as we love each other, let the world talk as it will!"); and "swore each other to silence" (a paraphrase for narrative meaning) is from *Kokinshū* 1108.

The rivalry between these two took some peculiar turns, though it would be a bore to describe them all.

It appears that in the seventh month Fujitsubo was elevated to Empress.[48] Genji became a Consultant. Soon His Majesty would act on his desire to step down from the throne, and he had the little Prince in mind for the next Heir Apparent. However, there was no one suitably placed to look after him when that time came. The Prince's maternal relatives were all imperial, hence excluded from governing, and His Majesty had therefore wished at least to make his mother's standing unassailable in order to strengthen his position.

All this compounded the Kokiden Consort's agitation, as well it might, but His Majesty assured her, "The Heir Apparent's reign is coming soon, and you will then be the Empress Mother. You need not worry." People had indeed been complaining, as one would expect, that His Majesty could not just set aside the Heir Apparent's mother, who had been his Consort for twenty years, in order to appoint someone else Empress over her.

Genji, the new Consultant, was in Her Majesty's escort on the night when she entered the palace in state. She whose own mother had been Empress glowed with the beauty of a jewel, even among the exalted company of past Empresses, and she enjoyed such unexampled esteem from His Majesty that everyone else, too, held her in the highest regard. No wonder, then, if the despairing Genji thought of her in her palanquin and knew that she had now well and truly passed beyond his reach. It was almost too much for him.

> "There can be no end to a darkness in my heart that blots out all things,
>   now that I must watch her go off to live among the clouds,"[49]

he murmured to himself. For him it was a tragedy.

48. The brevity and indirection of this announcement has to do with the solemnity of the event.
49. Into the "cloud dwelling" (*kumoi*), a noble expression for the palace.

The more the little Prince grew, the less one could tell him apart from Genji, but although this tormented Her Majesty, no one else seems to have noticed. In truth, one wonders how anyone could be born as handsome as Genji and yet at the same time look unlike him. They were to all as the light of sun and moon coursing through the sky.

8
(COMPLETE)

HANA NO EN
UNDER THE CHERRY BLOSSOMS

This chapter title, like the preceding one, is descriptive: the chapter begins with a party (*en*) to honor a blossoming cherry tree (*hana*).

The events in chapter 8 take place in the spring following those narrated in chapter 7.

A little past the twentieth of the second month, the Emperor held a party to honor the cherry tree before the Shishinden.[1] To his left and right were enclosures[2] for Empress Fujitsubo and the Heir Apparent, whose pleasure it was to be present according to his wishes. The Kokiden Consort took offense whenever Her Majesty received such respect, but she came, for she would not have missed the event.

It was a lovely day, with a bright sky and birdsong to gladden the heart, when those who prided themselves on their skill—Princes, senior nobles, and all—drew their rhymes and began composing Chinese verses.[3] As usual, Genji's very voice announcing, "I have received the character 'spring,'" resembled

---

1. *Sakon no sakura,* a cherry tree by the steps at the front (south) side of the Shishinden. This kind of party, like the one beneath the autumn leaves, was especially favored about a century before the author's time.
2. *Tsubone,* made by setting up curtains and screens around their places.
3. The gentlemen advanced in order of rank, each to draw a single rhyme character (as in a lottery) from those set out on a table; then, before retiring, each announced his clan name, his office, and his rhyme character. His poem developed this rhyme.

no other. Tō no Chūjō came next. He was nervous about how he might look, after Genji, but he maintained a pleasing composure, and his voice rang out with impressive dignity. Most of the rest appeared tense and self-conscious. Naturally, those belonging to the lesser ranks were still more in awe of the genius of the Emperor and the Heir Apparent, which stood out even then, when so many others excelled at that sort of thing. They advanced in dread across the immaculate expanse of the broad court, only to make a painful labor of their simple task. His Majesty was touched by seasoned performances from the shabby old Doctors, and he derived great pleasure from them, too.

He had of course arranged the dances perfectly. The one about the warbler in spring[4] was charming as sunset approached, and after it the Heir Apparent, who remembered Genji under the autumn leaves, gave him his own blossom headdress and urged him to dance again. Genji, who could not refuse, rose and with casual ease went through the part where the dancer tosses his sleeves. The effect was incomparable. The Minister of the Left forgot all his displeasure and wept.

"Come, where is Tō no Chūjō?" His Majesty said. And so beautifully did Tō no Chūjō then dance "Garden of Flowers and Willows,"[5] rather more intently than Genji and evidently well rehearsed in case of need, that to everyone's wonder he received His Majesty's gift of a robe. The senior nobles then danced on into the evening, in no particular order, but none stood out for better or worse. When the time came to declaim the poems, the Reader could not get on with Genji's because the gathering repeated and commented admiringly on every line. Even the Doctors were impressed. His Majesty was undoubtedly pleased, since to him Genji was the glory of every such occasion.

The Empress wondered while she contemplated Genji's figure

4. "Song of the Spring Warbler" (Shun'ōden), a "Chinese" *bugaku* piece.
5. *Ryūkaen*—a "Chinese" *bugaku* piece last known to have been performed in 960.

how the Heir Apparent's mother could dislike him so, and she lamented that she herself liked him all too well.

> *"If with common gaze I could look upon that flower just as others do,*
> *why should it occur to me to find in him any flaw?"*

she murmured. One wonders how anyone could have passed on words meant only for herself.

The festival ended late that night. Once the senior nobles had withdrawn, once the Empress and the Heir Apparent were gone and all lay quiet in the beauty of brilliant moonlight, Genji remained drunkenly unwilling to grant that the night was over. His Majesty's gentlewomen all being asleep, he stole off toward Fujitsubo's residence, in case fortune should favor him at this odd hour, but the door through which he might have approached her[6] was locked, and so he went on, sighing but undeterred, to the long aisle of the Kokiden, where he found the third door open. Hardly anyone seemed to be about, since the Kokiden Consort had gone straight to wait on His Majesty. The door to the inner rooms was open, too. There was no sound.

This is how people get themselves into trouble,[7] he thought, stepping silently up into the hall. Everyone must be asleep. But could it be? He heard a young and pretty voice, surely no common gentlewoman's, coming his way and singing, "Peerless the night with a misty moon . . ."[8] He happily caught her sleeve.

"Oh, don't! Who are you?" She was obviously frightened.

"You need not be afraid.

---

6. More precisely, the door to where he might have found Ōmyōbu and persuaded her to take him to her mistress.

7. Genji's criticism, appropriate for himself, is probably aimed at the laxness of the Kokiden Consort's household. He has a low opinion of the household's mores.

8. *Shinkokinshū* 55, by Ōe no Chisato: "Nothing compares with the misty moon of a spring night, neither brilliant nor clouded." Oborozukiyo ("Night with a Misty Moon") is the name by which she has been known ever since.

> *That you know so well the beauty of the deep night leads me to assume*
>   *you have with the setting moon nothing like a casual bond!"*

With this he put his arms around her, lay her down, and closed the door. Her outrage and dismay gave her delicious appeal.

"A man—there is a man here!" she cried, trembling.

"I may do as I please, and calling for help will not save you. Just be still!"

She knew his voice and felt a little better. She did not want to seem cold or standoffish, despite her shock. He must have been quite drunk, because he felt he must have her, and she was young and pliant enough that she probably never thought seriously of resisting him.

She pleased him very much, and he was upset to find daybreak soon upon them. She herself seemed torn. "Do tell me your name!" he pleaded. "How can I keep in touch with you? Surely you do not want this to be all!"

With sweet grace she replied,

> *"If with my sad fate I were just now to vanish, would you really come—*
>   *ah, I wonder!—seeking me over grassy wastes of moor?"*[9]

"I understand. Please forgive me.

> *While I strove to learn in what quarter I should seek my dewdrop's dwelling,*
>   *wind, I fear, would be blowing out across the rustling moors.*[10]

We might be frank with each other. Or would you prefer to evade me?"

9. "If I were to vanish [die], would you fail to seek me only because I had not told you my name?"
10. "[I asked you to tell me who you are only because] if I come looking for you, people may notice and condemn us."

He had no sooner spoken than gentlewomen began rising noisily, and there was much coming and going between the Kokiden and His Majesty's apartments.[11] They were both in peril. He merely gave her his fan as a token, took hers, and went away.

Some of the many women at the Kiritsubo[12] were awake. "He certainly keeps up his secret exploring, doesn't he!" they whispered, poking each other and pretending all the while to be asleep.

He came in and lay down, but he stayed awake. What a lovely girl! She must be one of the Kokiden Consort's younger sisters—the fifth or sixth, I suppose, since she had not known a man before. He had heard that the wife of the Viceroy Prince[13] and the fourth sister, the wife who meant so little to Tō no Chūjō, were both beauties, and it certainly would have been rather more of a lark if she had been either of them. As for the sixth, her father intended her for the Heir Apparent—yes, that *would* be unfortunate. It was all very difficult, and he was unlikely to find out which one she was even if he tried. She did not seem eager to break it off, though—so why did she not leave me any way to correspond with her? These ruminations of his no doubt confirmed his interest in her, but still, when he thought of *her,* he could not help admiring how superbly inaccessible she was in comparison.

The second party[14] was to be today, and he was busy from morning to night. He played the *sō no koto*. The event was more elegant and amusing than the one the day before. Dawn was near when Fujitsubo went to wait on the Emperor.

Desperate to know whether she of the moon at dawn[15] would

11. The Kokiden Consort is about to return; some gentlewomen precede her, while others go out from her own apartments to meet her.
12. Genji's own rooms at the palace.
13. Genji's younger brother, a Prince who is Viceroy of Kyushu (Dazai no Sochi).
14. *Goen,* a "follow-up party" held for a smaller circle of the highest rank. The absence of the lower ranks made it less formal and more elegant than the earlier one.
15. Oborozukiyo. Genji calls her *ariake* ("moon at dawn") by association with "misty moon," and also because this is the time of the lunar month (the twentieth and after) for the *ariake* moon, to which he refers again in a poem below.

now be leaving the palace, he set the boundlessly vigilant Yoshikiyo and Koremitsu to keep watch. When he withdrew from His Majesty's presence, they gave him their report. "Several carriages have just left from the north gate,[16] where they were waiting discreetly," they said. "Relatives of His Majesty's ladies were there, and when the Fourth Rank Lieutenant and the Right Controller[17] rushed out to see the party off, we gathered that it must have been the Kokiden Consort who was leaving. Several other quite distinguished ladies were obviously in the party, too. There were three carriages in all."

Genji's heart beat fast. How was he to learn which one she was? What if the Minister of the Right, her father, found out and made a great fuss over him?[18] That would be highly unwelcome, as long as he still knew so little about her. At any rate, he could not endure his present ignorance, and he lay in an agony of frustration about what to do. He thought fondly of Murasaki. How bored she must be, and probably dejected as well, since he had not seen her for days!

The keepsake fan was a triple cherry blossom layered one[19] with a misty moon reflected in water painted on its colored side—not an original piece of work but welcome because so clearly favored by its owner. Her talk of "grassy wastes of moor" troubled him, and he wrote on the fan, which he then kept with him,

> "All that I now feel, I have never felt before, as the moon at dawn
> melts away before my eyes into the boundless heavens."

It had been too long since his last visit to the Minister of the Left's, as he well knew, but anxiety over Murasaki won out, and he went to Nijō to cheer her up. The more he saw of her,

16. Kita no jin (also called Sakuheimon), the north gate to the palace compound.
17. Brothers of the Kokiden Consort, not mentioned elsewhere.
18. As a son-in-law.
19. "Triple" because the fan, with its eight cypress ribs, folds into three panels together. The fan is white on one side and scarlet on the other.

the lovelier she became, and she also had exceptional intelligence and charm. Her unblemished perfection certainly made her the right girl for him to bring up on his own, as he so longed to do. The only worry was that having a male teacher might make her a little too familiar with men. Genji spent the day telling her what he had been up to lately and giving her a koto lesson, and although she was as sad as ever when he went out again, she was used to it now and did not cling to him as before.

At His Excellency's, Aoi refused as usual to see him straightaway. Caught up in his idleness by a swarm of thoughts, he toyed a while with a *sō no koto* and sang, "I never sleep at ease . . ."[20]

The Minister joined him and told him how much he had enjoyed the other day. "At my advanced age I have witnessed the reigns of four enlightened Sovereigns," he said, "and yet what with the quality of the verse and the harmony of the music and dances, the years never lay so lightly upon me. We have so many now who are expert in all the arts, and I am sure it was you who selected and guided them. Even I, an old man, felt like stepping out and stumbling through a dance."

"I did nothing at all to prepare them. It was simply my duty to find them the best instructors, whoever that might be. To my eye, 'Garden of Flowers and Willows' so far outshone the rest that the performance must stand for all time; and if you yourself had ventured to show off your skill, Your Excellency, in defiance of the years, the glory of His Majesty's reign would have shone more brightly still."

Tō no Chūjō and his brothers arrived. With their backs against the railing they tuned their instruments together and played away in concert very nicely indeed.

The lady of the misty moon, Oborozukiyo, remembered that fragile dream with great sadness. Her father had decided that her presentation to the Heir Apparent was to take place in the fourth month, and the prospect filled her with despair.

20. From a *saibara* song; the singer is a young woman in love (quite unlike Aoi).

Meanwhile her lover, who thought he knew how to pursue her if he wished, had not yet actually found out which sister she was, and besides, he hesitated to associate himself with a family from which he had nothing but censure. Then, a little after the twentieth of the third month, the Minister of the Right held an archery contest attended by many senior nobles and Princes and followed immediately by a party for the wisteria blossoms.[21]

The cherry blossom season was over, but two of the Minister's trees must have consented to wait,[22] for they were in late and glorious bloom. He had had his recently rebuilt residence specially decorated for the Princesses' donning of the train.[23] Everything was in the latest style, in consonance with his own florid taste.

The Minister had extended an invitation to Genji as well, one day when they met at court, and Genji's failure to appear disappointed him greatly, for to his mind this absence cast a pall over the gathering. He therefore sent one of his younger sons to fetch him, with the message

> "If in their gay hues the flowers that grace my home were like all others,
>   why should I so eagerly be waiting to welcome you?"

Genji, at the palace, told His Majesty. "He certainly is pleased with himself!" His Majesty remarked with a smile, "Go then, since he seems so eager to have you. After all, he is bringing the Princesses up there; so you are hardly a stranger to him."[24] Genji dressed with great care, and the sun had set by the time he arrived to claim his welcome.

He wore a grape-colored train-robe under a cherry blossom

21. Wisteria (*fuji*) was the emblem of the Fujiwara clan.
22. *Kokinshū* 68, by Ise: "O cherry tree in a mountain village with no one to admire you, wait to bloom until the flowers elsewhere are gone."
23. Two imperial daughters of the Kokiden Consort, hence the Minister's granddaughters.
24. They are Genji's half sisters as well as the Minister's granddaughters.

dress cloak of sheer figured silk.[25] Among the formal cloaks worn by everyone else, his costume displayed the extravagant elegance of a Prince, and his grand entry was a sensation. The very blossoms were abashed, and the gathering took some time to regain its animation.

He played beautifully, and it was quite late by the time he left again, on the pretext of having drunk so much that he was not well. The First and Third Princesses were in the main house, and he went to sit by the door that opened from there toward the east. The lattice shutters were up, and all the women were near the veranda, since this was the corner where the wisteria was blooming. Their sleeves spilled showily under the blinds as though for the New Year's mumming, but Genji disapproved and only found his thoughts going to Fujitsubo.

"I felt unwell to begin with," he said, "and then I was obliged to drink until now I am quite ill. May I be allowed to hide in Their Highnesses' company, if it is not too forward of me to ask?" He thrust himself halfway through the blind in the double doorway.

"Oh, no, please!" one cried. "Surely it is for little people like us to claim protection from the great!"

Genji saw that these ladies, although not of commanding rank, were not ordinary young gentlewomen either. Their stylish distinction was clear. The fragrance of incense hung thickly in the air, and the rustling of silks conveyed ostentatious wealth, for this was a household that preferred modish display to the deeper appeal of discreet good taste. The younger sisters had no doubt taken possession of the doorway because Their Highnesses wished to look out from there.

He should not have accepted the challenge, but it pleased him, and he wondered with beating heart which one she was.

25. His dress cloak (*nōshi*) is of a "cherry blossom" (*sakura*) layering, suitable for a young man in spring. Under that he has on an *ebi* dyed *shita-gasane*, which normally went under the formal cloak (*hō*) for a solemn court occasion. A dress cloak is relatively informal, and its color does not convey rank. Genji is flaunting his exalted station.

"Alas," he sang as innocently as could be, still leaning against a pillar, "my fan is mine no more, for I have met with woe . . ."[26]

"What a very odd man from Koma!" The one who answered seemed not to understand him.

Another said nothing but only sighed and sighed. He leaned toward her, took her hand through her standing curtain, and said at a guess,

> *"How sadly I haunt the slopes of Mount Irusa, where the crescent sets,*
> > *yearning just to see again the faint moon that I saw then!*

Why should that be?"

This must have been too much for her, because she replied,

> *"Were it really so that your heart goes straight and true, would you lose your way*
> > *even in the dark of night, when no moon is in the sky?"*

Yes, it was her voice. He was delighted, though at the same time . . . [27]

---

26. He intentionally misquotes a *saibara* song ("A man from Koma stole my sash, oh, bitter regret is mine . . ."), substituting "fan" for "sash."
27. Oborozukiyo, the daughter of a political enemy, is promised to the Heir Apparent. Besides, Genji already dislikes her family's shallow ostentation, and he may be disappointed by how easily she gave herself to him.

9

(ABRIDGED)

AOI

HEART-TO-HEART

The plant *aoi* (more precisely, *futaba aoi*), sacred to the Kamo Shrine, grows on the forest floor and consists of a pair of broad, heart-shaped leaves that spring from a single stem. At the Kamo Festival people decorated their headdresses and carriages with it. In its Heian spelling (*afuhi*), the word can also be read to mean "day of (lovers') meeting." This word-play and the plant's configuration suggest the translation "heart-to-heart."

As the chapter title, *Aoi* refers particularly to an exchange of poems at the Festival between Genji and the amorous Dame of Staff. Since Genji's wife bears the main responsibility for a famous incident at the Festival, she is traditionally known as Aoi.

There is a gap of two years or so between chapters 8 and 9. In the interval Genji's father has abdicated; Suzaku, his son by the Kokiden Consort, has become Emperor; and Fujitsubo's son by Genji has become Heir Apparent.

The change of reign made all things a burden for Genji, and perhaps his rise in rank[1] explains why he now renounced his lighter affairs, so that for many he multiplied the sorrows of

1. Suzaku, the son of the Kokiden Consort, has succeeded Genji's father as Emperor. This has brought the faction represented by the Kokiden Consort and her father, the Minister of the Right, to power. Moreover, Genji's father seems as a last gesture to have appointed Genji Commander of the Right, so that he must now travel with an escort of eight guards.

neglect even while he himself, as though in retribution, continually lamented his own love's cruelty.[2] Fujitsubo was so constantly at the Retired Emperor's side[3] that she might as well have been a commoner, and this seemed to displease the Empress Mother,[4] who kept to the palace and left her in peace. Now and again His Eminence might hold a beautiful concert or something of the sort, one that set the whole court talking, so that he shone more brightly than ever; but he sadly missed the Heir Apparent, whose lack of effective support worried him, and his request that Genji look after him moved the new Commander to mingled joy and dismay.

Oh, yes, Akikonomu, the late Heir Apparent's daughter by the Rokujō Haven, had been named High Priestess of Ise, and her mother, who doubted Genji's devotion, had quickly invoked concern over her daughter's youth as a reason for considering going down to Ise herself.

Genji's father remarked to him on learning of her plan, "The Heir Apparent thought very highly of her and showed her every attention, and I find it intolerable that you should treat her as casually as you might any other woman. I consider the High Priestess my own daughter, and I should therefore appreciate it if you were to avoid offending her mother, both for her father's sake and for mine. Such wanton self-indulgence risks widespread censure." The displeasure on his countenance obliged Genji to agree, and he kept a humble silence.

"Never cause a woman to suffer humiliation," His Eminence continued. "Treat each with tact and avoid provoking her anger."

Genji withdrew contritely from his presence, terrified to imagine his rebuke were he to learn the full impudence of his own inadmissible passion.

That even His Eminence should know of his misconduct and express himself on the subject showed how painfully the lady's

---

2. Fujitsubo's. *Kokinshū* 1041: "As though in retribution for my not loving the one who loves me, the one I do love does not love me."
3. Genji's father.
4. The former Kokiden Consort, whose son is now Emperor.

name as well as his own had been compromised in the affair, and he guiltily redoubled his attentions toward her, but he still showed no sign of acknowledging their tie openly. She herself remained constantly constrained by shame over the discrepancy between their ages, and he countered with matching formality. The affair had reached His Eminence's ears by now and was well known to one and all, but she still suffered acutely from his relative indifference toward her.

News of all this confirmed Princess Asagao in her resolve that nothing of the kind should happen to her, and she rarely gave him the simplest reply. Still, he often thought how unusual it was of her, and how like her, too, not to dismiss him outright.

At the Minister of the Left's there was no praise for Genji's obviously roving fancy, but Aoi did not hold it deeply against him, perhaps because the way he almost flaunted it was beneath comment. For a very touching reason she was sadly unwell.[5] Genji felt wonder and sympathy for her. Everyone was pleased, but her parents had penances done for fear of rejoicing too soon.[6] These things kept him fully occupied, and while he never forgot the Rokujō Haven, he must have failed more often than not to visit her.

The High Priestess of the Kamo Shrine resigned at this time, and her successor was the Retired Emperor's third daughter by the Empress Mother. This Princess's parents were sorry to see her life take this odd turn, since she was a great favorite of theirs, but no other would do. The attendant rites, although not unusual, were done with great pomp and animation. When the time for the Festival came,[7] the customary events received many embellishments, and there were all sorts of sights to see. The Princess's personal distinction seemed to explain it all.

On the day of the Purification[8] the senior nobles took part in

5. With morning sickness.
6. Ritual abstinences, performed by others on her behalf, to ensure safe child-birth.
7. The Kamo Festival, on the middle Bird (*tori*) day in the fourth month, one of the major annual events in the City.
8. Strictly speaking, the second Purification, held on the day of the Horse (*uma*) or Sheep (*hitsuji*) preceding the day of the Festival proper.

the requisite numbers,[9] but only the best-looking and most highly regarded among them. They were all perfect in the color of their train-robes, in the pattern of their outer trousers,[10] and even in their choice of saddle and mount. Genji took part as well, by His Eminence's special decree. The sightseeing carriages had been made ready well in advance. Ichijō Avenue was packed and terribly noisy. The viewing stands put up here and there were elaborately adorned, each according to its owner's taste, and even the sleeves spilling from under their blinds were a wonder to behold.

Aoi rarely went out for such events, and she had not even thought of going this time, since she was indisposed, but her younger gentlewomen protested, "Oh, come, my lady, we would not enjoy stealing off there on our own! All the world longs for a glimpse of Lord Genji at the Festival today, and they say even the poorest woodcutters will be there to see him. Some people are even bringing their families from far-off provinces! My lady, you simply cannot miss it!"

"You really are feeling better lately," Aoi's mother remarked to her daughter when she heard, "and your women seem so disappointed." The household therefore suddenly learned that she would see the Festival after all.

The sun was already high when she set out with as little fuss as possible. Her imposing train of carriages halted, since by now every place was taken and it had nowhere to go. Her grooms fixed on a spot occupied by many fine ladies' carriages but free of any press of attendants, and they began having them cleared away. Among them were two basketwork carriages, a little worn but with elegant blinds through which spilled a hint of sleeves, trains, and jackets in the loveliest colors worn by those seated deep within. The occupant clearly wished to go unrecognized.

9. According to the *Engi shiki,* the first Purification required a single Consultant as imperial envoy, while the second required one Grand Counselor, one Counselor, and two Consultants.
10. They had on full civil dress, with a formal cloak of a color to match their rank, contrasting train-robes, and two pairs of open-legged trousers (the inner pair of plain red silk, the outer of brocade).

"These carriages are *not* ones you can push aside this way!" her grooms insisted loudly, and they would not let them be touched, but by now the young men on both sides were drunk and rowdy and out of control. The more sober personal escort from the Minister of the Left's warned them in vain.

The Rokujō Haven, the mother of the High Priestess of Ise (for it was she), had come secretly for relief from her troubles. Her people said nothing about who she was, but the other side of course knew her. "Take no such nonsense from the likes of them! They must be counting on Lord Genji's protection!" shouted the men from the Miniser of the Left's. Some of them, Genji's own men, were disturbed to see what was happening, but they feigned indifference because it would have been too difficult to intervene.

By the time all the carriages were in place, the Rokujō Haven's had been pushed behind the least of the gentlewomen's, and she had no view at all. She was not only outraged but extremely put out that she had been recognized after all. With her shaft benches broken and her carriage shafts now resting willy-nilly on the wheel hubs of other carriages, she looked so ridiculous that she rued her folly and wondered helplessly why she had ever come. She would gladly have left without seeing the procession, but there was no room for her to get out, and her resolve must have faltered after all when she heard cries of "Here they come!" and understood that her own cruel lover would be passing by. And pass on by he did, to her bitter chagrin, without so much as a glance her way.[11]

Beneath the blinds of carriages far more elaborately done up than usual, many eager ladies had indeed put forth a bright display that Genji affected to ignore, but on some he bestowed a sidelong glance and a smile. The carriages from the Minister of the Left's stood out, and he rode gravely past them. The profound deference and respect shown by his own retinue

11. More literally, "And perhaps because this was not even Sasanokuma, he passed by with no sign of recognition . . ." *Kokinshū* 1080, attributed to the goddess at Ise: "At Sasanokuma, by the Hinokuma River, stop, let your horse drink, that I may look upon you!"

brought home to the Rokujō Haven the sting of her ignomin-
ious defeat.

"One fugitive glimpse as of a face reflected in a hallowed stream
tells me with new cruelty that I matter not at all!"

She did not like being seen to weep, but she knew how much she
would have regretted missing the dazzling beauty and presence
that on this great occasion shone more brilliantly than ever.

The gentlemen of Genji's escort were perfect in dress and deportment, each as his station warranted, and the senior nobles
among them especially so, but the brightness of that single light
seemed to eclipse them all. It was unusual for a Commander to
be specially guarded by a privy gentleman from the Palace
Guards, but this procession was so exceptional that that office
was filled for once by someone from the Right Palace Guards.
The rest of Genji's retinue was equally brilliant in looks and finery, until it seemed as though the very trees and grasses must
bow down before a beauty so universally admired. The way quite
respectable women in deep hats[12] or nuns to whom the world
was dross came lurching and stumbling along to see him would
ordinarily have merited cries of horrified disapproval, except
that today no one could blame them. Women with puckered
mouths and gowns over their hair[13] gaped up at him, palms
joined or pressed to their foreheads in idiot adoration, while
peasant simpletons grinned beatifically, innocent of any
thought of how they looked themselves. Even miserable Governors' daughters, girls beneath his notice, were there in cleverly
tricked-out carriages, preening and congratulating themselves.
Yes, there were many amusing sights to see. Of course, there
were also many whom Genji had secretly favored and who now
could only sigh that they meant so little to him.

12. *Tsubo sōzoku,* the attire for a respectable woman outdoors. She draped a
shift over her head and hair, then put on a deep, broad-brimmed hat. She also
hitched up her skirts a little for walking.
13. Women too modest in standing to wear *tsubo sōzoku* would still tuck their
hair under their outer robe when outdoors.

Princess Asagao's father, the Lord of the Bureau of Ceremonial, was watching from a stand. The older he grows, the more devastatingly handsome he becomes, he said to himself with a feeling of vague dread; surely he must catch the eye even of the gods! To his daughter, who well knew from the letters she had had from him all these years how little his sentiments resembled those of other men, Genji would no doubt have been pleasing enough even if quite ordinary in looks, and she wondered as she felt his attraction how he could possibly be so dazzlingly beautiful as well. Still, she desired no greater intimacy with him. Her young gentlewomen praised him until she wished they would stop.

There were no sightseers from the Minister of the Left's residence on the day of the Festival proper.[14] With shock and dismay Genji received from his men a full account of the quarrel the previous day over the placement of the carriages. Alas, he thought, despite her dignity Aoi lacks kindness and tact. She cannot really have meant this to happen, but I suppose she sees so little reason why the two of them should think warmly of each other that those men of hers then took it on themselves to act as they did. The Rokujō Haven is so fastidious and reserved by nature—it must have been a terrible experience for her.

He anxiously went straight to call on her, but her daughter, the Ise Priestess, was still at home, and she invoked respect for the sacred *sakaki* tree to turn him away.[15] He quite understood, yet he could not help whispering to himself, "But why? I do wish they would both be less prickly with one another!"

On the day, he sought refuge at Nijō, from where he went to watch the Festival. He crossed to the west wing[16] and had

14. On this day the High Priestess actually went to the Kamo Shrine.
15. Once appointed, the High Priestess moved to special quarters in the palace and there underwent purification until the seventh month of the following year, when at last she went on to Ise. In this case, however, her move seems to have been delayed. Meanwhile, her house has been purified, and branches of the sacred *sakaki* tree, hung with cloth or paper streamers, have been set up at the four corners and at the gate to mark the place as ritually pure.
16. Where Murasaki lives.

Koremitsu order the carriage. "Are you gentlewomen going, too?"[17] he asked and watched, all smiles, while the young lady got herself ready very prettily indeed. "Come along, then," he said, "let us see it together."

Her hair was lovelier than ever. "You seem not to have had it trimmed for ages," he observed while he stroked it. "I imagine today is a good day for that."[18] He called for a Doctor of the Almanac and had him questioned about the proper hour. "Out you come now, gentlewomen!" he said and surveyed the delightful picture the children presented. The line of their bewitching hair, boldly cut straight across, stood out sharply against their damask-patterned outer trousers.

"I shall trim your hair myself. But oh, dear, how thick it is! I wonder how long it will grow!" He hardly knew what to do next. "People with very long hair still seem to have it shorter at the sides, but you have no stray locks at all! I am afraid you are not going to look very nice!"[19] When he was done, he made the "thousand fathom" wish, while Shōnagon looked on with pleasure and deep gratitude.

He said,

"Rich seaweed tresses of the unplumbed ocean depths, a thousand fathoms long,
    you are mine and mine alone to watch daily as you grow."[20]

"How am I to know whether a thousand fathoms measure your love, too,
    when the ever shifting tides so restlessly ebb and flow?"

17. Genji playfully addresses Murasaki's playmates as adults.
18. An auspicious day according to the almanac.
19. Ladies with long hair, Genji says, still have shorter sidelocks (hitai gami, the hair that falls from the temples over the cheeks); but Murasaki's hitai gami seems as long as the rest of her hair. His lament that she "will not look very nice" is not serious.
20. It was apparently customary to wish that a girl's hair should grow "a thousand fathoms" long. Genji's poem compares the little girl's hair to seaweed in praise, and it plays on miru (a kind of seaweed) and miru ("see"—i.e., "possess" [a wife]).

she wrote on a bit of paper, looking so grown-up yet at the same time so fresh and young that she was a joy to behold.

Today again there was no room for one carriage more. Genji's found nowhere to go, and it waited by the riding ground pavilion.[21] "It is awfully crowded here, with all these senior nobles' carriages," he remarked, and he was wondering whether to pass on when from a very fine one overflowing with a bright profusion of sleeves there emerged a fan that beckoned to one of his men.

"Would you not like to put your carriage here?" the occupant inquired. "I cede you my place."

Genji wondered what sort of coquette she could be, but he had his carriage brought up to the spot, since it was indeed a good one. "I envy you having managed to find it," he replied.

At this she broke a bit off a prettily decorated fan[22] and wrote upon it,

> "Ah, it is too hard! Today when our heart-to-heart told me that the god
> blessed our meeting, I perceive that another sports those leaves.

I should not presume . . ."[23]

He knew the handwriting: it was the Dame of Staff's. How she will play the gay young thing, despite her years! He was sufficiently irritated to retort,

21. The riding ground ([sakon no] baba) was near the intersection of Ichijō and Nishi no Tōin; the pavilion (otodo) there was where the Captains and Lieutenants sat during the yabusame riding events that took place on the third and fifth days of the fifth month. For the Festival the High Priestess was to come down from her temporary residence north of the city and proceed eastward along Ichijō to the Kamo Shrine.

22. Presumably a hiōgi made of thin slips of cypress (hinoki) wood. She would have written on a piece of one of these.

23. Continuing the mood of the poem, "I should not presume" relies on vocabulary special to a sacred festival.

"Yours, so I would say, was a very naughty wish to sport heart-to-heart,
when this meeting place today gathers men from countless clans!"

She answered, deeply wounded,

"How I rue the day I wished to sport heart-to-heart, those perfidious leaves
that with no more than a name stir such foolish pangs of hope!"

Many ladies were disappointed to see that he had someone
with him and did not even raise his blinds. The other day he was
so correct, they said to themselves, but he certainly is making a
casual outing of it today. Who can she be? She must be worth
looking at, if she is with him.

What a dismal skirmish that was, over heart-to-heart! Genji
was annoyed. Certainly, anyone less shameless than that woman
would have deferred to the lady beside him and refrained from
tossing off rash repartee.

The Rokujō Haven had never through all the years known
such misery and turmoil. As to her cruel lover, she had given
him up, but she knew how badly she would miss him if she were
actually to break with him and go down to Ise, and she also
feared ridicule for doing so; yet the thought of staying after all
left her afraid of encountering once more the hideous contempt
that she had already suffered. "Am I the float on the fisherman's
line?"[24] she asked herself in anguish day and night, and perhaps
this was why she lived like an invalid, her mind seeming to her
to have come adrift.

Genji never insisted that it would be madness for her to go;
he only argued, "I quite understand that you should wish to see
the last of me, worthless as I am, but even if you are fed up with
me by now, it would still be much kinder of you to continue

24. *Kokinshū* 509: "Am I the float on the line of the fisherman, fishing in Ise
Bay, that I should be unable to make up my mind?"

receiving me." This made the storm of that day of Purification,[25] which she had attended only for relief from her indecision, more hateful to her than before.

At the Minister of the Left's a spirit, it seemed, was making Aoi extremely unwell, and her family was alarmed. This was therefore no time for Genji to pursue adventures elsewhere, and it was only at odd moments that he managed even to visit Nijō. It pained him deeply that someone who so commanded his consideration should suffer this way, especially in her already delicate condition, and he had many prayers and rites done for her in his own apartment within the residence.

Many spirits and living phantoms[26] came forth and identified themselves in one way or another, but one refused to move into the medium and clung instead to Aoi herself; and although it did her no great violence, it never left her. Its resistance even to the most potent healers was extraordinarily stubborn.

After considering all the women with whom Genji had a liaison, people began to whisper that only the Rokujō Haven and the lady at Nijō engaged his deeper feelings, so that either might be intensely jealous; but divination performed at His Excellency's insistence still yielded nothing clear. None of the other spirits was especially hostile. One appeared to be a deceased nurse, while others were entities that had haunted her parents' families for generations, but these were not serious, and they were manifesting themselves only at random because of her weakened condition. She herself just cried and cried, and sometimes retched, suffering such unbearable agony that her parents wondered in fear and sorrow what was to become of her.

There were constant inquiries from the Retired Emperor, whose most gracious solicitude, expressed in the prayers that he was kindly having offered on her behalf, made it seem still more urgent that she be saved. The Rokujō Haven was shaken to learn that all the world feared for Aoi's life. No one at His Excellency's guessed

25. Literally, "the violent rapids of the lustration stream" (*misogigawa*, the stream that runs before the Kamo Shrine).
26. "Spirits" (*mononoke*) are the spirits of the dead or other supernatural, generally troublesome entities. "Living phantoms" (*ikisudama*) are the malevolent spirits of living persons.

that that little quarrel over placement of the carriages had inflamed in her heart a rivalry hitherto dormant for many years.

Her troubled mood convinced her that she was simply not
herself, and she moved elsewhere to have healing rites done.
The news made Genji wonder with uneasy sympathy what state
of mind had prompted her to do this, and he resolved to go and
see her. He went very discreetly, since for once she was not at
her own home. He begged forgiveness at length for his recent,
quite unintentional neglect, and he appealed to her with an account of Aoi's condition.

"I myself am not all that worried," he earnestly explained,
"but I feel for her parents, who are desperately anxious, and so,
you see, I thought I should stay with her for the time being. I
would be grateful if you were to view my behavior more indul-
gently." He understood that she was suffering more than usual,
and was pained to see it.

His departing figure, at dawn after a night of distances, was
so enchanting that again she could not bear to leave him, but
now that he had reason to devote himself more than ever to the
one who commanded his first allegiance, he would doubtless
settle his affections upon her, and this endless waiting would
mean nothing but misery; his occasional visit would arouse
only fresh despair. These thoughts were running through her
mind when she had a letter from him—only a letter, and toward
sunset: "She had seemed a little better lately, but all at once she
took such a turn for the worse that I could not get away."

To her this was just another of his excuses, and she replied,

> "I knew all too well that no sleeve goes unmoistened by the mire of love,
>   yet in the slough of that field I labor in helpless pain.

How true it is, that line about the mountain spring!"[27]

27. Rokujō's poem develops a play on *koiji* ("mud-filled [flooded] rice field"
and "path of love"), and her final remark means, "It is true that you care little
for me." *Kokin rokujō* 987: "How bitterly I regret dipping water from the
mountain spring, so shallow that I only wetted my sleeves."

To Genji her writing stood out easily in any company. Ah, he thought, why must it be like this? He was caught agonizingly between his reluctance to give up both her spirit and her looks and his incapacity to commit himself to her. His reply reached her well after dark: "Only your sleeves are wet? So your feelings have no depth . . .

It is shallow, then, the field of your hard labors, not at all like mine,
for I am wholly immersed in the deep slough of love's mire.

Have I failed to answer you in person only because you mean so little to me?"

At the Minister of the Left's the spirit was very active, and Aoi was in agony. The Rokujō Haven heard that some were calling it her own living phantom or the ghost of her late father, but on reflection she found in herself only her own misery and no desire at all to see Aoi harmed, though she conceded that a soul wandering in distress, as souls were said to do, might well act in this manner. Despite years plumbing the depths of despair, she had never before felt, as now, utterly destroyed, and after the Purification, when in that foolish incident she had been as though singled out for contempt and treated as naught, she knew that her mind, which had then drifted briefly from her, was now indeed beyond her control; and perhaps this was why she dreamed repeatedly, on dozing off, that she went to where that lady (as she supposed) lay in her finery, pushed and tugged her about, and flailed at her with a baneful violence strange to her waking self. Time after time she felt that she was not herself and that to her horror she had wandered away from her own body, until she saw that even if she were wrong, the world so unwillingly speaks well of anyone that the rumor of it would be embroidered upon everywhere with glee. She would, she knew, be talked of far and wide. No doubt it was common enough to leave a still-active malevolence behind after death, and this alone, when told of another, would arouse repulsion and fear; but that it should be her tragic destiny to have anything so horrible said of herself while she was still alive! No, she could not remain attached to so cruel a lover. Such were her thoughts, but hers was a case of "trying too hard to forget."[28]

Akikonomu was to have gone to the palace the year before,[29] but various difficulties had prevented her from doing so until this autumn. She was then to move in the ninth month directly to the Shrine on the Moor,[30] which meant that preparations for the second Purification had to go forward urgently at the same time; but her mother was overcome by a strange lassitude and spent her time in despondent brooding, to the intense anxiety of the High Priestess's staff, who offered prayers of every kind.[31] Still, her condition was not actually dire, and she got through the days and months without displaying any clear symptoms. Genji called on her often, but Aoi was so ill that he remained deeply preoccupied.

It was still early, and the family were unprepared, when all at once Aoi began to show obvious signs and to suffer pain. Ever more potent prayers were commissioned in great numbers, but that single most obstinate spirit refused to move, until the mightiest healers were surprised to find their efforts frustrated. Their assault was nonetheless fierce enough that the spirit wept in misery and cried, "Oh, please be a little more gentle with me! I have something to say to Commander Genji!"

"What did I tell you?" the women whispered among themselves. "Now we shall know!"

They led Genji in to the curtain that stood near where she lay. She was so clearly dying that her parents withdrew a little,

28. From a riddling poem (*Genji monogatari kochūshakusho in'yō waka* 76) built on the multiple implications of the verb *omou*: "Trying too hard to forget, I only remember; why, when one tries to forget, does one not forget?"
29. An Ise Priestess was appointed by divination at the start of a new reign. She first purified herself on the bank of the Kamo River (first Purification), then entered the Shosai-in ("Hall of First Abstinence") within the palace compound. In the autumn of the next year she underwent the second Purification and then entered the Shrine on the Moor; she went to Ise in the ninth month of the following year, after further purification in the Katsura River.
30. Nonomiya, a temporary shrine built for the purpose on Saga Moor (Sagano), just west of the City.
31. If she became unambiguously ill, her presence would pollute the sacred space inhabited by her daughter.

understanding that she might have some last word for him. The priests chanting the Lotus Sutra lowered their voices, to awesome effect. He lifted the curtain and looked in. Anyone, not only her husband, would have been moved to see her lying there, so beautiful and with so vast a belly, and since she was indeed his wife, he was of course overcome by pity and regret. Her long, abundant hair, bound at the end, lay beside her, contrasting vividly with her white gown. He thought her dearer and more beautiful than ever before.

He took her hand. "This is dreadful! What a thing to do to me!" When weeping silenced him, she lifted to his face her expiring gaze, so filled in the past with reproach and disapproval, and tears spilled from her eyes. How could he not have been profoundly moved?

She wept so piteously that he assumed her thoughts were on her sorrowing parents, as well as on the pain of leaving him. "You must not make too much of all this," he said soothingly. "You are going to be well after all. At any rate, whatever happens, you and I will meet again. People do. Remember what a strong bond you have with your mother and father, because it will remain unbroken in lives to come, and you will be with them again."

"No, no, you do not understand," a gentle voice answered. "I only wished you to have them release me a little because I am in such pain. I did not want to come at all, but you see, it really is true that the soul of someone in anguish may wander away.

> This spirit of mine that, sighing and suffering, wanders the heavens,
> oh, stop it now, tie a knot where in front the two hems meet."[32]

The voice, the manner, were not hers but those of someone else. After a moment of shock he understood that he was in the presence of the Rokujō Haven. Alas, what he had dismissed so

32. An old poem-spell, to be repeated by one who has seen a ghost, enjoins the speaker to knot the overlapping hems at the front of his or her robe.

far as malicious rumor put about by the ignorant now proved to be patently true, and he saw with revulsion that such things really did happen. "I hear your voice, but I do not know you. Please make it clear to me who you are." To his understandable horror, the answer was not in doubt. He shuddered to imagine the gentlewomen coming to their mistress now.

When her cries died down a little, her mother brought the hot medicinal water in case she might be in reprieve; then she was lifted upright and quickly gave birth.[33] Her parents' joy knew no bounds, but the spirits expelled by the healers[34] now raised a wild clamor of jealous rage, and what remained to come[35] was still a great worry. When all finally ended well, no doubt thanks to urgent prayers renewed in numbers beyond counting, the Abbot of Mount Hiei and the other most holy monks wiped away their perspiration in triumph and hurried away.

Days of acute and widespread anxiety now gave way to a welcome lull, and at last her parents breathed easily. The Minister of the Left commissioned a new round of protective rites, but happiness reigned, and exceptional delight in the child put everyone off guard. The Retired Emperor, Their Highnesses the Princes, and the senior nobles all attended the splendid birth celebrations that enlivened the succeeding evenings.[36] These events were especially bright and gay because in the bargain the child was a boy.

This news shook the Rokujō Haven. Aoi was supposed to be near death, she silently exclaimed, and now she has actually given birth without a hitch! Curiously, she still felt unlike herself, and her clothing reeked of poppy seeds.[37] To allay her misgivings she tried washing her hair and changing, but the smell

33. Her gentlewoman lifted her to the then-normal squatting position. Hot medicinal water was provided for a birth.
34. Driven by the healers (male Buddhist clerics) into the attendant (female) mediums, through whom the healers interrogated and dismissed them.
35. The afterbirth.
36. Parties (*ubuyashinai*) were given on the third, fifth, seventh, and ninth evenings after a birth. The guests brought gifts of food and clothing for the child.
37. Poppy seeds were thrown on the sacred *goma* fire during the rite to quell a spirit.

lingered until she came to look on herself with horror and of course to mourn inwardly (for the matter was hardly one she could discuss) what others must be saying about her. As she did so, she sank into ever more disturbed states of mind.

Genji, who was now a little less anxious than before, shuddered to recall that dreadful moment when the spirit had so startlingly addressed him. He knew he had been wrong to neglect her for so long, but he had grave doubts about how he would feel in her presence, and after careful reflection (for he did not wish to be unkind) he only sent her a letter.

Aoi's parents were still apprehensive, since they feared the effects of so serious an illness, and Genji tactfully abstained from his private excursions. She was not yet well enough to receive him as she usually did. The little boy was so handsome, in fact disturbingly so, that Genji was soon captivated, while His Excellency rejoiced that things had turned out well after all, if it were not for the worry that his daughter had yet to recover; but this he attributed to the difficulty of getting over everything she had suffered, and in truth he had little reason to fear.

Seeing how closely the little boy's engaging looks resembled the Heir Apparent's, Genji gave in to fond memories and went to call at the palace. "I feel guilty not to have seen His Majesty for so long," he said reproachfully, "and now I am going at last, I hope that I may come a little nearer to talk to you. It is too unkind of you to keep yourself from me as you do."[38]

"Indeed, my lord," a gentlewoman replied, "you and my lady need no longer present yourselves flatteringly to each other, and although my lady is very reduced, there is no reason why a curtain should stand between you."

They arranged a seat for him near where she lay, and he went in to talk to her. She was very weak even now, as her few answers showed. Still, the memory of thinking her well and truly lost seemed a dream, and as he told her of his fears for her then, he was assailed by the grim recollection of how, while she lay all but lifeless, that flood of speech had suddenly burst from her. "Ah," he said, "I have so much more to tell you, but they

38. He speaks to Aoi through a gentlewoman.

tell me you are not up to it, you see. Do take your medicine," he went on, and in other ways, too, he made himself so useful that her gentlewomen were touched and wondered when he could have learned all this. The sight of her lying there, so beautiful yet so thin and weak that she hardly seemed among the living, aroused his love and his keenest sympathy. The hair streaming across her pillow, not a strand out of place, struck him as a wonder, and as he gazed at her, he found himself unable to understand how for all these years he could have seen any flaw in her.

"I shall call upon the Retired Emperor, too, and then I shall be back very soon. I would gladly stay with you like this all the time, but your mother is always beside you, and I am afraid that I have held back so far for fear of being indiscreet. In your usual room, though, once you have gradually recovered your strength . . . One reason why you do not get better is that you treat yourself too much like a child." When he had finished, he set out in his magnificent robes, while she lay there and watched him go for longer than ever before.

The Minister of the Left, too, left for court, since the autumn appointments were to be announced,[39] and all his sons, who had ambitions of their own and kept him close company, set off with him.

The residence was quiet, for there was hardly anyone about, when she was suddenly racked by a violent fit of retching. Before word could reach the palace, she was gone. All present there withdrew in shock. Appointments list evening or not, this disaster had clearly put an end to the proceedings. His Excellency could not call on the Abbot of the Mountain or on any other great monk because it was already night when the cry went up. The people of the household, who had thought the danger past, went stumbling about blindly in their horror. The messengers who crowded in from far and near found no one to talk to because all was turmoil, and the parents' desperate grief was truly frightening to see. The spirit had possessed her so

39. Appointments were announced each spring and autumn, and the Minister of the Left, the court's senior nonimperial official, presided over the event.

often in the past that they watched for two or three days, leaving her pillow and so on undisturbed,[40] until signs of change convinced them at last, in their misery, to give up hope.

Genji had now suffered blow on blow, and life was intolerable to him. Condolences from those closest to him aroused only irritated impatience. The expressions of sorrow and sympathy from the Retired Emperor were still a great honor, and the Minister of the Left, who had also reason to rejoice, wept without end. At the urging of those around him he commissioned solemn rites of every kind, in case his daughter should revive, and in his anguish he persisted even when the workings of change had become all too plain, but after the vain passage of several days he resigned himself at last, and they took her to Toribeno[41] amid scenes of heartrending grief.

[Aoi's funeral is performed. Her parents mourn her bitterly. Genji remains with them for a week and mourns her, too. Eventually, however, he returns to his Nijō residence and to Murasaki.]

Every room at Nijō was spic-and-span, and the whole staff, men and women alike, awaited his arrival. The senior gentlewomen were all back, and seeing each of them dressed and made up to her best advantage recalled to him with a pang the sorrowing company that he had just left. He changed and went straight to the west wing. The curtains and furnishings for the new season were bright and gay,[42] the handsome young gentlewomen and page girls, with their graceful airs and ways, made a most agreeable sight, and Shōnagon's warm welcome pleased him greatly.

His young lady was dressed extremely prettily. "See what a big girl you are, now I have been away so long!" He lifted her little standing curtain to see her, and her looks as she bashfully turned away were beyond reproach. Her profile in the lamplight, her hair—everything told him that she would exactly resemble that other lady for whom he pined, and he was overjoyed.

40. The pillow was the soul's resting place. If it was moved, the soul might fail to find the body again if life returned.
41. A burning ground just east of the City.
42. Curtains and other furnishings had been changed for winter, which began on the first of the tenth lunar month.

He sat beside her and described what had happened while he was gone.[43] "I so look forward to telling you all about it," he said, "but all that would be too much now. I shall go and rest a little first and then be back. I shall be seeing so much of you now that you may grow tired of me!"

Shōnagon was pleased to hear all this, but she still worried about him. That may not have been very nice of her, but he kept up with so many great ladies that she was afraid a new one might now appear and ruin everything.

Genji returned to his own apartments, where he had the gentlewoman Chūjō rub his legs before he fell asleep. The next morning he sent off a letter for his little son. The sorrowful reply filled him with melancholy.

With so little to occupy him now he remained very pensive, but he could not yet muster the ambition to set out on casual evening calls. It was a pleasure to see that his young lady had turned out to be all he could wish, and since he judged that the time had now more or less come, he began to drop suggestive hints; but she showed no sign of understanding.

He spent whole days with her, whiling away the time at Go or at character-guessing games,[44] and such were her wit and grace, so enthralling in quality her every gesture, that after those years of forbearance while her charm had offered nothing more, he could endure it no longer; and so despite his compunction it came to pass one morning, when there was nothing otherwise about their ways with each other to betray the change, that he rose early while she rose not at all.

"What can be the matter?" her women asked each other anxiously. "She must not be feeling herself."

Before leaving he put a writing box beside her, inside her curtains.[45] At last, when there was no one nearby, she lifted her

43. He addresses her very politely, despite his intimate tone.
44. The guessing game (*hen-tsugi*) involved guessing partly hidden characters or making up new ones by adding elements to given parts.
45. So that she can answer the poem he has left by her pillow. After a couple's first night together the man was supposed to leave the woman a poem, and she to respond. Being "knotted," Genji's note has visibly to do with love.

head and found a knotted letter at her pillow. Opening it uncomprehendingly, she read,

> *"Ah, what distances kept us so strangely apart, when night after night*
> *we two yet lay side by side in our overlapping clothes."*

He seemed to have dashed it off with the greatest of ease. She had never suspected him of such intentions, and she could only wonder bitterly why in her innocence she had ever trusted anyone with such horrid ideas.

Toward midday he returned. "You seem to be ill. What is wrong, then? Today will be no fun if we cannot play Go." He peeped in: she was still lying with the bedclothes over her head. The gentlewomen drew back as he went to her. "Why will you not talk to me? You do not like me after all, do you. Your gentlewomen must be wondering about all this." He pulled the covers off her and found her drenched in perspiration. Even the hair at her forehead was soaking wet. "Oh, dear, we cannot have this! What a fuss you are making!" She was still furious with him, though, despite his attempts to console her, and she refused him a single word in reply. "Very well, then," he said reproachfully, "I will not come anymore. I feel quite unwanted." He opened the writing box and peered inside, but there was nothing in it.[46] What a little girl she still is! He contemplated her fondly. He spent the whole day trying to make her feel better, and her refusal to yield only made her more precious.

That evening they were brought baby boar cakes.[47] The event was nothing elaborate, since Genji was in mourning, and the cakes were served only there in the west wing. When he saw them in all their colors, presented in pretty cypress boxes, he

---

46. She had not answered his poem on that morning.
47. Glutinous rice cakes, each shaped like a baby boar (*inoko mochii*), eaten for good luck at the hour of the Boar (about 9:00 to 11:00 P.M.) on the first day of the Boar in the tenth lunar month. The rice was mixed with ingredients like sesame, chestnut, or persimmon, so that the cakes came in seven different flavors and colors.

went out to the front of the house and called Koremitsu. "Bring me cakes like these tomorrow evening, although not nearly so many. Today was not lucky."[48]

Koremitsu, always so quick, noted his smiles and caught his meaning instantly. He asked no questions but only said with a perfectly straight face, "Certainly, my lord, a new couple should of course choose the right day to have them. How many baby rat cakes should I provide?"[49]

"About a third as many should do." Koremitsu, who understood him perfectly, withdrew. He certainly knows his way about! Genji thought. Koremitsu said nothing to anyone, and he all but made the cakes himself, at home.

Genji, at his wits' end to placate his darling, was highly amused to feel as though he had just stolen a bride. What she used to mean to me is nothing compared to what she means to me now! he reflected. How unruly the heart is! I could not bear one night away from her!

Discreetly, very late at night, Koremitsu brought the cakes that Genji had ordered. He was acutely aware that Shōnagon, who was older, might embarrass Genji's young lady, so he called for her daughter, Ben. "Take them these, quietly." He handed her the cakes in an incense jar box.[50] "They are to celebrate a happy event, and you are to put them beside the pillow. Be careful, now, do not do anything wrong."

"But I have never done anything wrong like that," Ben said in surprise as she took them.[51]

"Actually, avoid that word for now. Just don't use it."[52]

Ben was too young to grasp what he meant, but she delivered

---

48. Newlyweds were served white rice cakes on their third night together, the one when their marriage was sealed. However, the day of the Boar (only the second night in this case) was unlucky for the start of anything as important as marriage.

49. The day of the Rat followed that of the Boar, but "baby rat cakes" (*nenoko* [*no mochii*]) did not exist; the term is Koremitsu's invention.

50. Ben must be behind a curtain. The box serves to disguise its contents.

51. She mistakes Koremitsu's meaning. *Ada* ("wrong") can mean specifically something wanton.

52. *Ada* is too ill-omened to use at the time of a marriage.

the cakes, slipping them in through the standing curtain by their pillows. No doubt it was as always Genji who explained them.

The gentlewomen knew nothing of all this, but when Genji had the box removed early the next morning, those closest to their mistress understood what had happened. Where could those dishes have come from? The little carved stands were so delicate and the cakes themselves so beautifully made—it was all as pretty as could be.[53] Shōnagon, who had never dreamed Genji would go this far,[54] dissolved in tears of gratitude before such evidence of his unstinting devotion.

"I do wish he had quietly told *us*, though," the women whispered to each other. "What can that man of his have thought?"

Thereafter Genji missed her and worried about her whenever he called a moment at the palace or at His Eminence's, so much so that his feelings surprised even him. He was not insensitive to the bitter complaints addressed to him by the ladies he was visiting, but he was so reluctant to hurt his new wife by being away a single night that he arranged things to look as though he were ill. "I shall begin going out once I am again ready to face the world" was the only kind of answer he gave them.

Oborozukiyo still had her heart set only on Genji, and the Empress Mother did not at all like the feelings that their father, the Minister of the Right, expressed on the subject. "After all," he would say, "I see nothing wrong with her having what she wants, now that I gather that proud wife of his is no more." The Empress Mother, to whom there was nothing dishonorable about her sister's entering palace service as long as she did so with dignity, was determined to offer her to His Majesty.

Genji, who was so fond of her, found this prospect thoroughly disappointing, but he was in no mood just now to divide his affections. Why do that? He had learned, to his cost, the value of caution. Life is short enough as it is, he reflected, and besides, I have made my choice. I should never have provoked jealousy.

---

53. "Third-night cakes" were served on silver dishes, with silver chopsticks, silver chopstick rests in the shape of cranes, etc.
54. As to marry Murasaki relatively formally.

As to the Rokujō Haven, her plight affected him very much, but things would never go well if he acknowledged her formally, whereas she was just the woman to discuss things with now and again, if she would only let him go on seeing her as in the past. He could not bring himself to give her up even now.

It occurred to him that society still did not know who his new love was, and that that reflected poorly on her; and he decided accordingly to inform His Highness her father. He invited a chosen few to a donning of the train that he planned to bring off more amply than usual—which was all very well, except that she had now taken a keen dislike to him. She so bitterly rued giving him all those years of trust and affection that she would not even look him properly in the eye, and she displayed only aversion for his lightest remark. The change that had come over her both amused and pained him. "Those years when I was so fond of you have all gone to waste," he would complain, "and the way you keep yourself from me hurts me very much!" On this note the New Year came.

[. . .]

IO
(COMPLETE)

SAKAKI
THE GREEN BRANCH

Sakaki, a broadleaf evergreen, figures in Shinto ritual, hence in this chapter's best-remembered scene: Genji's visit to the Rokujō Haven at the Shrine on the Moor. She reproaches him when he arrives and slips a branch of *sakaki* under her blinds. The *sakaki* branch gave the chapter its title.

Chapter 10 follows chapter 9 in unbroken narrative sequence, from the ninth month of that year, when Genji is twenty-three, to the summer a year and a half later, when he is twenty-five.

As the High Priestess's journey to Ise approached, her mother, the Rokujō Haven, felt increasingly miserable. Now that Aoi, whose commanding rank she had so resented, was no more, people told one another that her time had come, and her own gentlewomen looked forward eagerly to the future; but when she considered Genji's subsequent silence and his shabby treatment of her, she recognized that something must really have happened to distress him, and she therefore put her feelings aside to prepare for a resolute departure.

No Priestess had ever gone down to Ise with her mother before, but the Rokujō Haven invoked anxiety over her daughter's welfare and held firm in her wish to put her troubled life behind her, even as Genji, disappointed that she really did mean to leave, now began at least sending her sympathetic letters. She felt unable to receive him in person. No doubt she sternly reminded herself that although he might think this decision unkind, seeing him would make things so much more difficult for her that she was not obliged to do so.

Now and again she went home for a time, but so quietly that Genji never knew when to find her there. He was not free to call on her where she was living at present, and days and months therefore went by without a visit from him. Meanwhile the Retired Emperor began often to feel unwell, although he was not alarmingly ill, and this burdened Genji with yet another care.

Concern that she might condemn his cruelty and fear that others might actually agree decided him after all to set out for the Shrine on the Moor. He knew that she would be leaving soon, for it was the seventh of the ninth month, and she did indeed have a great deal to occupy her, but his repeated appeals to give him a moment whether or not he even sat down, coupled with her wish to avoid appearing too distant, overcame her misgivings and persuaded her that yes, she might converse with him as long as she kept something between them; and in this mood she began privately to look forward to his coming.

Melancholy overwhelmed him as soon as he set out across the moor's vast expanse. The autumn flowers were dying; among the brakes of withering sedge, insect cries were faint and few; and through the wind's sad sighing among the pines there reached him at times the sound of instruments, although so faintly that he could not say what the music was. The scene had an intensely eloquent beauty. The ten or more close retainers in his escort were modestly outfitted, but he had dressed elaborately, despite the private character of his journey, and he looked handsome enough to give the setting a new charm for the young gallants with him. He asked himself why he had not come before, and regretted having failed to do so.

Within a low, frail brushwood fence stood a scattering of board-roofed buildings, very lightly built.[1] The unbarked *torii*[2] evoked a holy awe that reproved his own concerns, and the

---

1. They were temporary, for the shrine was rebuilt as needed at a new spot.
2. The gateway to a Shinto shrine, normally made of finished wood; this one emphasizes the shrine's temporary character.

priests clearing their throats[3] here and there or conversing with their fellows gave the precincts an air all their own. The fire lodge[4] glowed dimly. With so few people about, a deep quiet reigned, and the thought that she had spent days and months here alone with her cares moved him to keen sympathy.

He hid at a suitable spot by the north wing[5] and announced his visit, at which the music ceased and he heard promising sounds of movement within. She showed no sign of receiving him in person, and he was not at all pleased to exchange mere commonplaces with her through a go-between. "You would not persist in keeping the sacred rope between us if only you knew how hard it is for me now to get away on so personal a quest," he said earnestly. "A good deal is clear to me by now, you know."

His appeal moved her women to intercede for him with their mistress. "Yes, my lady," they said, "it is a shame to leave him just standing there; one must feel sorry for him."

Oh, dear, she thought, I do not like the spectacle I am making—he can hardly think well of me for it; I would much rather not go out to him at all. She did not have the courage to treat him coldly, though, and at last she emerged amid reluctant sighs, delighting him with the grace of her form.[6]

"I wonder whether, here,[7] I might be allowed up on the veranda," he said and promptly installed himself there. In the brilliant moonlight his movements had a charm unlike anyone else's. Too abashed now to make fluent excuses for his long silence, he slipped in to her under the blind a *sakaki* branch that he had picked, and he said, "This is the constant color[8] that led me to penetrate the sacred paling, yet now you cruelly . . ."

She answered,

3. Probably as a warning at Genji's approach.
4. Perhaps where the food offerings were prepared.
5. Where Rokujō lives. Her daughter occupies the main house.
6. A blind still separates them, but Genji sees her silhouette through it.
7. At the house rather than at the sanctuary proper.
8. That of the evergreen *sakaki* and of Genji's own constant heart.

"When no cedar trees stand as though to draw the eye by the sacred fence,
what strange misapprehension led you to pick sakaki?"[9]

"This was where she was, the shrine maiden, that I knew, and fond memories
made the scent of sakaki *my reason to pick a branch,"*[10]

he replied. Despite the daunting character of the surroundings
he came in halfway under the blind, and there he remained,
leaning on the lintel that bounded the room.

For years, while he could see her whenever he wished and she
herself thought of him with longing, a proud complacency had
made him somewhat indifferent to her; and then that shocking
discovery of her flaw had cooled the last of his ardor and turned
him away. Now, however, he was undone by all that this rare
meeting brought back to him from the past, and he wept helplessly over what lay behind them and what might yet be to
come. Her own failure to control emotions that she had seemed
resolved never to betray affected him more and more, and he
begged her to give up her plan after all.

As he laid his whole complaint before her, his eyes on a sky
perhaps lovelier still now that the moon had set, all the bitterness pent up in his heart melted away, and she, who had given
up clinging to him, was not surprised to find her feelings in
turmoil nonetheless. Meanwhile young scions of the great
houses passed the time with one another while they wandered
the grounds, presenting as they did so a scene of incomparable
elegance.

No one could ever convey all that passed between those two,

9. "Why have you come and why are you giving me this *sakaki* branch when I
have no wish to respond?" From *Kokinshū* 982, attributed to the Miwa deity,
to whom the cedar (*sugi*) is sacred: "My humble dwelling is below Miwa
Mountain: come, if you love me, to the gate where the cedars stand."
10. "Shrine maiden" (*otomego*) seems to mean Rokujō herself, though it
would better suit her daughter. It is an *engo* ("associated word") of *sakaki*.
The poem draws on *Shūishū* 1210, by Kakinomoto Hitomaro, and *Shūishū*
577.

who together had known such uncounted sorrows. The quality
of a sky at last touched by dawn seemed meant for them alone.

> *"Many dews attend any reluctant parting at the break of day*
> *but no one has ever seen the like of this autumn sky,"*

Genji said. Wavering and unwilling to leave, he very tenderly
took her hand. An icy wind was blowing, and the pine crickets'
faltering song so truly caught the mood of the moment that not
even someone free of care could have heard it without a pang;
no wonder, then, if in their deep anguish neither could find
words of farewell.

> *"There has never been a parting in the autumn untouched by sorrow,*
> *but oh, do not cry with me, pine crickets upon the moor!"*

she replied.

Genji, who knew the vanity of all his regrets, heeded the coming dawn and left at last. The path he followed home was a very
dewy one, while she, no longer resolute, mourned his going.
His figure so recently glimpsed in the moonlight, that fragrance
of his lingering nearby—her intoxicated young women threw
discretion to the winds to sing his praises. "Oh, how can my
lady set out on this journey," they tearfully asked each other,
"when to do so means leaving such a gentleman behind?"

Genji's unusually expansive letter bent her wishes well
enough to his own, but alas, she could not again reconsider her
plans. He was capable of such eloquence in the service of romantic ambition, even when the affair did not interest him
greatly, that regret and compassion must have truly inspired
him when he reflected that someone who meant so much to him
was now to leave and go her way.

He gave clothing for the journey to her and even to her gentlewomen, as well as other furnishings of the finest, most ingenious
design, but these things meant nothing to her. The nearer the
day came, the more continually she lamented, as though the
thought were ever new, the cruel reputation she would leave

behind and the sad fate that now awaited her. The High Priestess herself was young enough simply to be pleased that this often delayed departure should be settled at last. Some people in the world no doubt criticized the unprecedented step her mother was taking, even as others sympathized. Those whose standing spares them reproach in all they do are fortunate indeed. Alas, one singled out above the rest can act so seldom on her desires!

On the sixteenth the High Priestess of Ise underwent purification in the Katsura River.[11] His Majesty chose gentlemen of loftier ancestry and higher renown than usual for the imperial escort[12] and the party of senior nobles. The Retired Emperor's wishes, too, must have played their part in the matter.

A letter came from Genji as the Priestess was setting out, one filled with the usual endless entreaties. It was attached to a mulberry-cloth streamer[13] and addressed "To the High Priestess, in reverence and awe."[14] "The Thunder God himself would refrain, you know,"[15] Genji had written.

> "Ye great gods of earth, who guard this Land of Eight Isles, if you can be kind,
> judge in favor of a pair to whom parting means such pain!

I cannot think of you without wishing that you would not go."

He had answers, too, despite all there was to do. The Priestess had hers written by one of her senior women:

> "If the gods of earth from aloft in the heavens issued their decree,
> they might hasten to denounce the lightness with which you speak."

11. West of Kyoto.
12. A party of four nobles, headed by a Counselor or a Consultant, that accompanied the Priestess to Ise on the Emperor's behalf.
13. A streamer cut in zigzag pattern from mulberry-bark cloth, used in Shinto rites.
14. *Kakemakumo*, a formula of respect used in Shinto prayers.
15. *Kokinshū* 701 protests that even the fearsome Thunder God refrains from severing the relations between lovers.

Genji would have gladly gone on to the palace to witness what was to follow,[16] but he thought that it might look odd of him to see off someone who was leaving him, and he therefore gave up the idea and lost himself in his musings. The High Priestess's reply, so grown-up in tone, made him smile. His interest aroused, he imagined her attractive beyond her years. Seduced as he always was by strange complications, he now rued his failure to see her for himself while she was young enough for that to be easily possible, and he assured himself that the vicissitudes of life might in time allow him to meet her after all.

The personal distinction of mother and daughter had attracted many sightseeing carriages. The two arrived at the hour of the Monkey.[17] For the Rokujō Haven in her palanquin it was sad to see the palace again after so many years, and under circumstances so different from what her father, with his high ambition for her, had fondly brought her up to expect.[18] She had married the late Heir Apparent at sixteen and been widowed at twenty. Now, as she again beheld the Emperor's palace, she was thirty,[19] and this poem came to her:

> "No, I do not wish today to lament again a life I once knew,
>   but deep in my heart I feel a vague, pervasive sorrow."

Akikonomu, her daughter, was fourteen. She was very pretty already, and her mother's careful grooming had given her a beauty so troubling that His Majesty's heart was stirred. He shed tears of keen emotion when he set the comb of parting in her hair.[20]

A line of display carriages[21] stood before the Eight Bureaus,

---

16. The Priestess's farewell to the Emperor and her formal departure.
17. Roughly 3:00 to 5:00 P.M.
18. She had last come to the palace in a palanquin as a future Empress.
19. This age disagrees with the chronology for the other characters in the tale. If with her history she is now thirty, Genji is only fourteen.
20. When a Priestess set out, the Emperor put the "comb of parting" in her hair with the words "Set not your face toward the City again." She will remain at Ise until the Emperor abdicates.
21. *Idashiguruma*, carriages under the blinds of which gentlewomen allowed their sleeves to hang in a brilliant display of color.

waiting for the Priestess to come forth, and the sleeves spilling from them made a brilliant show that for many a privy gentleman evoked a painful parting of his own.[22] She set out by night, and when the turn from Nijō onto Tōin brought her before Genji's Nijō residence, he was moved to send her mother this poem, caught in a *sakaki* branch:

> *"Go then if you will, and abandon me today, but those sleeves of yours—*
> *will the Suzuka River not leave them wet with its spray?"*[23]

It was so dark then, and the commotion around the Haven so great, that Genji had no answer until the next day, from beyond the barrier:[24]

> *"Whether leaping spray from the Suzuka River wet my sleeves or not,*
> *whose thoughts will still follow me all the long way to Ise?"*

Her writing in this hasty note still conveyed great distinction and grace, but Genji wished that she might have shown a little more sympathy for his feelings. A thick fog shrouded all things this unhappy dawn as he stared before him, murmuring to himself,

> *"I shall let my gaze rest upon where she has gone: this autumn at least,*
> *O mists, do not hide from me the summit of Ōsaka!"*

22. These ladies will accompany the Priestess to Ise, and some have lovers who will not see them again for a long time. The Eight Bureaus (*Hasshō*), a compound housing the offices of the eight major government bureaus, was continuous with the Great Hall of State, the major ceremonial building in the palace precincts.

23. "You will soon be weeping with regret at having left me." The Suzuka River had to be crossed on the way to Ise.

24. The Ōsaka Barrier, a low pass with a tollgate at the summit, just outside the City on the main road toward the East. Its name suggests *au saka*, "hill of meeting."

He did not go to the west wing but chose instead to spend the day in lonely brooding. What torments she must have known on her journey!

By the tenth month the Retired Emperor's illness was serious, and all the world longed only to see him recover. His Majesty was acutely worried and called on him in person. His Eminence in his weakened condition spoke again and again of the Heir Apparent and then turned to the subject of Genji. "Keep nothing from him, great or small," he said, "but seek his support in all things, as I have done while I lived. Despite his youth I believe that you need not fear to entrust him with government. He has the mark of one born to rule. That is why, considering the complexity of his situation, I did not make him a Prince but decided instead to have him serve the realm as a commoner. I beg you not to disregard my intention."

His last touching injunctions were many, but a woman has no business passing them on, and the little said of them here is more than enough. His Majesty was deeply saddened and promised repeatedly never to contravene his father's wishes. He was so handsome and so agreeably mature that His Eminence looked on him with happy confidence. The visit then had to end, and His Majesty hastened homeward more than ever burdened with sad forebodings.

The Heir Apparent had wished to accompany the Emperor, but his doing so would have caused such a stir that he changed his visit to another day. He was very grown-up and attractive for his age;[25] and he loved his father so much that his innocent happiness when he saw him again made a touching sight. The Retired Emperor was greatly troubled to see Fujitsubo, his Empress, dissolved in tears. He instructed her son on a wide range of matters, but the future of so young a boy still worried him greatly. On Genji, too, he urged repeated advice on how to serve the realm, as well as admonitions to look after the Heir Apparent. The Heir Apparent withdrew only late in the evening, his visit having caused no less of a commotion than His

25. He is now five.

Majesty's own. Even then His Eminence could hardly bear to let his little son go.

The Empress Mother had meant to call on the Retired Emperor, too, but Fujitsubo's presence beside him gave her pause, and while she vacillated, he quietly passed away. The court was distraught. Despite having renounced the throne he had continued to wield the powers of government just as he had during his reign, and now, with His Majesty so young and His Majesty's grandfather, the Minister of the Right, so testy and impatient, the senior nobles and privy gentlemen all groaned to imagine what might await them when this Minister came into his own.

Fujitsubo and Genji were even more stricken with grief. It goes without saying that everyone was profoundly moved to see Genji, the most brilliant presence among all his father's Princes, so devotedly perform the memorial rites. His beauty was perfect even in drab mourning. Last year the spectacle of mortality had convinced him that this world is dross, and this year he learned the same lesson, but although this loss confirmed him in his resolve,[26] many ties yet restrained him.

The Late Retired Emperor's Consorts and others remained at his residence until the forty-ninth day, but they dispersed once it was past. On the twentieth of the twelfth month, under a lowering sky that threatened to seal off the world, Fujitsubo found herself beset by stubbornly gathering gloom. Knowing the Empress Mother's mind as she did, she understood how painful it would be to inhabit a palace subject to her will, and she saw that she could not remain forever as she was, absorbed in the memory of that noble presence whose intimate she had been for all those years. Now, when the others were going home, her sorrow knew no bounds.

She was to move to her Sanjō residence, and her brother, Prince Hyōbu, came to accompany her there. Snow was blowing on a stiff wind, and by the time Genji arrived, the departed's residence was all but deserted. He began to speak of the past. Prince Hyōbu observed that the five-needled pine

---

26. To leave the world.

before Fujitsubo's rooms was weighed down by snow and that its lower branches had died. He said,

> *"Alas, that great pine whose broad shade inspired such trust seems to live no more,*
> *for the year's last days are here, and the lower needles fall."*[27]

The poem was no masterpiece, but it caught their feelings so well that Genji's tears moistened his sleeves.

Seeing the lake frozen from shore to shore, Genji added,

> *"That face I once saw, clear in the spotless mirror of this frozen lake,*
> *I shall never see again, and I am filled with sorrow."*

His quite artless words merely gave voice to his heart.

Ōmyōbu offered,

> *"The year soon will end, the spring there among the rocks is caught fast in ice,*
> *and the forms we knew so well vanish from before our eyes."*

Many others put in poems of their own, but one could hardly record them all.

The protocol for Fujitsubo's return followed custom; perhaps it was her own state of mind that made the move unusually sad. She felt when she arrived that, far from having come home, she must have set out on a journey, because it came to her that she had hardly been back in all these years.

The New Year had come, but without any festive display. All was quiet. Genji had heart only for solitude at home. When the time came for the appointments list,[28] the horses and carriages

---

27. The "lower needles" are the members of Genji's father's household, who are dispersing.

28. *Jimoku,* the list of appointments (generally to regional posts) and promotions announced in the first month. Candidates once flocked to Genji for his favor.

that had of course thronged to his gate during his father's reign, and even more so in recent years, were few and far between, and few, too, the sets of bedding put out for his retainers on duty; instead, the sight of no one but trusted household officials, obviously with little urgent to do, reminded Genji unpleasantly that this was what things were to be like henceforth.

In the second month Oborozukiyo, formerly the Mistress of the Wardrobe, was named Mistress of Staff,[29] her predecessor having been moved by mourning for the Late Retired Emperor to become a nun. Distinguished of manner and imposing in rank, she among all His Majesty's ladies enjoyed his greatest regard. The Empress Mother, who spent more and more time at home, adopted the Umetsubo as her palace residence, while Oborozukiyo occupied the Kokiden. She who had once languished in the gloom of the Tōkaden[30] now lived gaily amid countless gentlewomen, and yet in her heart she grieved, for she could not forget what had begun so unexpectedly. Her secret correspondence with Genji must have continued. He dreaded the consequences if their affair should become known, but that familiar quirk of his probably made him more eager than ever. The Empress Mother, with her sharp temper, had restrained herself while the Late Retired Emperor lived, but now she seemed bent on revenge for every grudge she nursed against him. He met nothing but disappointment, and although this was no surprise, being so strangely at odds with the world robbed him of any wish to appear among people.

The Minister of the Left was similarly disheartened and made no effort to appear at the palace. The Empress Mother resented it that he had withheld his late daughter from the then–Heir Apparent and reserved her for Genji instead, and she had no use for him. His relations with His Excellency of the Right, too, had always been prickly, and whereas fortune had previously smiled on him, times had changed, and it was he of the Right

29. Naishi no Kami. In principle, the incumbent supervised female palace staff, palace ceremonies, and the transmission of petitions and decrees. In practice, she was a somewhat junior Consort.
30. The pavilion north of the Kokiden, hence farther from the Emperor and less advantageous.

who now lorded it as he pleased. No wonder Genji's former father-in-law felt bitter.

Genji called upon him as always. He was if anything more attentive to the women who had once served him there, and he showed great devotion to his little son; and all this so pleased and surprised the old gentleman that he still did for Genji whatever lay in his power. Once Genji's exalted standing had put far too many demands on his time, but now he lost touch with several ladies he had been visiting, and he also gave up as unbecoming the more lighthearted of his secret adventures, so that for once his leisured life suited him perfectly.

All the world admired the good fortune enjoyed by Murasaki. Privately, Shōnagon attributed it entirely to the prayers of her mistress, the late nun. Murasaki's father corresponded with his daughter as he pleased, no doubt to her stepmother's chagrin, since the daughters this lady had thought destined to rise high had failed instead and were only a disappointment. The happy fate of Genji's darling was just like a fiction in a tale.

Mourning had obliged the High Priestess of the Kamo Shrine to resign, and she was succeeded by Princess Asagao. Few precedents authorized an imperial granddaughter to serve as Kamo Priestess, but presumably there was no qualified daughter. Genji had not given her up, despite the passage of time, and he was sorry to see her life take so unusual a course. He was presumably still writing to her, his letters reaching her as before through Chūjō. A change of fortune had failed to impress him, but he now wavered painfully between two capricious affairs that gave him little consolation.

The Emperor thought well of Genji, as his father on his deathbed had enjoined him to do, but his youth made him still too weak and pliable successfully to oppose anything undertaken by the Empress Mother or by the Minister his grandfather, and the ways of the court therefore seemed greatly to displease him.

Life brought Genji trouble upon trouble, but thanks to his secret understanding with Oborozukiyo, the two were not wholly parted, despite the risk. Genji saw His Majesty enter seclusion at the start of a Five Altar Rite[31] and immediately met her in what, as always, seemed a dream. Chūnagon managed to lead them undetected into the hall they remembered so well. There were many people about at the time, and they were frightened to be so near the veranda. She cannot have been indifferent to him, for he never wearied even those who saw him day in and day out. She herself was in full womanly bloom, and despite perhaps a certain want of gravity, the delightful youth and grace of her looks made her thoroughly desirable.

It must have been nearly dawn when a man cleared his throat directly beside them and cried, "Present at your service, my lord!" Genji gathered that another Palace Guards officer was concealed nearby and that some wag among his colleagues had sent the fellow to report.[32] He was amused but also upset. They heard the fellow hunting his superior high and low and calling, "Hour of the Tiger, first quarter!"[33]

> "My own heart alone explains the many reasons why I wet my sleeves,
> when cockcrow warns me of dawn and of your drifting away,"[34]

she said, lovely in her frail distress.

Genji replied,

> "Do you mean to say I must live my life this way amid endless sighs?
> There will never come a dawn when you do not have my heart."

31. *Godan mizuhō*, an elaborate protective rite to ward off misfortune and promote vital force. It was performed by five officiants before altars to the deity Fudō and his four directional, protector deities.
32. During the first half of the night the Left Palace Guards were on duty, to be followed in the second half by those of the Right. This guardsman, jokingly sent to report to his superior officer (apparently occupied like Genji), would have announced his name as well. Genji, who commands the Right Palace Guards, knows him and for a moment fears that the man has been sent to *him*.
33. Roughly 3:00 A.M.
34. Her poem, like Genji's reply, plays on *aku*, "[day] dawns" and "be weary of."

He hastened away. With everything so beautifully misty under a dawn moon, the very thoroughness of his disguise made him incomparable as he passed—alas, without realizing it—the Shōkyōden Consort's elder brother,[35] who was standing by a shutter, a little out of the moonlight. Genji could easily have become a figure of fun.

This sort of thing sometimes led him to admire Fujitsubo, who kept herself at such a distance from him, but as far as his own wishes went, he often was more inclined to hold her discretion against her. She herself now felt too constrained and out of place to go to the palace, and she was upset that she could no longer see the Heir Apparent. Lacking anyone else to trust, she looked only to Genji in all things, and his failure to give up his unfortunate obsession often reduced her to despair. Meanwhile the mere idea that the Late Retired Emperor had noticed nothing terrified her, and in fear that some hint of the truth might spread at any moment, with grave consequences for the Heir Apparent (since she hardly cared what it might mean for herself), she commissioned prayers and used every device to stay out of Genji's way, in the hope that he would give up. In time, though, to her horror, he found his way to her after all, after plotting so deep a stratagem that nobody knew. It was like a dream.

He talked for so long that no one could ever repeat all he said, but she steadfastly withheld any response until sharp chest pains alarmed Ōmyōbu and Ben, her intimate gentlewomen, into giving her urgent care. Bitterness and despair so blinded him to all thought of past or future that he lost his head and failed to leave even when dawn was upon him.

In the confusion while anxious gentlewomen clustered around their stricken mistress, a distraught Genji found himself thrust hastily into the retreat.[36] Frantic women rushed to get his clothes out of sight. Fujitsubo was faint with anguish and in fact quite ill. Prince Hyōbu and her Commissioner of the Household

35. The identities of this Consort and her brother are unclear.
36. *Nurigome*, a completely walled room, continuous with the chamber, with hinged, double doors. It could serve as a sleeping room or for storage.

arrived, and Genji was aghast to hear them calling loudly for a priest. Not until the day was almost over did she revive. She had no idea that Genji was still shut up nearby, and her women were too afraid of upsetting her again to tell her.

She had moved to her day sitting room. Prince Hyōbu had gone, believing her now to be well, and she was nearly alone. Most of her women were discreetly out of sight behind curtains and screens, for she usually kept only a few beside her.

"How can we get his lordship away from here?" Ōmyōbu and Ben whispered to each other. "It would be too awful if my lady were to feel faint again tonight."

Meanwhile, Genji silently opened the door of the retreat, which was already slightly ajar, and came in upon Fujitsubo through the gap between two screens. The joy of so rare a sight started tears from his eyes.[37] She was gazing outside, thinking how unwell she still felt and how little time she might yet have to live, offering him as she did so a profile of inexpressible beauty. Fruit lay beside her in case she should wish to eat. The way it was arranged in a box lid[38] made it look tempting enough, but she had never even glanced at it. Absorbed as she was in anxiety over the course her life was taking, she struck him as touchingly frail. Her hairline, the shape of her head, the sweep of her hair—all in their lovely way recalled precisely the lady in his own west wing.

After so many years he had begun to forget how extraordinarily the two resembled each other, and this fresh reminder helped to console him. In noble dignity, too, they were indistinguishable, but perhaps because he had loved the one before him so deeply and so long, he saw her now matured to the greater perfection, and the conviction that she really was peerless troubled him until he stole in beneath her curtains and rustled his robe. It was he, his fragrance told her so. In fright and surprise she sank facedown to the floor. "At least look at me, won't you?" he cried, thwarted and angry, and drew her to him. She slipped off her dress robe to escape, only to discover with horror that

37. He has probably not seen her in daylight since before coming of age.
38. Fruit and nuts were often served in a writing box lid.

he had accidentally caught her hair as well, and with a sinking heart she knew the force of her fate.

The self-control that Genji had so fought to maintain now broke down. Lost to reason, he poured forth a thousand miseries and complaints, in a flood of tears, but she was repelled and did not even deign to reply. "I am not feeling at all well, and I prefer to answer you at another time," she said, but he pressed on with his endless recital of woe. Some of his words undoubtedly struck home. Not that all this had not happened before, but she so shrank from having it repeated that despite her tender feelings for him she managed to talk him past anything worse, until dawn broke at last.

Genji was ashamed to have willfully disobeyed her and sufficiently daunted by her dignity to seek to placate her. "I would do nothing I might regret," he pleaded, "if only I could sometimes tell you like this all I suffer." Love like theirs must be fraught with pain, and their feelings were beyond any comparison.

Both gentlewomen desperately urged him to go now that it was light. In dismay at seeing her half expiring, he said, "I would gladly die of shame to have you hear I am still alive, if it were not that this sin of mine will last beyond this life." He spoke from a disturbing reverie.

> "If there is no end, today and forevermore, to what severs us,
>   I wonder how many lives I shall spend in misery,"

he went on, "and my clinging will shackle you as well."

She answered with a sigh,

> "Leave me, if you will, burdened with your bitterness through all lives to come,
>   but know your real enemy is your heart, and yours alone."

The simplicity of her words was beyond all praise, but respect for her feelings and fear for his own situation now led him, dazed, to take his leave.

How could he have the face ever to appear before her again? To let her know how sorry he was, he did not even send her a letter. Calling on neither the Emperor nor the Heir Apparent, he shut himself up at home, where the thought of her cruelty kept him prisoner to the sad torments of longing until he fell ill, for the spirit was indeed gone from his body. He asked himself in misery why in life woe should only pile upon woe, and he resolved to accept these trials no more—only to remember how dear his own young lady was, how sweetly she depended upon him, and how impossible she would be for him to leave.

The aftermath still left Fujitsubo unwell. She gathered from the grieving Ōmyōbu that Genji had shut himself up at home and had sent no note. For the Heir Apparent's sake she feared that he might now have turned alarmingly against her, and that if he had had enough of worldly life, he might even act to renounce it. She at last decided that unless this sort of thing ceased, her name would soon be bandied about to her dishonor in a world that in any case brought her nothing but misery, and she preferred to give up a title that the Empress Mother (so she was told) felt should never have been hers in the first place. The memory of the Late Retired Emperor's exceptional regard brought home to her how profoundly all things had changed. She might be spared the fate of Lady Seki,[39] but she was nonetheless sure to suffer widespread ridicule.

These bitter musings on the hatefulness of worldly life decided her to reject it, but it so pained her to go through this change without seeing the Heir Apparent that she first went quietly to the palace. Genji always waited thoughtfully on her on the least occasion, but this time he pleaded indisposition to absent himself from her cortège. He saw to her needs as correctly as ever,[40] but those who understood felt very sorry for him.

The Heir Apparent had grown into a beautiful little boy, and the joy of seeing his mother again made him very affectionate, but although love for him shook her resolve, she perceived well enough that shifting fortunes had taken their toll and that little now remained of the court she had once known. The constant

39. Lady Qi (Japanese Seki) was loved by the Han dynastic founder, Emperor Gaozu. She and her son were killed by Gaozu's jealous Empress after his death.
40. By sending retainers and members of his household to help Fujitsubo.

threat of displeasing the Empress Mother made it perilous even to visit the palace this way, and there were indeed moments sufficiently awkward that fear for her son came to trouble her deeply.[41]

"How would you feel, Your Highness, if you did not see me for a long time, and then afterward I looked different and not very nice?"[42]

He studied her face. "Like Shikibu?[43] But how could you look like that?" he answered, smiling.

Alas, he was too young to understand. "Shikibu is ugly because she is old." She was weeping. "No, no, the thing is that I am going to cut my hair even shorter than hers and wear a gray robe like the priests on night watch,[44] and I shall not be able to see you nearly as often as I do now."

"But I shall miss you if you are gone that long!" His tears caused him to turn bashfully away from her with a sweep of his lovely hair. The older he grew, the kinder his eyes became, as though Genji's face had slipped over his own. Mild decay affected his teeth, darkening the inside of his mouth and giving him a smile so winsome that she would gladly have seen such beauty in a girl.[45] This distressing resemblance to his father, which was his single flaw, put her in fear of the world and its censorious gaze.

Genji missed him badly, but the wish to make his mother regret her cruelty led him to restrain himself, until concern that such idleness ill became him prompted him to set out on a trip through the autumn fields and, by the way, to visit Urin'in.[46] He spent two or three days in the hall of a certain Master of Discipline,[47] his maternal uncle, reading the scriptures and performing

41. In the palace she is treated with disdain, and she fears plots to depose her son. An early commentary cites the Han dynasty story of an Empress who poisoned the Heir Apparent while the Emperor was out hunting.

42. In a nun's short hair and sober habit.

43. Presumably an aged gentlewoman.

44. *Yoi no sō*: priests who performed rites during the night for the Emperor's health.

45. His mouth looks as though his teeth have been blackened like a girl's.

46. A popular temple north of the City.

47. *Risshi,* the first rung on the ladder of ranks held by the highest class of Buddhist priests.

rites of devotion, and while he was there he often felt very moved. All the leaves had turned by now, and he nearly forgot the City before the beauty of the autumn fields.

He summoned the most gifted of the temple monks and set them to debating before him. In such a place he spent the night absorbed in the vanity of all things, but toward dawn he again remembered her who to him meant suffering. Meanwhile the monks clattered about offering holy water beneath a lingering moon, scattering chrysanthemums and red leaves dull or bright—modest occupations, no doubt, but, he felt, sufficient to relieve the tedium of this life and of course to assure a happy prospect for the life to come. He kept thinking how dismally he was squandering his own existence. "All who call his Name, he will gather to himself, nor once cast them aside,"[48] his host slowly chanted in lofty tones while Genji asked himself in intense envy, Why not make this life my own?—only to be most ignominiously caught up in troubled thoughts of his darling at home.

He was rarely away from Murasaki for so many days, and he was worried enough to send her a flurry of letters. "I thought I might see whether I really could give it all up," he wrote, for example, "but time drags by all too slowly, and I am gloomier than ever. I still have more questions, and I am uncertain what to do. What about you?"

Even this from him, casually set down on Michinokuni paper,[49] was a pleasure to look at.

> "Having left you there, frailly lodged as a dewdrop trembling on a leaf,
> I am prey to many fears whenever the four winds blow,"

he had added with deep feeling, and his reader wept. On thin white paper she replied,

48. A passage in Chinese from the Kanmuryōju-kyō (Sutra on the Contemplation of Eternal Life), referring to Amida's vow to save all who call his Name.
49. A thick white paper of fiber from spindle-tree (*mayumi*) bark. Genji probably found this rustic paper more in keeping with his setting than the thinner, colored *torinoko* paper commonly used for such letters.

"Ah, when the winds blow, how the spider's thread that hangs on that fading leaf
quickly tangles, and my heart trembles lest it be betrayed!"[50]

That was all.

Her writing is prettier all the time, he said to himself, smiling with pleasure at how lovely she was. They corresponded so often that her writing looked very like his, though with an added touch of feminine grace. I seem to have brought her up quite nicely in every way.

He wrote also to the Kamo Priestess, Princess Asagao, since the breeze had so short a way to blow between them.[51] "Your mistress will never know how I have longed for her beneath these unfamiliar skies," he observed rather bitterly to Chūjō;[52] and to the Priestess herself:

"Far be it from me to offend the mighty gods, but your raiment now
cannot help reminding me of that autumn long ago.[53]

All I want to do, and foolishly, I know, is 'to turn the past to now';[54] yet I feel as though it should be possible . . ." He had written his letter, so familiar in tone, on green Chinese paper and attached it solemnly to a *sakaki* branch.

Chūjō replied, "Having so little to do I let my mind dwell on memories, and then, my lord, my thoughts often turn to you; but it really is no use." Her letter was long and thoughtful.

50. "I who have only you, with all your shifting moods and loves, cannot feel secure."
51. The wind figuratively carries messages, and Urin'in was near Kamo.
52. The gentlewoman through whom Genji corresponds with Asagao.
53. Genji seems to refer to a moment between himself and Asagao that the reader does not otherwise know about. "Raiment" conveys *yūdasuki:* cords of mulberry-bark fiber with which those in shrine service tied back their sleeves so as to busy themselves with the rites.
54. *Ise monogatari* 65, which expresses the wish to "spin" (as one spins thread) the past into the present.

The Priestess had written along the edge of a sacred streamer,

"Long ago, you say—what is it that happened then, that my raiment now
should arouse such memories and once more detain your heart?

More recently . . ." Her writing, which had no great character, nevertheless showed practiced skill, and her cursive letters[55] were nicely done. He was sacrilegiously stirred to imagine the bluebell now more richly beautiful than ever.[56]

The season, he remembered, was just the same as that sad time at the Shrine on the Moor, and in his deplorable way he reproached the gods for the strange coincidence. It was odd of him to have these regrets now, considering the years he had allowed to go by while he could have won her if he had really wished to. Asagao herself recognized his special interest in her and seems in her sporadic replies to have made little effort to discourage him, which was not entirely admirable of her.

All the monks of the mountain temple, down to the least of them, were pleased, because Genji's stay while he read the Sixty Scrolls[57] and sought help with perplexing passages seemed a bright reward for their prayers and a signal honor for their buddha.[58] Quiet reflection on the world and its ways should have discouraged him from turning home again, but the thought of one lady bound him, and he did not linger. Before leaving he generously commissioned scripture readings at the temple, bestowed gifts on all who deserved them—monks high and low and local mountain folk—and exhausted the sum of holy works. Ragged woodcutters gathered here and there, weeping,

55. *Sō*, cursive Chinese characters used for phonetic value in the *man'yōgana* writing style.
56. "Bluebell" (*asagao*) refers to the flowers that he once sent her and suggests, in context, that he then saw her plainly, hence that they were lovers.
57. The canon of doctrinal writings favored by the Tendai school of Buddhism.
58. The main image of Urin'in.

to see him on his way. Within his black-draped carriage he wore mourning,[59] so that one saw little of him, but the least glimpse showed that there was no one like him in the world.

Murasaki seemed to have grown still more beautiful during his absence, and on finding her so subdued and apprehensive about the state of his affections (for the undignified confusion of his feelings had no doubt been obvious to her), he was touched by her "fading leaf" poem and gave her more than his usual attention.

The autumn leaves he had sent her from the mountains were brighter in color than those from his own garden, and since he could not ignore the message of the dews that had stained them,[60] and deplored in any case his own prolonged silence, he sent some to Fujitsubo, ostensibly as a gesture of civility.

To Ōmyōbu he wrote, "I have been surprised to learn that Her Majesty is at the palace, but while I would not have her neglect the Heir Apparent, I have preferred not to cut short the days I had set aside for practice and prayer, and that is why you have had nothing from me for so long. Viewing autumn leaves alone reminds me of admiring brocade in the dark.[61] Please show Her Majesty these when you find the moment to do so."

They were indeed fine branches, and while examining them Fujitsubo noticed the usual tiny note. She paled, because her gentlewomen were watching, and she thought how hateful he was still to be pursuing her this way; surely they would wonder why so thoroughly tactful a man should suddenly take to doing this sort of thing. She was sufficiently annoyed to have the branches put in a vase and placed beside an outer pillar, and she gave him no more than a correct reply, confining herself to generalities and expressing her confidence in all that he had to say about the Heir Apparent. Her message conveyed her unrelenting vigilance, and he read it with bitter disappointment, but since he had always

59. For his father.
60. Autumn leaves are reddened by cold dews and rains (tears), so that especially bright leaves evoke intense, unhappy love. Genji thinks of Fujitsubo.
61. *Kokinshū* 297, by Ki no Tsurayuki: "Autumn leaves that fall in the mountains, with no one to see them, are like brocade in the dark of night."

done so much for her, he feared to arouse suspicion now, and he went to the palace on the day when she was to withdraw.

He called first on the Emperor, who was enjoying an idle moment, and they talked over old times. His Majesty looked very like their father, although he had an even sweeter grace, and his face was gentle and kind. They were extremely glad to see each other. His Majesty had heard of Genji's relations with Oborozukiyo, and he had noted signs of it himself, but he felt that the affair was after all not new and that since it had lasted so long already, they might as well continue to indulge their feeling for one another. He spoke never a word of reproach. After he had questioned Genji on a wide range of subjects, including passages of the classics that eluded him, the two began explaining to each other their love poems,[62] and His Majesty took this opportunity to observe how beautiful Akikonomu had been on the day when she set out as High Priestess for Ise. Genji then confided to him the story of that extraordinary dawn at the Shrine on the Moor.

The moon of the twentieth night rose at last,[63] inspiring His Majesty to observe that the moment called for music. Genji answered that he preferred to go and assist Fujitsubo, who was, he gathered, to leave that evening. "Our father charged me with looking after her, you see, and since she appears to have no other support, her welfare concerns me for the sake of the Heir Apparent."

"Our father urged me to accept him as my own son," His Majesty said, "and I try to keep an eye on him, but I do not see what more I can do. His handwriting and so on seem accomplished beyond his years; in fact, it is he who is a credit to me, for I do nothing well."

"On the whole he is very clever and behaves in a grown-up manner, but he still has far to go." Genji gave him an account of the young Prince.

As he withdrew, a certain gentleman, the son of the Empress Mother's elder brother, met the advance members of his escort,

62. That is, talking about their love affairs.
63. On this night in the ninth lunar month the moon rises at about 10:00 P.M.

who were discreetly clearing his path. A brilliant young man in high favor, he was on his way to his sister's in the Reikeiden.[64] He stopped for a moment and solemnly intoned, "A white rainbow curved across the sun; the Heir Apparent trembled."[65]

The shocked Genji could not very well reprove him. He often heard about the Empress Mother's alarming hostility, and he pretended to notice nothing, despite irritation that a close relative of hers should have such gall. He apologized to Fujitsubo for the lateness of the hour, having been in waiting on the Emperor until just a moment ago.

There was a brilliant moon, and Fujitsubo remembered how at such times His Late Eminence had called for music and shown a lively feeling for beauty. She grieved to see how much had changed, even if the palace remained the same. Through Ōmyōbu she sent her visitor,

> "Perhaps ninefold mists cut me off from all the world, for my longing goes
> to the moon so far away, riding high above the clouds."[66]

She was near enough that a glimpse of her, however faint, called up Genji's old feeling for her, and he wept, forgetting all the hurt that he had suffered.

> "The bright moon still shines as in autumns we once knew, all those years ago,
> but the mists that hide its light are a cruel trial to bear,"

64. An imperial Consort, a niece of Kokiden and Oborozukiyo, and a granddaughter of the Minister of the Right.
65. This *Shiji* passage insinuates that Genji, the Heir Apparent's protector, is plotting rebellion but will fail. A certain loyal subject plotted to assassinate the First Emperor of Qin on behalf of the Crown Prince of Yen, but Heaven revealed his plan by displaying a white rainbow that crossed the sun. (The sun stands for the Emperor, the white rainbow for weapons or warriors.) The Prince of Yen then feared that the plot would fail, as it did.
66. "Ninefold mists" are those of ill will who come between the speaker and the Emperor (the moon).

he replied. " 'The mists, like the heart,' they say[67]—it must have been the same long ago."

Fujitsubo did not wish to leave the Heir Apparent, and she gave him lengthy advice about what to do and what not, but she was disappointed to find that he did not take it all in very well. Usually he retired early, but he seemed to want to stay up until she left. She was especially touched to see that he refrained from begging her to stay, despite being indignant that she meant to go away again.

Genji reflected on that gentleman's pointed allusion and was moved by the prick of conscience to feel the world's censure keenly. For a long time he did not correspond with Oborozukiyo. The skies were promising the first early-winter rains when it was she who sent him word, for reasons of her own.

"While autumn wore on, bitter winds set in to blow, and I languished still,
your silence, and nothing else, pervaded day after day,"

she had written. He was not displeased that she should feel deeply enough in this saddest of seasons to contrive a secret note, so he had the messenger wait, opened the cabinet where he kept his Chinese paper, chose a particularly fine sheet, and prepared his brush with great care. The gentlewomen present nudged each other and wondered who the lady could be, for his every gesture was a lover's.

"I gave up once I understood that no correspondence with you could lead further," he wrote. "And while I suffered on,[68]

Are my tears to you, wept in longing memory while we do not meet,
no more than the common rain shed by early-winter skies?

67. In an otherwise unknown poem cited by an early commentary (*Genji monogatari kochūshakusho in'yō waka* 464), the speaker compares the mists that hide a distant cherry tree to the cruel heart of one who keeps lover from beloved.
68. *Gosenshū* 1260: "While I who hardly count only suffer on, it has been so long that even I am missed."

If only we were really in touch, how easily we might forget this dreary rain!" It had become quite a passionate letter. A good many ladies must have claimed his attention this way, and he made sure that his replies were not discouraging, although he felt deep attachment for none.

Fujitsubo was variously occupied with preparations for her Rite of the Eight Discourses,[69] which was to follow the anniversary observances for the Late Retired Emperor. A heavy snow fell on the anniversary day, early in the eleventh month. From Genji she had this:

> "That unhappy day when he was taken from us has come round once more,
>   but when shall we see again the man we once knew so well?"

Today was so sad for her, too, that he had a reply:

> "Living on this way is a burden while it lasts, but to meet again
>   this day among all others makes him seem present once more."

She had made no effort to dress up her writing, but to him it certainly conveyed supreme distinction. Although not strikingly unusual or fashionable, it resembled no one else's. He quelled his thoughts of her today and gave himself up to offices of prayer, wet with drops from the evocative snow.

The Eight Discourses were held a little past the tenth of the twelfth month. It was an imposing event. By Fujitsubo's order the scripture scrolls dedicated each day, with their jade rollers, their silk gauze covers, and their beautifully decorated wrapping, were more splendid than any ever seen before. Since even as a matter of common practice she made it a point to do things exceptionally well, her arrangements this time were obviously a marvel. The altar furnishings and the very

69. Mi-hakō, a four-day rite celebrating the Lotus Sutra. Each day a formal debate, held in morning and afternoon sessions, developed the content of two of the sutra's eight scrolls.

cloths on the altar tables brought to mind thoughts of paradise.

The first day was dedicated to the former Emperor, the donor's father, the second to the Empress her mother, and the third to the Late Retired Emperor. On the day for the Fifth Scroll[70] the senior nobles overcame their fear of giving offense[71] and attended the rite in great numbers. Fujitsubo had chosen the day's Lecturer so well that the familiar passages, beginning with the one about gathering firewood and so on, were profoundly inspiring.[72] The Princes in the procession bore offerings of many kinds,[73] but those prepared by Genji far surpassed the others. Perhaps I seem only to repeat the same praises about him, but I cannot help it, because he was a wonder to behold whenever one had the good fortune to do so.

Fujitsubo reserved the last day's merit for herself, and everyone was astonished when she had it announced to the Buddha that she would renounce the world. Prince Hyōbu and Genji were both aghast. His Highness went in to her halfway through. After insisting that her mind was made up, she summoned the Abbot of the Mountain, and when the rite was over, she had him informed that she wished to receive the appropriate Precepts.

A commotion spread when the Abbot, her uncle, approached and cut off her hair,[74] and her residence filled with loud weeping. It is strangely moving whenever anyone, however insignificant and however obviously old, takes the great step of leaving the world, and that so great a lady should do so without having ever hinted at her plan gave her brother still more reason for ceaseless tears. Those present had found the rite itself sufficiently stirring, and they all left with wet sleeves.

70. A key scroll, expounded during the morning session on the third day.
71. Offense to the Kokiden Consort and to the Minister of the Right.
72. The Lecturer (Kōji) was central to each day's debate. The sutra's "Devadatta" chapter describes how the Buddha served his teacher by picking fruit, drawing water, and gathering firewood, until he received the Lotus Sutra teaching.
73. The assembly probably moved in procession around the garden lake (assimilating it to the lake in paradise) while bearing bundles of firewood, buckets of water, and offerings attached to artificial gold or silver branches.
74. To just past shoulder length.

The Late Retired Emperor's sons felt even sorrier for her when they recalled her better days, and each gave her a message of sympathy. Genji stayed behind, at a loss for what to say and in a state of dark confusion, but he went to her after the Princes had left, since people were sure to wonder otherwise what had come over him.

The household was quiet at last, and the women were clustered here and there, sniffling and blowing their noses. Brilliant moonlight on the snowy garden brought back unbearably scenes from days gone by, but he mastered himself sufficiently to ask, "What was it that decided you and made you so suddenly . . . ?"

She replied through Ōmyōbu, as always, "There was nothing abrupt about my decision, but I knew that it would cause a stir, and I was afraid I might falter."

Genji divined her presence behind the blinds, caught a rustling of silks from the women waiting on her as they moved quietly about, and was touched, although not surprised, to gather from certain other sounds that their grief had not yet abated. Outside, the wild wind blew, but within her blinds the air was fragrant with her intense, "deep black" scent[75] and with a trace of her altar incense. Genji's own fragrance mingled so beautifully with both that one could think only of paradise.

A messenger came from the Heir Apparent. The memory of talking with her son so shook her fortitude that she could not answer, and it was Genji who provided her reply.

The household was too agitated for him to be able to tell her all he wished.

> "Though I, too, aspire to give my heart to those skies where a clear moon shines,
> I should only wander still in the darkness of this world,"[76]

he said; "I so wish it were possible, but alas . . . I envy you your decision!" That was the best he could do, while she, with

75. *Kurobō*, a blend of six incenses used to scent clothing, especially in winter.
76. Both Genji and Fujitsubo (below) allude by a discreet wordplay to their child, the Heir Apparent.

her women nearby, could convey nothing to him of her own suffering.

Her heart was very full.

"What I have renounced covers the common troubles that beset us all,

but, ah, when will even I truly give up all the world?

Its worries are still mine," she answered, some of what she said having no doubt been tidied up by her messenger. Genji withdrew sick at heart, in thrall to boundless sorrow.

At home again he lay down alone in his own room, but his eyes would not close, and each time disgust with the world invaded him, he was assailed by anxiety for the Heir Apparent. It had been his father's wish to have the young Prince's mother, at least, uphold her son's dignity before all, but now that her unhappiness had led her so far, she could never reclaim her former rank; and what if he, too, were to abandon him? So ran the thoughts that kept him wakeful hour after hour.

He wanted her to have the furnishings for her new life from him, and he therefore hastened to have them ready before the end of the year. His generosity included Ōmyōbu as well, since she had taken vows with her mistress. A full account of all this seems not to have reached me; there would have been just too much to tell. That is a shame, though, because this is just the sort of occasion that may yield fine poetry.

Genji could now call on Fujitsubo more openly than before, and at times he even spoke to her in person. Not that that secret yearning had left him, but what he desired was even less possible now.

The New Year had come, and with it new life to the court, but news of the privy banquet and the mumming only confirmed Fujitsubo in her present solitude, and while she went quietly about her litanies and prayers, keeping her thoughts on the life to come, she felt as though she was putting behind her at last all that had so troubled her before. Apart from the chapel that had always been hers she had built another specially, south of her west wing, and she now moved to this rather isolated retreat in order to pursue her intent devotions.

It was there that Genji visited her. The breath of the New
Year had not touched her silent, all but deserted dwelling, where
one now encountered no more than a few faithful members of
the Empress's household,[77] their heads bowed and to all appearances sadly downcast. Only the Blue Roans came round as
usual,[78] and her women went to see them. No wonder the senior
nobles, who once had flocked to her, now took another path to
gather at the residence across the avenue.[79] This did not surprise
her, but it was very sad, and the vision of Genji, who had come
all the way to find her—a sight splendid enough to be worth a
thousand callers—somehow brought tears to many an eye.

Her visitor himself seemed deeply affected, and after glanc-
ing about he sank into silence. In this new life of hers the bor-
ders of her blinds and the standing curtains around her were
blue-gray, and through the gaps between them he glimpsed
sleeves of gray or yellow:[80] a prospect that for him evoked only
greater depths of grace and beauty. "Indeed, a most discerning . . . ," he murmured,[81] pensively noting how the outdoor
scene alone—the thin ice now gone from the lake, the willows

77. *Miyazukasa*: members of the Empress's household staff (*chūgū shiki*) with
a personal tie to Fujitsubo or her family.
78. On the seventh of the first month, twenty-one horses, the sight of which
was held to ward off misfortune, were led before the Emperor, then before the
Retired Emperor, the senior imperial ladies, and the Heir Apparent. The custom was originally Chinese. They were blue roans up to Murakami's reign
(946–67), which corresponds to the present in the tale, but after that they were
white. This was the only New Year observance retained when an Emperor was
in mourning, which is probably why the horses went to Fujitsubo's residence,
too, even though she was now a nun.
79. That of the Minister of the Right, across Nijō (Second Avenue).
80. Blue-gray (*aonibi*) was normal for a nun; other possibilities were gray
(*usunibi*) or yellow (*kuchinashi*), worn here by gentlewomen who had taken
vows with their mistress.
81. "Indeed, she shows the same discerning taste as that imperial nun of old."
Gosenshū 1093, by Sosei: "Today I see with my own eyes the celebrated Isle of
Pines and, indeed, find dwelling here a most discerning *ama*." *Ama* in this
poem and the next means both "shore-dweller" and "nun." The Isle of Pines
(Matsu no Urashima) was in Shiogama Bay in northern Honshu. Sosei wrote
his poem on pine bark from the artificial island in the garden lake of an Empress who had just become a nun.

on the bank—kept faith with the seasons. He looked incomparably elegant as he did so.

> *"Now that I perceive a nun lives here, gathering sea-tangle sorrows,*
> *briny drops spill from my eyes upon this, the Isle of Pines,"*[82]

he said; and since her rather small room was given over to the altar, her low answer sounded quite near:

> *"Of the world I knew there remains no trace at all on this Isle of Pines,*
> *and it is a miracle any wave should come to call."*[83]

He could not stop his tears, and he said little else before he left, for the gaze of nuns who had renounced worldly ways embarrassed him.

"What an absolute marvel he has turned out to be!" the old nuns cried to their mistress in tearful praise. "When all the world was his and he had not a care in it, one wondered how anyone that fortunate could know much of life; but he is very thoughtful now, and almost anything makes him look so sad that one's heart goes out to him." Memories flooded through their mistress, too.

Fujitsubo's retainers failed to receive their due when the appointments list was announced, and to the bitter disappointment of many, promotions that should have come to them as a matter of course or as their patron's normal prerogative[84] were withheld. There was no reason why in her new condition she should lose her former dignity or be deprived of her established emoluments,[85] but that condition was nonetheless the pretext

---

82. "Sea-tangle sorrows" are *nagame,* "sorrow" and also a kind of seaweed.
83. The "wave" is her visitor, Genji.
84. A prerogative involving benefices that accrued to persons of Fujitsubo's standing through provincial sinecures awarded to their retainers.
85. An Empress normally enjoyed production and labor imposts from fifteen hundred households.

for the many changes that now came upon her. Despite having given up just such concerns, she was often pained to see her retainers in distress, as though cast adrift, but her one heartfelt wish was to have the Heir Apparent's accession proceed smoothly, even at the cost of her own ruin, and to this end she dedicated her unflagging devotions. Having a secret reason to dread the worst, she calmed her fears by begging the Buddha to lift her burden of sin from her and grant her forgiveness. Genji saw her feelings and understood them well. His own people often encountered similar disappointments, and he therefore shut himself up at home in disgust with the world.

The Minister of the Left was sufficiently upset by the change that now pervaded his own world, public or private, to tender his resignation, but the Emperor remembered how greatly his father had trusted this adviser, and how at the last he had commended him to his successor as an enduring pillar of the realm, and accordingly he considered him too valuable to release. Although he repeatedly declined to accept the resignation, the Minister stubbornly resubmitted it again and again, until at last he was able to withdraw to his residence. Now that single faction flourished as never before. His Majesty was left forlorn once the Minister whose weight steadied the realm had removed himself from its affairs, and the wise everywhere groaned.

The Minister's sons had all enjoyed the world's esteem and lived free of care, but now they were brought low, and the future promised Tō no Chūjō only gloom. Now and again he still visited the Minister of the Right's fourth daughter, but his poor treatment of her led her father to exclude him from among his favored sons-in-law. His omission from the recent promotions list, perhaps in warning, did not upset him unduly. With Genji himself idle and life so obviously treacherous in any case, his situation hardly surprised him; and in this spirit he visited Genji often, sharing with him both study and the pleasures of music.

Remembering how madly he had once set himself to challenge Genji, he now vied again with his friend in all things, however small. Genji commissioned the most imposing rites for the spring and autumn scripture readings, of course, but also for lesser, irregular occasions of a similar kind,[86] and he convened those Doctors who seemed otherwise to be idle, so as to pass the time composing Chinese poems, guessing rhymes, and so on.[87] In short, he took his ease, and instead of presenting himself for service at court, he amused himself exactly as he pleased, so much so that some must have begun talking very unpleasantly about him.

One lazy day of quiet summer rain, Tō no Chūjō turned up with a bearer carrying a suitable choice of poetry collections. Genji, too, had his library opened. After ordering a few rare and curious old volumes from cases never examined before, he discreetly called together those whose interests inclined them that way. The many present from the Academy and from among the privy gentlemen were divided at Genji's order into a company of the Left and one of the Right. The superb prizes on offer aroused intense competition. Difficult rhymes predominated as the guessing went on, and Genji's way now and again of proposing the right one when even renowned scholars were stumped made his exceptional learning plain. "How is it possible that he should have every talent?" everyone murmured in praise. "It must simply have been his destiny to be far better at everything than anyone else!" In the end the Right lost.

Two days later Tō no Chūjō gave the loser's banquet. It was modest enough, but the cypress boxes were handsome and the prizes varied, and he invited the same gathering as before to compose Chinese verses and so on. The roses below the steps were then just coming into bloom,[88] and in so mild a season, more peaceful than those of the spring and autumn flowers, all joined happily in music making.

86. In the palace and the great houses, solemn readings of the *Daihannya-kyō* were a regular spring and autumn event, but Genji seems to have added other, similar events of his own.
87. "Doctors" are the scholars of the Academy for young men of the aristocracy. "Guessing rhymes" (*in futagi*) involved guessing the rhyme words in a Chinese poem unknown to the contestant.
88. This phrase recalls two poems by Bai Juyi and evokes the mood of Chinese poetry. The steps led down to the garden from the main building of the Minister of the Left's residence.

One of Tō no Chūjō's sons, a boy of eight or nine who had only this year begun to frequent the privy chamber, sang and played the *shō*[89] prettily enough to attract Genji's delighted attention. He was the second son born to the Minister of the Right's fourth daughter. All the world had high hopes for him and treated him fondly, since he had his wits about him and was also pleasing in looks. When the music picked up a little, he gave full voice to a very fine rendition of "Takasago."[90] Genji took a layer from his costume and placed the garment over the boy's shoulders.[91] His face, flushed with unaccustomed excitement, gave forth a beauty beyond any in the world, and his skin glowed wondrously through the silk gauze dress cloak and shift, until the ancient scholars watching him from their distance wept.

"How I long for you, my lily flower!" the boy's song ended, and Tō no Chūjō gave Genji a cup of wine.

"All have longed to see those first blossoms this morning burst into full bloom,
yet I contemplate in you beauty just as great as theirs!"[92]

he said.

Genji took it, smiling.

"Those flowers in bloom this morning out of season, in the summer rain
seem to have drooped and wilted before their beauty could show.

I am not what I used to be, you know," he bantered, resolutely

89. An instrument, originally Chinese, consisting of seventeen slender bamboo pipes rising from a central wind chamber.
90. A *saibara* folk song in which a lover addresses a passionate appeal to his beloved.
91. A gesture of special appreciation. Genji has given the boy a gown, worn under the dress cloak.
92. Tō no Chūjō's poem quotes the song that his son has sung and even alludes to the roses described as "then just coming into bloom."

taking this tribute for tipsy civility, but Tō no Chūjō only reproved him and urged more wine upon him. As Tsurayuki warns,[93] there is no point in recording all the faulty poems spoken at such times, and I have therefore obediently and conveniently left them out.

In both Chinese and Japanese verse the guests pursued no theme but Genji's praise, and Genji, swept up in visions of his own glory, went so far as to declaim on his own behalf the line "The son of King Bun I am, King Bu's younger brother." It was a great moment, but what might he have said about King Sei? Perhaps that still gave him pause.[94]

Fujitsubo's brother, too, often called on Genji, and he played so beautifully that he made Genji a perfect partner in music.

Oborozukiyo now withdrew from court. Having long suffered from a recurrent fever, she wanted the freedom to commission healing rites. Her whole family rejoiced to find her better once the rites had begun, and meanwhile, in concert with Genji, she managed by hook or crook to receive him every night.

A stylishly engaging young woman in full flower, she was slimmer now because of her slight illness, and extremely attractive. Genji feared discovery because the Empress Mother was then at home as well, but as usual, danger only spurred him to pursue his visits in deep secrecy. Some gentlewomen must have noticed these goings-on, but they neglected to inform the Empress Mother lest they cause trouble.

The Minister of the Right of course knew nothing about all this when one night, just before dawn, rain suddenly came pelting down and thunder roared, alarming his sons and the Empress Mother's staff. People were everywhere, the gentlewomen

93. No such injunction survives in the works of the early-tenth-century man of letters Ki no Tsurayuki.

94. The Duke of Zhou declares in the *Shiji*, "The son of King Wen [Japanese, Bun] I am, King Wu's [Japanese, Bu] younger brother, and uncle to King Cheng [Japanese, Sei]. In this realm I am not to be despised." These figures are all sage rulers of Chinese antiquity. King Wen apparently corresponds to the Kiritsubo Emperor, King Wu to his son Suzaku, and the Duke of Zhou to Genji. If so, King Cheng matches the Heir Apparent, who is actually Genji's own son.

gathered nearby in terror, and the desperate Genji found no escape before daylight was upon him. There were enough women
even around their mistress's curtained bed to set his heart pounding. The two who knew were frantic.

When the thunder stopped and the rain let up, the Minister
went first to call on the Empress Mother. Then, while a sudden
shower drowned out the sound of his arrival, he stepped
abruptly up to his younger daughter's room and lifted the
blinds.[95]

"Are you all right? It was an awful night, and I kept thinking
of you—I should really have come round before. Has the Captain or the Empress Mother's Deputy[96] looked in on you?" he
rattled on breathlessly, and even in this crisis Genji could only
smile at the difference when the image of the Minister of the
Left sprang to mind. At least the man could have saved his remarks until he was all the way into the room!

In panic Oborozukiyo slipped out through her curtains,
blushing so profusely that her father assumed she was still ill.

"What is wrong with you? These spirits are a menace! We
should have kept those rites going longer," he went on, until he
was surprised to see a violet sash, which had emerged with her,
entangled in her skirts. There was also a piece of folding
paper[97] with some sort of writing on it lying by her standing
curtain. "Whose are these?" he said, startled to contemplate
what they suggested. "What are they doing here? Give me that.
Here, pick it up, and I'll see whose it is."

Only then did she glance behind her and see the paper, too.
What could she answer, when there was no hiding the truth? A
man of his standing should have seen her embarrassment and
restrained himself in consideration of her acute discomfort,

95. The Empress Mother is in the main house and Oborozukiyo in the chamber
of one of the wings. The Minister comes straight across the aisle room to the
blinds hanging between it and the chamber.
96. The Captain is one of the Minister's sons; the Deputy (Miya no Suke) is the
second-ranking officer in charge of the Empress Mother's personal staff.
97. *Tatōgami*: a general purpose paper, folded for convenience, on which gentlemen wrote notes or blew their noses.

even if she was his own daughter; but no, he was too hotheaded and irascible for that. Paper in hand, he peered past the curtain and saw, sprawled shamelessly within it, a young man who only now stealthily covered his face and moved to hide. For all his shock and outrage he could not very well bluntly require the young man to identify himself. In a blind fury he strode off with the paper toward the main house. Oborozukiyo, all but fainting, thought she would die. Genji regretted a series of pointless escapades that now was certain to burden him with widespread condemnation, but he did what he could to console her in her all too obvious distress.

Ever a willful man, incapable of discretion, her father had gained nothing from the passing years but the testiness of age, and he was not one to waver now. He laid his whole complaint before the Empress Mother.

"This is what has been going on, you see. The writing on this paper belongs to Lord Genji. All this began long ago and without my leave, but I forgave him, considering who he was, and told him I would accept him anyway,[98] but he turned up his nose at the proposal and behaved so badly that I was extremely displeased. Still, I dismissed it as fate and offered her to His Majesty after all, trusting him not to consider her tainted. In the end, however, the cloud she is under has kept her from being appointed a Consort, which is a very great shame, and this latest incident disgusts me more thoroughly than ever. This is what men are like, I know, but it just shows how despicable that Genji really is. They say he has the audacity even now to pursue the Kamo Priestess, and that he corresponds secretly with her and encourages certain suspicions, which is so obviously a risk not only for the realm[99] but for himself that no one can believe such lunacy of him; he seems to have the world in awe as though he were the paragon of our time."

The Empress Mother was even more vehement on the subject

98. As a son-in-law.
99. In pursuing Asagao, Genji violated a religious prohibition and so perhaps endangered the realm, for the Kamo Shrine protected the City, and the deity's displeasure might cause disaster.

than he. "My son may be the Emperor," she said, "but no one has ever granted him any respect. That Minister of the Left did not offer his precious only daughter to *him,* the elder brother and the Heir Apparent; no, he gave her to the younger, a commoner and a stripling not yet even of age. And when we were so hoping to send our girl into palace service, did anyone object to the ridiculous position this Genji had left her in? It seems everyone admired him so much that she is in service there anyway, even though our first plan for her failed, but I have still felt obliged to ensure that the poor thing could hold up her head properly, if only to show that miserable man who is who; except that now she has taken it on herself to follow her own secret inclination. What they say about the Kamo Priestess is undoubtedly quite true. Yes, there is every reason to fear for His Majesty, considering the way this man counts on the Heir Apparent reigning!"

Her father found this merciless tirade so painful that he wondered why he had brought up the matter at all. "At any rate," he said in an effort to calm the waters, "for the time being I would like knowledge of this to go no further. Do not tell His Majesty. Yes, she is guilty, but I suppose she is counting on his indulgence to escape rejection. Warn her in private, and I shall have to take the blame myself if she will not listen."

The Empress Mother's countenance nevertheless failed to lighten. She could not have Genji pointedly mocking and belittling her by brazenly invading her house while she herself was at home, so nearby, and this gave her a fine reason to set in train the measures to accomplish his downfall.

12
(ABRIDGED)

SUMA

SUMA
SUMA

Suma, a stretch of shore backed by hills, is now within the city limits of Kobe. *Ama* ("seafolk") lived there, and in poetry the typical *ama* was a young woman, a saltmaker, whose burning love was betrayed by the smoke from her salt fire. Suma was also famous as the place where Ariwara no Yukihira (818–893) was sent into exile. It comes to Genji's mind for this reason when he thinks of leaving the City.

The chapter is exceptionally rich in allusions to literature in Chinese, especially the poetry of two other famous literary exiles: Bai Juyi and the Japanese scholar-statesman Sugawara no Michizane (846–903).

Chapter 12 begins in the spring of the year that follows chapter 10. It ends in the spring of the year after that, when Genji is twenty-seven.

He faced mounting unpleasantness in a hostile world, and he knew that to ignore it might well provoke still worse. There was Suma, yes, but while someone had lived there long ago, he gathered that the place was now extremely isolated and that there was hardly a fisherman's hut to be seen there—not that he can have wished to live among milling crowds. On the other hand, merely being away from the City would make him worry about home. His mind was in undignified confusion.

He reflected at length on what was past and what was yet to come, and the effort brought many sorrows to mind. Now that he was considering actually removing himself from the world he rejected, a great deal of it seemed impossible to give up,

especially Murasaki, who suffered more with each passing
night and day. A day or two away made him anxious about her,
even when he had faith that "time once more would join them,"[1]
and she herself was forlorn; and now they despaired that he
would be gone for years and years and that despite their longing
to be reunited, life might play them false and he might be setting out for good. He therefore wondered sometimes whether
he should quietly take her with him; but it would be wrong
of him to bring anyone so lovely to so dreary a seaside, where
she would have no company but the wind and the waves, and
he knew that he, too, would only worry if he did. "Never mind
the terrors of the journey," she would hint, clearly hurt, "if
only I could be with you!"

*[Genji sets out on a round of farewell visits, mainly to
women. He spends the night with one of them.]*

At home again he found his own gentlewomen, who seemed
not to have slept, clustered here and there in acute distress.
There was no one in his household office; the men in his intimate service were no doubt busy with their own farewells, in
preparation for accompanying him. It amounted to grave misconduct for anyone to visit him, and to do so more and more
to risk reprisal, so that where once horses and carriages had
crowded to him, a barren silence now reigned, and he felt the
treachery of life. Dust had gathered here and there on the serving tables, some of the mats had been rolled up, and he was not
even gone yet. He could imagine the coming desolation.

He crossed to the west wing. Murasaki's page girls had
dropped off to sleep on the veranda and elsewhere, for she had
spent a sad, sleepless night with the lattice shutters open, and they
were only now bustling about getting up. He watched them
sadly, so pretty in their nightclothes, when otherwise he might
not have given them a glance, and he reflected that with the
years they would all drift away.

"I stayed very late, you see, what with one thing and another," he said. "You must be imagining strange things as usual.

1. *Kokinshū* 405, by Ki no Tomonori: "As the undersash goes two ways to
come round and join again, so I long for time again to join us."

I would much prefer not to leave you at all at a time like this, but now that I am going so far away I naturally have many urgent concerns, and I cannot be here all the time. The world is cruel enough as it is, and I could not bear to have anyone think me unkind."

"Strange things? Could anything be stranger than what is happening already?" She said no more.

No wonder she grieved more than anyone else. Her father was so distant that she had long loved Genji instead, and now fear of rumor discouraged him from ever writing or visiting, which shamed her before her women and made her sorry that he had ever found out where she was. She happened to know that her stepmother had remarked, "Her luck did not last, did it! She is accursed! She loses anyone who loves her, every time." This hurt her so badly that she then gave up all communication with her father. She really was in a sad plight, since Genji was all she had.

"If years from now there is still no pardon for me, I will bring you to join me, yes, even 'among the rocks,' "[2] Genji went on. "It would start unwelcome gossip, though, if I were to do so now. A man suffering his Sovereign's displeasure shuns the light of sun and moon, and it would be a serious offense for him to live as he pleases. I am blameless, but I know that this is the sort of trial destiny brings, and no precedent allows me to take someone I love with me; no, in a world evermore gone mad that would only make things worse."[3] After he had spoken, they slept until the sun was high in the sky.

Prince Hotaru[4] and Tō no Chūjō came. Genji put on a dress cloak to receive them: an unpatterned one, since he had no rank, but which by its very plainness showed him off to still better advantage. Approaching the mirror stand to comb his sidelocks, he noted despite himself the noble beauty of the

2. From *Kokinshū* 952: "Where could I live, among the rocks, that I should hear no more of the world and its troubles?"
3. Heian law allowed a man to take his wife into exile, but Genji seems to mean that no one had ever actually done so.
4. Genji's younger half brother.

wasted face he saw. "I am so much thinner now!" he said. "Just look at my reflection! It really is too hard!" She turned on him eyes brimming with tears. He could not bear it.

> "I may have to go and wander far, far away; yet, forever near,
>   this your mirror will retain the presence I leave with you."

> "Were it only true that the image may linger when the person goes,
>   then a glance in this mirror would be comforting indeed."

She was sitting behind a pillar to hide her weeping. The sight reminded him afresh that she alone, among all the women he had known, was beyond compare.

Prince Hotaru pursued their melancholy conversation until he left at dusk.

[Genji makes another farewell overnight visit.]

He put his affairs in order. Among the close retainers who resisted the trend of the times he established degrees of responsibility for looking after his residence. He also chose those who would follow him. The things for his house in the mountain village,[5] items he could not do without, he kept purposely simple and plain, and he added to his baggage a box of suitable books, including the *Collected Poems*,[6] as well as a *kin*. He took no imposing furnishings with him and no brilliant robes, for he would be living as a mountain rustic. To Murasaki he entrusted his staff of gentlewomen and everything else as well, and he also gave her the deeds to all his significant properties—estates, pastures, and so forth. As to his storehouses and repositories, Shōnagon struck him as reliable, and he therefore instructed her on their care, assigning her for the purpose a staff of close retainers.

He had never been attentive to Nakatsukasa, Chūjō, or other such gentlewomen of his own, but it was comfort enough for

5. Although most obviously by the sea, Suma is referred to as a *yamazato*, a "mountain village." Hills rise behind the shore.
6. Of Bai Juyi. Bai Juyi, too, took a *kin* with him into exile.

them to see him, and they wondered where they would turn for solace now. "I will certainly be back, if only I live long enough," he said, "and those of you who wish to wait must serve your mistress." He had them all, high or low, go to join her.

[. . .]

He managed to get a message to Oborozukiyo. "I am not surprised to have heard nothing from you," he wrote, "but I am sorrier and more disappointed than words can say now that I am leaving all my world behind.

> *Did the way I drowned in a sad river of tears that we could not meet*
> *set running the mighty flood that has now swept me away?*

I know when I look back that I must take the consequences." He wrote little, for the letter would have a perilous journey.

She was very upset, and the tears overflowed her sleeves despite her attempt at self-control.

> *"Ah, river of tears! The froth floating on that stream will vanish quite soon,*
> *long before the current runs laughing over happier shoals."*[7]

What she had written through her tears was very beautiful. He wondered whether he might not try to see her again after all, but then he thought better of the idea, and since she was surrounded by relatives who detested him and was herself keeping very quiet, he renounced any heroic attempt to correspond with her further.

The evening before he was to leave he went to the Northern Hills to salute his father's tomb, but first he visited Fujitsubo, since at this time of the month the moon would still be up at dawn. She seated him directly before her blinds and spoke to him in person. The Heir Apparent worried her acutely. The conversation of a pair so deeply engaged with one another must have been extremely moving.

---

7. "Shoal" (*se*) suggests also "change of fortune" and "lovers' meeting."

The sweet promise of her presence was what it had always been, and he felt a wish to chide her for her cruelty, but she would only have disliked him for it. He calmed the renewed clamor in his heart and said only, "There is one thing that comes to mind, now that a punishment so unforeseen has come upon me—one thing for which I still fear the heavens above. I would gladly give my life to assure the Heir Apparent's smooth accession." One could hardly blame him. Fujitsubo, who fully shared his feelings, was too moved to reply. He wept as he thought back over the past, making as he did so a vision of infinite beauty.

"I am going to my father's tomb," he said. "Have you any message for him?" But she could not immediately speak, and she seemed to be struggling to master her emotions.

> "The man I once knew is gone now, and he who lives bears many sorrows:
>   all in vain I left this world to live out my life in tears,"

she said. Their hearts were too troubled to allow their teeming thoughts to find voice.

> "When he went away, I discovered just how far grief and pain may go,
>   yet the sorrows of this life only rise and rise anew,"

Genji replied.

He left once the moon had risen, with a mere half dozen companions and only the closest servants. He rode.[8] Needless to say, everything was so different from his excursions in happier days that those beside him were very downcast.

One of them, a junior officer in the Right Palace Guards, had been assigned to his escort that Purification Day; he had been denied due promotion, barred from the privy chamber, and stripped of his functions, and that was why he was with Genji

8. In acknowledgment of his disgrace, rather than travel in a carriage.

now. The sight of the Lower Kamo Shrine in the distance brought that moment back to him. He dismounted, took the bridle of his lord's mount, and said,

> *"I recall the days when we all in procession sported heart-to-heart,*
> *and the Kamo palisade calls forth a great bitterness."*[9]

Genji could imagine the young man's feelings, and he grieved for him, since he had once shone brighter than the rest. He, too, dismounted and turned to salute the shrine. Then he said in valediction,

> *"Now I bid farewell to the world and its sorrows, may that most wise god*
> *of Tadasu judge the truth in the name I leave behind."*[10]

Watching him, these young men so enamored of beauty were filled with the wonder of his stirring grace.

He reached the tomb, and there came into his mind the image of his father as he had once been. Only ineffable sorrow remained now that even he, who had been beyond rank, was gone. Genji reported in tears what had befallen him, but his father's judgment remained inaccessible. Alas, what had become of all his parting injunctions?

Wayside grasses grew thickly by the tomb, which Genji had approached through gathering dews, and meanwhile clouds had covered the moon and the darkness of the forest weighed upon him. He felt as though he might never find his way back again. While he prayed, he shivered to behold a vision of his father as he had seen him in life.

9. The "palisade" (*mizugaki*) is the sacred fence around the shrine. The syllables *sono kami* ("then") mean also "(remember) that divinity (with bitterness)."

10. The Lower Kamo Shrine is in Tadasu Grove, a name homophonous with the verb for "ascertain the truth."

"*What is it his shade beholds when he looks on me—I, before whose eyes*
the moon on high, his dear face, hides from sight behind the clouds?"

[Genji sends the Heir Apparent a letter of farewell.]

No one who had laid eyes on Genji could see his affliction
without grieving for him, and of course those in his personal
daily service, even maids and latrine cleaners[11] he would never
know but who had been touched by his kindness, particularly
lamented every moment of his absence.

Who could have remained indifferent to him, even in the
world at large? He had waited day and night on His Majesty
since he was seven, he had told him no wish that remained un-
fulfilled, and all had therefore come under his protection and
enjoyed his generosity. Many great senior nobles or court officials were among them, and lesser examples were beyond
counting. Although they did not fail to acknowledge their debt,
they did not call on him, for they were cowed by the evil temper
of the times. People everywhere lamented his fate and privately
deplored the court's ways, but apparently they saw no point in
risking their own careers to express their sympathy, for many
of them disappointed or angered him, and all things reminded
him how cruel the world can be.

On the day, he talked quietly with Murasaki until dark and
then set out late at night, as people do. He had kept his traveling
costume—hunting cloak and so on—very plain. "The moon is
up," he said. "Do come out a little farther and see me off. There
will be so much I will wish I could tell you! Somehow, you
know, I have no peace when I am away from you only a day or
two." He rolled up the blinds and beckoned her out to the edge
of the aisle. Dissolved in tears, she paused before she slipped
out to sit like a lovely vision in the moonlight. What would become of her once he was gone from the dreary world around
them? The matter desperately worried him, but in her present
state he only feared to upset her more.

11. Men used outside latrines and women chamber pots.

"Even while alive, people may yet be parted: that I never knew,
even as I swore to you to stay by you till the end.

So much for promises . . ." he said, striving to take it lightly.

"I would soon give up this unhappy life of mine if that might just stay
a little while the farewell now suddenly upon us."

He did not doubt that she had spoken truly, and he could hardly bear to leave her, but he did not wish dawn to find him there, and he hastened away.

Her image was with him throughout the journey, and he boarded his ship with a stricken heart.[12] The days were long then, and with a following wind he reached his destination at the hour of the Monkey.[13]

Having never traveled this way before, even for pleasure, he experienced mingled desolation and delight. The place called Ōe Hall was sadly ravaged, for only its pine trees showed where the building had stood.[14]

"Is it then my lot even more than his, who left his name in Cathay,
to roam on and never know anywhere to call my home?"[15]

Seeing the waves washing the shore and slipping back to the sea, he murmured, " 'With what envy . . .' ";[16] and on his lips the old poem sounded so fresh and true that sorrow overwhelmed his companions. Looking back, he saw the mountains

12. He would have ridden to Fushimi and then taken a boat down the Yodo River to Naniwa (now Osaka), a day's journey. He probably "boarded his ship" the next morning at Naniwa, to sail the thirty miles westward to Suma.
13. Roughly 4:00 P.M.
14. It is unclear what this building was or had been.
15. An allusion to a Chinese poet (Qu Yuan, 340–278 B.C.) who also wandered in exile.
16. *Ise monogatari* 8 (section 7): "My heart so longs to cross the distance I have come: with what envy I watch the waves as they return!"

behind them melting into the mists and truly felt "three thousand leagues from home."[17] He could not bear the drops from the boatman's oar.

> "Mist over the hills may conceal my home from me, yet perhaps that sky
> my eyes turn to in longing is hers, too, beyond the clouds."

All things weighed upon him.

He was to live near where Ariwara no Yukihira had lived before him, with the "salt, sea-tangle drops falling as he grieved."[18] The place stood a little back from the sea, among lonely hills. Everything about it, even the surrounding fence, aroused his wonder. The miscanthus-thatched pavilions and what seemed to be galleries thatched with rushes were nicely done. At any other time a dwelling so novel and so in keeping with the setting would have delighted him, and his thoughts returned to pleasures past.

He summoned officials from his nearby estates, and it was sad to see Lord Yoshikiyo, now his closest retainer, issuing orders for all there was to be done.[19] In no time the work was handsomely finished. The streambed had been deepened, trees had been planted, and Genji felt to his surprise that he could actually live there. The Governor of the province[20] was another of Genji's familiar retainers, and he quietly did all he could to help. The place was lively with visitors even though Genji had just arrived, but he still felt lost in a strange land, for he had no

17. From a poem by Bai Juyi.
18. From *Kokinshū* 962, by Ariwara no Yukihira, the poem that provides the poetic authority for Genji's exile at Suma: "Should one perchance ask after me, say that, on Suma Shore, salt, sea-tangle drops are falling as I grieve." The "salt, sea-tangle drops" are Yukihira's tears and the brine that drips from those who gather seaweed along the Suma coast. Suma was known for its saltmakers, and seaweed was used in the saltmaking process.
19. Sad presumably because in the capital Yoshikiyo never had to speak to anyone as lowly as an estate official. One of Genji's men, he is the son of the Governor of the neighboring province of Harima, in which Akashi was located.
20. Settsu, where Suma was.

one with whom to discuss things properly, and he wondered how he would get through the years ahead.

The rainy season came as life began at last to take on a normal rhythm, and Genji's thoughts turned to the City: to the many there whom he loved, to Murasaki in her sorrow, to the Heir Apparent, and to his little son at innocent play. He sent off messengers. It was beyond him to complete the letters to Murasaki and to Fujitsubo, for tears blinded him. To Fujitsubo he wrote,

"How, then, fares the nun in her seafolk's hut of rushes at Matsushima,
these days when brine is dripping from the man of Suma Shore?[21]

Amid my prevailing sorrows, the past and the future lie in darkness, and, alas, the floodwaters are rising . . ."[22]

To Oborozukiyo he wrote, as always, as though addressing himself privately to Chūnagon, but he enclosed, "Now that I have such leisure to dwell on the past, I wonder,

While, all unchastened, I on Suma Shore still miss sea-tangle pleasures,
what of you, O seafolk maid, whose salt fire never burns low?"[23]

One easily imagines his passionate eloquence.
[. . .]

21. *Ama* ("nun") also means someone who lives from the sea; and Matsushima, like Suma, is poetically famous for its saltmakers. This wordplay therefore assimilates Fujitsubo's condition to Genji's own as a "man of Suma Shore."
22. The flood of my tears. *Kokin rokujō* 2345: "Because you are gone, my tears fall and fall, and the river will soon overflow its banks."
23. "I should have learned my lesson, even now I want to see you—would you want that, too?" The marine wordplays in the poem include even the hidden name of Suma. The chief play is on *mirume,* a kind of seaweed, but also "lovers' meeting." Genji likens Oborozukiyo, too, to a saltmaker.

In the City his letters aroused strong feelings in most of those who read them. Murasaki lay down at once, grieving and yearning, and she would not rise again, until the women in her service were at their wits' end to console her. An accessory he had favored in daily use, a koto he had played, the scent of a robe he had worn: these only recalled him to her now, as though he had passed beyond her world, with consequences so ominous that Shōnagon asked the Prelate[24] to pray for her. The Prelate did a protective rite for her and Genji, and he begged, "Oh, let her cease to mourn as she is doing and enjoy a life free from care!"

She made him nightclothes to wear while he was away. A dress cloak and gathered trousers of plain, stiff silk were so different and strange that the face of which he had spoken, the one "forever near in your mirror" (and indeed it was) was no comfort at all. It broke her heart to see a doorway he had come through, a pillar he had leaned on. She would still have been unhappy even if she had been old enough to have thought things over better and known more of life, and no wonder she missed him keenly, considering how close she was to him and how he had been both father and mother to her while she grew up. If he really had no longer been among the living, that would have been that, and she might have begun to forget, but although she knew that Suma was not far away, she could not know how long they would be parted, so that she had no relief from her sorrow.

Needless to say, Fujitsubo grieved, too, because of the Heir Apparent.[25] How could it leave her indifferent to ponder her karma from past lives? Fear of rumor had kept her wary all these years, for if she had shown Genji affection, the result might have been censure, and she had often ignored his own to remain impassively formal; but despite the world's cruel love of gossip he had so managed things in the end that nothing was said; he had resisted his unreasoning passion and kept the affair decorously concealed. Could she then fail to remember him

24. Murasaki's great-uncle, prominent in chapter 5.
25. She fears that the Heir Apparent's position may suffer in Genji's absence.

with love? Her answer was unusually warm. "More and more, lately,

> *Her every labor goes to firing dripping brine: at Matsushima,*
> *while her years go by, the nun heaps up the sad fuel of sighs."*

Oborozukiyo replied,

> *"She whose love this is, the saltmaker with her fire, dares not have it seen,*
> *and for all her smoldering the smoke has nowhere to go.*

I shall not repeat things that need not be said . . ." Her short note was enclosed in the one from Chūnagon, who vividly conveyed her mistress's sorrow. Some passages were so affecting that Genji wept.

The letter from Murasaki, her reply to a long and passionate one from him, was often very moving. She had written,

> *"Hold up to your sleeves ever wet from dipping brine, O man of the shore,*
> *the clothes I wear every night that watery road parts us."*

The things she had sent were lovely in both color and finish. She was so skilled at every task that he could not have wished for more, and he bitterly regretted not having her with him now that other absorbing affairs no longer claimed him and he should have been living in peace. Her image was before him day and night, and her memory haunted him unbearably until he quietly considered bringing her down after all, only to dismiss the idea again as hopeless and to aspire instead to erase his sins at least in this blighted lifetime. He went straight into continual practice of purifying fasting.

[. . .]

Oh, yes, in all the confusion I left something out. Genji had also sent a messenger to the Ise Shrine, and he had had one from there as well. The Rokujō Haven had written with great warmth. Her turn of phrase and the movement of her brush showed exceptional mastery and grace. "News of the conditions under which you are living, and which I can scarcely believe, leaves me, so to speak, caught in the night without a dawn;[26] yet I take it that you will not be away long, whereas I, deep in sin,[27] will speak to you again only in the far future.[28]

> Give thought when you can to the Ise saltmaker gathering sorrows,
>   you who are of Suma Shore, where I hear the brine drips down.[29]

Oh, where will it lead, this life that is so painful in every way?" It was a long letter.

> "Though I scour the strand at low tide on Ise Bay, there is not a shell
>   nor anything such as I can do in my affliction."[30]

She had joined four or five sheets of white Chinese paper into a scroll, on which she had written fitfully, as her sorrows moved her, and there was a lovely quality to the strokes of her brush.

The thought that he had turned against her in an unkind moment, when she meant so much to him, that he had hurt her and driven her away, made her timely letter especially moving. He felt so grateful and so sympathetic that her very messenger was welcome, and he detained him for several days to learn all about her life. The messenger was a young and most accomplished member of his mistress's household. In his present reduced circumstances Genji did not keep even a man like him too far away, and the dazzled messenger wept at his glimpses of Genji's beauty.

26. The (Buddhist) night of subjection to the passions.
27. The sin of doing no Buddhist devotions. At Ise, as at the Shrine on the Moor, contact with Buddhism was taboo.
28. When a change of reign occurs and the Ise Priestess returns to the City.
29. *Ukime* ("gathering sorrows") also means "harvesting seaweed."
30. The poem plays on *kai,* "shellfish" and "reward."

Genji framed a reply. His words are easily imagined: "If I had known that I was to leave the City in any case, I would have done better to follow you after all," and so on. Bored and lonely, he wrote,

> "If only I, too, had boarded the little boat she of Ise rows
> lightly out over the waves, and gathered in no sorrows![31]

> How long, languishing here at Suma on the shore, must I dream and mourn
> while the briny drops rain down on the seafolk's fuel of care?

I cannot get over not knowing when I shall speak to you again."

In this way he kept consolingly in touch with all his ladies.

[. . .]

Oborozukiyo was extremely unhappy to be laughed at, and her father, the Minister of the Right, who was very fond of her, made such strenuous representations to the Empress Mother and the Emperor that His Majesty reconsidered; after all, she was neither a Consort nor a Haven but merely a palace official, and besides, that lapse of hers had already caused her trouble enough. She gained His Majesty's pardon and could once more go to court, though even now her sole desire was the one who had claimed her heart.

She went to the palace in the seventh month. His Majesty, who still thought highly of her, ignored the vicious gossip and kept her constantly with him as before, now chiding her for this or that, now asserting his love, and he did so with great beauty and grace; but alas, her heart had room only for memories of Genji.

Once when there was music, His Majesty remarked, "His absence leaves a void. I expect many others feel it even more than I do. It is as though all things had lost their light"; and he went

31. A partial variation on a folk song: "The people of Ise are odd ones, and why? In little boats they row over the waves, row over the waves."

on, "I have not done as my father wished. The sin of it will be upon me." Tears came to his eyes and, helplessly, to hers as well. "I have no wish to live long, now that I know life only becomes more cruel as one ages. How would you feel if something were to happen to me? I cannot bear it that such a parting would trouble you less than another, more benign, does already. No, I cannot think well of him who wrote, " 'While I am still alive . . .' "[32]

His manner was so kind, and he spoke from such depth of feeling, that her tears began to fall. "Ah, yes," he said, "for which of us do you weep?" He continued, "I am sorry that you have not yet given me any children. I should like to do for the Heir Apparent as my father asked, but that, I am afraid, would only have unpleasant consequences." Those whose manner of governing offended him gave him many reasons to regret being still too young to have any strength of will.

At Suma the sea was some way off under the increasingly mournful autumn wind, but night after night the waves on the shore, sung by Yukihira in his poem about the wind blowing over the pass,[33] sounded very close indeed, until autumn in such a place yielded the sum of melancholy. Everyone was asleep now, and Genji had hardly anybody with him; he lay awake all alone, listening with raised pillow[34] to the wind that raged abroad, and the waves seemed to be washing right up to him. Hardly even knowing that he did so, he wept until his pillow might well have floated away.[35] The brief music he plucked from his *kin* dampened his spirits until he gave up playing and sang,

32. *Shūishū* 685, by Ōtomo no Momoyo: "What do I care for the future once I have died for love? My longing to see you is for while I am still alive."

33. A somewhat confused reference to *Kokinshū* 184 ("mournful autumn wind"), *Shoku Kokinshū* 868, by Ariwara no Yukihira ("wind blowing on the pass"), and *Shin Kokinshū* 1599, by Mibu no Tadami (the waves along the shore joining the sighing of the wind).

34. A wooden or ceramic pillow that Genji has turned so that it keeps his head higher than normal.

35. *Kokin rokujō* 3241: "With all the tears that fall upon the bed of one who sleeps alone, even a pillow of stone might well float away."

"Waves break on the shore, and their voices rise to join my sighs of yearning:
can the wind be blowing then from all those who long for me?"

His voice awoke his companions, who sat up unthinkingly here
and there, overcome by its beauty, and quietly blew their noses.
What indeed could their feelings be, now that for his sake
alone they had left the parents, the brothers and sisters, the families that they cherished and surely often missed, to lose themselves this way in the wilderness? The thought pained him, and
once he had seen how dispiriting they must find his own gloom,
he purposely diverted them with banter during the day and enlivened the hours by joining pieces of colored paper to write poems on, or immersed himself in painting on fine Chinese silk,
which yielded very handsome panels for screens. He had once
heard a description of this sea and these mountains and had
imagined them from afar; and now that they were before him,
he painted a set of incomparable views of an exceptionally
lovely shore.

"How nice it would be to call in Chieda and Tsunenori, who
they say are the best artists of our time, and have them make
these up into finished paintings!" his impatient companions
remarked.[36] He was so kind and such a delight to the eye that
the four or five of them forgot their cares and found his intimate
service a pleasure.

One lovely twilight, with the near garden in riotous bloom,
Genji stepped onto a gallery that gave him a view of the sea,
and such was the supernal grace of his motionless figure that he
seemed in that setting not to be of this world at all. Over soft
white silk twill and aster[37] he wore a dress cloak of deep blue,
its sash only very casually tied; and his voice slowly chanting

36. A painter named Tsunenori lived in the time of Emperor Murakami
(reigned 946–67), and perhaps a Chieda did, too. Genji's paintings (in ink
only) would serve these artists as *shitagaki* (design sketches) for finished paintings in color.
37. He seems to have on a shift of white silk twill (*aya*) and gathered trousers
of *shion* color.

"I, a disciple of the Buddha Shakyamuni . . ."[38] was more beautiful than any they had ever heard before. From boats rowing by at sea came a chorus of singing voices. With a pang he watched them, dim in the offing, like little birds borne on the waters, and sank into a reverie as cries from lines of geese on high mingled with the creaking of oars, until tears welled forth, and he brushed them away with a hand so gracefully pale against the black of his rosary that the young gentlemen pining for their sweethearts at home were all consoled.

"Are these first wild geese fellows of all those I love, that their cries aloft
on their flight across the sky should stir in me such sorrow?"

Genji said.
 Then Yoshikiyo:

"How all in a line one memory on the next streams across the mind,
though the wild geese never were friends of mine in that far world."

Koremitsu:

"The wild geese that cry, abandoning of their own will their eternal home,
must find their thoughts returning to that world beyond the clouds."

The Right Palace Guards officer:

"The wild geese that leave their eternal home to fly high across the sky
surely find it comforting at least not to lag behind."

38. Words likely to begin a Buddhist prayer or the chanting of a sacred text.

What would happen to one that lost its companions?" His father[39] had gone down to Hitachi as Deputy Governor, but he had come with Genji instead. At heart he was probably in despair, but he put up a brave show of unconcern.

Genji remembered when a brilliant moon rose that tonight was the fifteenth of the month.[40] He longed for the music at the palace, and the thought of all his ladies with their eyes to the heavens moved him to gaze up at the face of the moon. "Two thousand leagues away, the heart of a friend . . ."[41] he sang, and as before his companions could not contain their tears. There came back to him with unspeakable yearning the occasion[42] of Fujitsubo's poem, "Perhaps ninefold mists," and he wept bitterly to remember his times with her. "It is very late," they said, but he still would not go in.

> "That vision alone comforts me a little while, though it will be long
> till time brings me round again to the city of the moon."[43]

Genji recalled fondly how intimately that night His Majesty had spoken of the past and how much he had then resembled their father, and he went in, singing, "Here is the robe he so graciously gave me . . ."[44] It was true, he really was never parted from his father's robe but kept it constantly with him.

> "Bitterness alone: no, that is by no means all I feel in my heart,
> for the left sleeve and the right, both, are wet at once with tears."[45]

39. The Iyo Deputy.
40. The fifteenth of the eighth lunar month, the great full moon night of the year.
41. A line from a poem by Bai Juyi (*Hakushi monjū* 0724), also written on the fifteenth night of the eighth month.
42. In "Sakaki."
43. The imperial city was poetically associated with the moon.
44. A line from a poem in Chinese by Sugawara no Michizane, written in exile. Michizane had received the gift of a robe from Emperor Daigo.
45. "I am angry with the Emperor, but I also miss him: hence bitter tears on one side, tears of love on the other."

[. . .]

As the days and months slipped by, many in the City, not least the Emperor himself, had frequent occasion to regret Genji's absence. The Heir Apparent, who naturally thought of him constantly, quietly wept—a sight that aroused sharp pangs of sympathy in his nurses and even more in Ōmyōbu herself.

Fujitsubo had always trembled for the Heir Apparent, and her alarm was very great now that Genji himself had been banished. His brothers the Princes and the senior nobles closest to him had all at first inquired after his health, but their affectionate correspondence with him, and the resulting evidence that he still enjoyed the world's esteem, drew strong words from the Empress Mother when she heard of it. "It is my understanding that one under imperial ban does not properly enjoy even the taste of food," she said, "and for him to inhabit a fine house, to mock and slander the court, and to have his flatterers spouting the same nonsense as those who, they say, called a deer a horse . . ."[46] Word of trouble spread, and for fear of the consequences Genji's correspondents lapsed into silence.

The passage of time brought Murasaki less and less comfort. When his gentlewomen from the east wing first went to serve her, they wondered what all the fuss could be about, but the more they knew her, the more they were drawn to her kindness, her pleasant manner, her steadiness of character, and her profound tact, and not one of them left. Now and again she saw the more senior ones in person, and they were not surprised that he loved her more than he did anyone else.

The longer Genji spent at Suma, the less he felt that he could bear it, but he kept reminding himself that since life there was hard penance even for him, it would be quite wrong to bring her there as well. Everything at Suma was different, and the very presence of the mountain folk, who were a mystery to him, constituted an affront and an offense. There was always smoke drifting past. He had assumed it was from their salt fires, but

46. The *Shiji* tells of an evil official who tested his men's loyalty by seeing whether they would agree with him in public that a deer was a horse.

now he found that it was what people called "brush" burning on the slope behind his house. He said in wonder,

> *"Ever and again, as the mountain folk burn brush on their humble hearths*
> *day after day, how I long for news of my love at home."*[47]

Winter came, and blowing snow. Eyes on the forbidding skies, he made music on the *kin* while Yoshikiyo sang for him and Koremitsu played the flute. Whenever he put his heart into a beautiful passage, the others stopped to dry their tears. His thoughts went to that lady long ago, sent off to the land of the Huns,[48] and he wondered what *that* was like, to send away one's only love; the thought was so chillingly real that he sang "A dream after frost."[49] Bright moonlight shone in, illumining every corner of his poor refuge. The floor afforded a view of the night sky,[50] and the sinking moon evoked such solitude that he repeated to himself, "I merely travel westward";[51] and he said,

> *"Where am I to go, wandering what unknown lands down what cloudy ways?*
> *Coming under the moon's gaze, I find myself filled with shame."*

While as so often he lay sleepless beneath the dawn sky, he was moved by the plovers' piping:

47. The poem is built on a play on *shiba* ("brush") and *shibashiba* ("often").
48. A Han Emperor was persuaded by a ruse to present the concubine he loved to a Hun ruler.
49. From *Wakan rōei shū* 703, a Chinese poem on the same theme by Ōe no Asatsuna. According to an early gloss, "a dream after frost" means the lady's dream of home, from which she wakes after a night of frost.
50. Probably because from there one could look up past the eaves. From *Wakan rōei shū* 536, a Chinese poem by Miyoshi no Kiyoyuki.
51. A line of Chinese verse written by Sugawara no Michizane as he went into exile (the speaker is the moon): "I merely travel westward: no banishment is this." The sentiment in Genji's poem also echoes Michizane.

"While into the dawn plovers flocking on the shore lift their many cries,
all alone I lie awake, knowing just a moment's peace."

No one else was up, and he said it to himself over and over again as he lay there. In the depths of the night he would rinse his hands and call the Buddha's Name, which to his companions was so wonderful and so inspiring that they never left him. They did not make even short visits to their homes.

The Akashi coast was close enough[52] that Lord Yoshikiyo remembered the Akashi Novice's daughter and wrote to her, but he got back only a message from her father: "I have something to discuss with you, and I would be grateful for a moment of your time." He will never consent, though, Yoshikiyo reflected gloomily, and going to talk to him would only mean leaving empty-handed, looking foolish. He did not go.

The Novice aspired to unheard-of heights, and although in his province an alliance with him was apparently thought a great prize, his eccentric mind had never in all the years considered a single such proposal; but when he learned of Genji's presence nearby, he said to his wife, "I hear that Genji the Shining, who was born to the Kiritsubo Intimate, is living in disgrace at Suma. Our girl's destiny has brought us this windfall. We must seize this chance to offer her to him."

"What an idea!" her mother replied. "According to people from the City, he already has a large number of distinguished women and he has in fact secretly violated one of the Emperor's. Would anyone who can start a scandal like that take any interest in a miserable country girl?"

The Novice was angry. "You do not know what you are talking about," he retorted with unrepentant and all too visible obstinacy. "I disagree. You must understand that. I will have to find a chance to bring him here."

The way he looked after both his house and his daughter yielded dazzling results.

52. About five miles away, across the border between Settsu and Harima Provinces.

"But why must we start out with our hopes on a man, however magnificent, who has apparently been banished for his crimes?" her mother objected. "Besides, even if he does take a liking to her, nothing can possibly come of it."

The Novice's only reply was angry muttering. "In our realm or in China, people who stand out or who differ at all from the rest always end up under a cloud. What sort of man do you take this Genji for? His late mother was the daughter of my uncle the Inspector Grand Counselor. When she became known as an extraordinary beauty, they sent her to the palace, where His Majesty singled her out for favor until she died under the burden of others' jealousy. Fortunately, however, her son survived her. A woman must aim high. He will not spurn her just because I live in the country."

His daughter had no remarkable looks, but she was attractively elegant and had wit enough to rival any great lady. Knowing full well that her station left much to be desired, she took it for granted that no great lord would deign to notice her and that no worthy match would ever be hers; if in the end she outlived her parents, she would become a nun or drown herself in the sea. Her father overwhelmed her with fond attentions and sent her to Sumiyoshi[53] twice a year. What he secretly expected was a boon from the gods.

At Suma the New Year brought lengthening, empty days, and the little cherry trees that Genji had planted came into first faint bloom. Such memories assailed him under those mild skies that he often wept. The twentieth of the second month was past, and he desperately missed those who had aroused his sympathy last year when he left the City. Yes, the cherry tree before the Shishinden would now be in its glory. Everything now came back to him: his father that other year at the party under the cherry blossoms, and the then–Heir Apparent's beauty and grace, and the way he had chanted Genji's own poem.

---

53. On the coast near Naniwa; the present shrine is surrounded by the city of Osaka.

"Never do I fail to call to mind with longing those of the palace,
yet today more than any, when I wore cherry blossoms."[54]

Life was very dull. Tō no Chūjō, now also a Consultant, was a sufficiently fine young man to enjoy great esteem,[55] but he still found the world a dreary place and missed Genji constantly, until he made up his mind that he did not care if he were discovered and charges were laid against him; suddenly he appeared at Genji's door. The sight of his friend aroused such joy and sorrow that tears of both spilled from his eyes.

Genji's house looked indescribably Chinese. Not only was its setting just like a painting, but despite their modesty the woven bamboo fence around it and its stone steps and pine pillars were pleasingly novel.[56] One could only smile before Genji's beauty, for he dazzled the eye in his purposely rustic blue-gray hunting cloak and gathered trousers, worn over a sanctioned rose[57] veering toward yellow, and all in the simple manner of a mountain peasant. He had kept his furnishings unpretentious, and his room lay open to view. Boards for Go and backgammon, assorted accessories, the wherewithal for *tagi*:[58] he had chosen everything to remain in keeping with country life, and Buddhist implements showed that he called the Name.

Genji made sure that their meal offered the delicacies proper to the place. The seafolk had brought a harvest of shellfish, and he invited them to come and show it off. When he had them questioned about their life on the shore, they told him of their perils and sorrows. Despite their impenetrable jargon[59] he

54. In chapter 8, when the Heir Apparent "gave [Genji] his own blossom headdress." The language of Genji's poem alludes to *Wakan roei shū* 25: "The denizens of His Majesty's palace must be at leisure, for all day long they have worn cherry blossoms in their hair."

55. His father, the former Minister of the Left, is out of power, but he is also a son-in-law of the Minister of the Right.

56. This description is derived from the poetry of Bai Juyi.

57. *Yurushi-iro no ki-gachi*: a color in the range of light pink.

58. Go and backgammon (*sugoroku*) are board games. *Tagi* seems to have involved skipping stones, rather as in tiddlywinks.

59. *Saezuru*, used for the song of the spring warbler, refers also to incomprehensibly foreign speech.

grasped sympathetically that their hearts moved as did his own, and that it must be so. He had them given robes, and in their joy they felt as though they had not lived in vain.[60]

Genji's horses were then led to a spot nearby and fed un-threshed rice from a structure, visible some way off, vaguely resembling a granary. His fascinated friend sang a bit of "Asukai,"[61] and they talked on amid tears and laughter about the life they had been leading. "His Excellency finds your little boy's utter innocence so sad that he sighs about it day and night," he said, and Genji was overcome. To repeat their whole conversation or even a part of it would be impossible. They spent the night not sleeping but making Chinese poems. Still, Tō no Chūjō was sensitive to rumor after all, and he made haste to leave, which only added to Genji's pain. Wine cup in hand, they sang together, "Tears of drunken sorrow fill the wine cup of spring."[62] Their companions wept. Each seemed saddened by so brief a reunion.

In the first light of dawn a line of geese crossed the sky. Genji said,

> "O when will I go, in what spring, to look upon the place I was born?
> What envy consumes me now, watching the geese flying home!"[63]

Tō no Chūjō still had no wish to go.

> "With lasting regret the wild goose knows he must leave his eternal home,
> although he may lose the way to the City of blossoms."[64]

60. The robes are a reward for the shellfish. This sentence plays on the word for shellfish (*kai*) and the business of diving for them (*kazuku*).
61. A *saibara* song: "You must stop at the Asukai spring, for you will have shade, the water is cool, the grazing is of the best . . ."
62. A line from a poem by Bai Juyi, written when a friend came to visit him in exile.
63. The motif of the departing geese (the departing friend) is from a poem in Chinese by Sugawara no Michizane.
64. The wild goose is Tō no Chūjō, who likens Genji to the "eternal home" of the geese.

The presents he had brought Genji from the City were superb. When they parted, Genji gave him a black horse in thanks. "This may be an awkward gift,"[65] he said, "but you see, he neighs whenever the wind blows."[66] The horse was a very good one.

"Keep this to remember me by," his visitor said, and he gave him among other things a fine flute of considerable renown, although that was all, for they exchanged nothing that might stir criticism.[67] By and by the sun rose, and Genji's friend set out in haste, with many a backward glance. Genji only looked sadder than before as he watched him go.

"When will I see you again?" his friend asked. "Surely this is not to be your fate forever."

"You who soar aloft so very close to the clouds, O high-flying crane,
look down on me from the sky, blameless as the sun in spring,"[68]

Genji replied. "Yes, I keep up hope, but men like me, even the wisest in the past, have never really managed to rejoin the world, and I remain doubtful; in truth, I have little ambition to see the City again."

"Forlorn in the clouds, I lift in my solitude cries of loneliness,
longing for that old, old friend I once flew with wing to wing,"

Tō no Chūjō answered. "I now so often regret, after all, having enjoyed the undeserved privilege of your friendship!" His

---

65. Since it is from someone in disgrace.
66. Genji's present of a black horse alludes to a story told in the *Han shu*, and the horse's neighing (whenever the wind blows from the direction of the capital) to a poem in the Chinese anthology *Wenxuan*. The customary gift to a departing visitor was called *uma no hanamuke*, a gift to "turn the horse's nose toward home."
67. Because too lavish for someone in exile to give or to receive.
68. "You who have the privilege of frequenting the palace . . ." The "clouds" allude to the place (*kumoi*, the "cloud dwelling").

departure was not easy, and it left Genji blank with sorrow the rest of the day.

On the day of the Serpent that fell on the first of the third month, an officious companion observed, "My lord, this is the day for someone with troubles like yours to seek purification"; so Genji did, since he also wanted a look at the sea. After having a space roughly curtained off, he summoned the yin-yang master who came regularly to the province, and had him begin the ritual. He felt a sense of kinship as he watched a large doll being put into a boat and sent floating away:[69]

> "I, sent running down to the vastness of a sea I had never known,
> as a doll runs, can but know an overwhelming sorrow."[70]

Seated there in the brilliance of the day, he displayed a beauty beyond words.

The ocean stretched unruffled into the distance, and his thoughts wandered over what had been and what might be.

> "Myriads of gods must feel pity in their hearts when they look on me:
> there is nothing I have done anyone could call a crime,"

he said. Suddenly the wind began to blow, and the sky darkened. The purification broke off in the ensuing confusion. Such a downpour followed that in the commotion the departing gentlemen could not even put up their umbrellas. Without warning a howling gale sent everything flying. Mighty waves rose up, to the terror of them all. The sea gleamed like a silken quilt beneath the play of lightning, and thunder crashed. They barely managed to struggle back, feeling as though a bolt might strike them at any moment.

"I have never seen anything like this!"

69. This kind of purification (harae) involved transferring disruptive influences into a doll that was then sent floating down a river or out to sea.
70. The poem plays on hitokata ("doll") and hitokata naku ("completely").

"A storm gives warning before it starts to blow! This is terrible and strange!"

Through their exclamations the thunder roared on, and the rain drove down hard enough to pierce what it struck. While they wondered in dismay whether the world was coming to an end, Genji calmly chanted a scripture. At dark the thunder fell silent for a time, but the wind blew on through the night.

"All those prayers of mine must be working."

"The waves would have drowned us if that had gone on any longer!"

"I have heard of people being lost to what they call a tidal wave, but never of a storm like this!"

Toward dawn they finally rested. When Genji, too, briefly dropped off to sleep, a being he did not recognize came to him, saying, "You have been summoned to the palace. Why do you not come?" He woke up and understood that the Dragon King of the sea, a great lover of beauty, must have his eye on him.[71] So eerie a menace made the place where he was now living intolerable.

71. Early commentaries observe that the Dragon King, whose daughter is famous in myth, desires a beautiful son-in-law.

13
(SLIGHTLY ABRIDGED)

AKASHI

AKASHI

Akashi, like Suma, is a stretch of shore backed by hills. It was then in Harima Province, while Suma, only five miles to the east, was in Settsu. The border between them divided Harima from the "home provinces" that were at least nominally under direct imperial rule.

Chapter 13 begins in the third month when Genji is twenty-seven.

It rained and thundered for days on end. Genji's miseries multiplied endlessly until his unhappy history and prospects made it too hard for him to be brave, and he wondered in despair, What am I to do? I will be more of a laughingstock than ever if this weather drives me back to the City before I have my pardon. No, let me rather disappear far into the mountains—although if they then start saying I could not take a little wind and a few waves, future generations will know me only as a fool.

The same being kept haunting his dreams. Day followed day without a break in the clouds, and he worried more and more about the City, meanwhile fearing miserably that he himself might well be lost; but no one came to find him, for the weather was too fierce to put one's head outdoors.

Someone from Nijō struggled through, though, barely recognizable and soaking wet. Genji's rush of warm feeling for the man, whom he might have swept from his path if he had met him on the road, wondering whether he was really human, struck even him as demeaning and brought home to him how low his spirits had sunk.

Murasaki had written, "There is never a lull in this terrifying storm, and the very heavens seem sealed against me, for I cannot even gaze off toward where you are.

How the wind must blow, where you are, across the shore, when the thought of you
sends such never-ending waves to break on my moistened sleeves."

Her letter was full of sadly distressing matters. Darkness seemed to engulf him as soon as he opened it, and the floodwaters threatened to overflow their banks.

"The City, too, takes this wind and rain for a dire, supernatural warning," the man said haltingly, "and I gather that there is to be a Rite of the Benevolent King.[1] For senior nobles on their way to the palace the streets are all impassable, and government has come to a halt." His none too clear account disturbed Genji, who summoned him and had him questioned further.

"It is strange and frightening enough that for days now there has been no letup in the rain, and that the wind has kept blowing a gale," the man said, "but we have not had hail like this, such as to pierce the earth, or this incessant thunder." His face as he sat there betrayed sheer terror, and their gloom only deepened.

At dawn the next day Genji wondered whether the world was coming to an end; a mighty tempest howled, the tide surged in, and it seemed amid the waves' furious roar as though neither rocks nor hills would be spared. Thunder boomed, lightning flashed with such awesome violence that they feared a strike at any time, and none of them remained calm. "What have I done to deserve such a fate?" they groaned. "To think I must die without ever seeing my father or mother, without setting eyes on my dear wife and children!"

With his companions in such panic Genji collected himself.

---

1. Ninnō-e, a solemn Buddhist rite performed in the palace for the protection of the realm.

Despite his conviction that no misdeed of his required him to end his life on this shore, he had many-colored streamers[2] offered to the gods and made plentiful vows, praying as he did so, "O God of Sumiyoshi,[3] your dominion embraces all these lands nearby. If you are a god truly present here below, I beg you, lend me your aid!"

His companions forgot their own troubles to grieve bitterly that such a gentleman should face so unexampled a doom. Those still somewhat in possession of their senses roused their courage and called out to the buddhas and gods that they would give their lives to save their lord's. "Reared in the fastness of our Sovereign's palace and indulged with every pleasure, he has nonetheless extended his profound compassion throughout our Land of Eight Isles,[4] and he has raised up many who were foundering! For what crime is this prodigy of wind and wave now to swallow him? O Heaven and Earth, discern where justice lies! Unjustly accused, stripped of rank and office, torn from his home to wander afar and to lament his lot dawn and dusk beneath cheerless skies, does he meet this dire fate and now face his end to atone for lives past or for crimes in this one? O gods, O buddhas, if you are wise, we beg you to grant this, our anguished prayer!"

Genji turned toward the shrine[5] and made many vows. He had vows made also to the Dragon King of the sea and to countless other divinities, whereupon the heavens redoubled their thunder and a bolt struck a gallery off his own rooms. Flames leaped up and the gallery burned. Everyone was struck witless with terror. They moved him to a structure in the back, one that he took to be the kitchen, where they all huddled, high and low together, weeping and crying out to rival the thunder. The day ended beneath a sky as black as well-ground ink.

2. Strips (*mitegura*) of paper or cloth in the five colors (green, yellow, red, white, black).
3. The Sumiyoshi cult was strong all along this coast. A patron of seafaring and of poetry, Sumiyoshi had a strong link with the imperial house.
4. A noble name for Japan.
5. Of Sumiyoshi.

At last the wind fell, the rain let up, and stars appeared. Mortified to see Genji so strangely lodged, they considered moving him back to the main house. "The remains of the fire are horribly ugly, there are all sorts of people still tramping aimlessly about, and besides, all the blinds have been blown away," one objected; and another, "We should wait until morning."

While they wavered, Genji pondered what had happened and meanwhile called in great agitation on the buddhas. The moon came out, and the high-tide mark showed just how close the tide had come. He opened his brushwood door and contemplated the still-violently lunging and receding surf. In all the surrounding region there was no one wise, no one familiar with past and future and able to make sense of these things.

The humble seafolk now gathered where the gentleman lived, and despite the strangeness of the jargon they spoke among themselves, one he found impenetrable, no one drove them away. "If the wind had gone on much longer, the tide would have swallowed up everything," they were saying. "The gods were kind."

"Despair" is a pale word for the listening Genji's feelings.

> "Had I not enjoyed divine aid from those great gods who live in the sea,
> I would now be wandering the vastness of the ocean."

He was so exhausted after the endless turmoil of the storm that without meaning to he dropped off to sleep. While he sat there propped upright, for the room was unworthy of him, the Late Retired Emperor, his father, stood before him as he had been in life, took his hand, and drew him up, saying, "What are you doing in this terrible place? Hasten to sail away from this coast, as the God of Sumiyoshi would have you do."

Genji was overjoyed. "Since you and I parted, Your Majesty, I have known so many sorrows that I would gladly cast my life away here on this shore."

"No, you must not do that. All this is simply a little karmic retribution. I myself committed no offense during my reign, but of course I erred nevertheless, and expiation of those sins now so absorbs me that I had given no thought to the world;[6] but it was too painful to see you in such distress. I dove into the sea, emerged on the strand, and despite my fatigue I am now hurrying to the palace to have a word with His Majesty on the matter." Then he was gone.

Genji, who could not bear him to leave, wept bitterly and cried out that he would go with him; but when he looked up, no one was there, only the shining face of the moon. He did not feel as though it had been a dream, because that gracious presence seemed still to be with him; and meanwhile, lovely clouds trailed aloft across the sky. He had seen clearly and all too briefly the sight he had longed for through the years but always missed, even in his dreams; and with that dear image now vivid in his mind he reflected wonderingly how his father had sped to save him from dire affliction and impending death, until he was actually grateful for the storm, for in that lingering presence he felt boundless trust and joy. With his heart full to bursting, he forgot in this fresh turmoil every grief of his present life, and dream or not, he so regretted not answering his father better that he disposed himself to sleep again, in case he should return; but day dawned before his eyelids would close.

Two or three men had brought a little boat up on the beach and were now approaching the exile's refuge. His companions asked them who they were. "The Novice is here from Akashi," they said. "He would be grateful to see Lord Yoshikiyo, if he is present, and explain."

Yoshikiyo could not get over it. "I knew the Akashi Novice well when I was in his province, and I talked to him often over the years, but then he and I fell out a little and have not corresponded for ages. What can have brought him here through such seas?"

Genji remembered his dream. "Go and meet him," he said; and so Yoshikiyo went to see the Novice in his boat. He could

6. Emperor Daigo (to whom Genji's father corresponds) was reputed to have suffered in hell for his misdeeds, which included exiling Sugawara no Michizane in 901. The monk Nichizō saw him there, "squatting on glowing coals," in a famous vision that Nichizō recorded in 941.

not imagine how the man had set sail so quickly through so violent a storm.

"In a dream early this month a strange being gave me a
solemn message that I found difficult to believe," the Novice
began, "but then I heard 'On the thirteenth I will give you another sign. Prepare a boat and, when the wind and rain have
stopped, sail to Suma.' I got a boat ready just in case, and then
I waited until fierce wind, rain, and lightning made me fear sufficiently for his lordship that I have now kept the appointed day
and brought him my message, though he may not heed it, because in other realms, too, faith in a dream has often saved the
land. An eerie wind followed my boat when I set out, and my
arrival shows how truly the god spoke. I wonder whether here
as well his lordship might have had a sign. I venture to hope
that you will be good enough to tell him."

Yoshikiyo quietly informed Genji, who considered the matter.
Neither his dreams nor his waking life encouraged complacency,
and in the light of these apparent warnings he contemplated
what was past and what yet to come. I do not want to risk
calumny from those who will eventually pass my story on, he
reflected, but if I ignore what may really be divine assistance, I
may, worse yet, become a mere laughingstock. One avoids
crossing even mortals. I should certainly have been more cautious in small things, too, and heeded those older than I am or
higher in rank and more generally respected. There is no blame
in yielding, as a wise man once observed. Just now I was in mor-
tal danger and witnessed disasters of all kinds. No, it hardly
matters, even if my name suffers in the end. After all, my father
and my Sovereign admonished me even in my dreams. Can I
doubt any longer?

He replied in this spirit. "In this wilderness where I am a
stranger I have suffered every outlandish affliction, and yet no
one brings me words of comfort from the City. Your fishing
boat is a welcome refuge,[7] when my only old friends here are

---

7. *Gosenshū* 1224, by Ki no Tsurayuki: "To one ever wet from the waves, a
fishing boat offers a welcome refuge."

the sun and the moon in their course across the sky! Could your shore offer me a quiet place to hide?"

The Novice was very pleased and expressed his thanks. "At any rate, my lord, do go aboard before it is day," Genji's men said to him; and so he did, with the usual four or five close companions. The same wind blew, and the boat fairly flew all the way to Akashi. So short a journey took hardly any time, but one could only marvel at the will of the wind.

The coast there was indeed exceptional, its only flaw being the presence of so many people. By the sea or among the hills, there stood on the Novice's land here a thatched seaside cottage for the pleasures of the seasons; there, by a stream that invited pure thoughts of the next life, an imposing chapel for his meditation practice; for the needs of this life rows of rice granaries replete with sufficient bounty from the autumn fields to last him through the fullness of his age; and, elsewhere, whatever pleasant feature the setting and the season might suggest. He had lately moved his daughter to the house below the hill, in fear of the monstrous tides and also so that Genji might freely occupy the mansion on the shore.

The sun slowly rose as Genji stepped from the boat into a carriage, and at this first faint glimpse of him the Novice felt age dissolve and the years stretch out before him; he bowed at once to the God of Sumiyoshi, wreathed in smiles. The light of sun and moon seemed to him now to lie in his hand. No wonder he danced attendance on his guest.

The setting of the house, of course, but also its style, the look of the groves, the standing stones and nearby garden, the lovely inlet—all would have required exceptional genius to do them justice in painting. This was a brighter and more welcoming place by far than the one where Genji had spent the recent months. The furnishings were superb, and the Novice did indeed live among them like the mightiest grandees in the City. In fact, in grace and brilliance his mode of life rather outdid theirs.

Genji rested and then wrote to the City. The messenger from home was still at Suma, bewailing the miseries he had had to endure on his hard journey. Genji summoned him and sent him back loaded with gifts beyond his station. He probably addressed a detailed account of recent events to favored monks adept at intercession, and to many others as well. It was only to Fujitsubo that he described his miraculous escape from death.

The deeply moving letter from Murasaki was too much for him to answer, and the way he put down his brush again and again to wipe his eyes betrayed intense feeling. "After surviving so long a catalog of horrors I want now more than ever to put this world behind me, but the face you spoke of seeing in the mirror is always present to me, and fear that this anxiety may be all I ever have of you is driving every other trouble from my mind.

How my longing flies, over what new distances, now that I have moved
far along that other shore to a shore I never knew!

All this makes me feel I am in a dream, and as long as I have not woken up from it, I wonder what nonsense I may talk." The lengthy, troubled wanderings indeed obvious in his writing were just what made them deserve a stolen glance, and his companions took it as proof of his supreme devotion. No doubt each had his own unhappy message to send home.

The sky that had rained and rained was now one perfect blue, and the seafolk seemed to be fishing in high spirits. Suma, where there was hardly a fisherman's shelter anywhere against the rocks, had been extremely dreary, and while Genji disliked finding so many people here, the spot offered such beauty that he felt a great deal better.

To all appearances the Akashi Novice was fiercely devoted to his practice, but he had one serious worry: his only daughter, who entered his talk with distressing regularity whenever he was with Genji. Genji had already noted her existence with interest, and he saw that his unlikely presence here might indicate a bond of destiny between them, but he intended only piety while still in disgrace, and he was so ashamed to imagine his love in the City charging him with broken promises that he betrayed no such thought to his host. Not that on occasion he did not avidly imagine the excellence of her person and her looks.

The Novice, who was afraid of intruding, seldom visited

Genji and confined himself to an outbuilding some distance off. Still, his only wish was to be with Genji from morning to night, and he redoubled his prayers to the buddhas and gods that he might somehow have his desire. Although sixty, he was still a fine-looking man, pleasingly lean from his practice and distinguished in temper, and perhaps for that reason his considerable qualities, as well as his knowledge of the ways of the past, sufficiently outweighed his vagueness and his eccentricities that his conversation helped to relieve Genji's tedium.

Little by little he treated Genji to tales of bygone days, ones that Genji had never really heard, having been taken up by his own affairs or those of the court; until Genji was sufficiently intrigued to feel at times as though it might have been a shame never to have come and met the man. For all the Novice's ready talk, however, Genji's courtliness daunted him, and despite his earlier tirades he was too abashed to bring up, as he longed to do, what he really had in mind. With many sighs he told his daughter's mother about his worry and disappointment.

As for the young lady, the sight of Genji in this desert where no one, however ordinary, seemed in the least presentable taught her at last that such a man could exist and made it all too plain where she stood herself; for she thought of him as far, far beyond her. When she learned about her parents' plans for her, they struck her as preposterous, and she felt more forlorn than ever before.

The fourth month came, and Genji got fine clothes and bed curtains for the new season. These ceaseless attentions oppressed and embarrassed him, but his host was so unfailingly noble and courteous that he let the matter pass.

A constant stream of letters arrived from the City. One quiet evening, with the moon still in the sky and the whole vast sea before him, he saw, as it were, the lake in his own garden, where he had always been at home, and with the island of Awaji looming in the distance an ineffable yearning seemed to fill all the world. "Alas, how far away . . ." he murmured.[8]

8. *Shinkokinshū* 1515, by Ōshikōchi no Mitsune: "The moon that on Awaji seemed, alas, so far away, tonight—it must be the setting—seems very near." The "setting" is the City, which was associated with the moon.

*"Ah, how grand a sight! The island of Awaji calls forth every shade
of beauty and of sorrow tonight under this bright moon."*[9]

He took from its bag the *kin* he had not touched for so long and
drew a little music from its strings, while emotion surged
through those sadly watching him. His full, masterly rendering
of "Kōryō" reached that house below the hill through the murmuring of the pines and the sound of waves, no doubt thrilling
the bright young women there. Here and there mumbling old
people who could not tell one note from another found themselves wandering the beach in defiance of the wind. The Novice
helplessly gave up his prayers and hastened to Genji's side.

"I think the world I left will claim me after all," he said,
weeping with delight. "I cannot help seeing tonight the land
where I pray to be reborn." Genji found his mind going back to
the music on this or that occasion—the koto of one, the flute of
another, a voice raised in song; to the praise he had received so
often and to the way he had been preferred and feted by one
and all, not least His Majesty himself; and to people he remembered and his own fortunes then. The present seemed so dreamlike that the strings as he touched them rang strangely loud.

The Novice could not stop the tears of age, and after sending to
the house below the hill for a *biwa* and a *sō no koto* he became a
biwa minstrel,[10] playing one or two rare and lovely pieces. Genji,
when pressed, played the *sō no koto* a little, leaving his host in
awe of his accomplishments. Even a fairly dull instrument may
sound splendid in its time, and these notes rang out across the sea
while depths of leafy shadow here and there surpassed in loveli-
ness spring blossoms or autumn colors, and a moorhen's tap-tap-
tap called up stirring fancies of "the gate favored tonight."[11]

9. Genji's poem alludes to Mitsune's (above) and repeats three times the syllables *awa* of "Awaji."
10. *Biwa hōshi*: a strolling musician in Buddhist robes, who sang to his own
biwa accompaniment.
11. The cry of the *kuina* (a kind of moorhen or water rail) sounds like someone
knocking lightly on a gate, and the hearer may think of a young man secretly
visiting his love. For this phrase early commentaries cite an otherwise unknown
poem (*Genji monogatari kochūshakusho in'yō waka* 120).

The Novice's sweet music on instruments so superb in tone delighted Genji. "It is on this instrument[12] that a charming woman's casual music is most pleasing," he remarked conversationally, to which his host replied with a curious smile, "Where would one find playing more charming than your own? For myself, I have my skill in the third generation from the Engi Emperor,[13] and being so hopeless, you see, and unable ever really to forget the world, I turn to it often when I am deeply troubled—so much so that to my surprise someone else here has picked up what I play. Her style recalls the Prince who taught me, unless my poor ears have simply misheard the wind's sighing among the pines. I wish I could discreetly arrange for you to hear her!" He was trembling and seemed on the verge of tears.

"For you, then, to whom my koto can be nothing . . . [14] I have made a great mistake," Genji said, pushing the instrument from him. "Somehow the *sō no koto* seems always to have been a woman's instrument. In Emperor Saga's[15] tradition it was his own Fifth Princess who stood out in her time, although no one has really continued her line. People who enjoy some renown nowadays play only desultorily, for their own amusement, and I am delighted that someone hidden away here should have kept it alive. But how could I possibly hear her?"

"I see no reason why you should not. You might even call her to play for you. After all, even among merchants someone once heard the old music with pleasure.[16] Speaking of the *biwa*, few

12. A *sō no koto,* the one the Novice has just been playing.
13. Emperor Daigo, whose reign (897–930) included the Engi era (901–23). The Novice would therefore have learned from one of Daigo's sons.
14. With "unless my poor ears have simply misheard . . ." the Novice apparently alludes to a poem cited in an early commentary (not included in *Genji monogatari kochūshakusho in'yō waka*): "He whose ears, because he lives in the mountains, are accustomed to hearing the wind in the pines, does not even recognize [the music of] a koto as [the music of] a koto." The Novice is modestly calling himself a hopeless rustic. Genji, with equally ceremonious modesty, takes him to have said that the sound of a koto means nothing to him because he is accustomed to the higher music of nature.
15. Reigned 809–23.
16. The exiled Bai Juyi described in a poem (*Hakushi monjū* 0603) hearing a woman play the *biwa* one night on a boat moored along a river. A former courtesan of the capital, she had then married a provincial merchant.

in the old days either managed to elicit its true sound, but she plays it very beautifully and makes no mistakes. I wonder how she does it. I am sorry to hear her music through the crash of great waves, but what with all the sorrows one has to bear, it is often a great consolation." His discernment delighted Genji, who gave him the *sō no koto* and took back the *biwa*.

The Novice did indeed play the *biwa* exceedingly well. His style was one no longer heard, his fingering was thoroughly exotic,[17] and the quaver he gave the strings yielded deep, clear tones. Though the sea off Ise was far away, Genji had a man of his with a good voice sing, "Come now, all to gather shells on the pristine strand!"[18] He often picked up the clappers and joined in the song himself, while the Novice took his fingers from the strings to speak his praise. The Novice called for most unusually presented refreshments and pressed wine upon his guests until the night soon became one to banish every care.

It was late. The sea breeze had cooled, and the sinking moon shone with a pure light. When all was quiet, the Novice poured forth his tale to Genji, little by little describing his plans when he first moved to this shore, his practice for the life to come, and, all unasked, his daughter herself. Although amused, Genji was often touched as well.

"If I may allow myself to say so, my lord," his host went on, "I believe that your brief stay in a land so strange to you may be a trial devised by the gods and buddhas in compassionate response to an old monk's years of prayer. I say this because for eighteen years now I have placed my trust in the God of Sumiyoshi. I have entertained certain ambitions for my daughter ever since she was small, and twice a year, in spring and autumn, we go on pilgrimage to his shrine. Quite apart from my own prayers for birth on the lotus,[19] in all my devotions through the hours of day and night I beg only to be granted my high aims on her behalf. It must be for my sins in lives past that I have become, as you see, a hopeless mountain rustic, but my

---

17. Reminiscent of the continent. The *biwa* came ultimately from Persia.
18. From "Sea of Ise" ("Ise no umi"), a *saibara* song.
19. In paradise.

father held the office of Minister. Yes, I myself now belong to the country, and I sadly wonder what life awaits those who will come after me if we remain this low; but I have had hope ever since she was born. I want a great lord from the City to have her, and that desire runs so deep that I have incurred the enmity of many and suffered much unpleasantness because of my pretensions. None of that matters to me, however. I tell her, 'As long as I live, I will do my poor best to look after you. If I go while you are still as you are now, then drown yourself among the waves.'" Between frequent spells of weeping he told Genji this and much else that defies a full account.

This was a troubled time for Genji, too, and he listened with tears in his eyes. "I had been wondering for what crime I was falsely accused and condemned to wander an alien land, but all that you have said tonight leaves me certain and, I may say, moved that this is indeed a bond of some strength from past lives. Why did you not tell me of what you have seen so clearly? I have been sickened by the treachery of life ever since I put the City behind me, and with only my devotions to occupy my months and days my spirits have sunk very low. Distant rumor had told me of such a lady, but I had sadly assumed that she would recoil from a ne'er-do-well. Now, however, I gather that you wish to take me to her. Her solace will see me through these lonely nights."

The Novice was transported with delight.

> "Do you know as well what it is to sleep alone? Think, then, how she feels,
> wakeful through the long, long nights by herself upon this shore!"[20]

he said. "And please imagine my own anxiety all these years!" Despite his trembling he did not lack dignity.

"But surely, someone accustomed to the shore . . .

20. The poem plays on *akashi*, the place name and "be awake through the night."

How traveling wears through the long melancholy of the wakeful nights
that keep a pillow of grass from gathering even dreams!"[21]

Genji's casual demeanor gave him intense allure and a beauty beyond all words.

The Novice talked on and on about all sorts of things, but never mind. Having got wrong everything I have written, I must have made him seem even odder and more foolish than he was. He was enormously relieved to see his hopes on the way to fruition.

Meanwhile, near noon the next day, Genji sent off a letter to the house below the hill. He was acutely aware that with her reputedly daunting standards the lady might be a startling rarity in these benighted wilds, and he did it very beautifully on tan Korean paper:

"Gazing in sorrow at skies so wholly unknown that near and far merge,
through the mists I seek the trees above your whispered refuge.

My longing heart . . ."[22] That may well have been all. The Novice was of course there already, eagerly waiting, and he plied Genji's envoy with astonishing quantities of wine.

When his daughter took a very long time to reply, he went in to her to urge her on, but she refused to heed him. Genji's dazzling missive so awed her that she shrank from revealing herself to him, and agonized thoughts of his station and hers made her sufficiently unwell that she had to lie down. Her father, at his wits' end, wrote it himself.

"Alas, your most gracious letter has proven overwhelming to someone so much of the country. She is too awestruck even to read it. Still, I believe,

21. This poem plays on *akashi* and also on words associated with clothing. The "pillow of grass" is a stock image for travel, while "dream" hints at sexual union.
22. *Kokinshū* 503: "My longing heart at last has bested me, though I had sworn never to show my love."

That your gaze like hers rests upon these very skies she has always seen
surely means that you and she are one also in your hearts.

But perhaps I am too forward . . ." He had written it on Michinokuni paper, in a style old-fashioned but not without its airs
and graces. Forward? Yes, thought Genji, mildly shocked. His
envoy enjoyed the gift of a splendid woman's robe.

"I know nothing of decrees issued through a secretary,"[23] he
wrote the next day.

"Ah, how cruelly I am required to suffer in my secret heart,
for there is no one at all to ask me, How do you feel?

The words will not come . . ."[24] He had made his writing very
beautiful. If it did not impress her, she must, young as she was,
simply have been too shy; and if it did, she no doubt still despaired when she measured herself against him, so much so that
the mere thought of his noticing her enough to court her only
made her want to cry. She therefore remained unmoved, until at
her father's desperate urging she at last wrote on heavily perfumed purple paper, in ink now black, now vanishingly pale,

"Your heart's true desire: hear me ask you its degree and just how you feel.
Can you suffer as you say for someone you do not know?"

The hand, the diction, were worthy of the greatest lady in the
land.

All this reminded him pleasantly of life in the City, but it did
not become him to write too often, and every two or three days
he would therefore seize the pretext of a languid evening or a
lovely dawn (moments likely to appeal to her as well) and soon

23. Decrees composed by a secretary at the Emperor's direction, hence answers
written by someone else.
24. From a poem cited in an early commentary, attributed to Emperor Ichijō:
"I am sick at heart, for the words will not come, to tell one whom I have never
seen that I am in love."

decided—since she was far from an unworthy correspondent—
that he did not wish to miss knowing someone so deeply proud;
and yet Yoshikiyo's possessive talk about her offended him, and
he did not like to ruin years of hope before the man's very eyes.
After some thought he decided to go further only when someone came forward toward him. Alas, she whose pride surpassed
the greatest lady's remained so maddeningly reticent that they
spent their days in a contest of wills.

Now that the pass[25] stood between him and the distant City,
he worried more and more about Murasaki there and wondered
what he really should do. Not having her was indeed no joke.[26]
Should he have her come to him in secret? His resolve wavered
now and then, but he told himself that he would not be there
forever and that in any case it would not look well if he did.

That year there were frequent omens and repeated distur-
bances at the palace. On the thirteenth of the third month, the
night when lightning flashed and the wind roared, the Emperor
dreamed that his father, the Late Retired Emperor, stood below
the palace steps, glaring balefully at him while he himself cow-
ered before him in awe. His father had much to say, and no
doubt he spoke of Genji. His Majesty described his dream in
fear and sorrow to the Empress Mother. "One imagines all sorts
of things on a night when it is pouring and the skies are in tumult," she said. "You must not allow it to disturb you unduly."

Something now went wrong with His Majesty's eyes, perhaps because he had met his father's furious gaze, and he suffered unbearably. Penances of all kinds were ordered, both at
the palace and at the Empress Mother's home.

The Chancellor[27] passed away, which was natural enough at
his age, but to add to this series of crises the Empress Mother
herself became vaguely indisposed, and she grew weaker with
time. Thus varied sorrows afflicted the court.

25. The *seki* ("pass," "barrier") mentioned in Yukihira's poem on the wind,
hence poetically associated with Suma and its region. Nothing is known
about it.
26. *Kokinshū* 1025: "When I do not go to see her, just to find out whether it is
true, I so long for her that it is no joke."
27. The previous Minister of the Right, the Emperor's grandfather.

"I do think there will be retribution, though, if Genji really is in disgrace when actually he is blameless," His Majesty would often remark. "I have a mind to restore him to his offices."

"You would gain no respect by doing so," the Empress Mother would strenuously insist. "What will people say if before even three years are out you pardon a man whose offenses have driven him into banishment?"

Days and months passed while His Majesty wavered, and meanwhile both his condition and the Empress Mother's grew worse.

At Akashi there was as always something new in the autumn wind, and Genji found sleeping by himself so horribly lonely that he now and then approached his host. "Do find one reason or another to bring her here," he would say; for he did not feel that he could go to her, and she herself showed no sign of encouraging him. She had heard that miserable country girls were the ones who foolishly surrendered that way to the flattering talk of a gentleman briefly down from the City. He could not possibly have any respect for me, she said to herself, and I would only burden myself with grief. I suppose that as long as I remain unmarried, my parents, with their impossible ambitions for me, entertain affectionately fanciful visions of my future, but I myself will only suffer for them. No, it is quite enough for me to correspond with him like this while he remains here on this shore. After years of listening to rumors about him she had never expected to catch the least glimpse of anyone like him where she actually lived, but she had nonetheless had a glimpse of him, she had heard on the wind the music of his koto, which was said to be superb, and she knew a good deal about how he spent his time; and the very idea that he should deign to notice her sufficiently to court her was simply too much for one whose life had been wasted among seafolk like these. Such were her thoughts, and the more embarrassed she felt, the less she could even contemplate allowing him nearer.

Her parents, who saw their long-standing prayer close to fulfillment, began anxiously imagining the grief that would follow, now that they had rashly given him their daughter, if he were to scorn her, for however great a lord he might be, that would be a bitter blow. Yes, they constantly fretted, we trusted the invisible buddhas and gods in ignorance of his feelings and of our daughter's karma.[28]

"I so long to hear her music against the sound of the waves we have had lately," Genji would often say. "It will be a great shame if I cannot."

The Novice quietly chose a propitious day, ignored her mother's varied objections, all on his own and without a word to his acolytes did up her room until it shone, and once the almost full moon[29] had risen in glory lightly remarked to his guest, "On so lovely a night . . ."[30]

You're a rascal, aren't you! thought Genji; but he put on a dress cloak, tidied himself up, and set out at a very late hour. His carriage was splendidly ready, but that seemed a little too much, and he rode instead. He took only Koremitsu and one or two others with him. It was quite a long way. From the path he looked out over distant stretches of shore, and the moon shining from waters dear to lovers of beauty[31] only recalled the lady he missed, until he felt as though he would ride on by and go straight to her.

> "On this autumn night, O steed with coat of moonlight, soar on through the skies,
> that for just a little while I may be there with my love!"[32]

he murmured to himself.

The house, a fine one, was magnificently situated deep among the trees. The mansion by the sea was curious and imposing, but here, he felt with a pang, life would be lonely and one would know every shade of melancholy. The bell of the nearby meditation hall rang mournfully while the wind sighed among

28. Karma that would in principle determine her marriage partner.
29. The moon of the twelfth or thirteenth night, two or three nights before the full.
30. *Gosenshū* 103, by Minamoto no Saneakira: "On so lovely a night, how gladly I would share the moon and the flowers with one who knows their beauty as I do."
31. *Genji monogatari kochūshakusho in'yō waka* 126: "Come, then, O lovers of beauty, to see the moon in the depths of the waters at Tamatsushima!"
32. A "moon-colored horse" (*tsukige no koma*) was a rose gray roan.

the pines, and the pines' roots gripping the rocks had a dignity all their own. Insects of many kinds were singing in the near garden. He looked carefully about him. The part where his host's daughter lived was done up with special care. The handsome door had let in the moonlight and still stood a little ajar.[33]

Her reluctance to expose her person to any liberties from him ran so deep that his hesitant tries at conversation met only mournful resistance. What airs she puts on! he thought. The most inaccessibly grand lady would have yielded with good grace after all this courting, but no, not she. Does she despise me, then, for being out of favor? He was annoyed and pondered varied misgivings. Heartlessly to force her would confound good sense, but he would gain no credit from losing a contest of wills. One would have wished to show him off in his trouble and anger to someone who really did know something of beauty. A ribbon on a nearby standing curtain brushed the strings of a *sō no koto,* which called up a pleasant picture of her playing alone for her own pleasure. "Will you not at least allow me to hear your famous koto?" he asked, multiplying his attempts to draw her out.

> "O for a dear friend to join me in the pleasure of sharing sweet talk,
> that I might perhaps awake from the dream of this sad life."

She answered,

> "How could I who roam the long darkness of a night unbroken by dawn
> even know what is a dream, that I should join in your talk?"

Her shadowy form was very like the Rokujō Haven's. Having been comfortably alone, thinking no harm, she now found the surprise too great a shock; entering the neighboring room, she

33. This partly opened door that has already admitted the moonlight and that will in a moment admit Genji himself was praised as sublime by Fujiwara no Teika (1162–1241), the great poet and scholar who edited the Genji text fundamental to most later editions.

somehow fastened the sliding panel so securely that he made no move to force it open. Yet that could not very well be all.

Elegantly tall, she had daunting dignity. It greatly saddened him to consider the contrived character of their union.[34] Now that he knew her, he surely felt still more deeply about her. The always tediously long night seemed to pass in an instant into dawn. Anxious to be gone before anyone should notice him, he left her with heartfelt assurances of love.

His letter came that day, very privately. Could he have been suffering, alas, from pangs of conscience? She did not wish anyone to know, and she gave his messenger no festive welcome. Her father could hardly bear it.

After that, Genji sometimes called on her in secret. Since her house was some way off, he restrained himself, lest gossiping seafolk turn up on his way, and this so sadly confirmed her fears that the Novice, too, in sympathy, forgot to long for paradise and waited only for signs of Genji's visits. It was a shame that his thoughts should be so troubled even now.

Genji suffered and smarted that Murasaki might somehow catch wind of all this and be hurt to imagine his heart straying, even in a flight of folly; which no doubt gave the measure of his extravagant love. Whenever she had occasion to note and, in a manner quite unlike her, to protest goings-on of this kind, he would wonder why he had let a silly amusement provoke her, and want to undo it all. The thought of the lady at issue this time therefore only aroused a longing that nothing could slake, until he wrote to Nijō more expansively than usual and appended this note: "I should add that although it is agony to remember how my foolishness has sometimes earned me your displeasure, when it disappoints even me, I have again strangely enough dreamed a little dream. Please understand from this unprompted confession how wholly I am yours. 'If my promise . . .' "[35] And he continued, "At each thought of you,

34. Contrived because he and she were brought together only by a highly unusual set of influences. Normally they would never have met.
35. *Genji monogatari kochūshakusho in'yō waka* 475: "If my promise never to forget you should lapse, may the judgment of the God of Mount Mikasa be upon me."

Salty streams of brine spring to his eyes and he weeps: the man of the shore
harvesting seaweed pleasures followed just a passing whim."

Her answer, written with engaging artlessness, had at the end, "The dream that you felt obliged to mention brings many thoughts to mind:

How innocently I let you have all my trust that once we were joined,
waves would never sweep across any height covered with pines."[36]

This hint, piercing through the mildness of her tone, so affected him that he could not put her letter down. The mood lasted, and he renounced the traveler's secret nights.

The object of his visits was not surprised, and now she really did feel like throwing herself into the sea. Lacking anyone but her aging parents, she had never expected to command the respect others enjoyed, but during the months and years that had drifted by, nothing after all had happened to cause her anguish. Now that she knew what cares life can bring, they seemed far worse than anything she had imagined, but she retained her composure and received Genji gracefully enough. She meant more to him as time went by, but he felt very sorry that a far greater lady should spend years of anxious waiting, tenderly thinking of him, and more often than not he slept alone.

He painted a varied collection of pictures and wrote his thoughts on them so that Murasaki could add her replies.[37] No one who saw them could have failed to be moved. Across the heavens their hearts must somehow have touched, for Murasaki, too, when excessively burdened by her sorrows, began to paint pictures of her own and to set straight down on them, as though in a diary, the telling moments of her life. What future did they have in store?

36. "That you would never be unfaithful." *Kokinshū* 1093: "Should I ever prove fickle and leave you, may waves wash over the pine-clad hill of Sue."
37. He wrote poems on the paintings, leaving room for Murasaki to add poems of her own.

The New Year had come, and to the court's loud distress His Majesty required treatment. One of his children was a son born to the Shōkyōden Consort, a daughter of the current Minister of the Right; but the boy was now in his second year and still too young.[38] His proper course was to abdicate in favor of the Heir Apparent, and when he pondered who might then govern in the service of the realm, Genji's disgrace so shocked and offended him that at last he ignored his mother's remonstrances and decreed that Genji was to be pardoned. The previous year the Empress Mother had begun to suffer from an afflicting spirit, and frequent oracles had disturbed the court, while recently the eye trouble that strict penances seemed to have relieved had worsened again, causing His Majesty such misery that after the twentieth of the seventh month he issued another decree recalling Genji to the City.

Genji had counted on this happening in time, although this treacherous world did not encourage him to look forward to what might follow, but the moment came so suddenly that his joy was mixed with sorrow at having now to give up this shore. The Novice, who wholly approved, still found his heart full at the news. He soon thought better of that, though, since the fulfillment of Genji's ambitions also meant success for what he himself desired.

By now Genji was with the Novice's daughter every night. In the sixth month she began to look and to feel sadly unwell.[39] Now that he was to leave her, he seemed unfortunately to value her more than before, and he was troubled to see her destined inexplicably for sorrow. Needless to say, she herself despaired, and for that no one could blame her. After undertaking this strangely melancholy journey Genji had always found comfort in the belief that he would return one day, but with that happy prospect now before him he reflected unhappily that he might never see the place again.

The men in his service rejoiced, each as his circumstances moved him to do. A party came from the City to greet him,

38. To displace the Heir Apparent.
39. With morning sickness.

which was pleasant, but the Novice wept and wept; and meanwhile the eighth month arrived. Under these autumn skies, sad enough in themselves, Genji wondered wretchedly why now as in the past he still gave himself up to these reckless adventures, until those who knew what the matter was grumbled, "Look at that! There he goes again!" Nudging each other, they went on, "All these months, without a word to anyone, he has been stealing off to see her, and now he has just made her unhappy after all." To Yoshikiyo's great discomfort they whispered that he was the one who had first told Genji about her.

Genji went to her earlier than usual in the evening, since he was to leave the day after tomorrow. This was the first time he had seen her properly, and her poised dignity so impressed him that he found it very painful to leave her behind. He wished she would come and join him in some suitable manner and sought to console her with assurances to this effect. His looks and bearing needed no description, but his devotions had given him a fine leanness of feature that lent him inexpressible grace, and while he poured forth in tears the tenderest promises, she may even have wondered whether this was not happiness enough, and whether she should not now renounce the thought of more. His very beauty made her own insignificance painfully obvious.

The noise of the waves had changed in the autumn wind. Smoke from the salt fires drifted thinly by, and all that gave the place its character was present in the scene.

> "Our parting has come, and for now I must leave you, but I pray the smoke
> rising from your salt fires here may still lean the way I go."

She replied,

> "Sea-tangle sorrows the saltmaker gathers in to heap on her fires
> are no more than what life brings; she has no wish to complain."

Although hardly able to speak through her tears, she could still give him an eloquent reply when one was needed.

Genji, who had always longed to hear her play for him, was very disappointed that she had not done so. "Just a little, then," he said, "to remember you by." He sent for the *kin* he had brought from the City and softly plucked its strings in a lovely tune that ineffably filled the clear depths of the night. This was too much for the Novice, who took the *sō no koto* and slid it through the curtains to his daughter. His invitation must have elicited as well tears that flowed freely while her quiet playing revealed what she could do. Fujitsubo's touch struck him as peerless in his time, for her brilliance, which often gave the listener a thrill of pleasure, also conveyed an image of herself, and that made her music truly supreme. In contrast, this lady excelled thanks to unfailing mastery and an enviably absorbing tone. Her music, too, called up deep, fond feelings, and while she played pieces he had never heard before, pausing so often that he could hardly bear it, he longed for more and wondered bitterly why for months he had failed to insist on her giving him this pleasure.

He poured forth promises about the future. "You must have this *kin* until we can play together again," he said.

> "That casual gift you give to make me believe you will remain true
> I shall honor in my thoughts with a long music of tears,"[40]

she replied, so low that he could hardly hear her; and he, nettled,

> "This koto is yours, that you may remember me till we meet again,
> and I hope you will not change the pitch of the middle string.[41]

We will see each other before it loses its tuning," he went on, to

40. The poem plays on *hitokoto* ("one word" and "a koto" [Genji's *kin*]) and *ne* ("music" and "sound of weeping").
41. It is unclear what the "middle string [or strings]" of the instrument is, but metaphorically it both links the lovers and confirms their separation.

encourage her trust; but she was understandably lost in tears of anguish at the prospect of his going.

On the day, he left her in the darkness before dawn. Even when caught up among those who had come to escort him, he still found a lull to send her,

"*Alas that the wave is to rise now and withdraw, leaving you behind to what sorrows of your own I imagine all too well.*"

She answered,

"*This house of rushes, where I have lived all these years, will be desolate— ah, how I long to follow after the withdrawing wave!*"[42]

The words said what she meant, and tears spilled from his eyes, though he tried to stop them. Those who did not know the circumstances thought this natural enough, despite the sort of place it was, considering that he had lived there a long time by now and that he was leaving forever. Such evidence of serious attachment did not at all please Yoshikiyo. The others were happy but also sad, for today really was to be their last by the sea, and their talk among themselves suggested that they, too, had their reasons to weep—not that one need go on about them, though.

The Novice's preparations for the day were grand indeed. Everyone, down to the least of Genji's men, had clothes of the best for the journey.[43] One wondered when he could possibly have had them made. Genji's own costume was finer than words can describe, and uncounted chests of clothing joined his train. Each gift was worthy of presentation in the City, and each had its own merit, for the donor had neglected nothing.

On the hunting cloak given him to wear, Genji found,

42. "I would willingly drown myself in the sea" or "I would willingly follow you to the City." The common people on the shore lived in *tomaya,* houses thatched with rushes.
43. Each must have got a hunting cloak and gathered trousers.

> "Perhaps you will spurn this travel cloak after all for its saltiness,
>   washed as it has often been by the brine of wave on wave."

Despite his agitation he still managed to reply,

> "Yes, let us exchange something to give each of us the other's presence:
>   a robe to be between us till the day we meet again";[44]

and he put it on in acknowledgment of her kindness. He sent her the things he had been wearing, and they did indeed make a keepsake for her to remember him by just that much better. How could the fragrance suffusing his exquisite cloak not permeate her own thoughts as well?

"Having at last put this world behind me, I still regret that I cannot go with you today," the Novice said. He made a sad sight, with his mouth turned down at the corners, but the younger people must have laughed.

> "Weary of the world, I have lived by the salt sea many, many years,
>   yet it is true even now that I cannot leave this shore,"[45]

he said to Genji. "Perhaps to the border, at least, since the heart's darkness is certain to claim me . . ."[46] And he went on ingratiatingly, "Please forgive my presumption, but if you ever chance to think of her . . ."[47]

Genji was very deeply moved, and the flush here and there on his face gave his looks an inexpressible charm. "I have good reason not to forget her, you know. You will very soon know

44. The "robe to be between us" (naka no koromo) parallels the "middle string" (naka no o) of an earlier exchange.
45. The "shore" is both Akashi and "this shore" (i.e., "this world") as opposed to "the other shore," paradise.
46. The darkness that engulfs the heart of a father worried about his child. The border is the one between Harima and Settsu Provinces.
47. "I hope that she may expect a letter from you."

me better than that. But it is so difficult for me to leave your house! What am I to do?" he said, and, wiping his eyes,

> *"Was that sorrow worse, setting out to go that spring far from the City,*
> *than this one, when in autumn I leave a familiar shore?"*

The Novice was beside himself and only wept the more. He could hardly even stand.

His daughter's state was beyond words. She calmed herself to keep it from showing, but fairly or unfairly, her plight drove her to helplessly bitter resentment at his leaving, and with his image always before her she could only collapse in tears after all.

Her mother did not know how to comfort her. "Why did we ever think of causing you this misery?" she said. "It is all my fault for having listened to anyone so mad."

"Stop it!" her father said. "He has every reason not to neglect her, and I am sure he still has something in mind for her"; and, to his daughter, "Take hold of yourself and drink your medicine. What a way to behave!" However, he himself was slumped in a corner.

Her nurses and her mother all condemned his delusions. "He has been so eager for years to see her as he wants her to be," they said, "and we thought he *had* managed it this time, but no, it is a disaster already!" Their distress and hers upset him so much that he became more and more confused, sleeping through the day and rising briskly at night to sit there, praying and rubbing his hands together, muttering, "My rosary has just vanished!" One moonlit night, after the servants had mocked him, he went outside to do his circumambulations, fell into the garden brook, bumped his backside on a picturesque rock, and went to bed to recover, which at last gave him something else to think about.

Genji traveled to Naniwa, where he underwent purification, and through a messenger he also announced to Sumiyoshi that he would give thanks for his safe journey and for the blessings received in response to his vows.[48] His entourage had suddenly

48. At the time of the storm.

grown too large to allow him for now to go in person, and he hastened to enter the City without pausing for any further excursions.

When he reached his Nijō residence, the people of his household and those traveling with him met in what felt to them like a dream, and there arose an alarming tumult of tears and laughter. Murasaki must have valued after all the life that had meant so little to her. She had grown up to be absolutely lovely, and to her great advantage the weight of her sorrows had slightly thinned her once overabundant hair. He was now deeply content to see that she would always be his this way, but at the thought his heart went out with a pang to the one whom he had so unwillingly left. Yes, such things would clearly never give him any rest.

He began talking about her, and the memories so heightened his looks that Murasaki must have been troubled, for with "I care not for myself"[49] she dropped a light hint that delighted and charmed him. When merely to see her was to love her, he wondered in amazement how he had managed to spend all these months and years without her, and bitterness against the world rose in him anew.

Very soon he was awarded a new office, that of Acting Grand Counselor. All his followers for whom it was proper to do so were restored to their former functions and privileges, until in both mood and manner they resembled wintry trees at last touched by spring.

An invitation came from His Majesty, and Genji called on him. The gentlewomen wondered while he was in the presence how a man of his now mature dignity could have endured all those years in so strange a place. The ancient women in service there since Genji's father's reign mourned again with tears and cries, and they sang Genji's praises. Even His Majesty felt called upon to mind himself, and he came forth attired with special care. Although greatly reduced because of

---

49. *Shūishū* 870, by Ukon: "I care not for myself, who am forgotten, but I grieve for the life of him who made me those vows."

his long illness, he had lately been feeling a little better. They talked quietly on into the night. The moon of the fifteenth night[50] hung aloft, lovely and tranquil, while fragments of the past drifted through His Majesty's mind, and perhaps in dread of the future he wept. He said, "How long I have gone without music and missed the sound of instruments once so familiar!"

"Feebly languishing in disgrace beside the sea, the forlorn Leech Child
for year after endless year could not stand on his own feet,"[51]

Genji replied.

Deeply moved, and also ashamed, His Majesty replied,

"Now that we at last have circled to meet again around the sacred pole,
O forget the bitterness that spring when we were parted!"[52]

He spoke with the most engaging kindness.

Genji hastened to arrange a Rite of the Eight Discourses for his father. He was extremely pleased to find that the Heir Apparent had grown up very nicely indeed, and he looked upon him with great emotion. The Heir Apparent's brilliant success in his studies made him obviously able to assume with confidence the duties of the Sovereign. Once Genji had composed himself a little, he called on Fujitsubo, too, and their conversation must have touched on many a moving theme.

50. Of the eighth month. Genji saw this moon at Suma just two years ago.
51. Genji likens himself to the first, defective offspring of Izanagi and Izanami, the primordial pair in the Japanese creation myth. The Leech Child had no bones and was therefore sent drifting out to sea. *Nihon shoki* 66, by Ōe no Asatsuna: "Do his parents not pity him? The Leech Child has reached his third year and still cannot stand."
52. The Leech Child was defective because after Izanagi and Izanami circled in opposite directions around a sacred pole, Izanami (the female) spoke first to invite Izanagi to intercourse. When they repeated the circling and Izanagi (the male) spoke first, the resulting children were sound.

Oh, yes, on the retreating waves he sent a letter down to Akashi.[53] It seems to have been a long one, stealthily written. "How are you getting on, when waves night after night . . . ?

> *My thoughts go to you, imagining morning mists rising down the shore*
> *while you at Akashi spend sleepless nights lost in sorrow."*

[. . .]

53. With the Akashi men who had escorted him to the City and were now re-turning.

14
(SLIGHTLY ABRIDGED)

MIOTSUKUSHI
THE PILGRIMAGE TO SUMIYOSHI

The syllables *mi-o-tsu-ku-shi* occur in the poetic exchange by which this chapter has often been remembered. Their primary meaning is "channel marker" (a pole set in an estuary bottom to mark the channel), but they also convey "give my all" (for love).

Chapter 14 continues chapter 13, beginning in the tenth month when Genji is twenty-eight and extending to the eleventh month of the following year.

Genji thought of his father often after that clear dream, and he sorrowfully wished somehow to save him from the sins that had brought him so low. Once he was back in the City, he quickly prepared to do so, and in the tenth month he held a Rite of the Eight Discourses. All the world bowed to his wishes, as it had done before.

The Empress Mother, even gravely ill, took it hard that she must fail to suppress this Genji, but His Majesty, who recalled his father's last wishes and foresaw certain retribution, was greatly relieved to have raised him up again. The eye trouble that had so often afflicted him was now gone, but his doubt that he would live much longer weighed heavily on him, and the knowledge that he had little time left prompted him to call Genji constantly to his side. He derived such obvious satisfaction from discussing all things openly with him that his pleasure brought happiness in turn to the whole court.

With his planned abdication rapidly approaching, his sympathy went to Oborozukiyo, whose experience of life had been so painful. "His Excellency your father is no more," he said to her, "the Empress Mother's health gives every cause for concern, and now that I feel my own time is coming, I am afraid of leaving you sadly on your own in a very different world. You have never thought as well of me as of a certain other, but my greater affection has always moved me to care for you above all. The one you prefer may take pleasure in you, too, but I do not think that his feeling for you approaches mine, which is far stronger, and this alone is very painful." He began to weep.

She blushed scarlet, in all the full, fresh ripeness of her beauty, and her tears spilled forth until he forgot her transgressions and looked on her only with pity and love. "I wonder why you would not even give me a child," he said. "That is a very great regret. I know you will have one for him, with whom your tie is so much stronger, and the thought makes me very sad indeed. After all, he is what he is and no more, and your child will have a commoner father."

This and other remarks from him about the future overwhelmed her with sorrow and shame. His face gave off such a lovely sweetness, and his behavior so clearly proved a boundless devotion that had seemed to grow with the passage of the years, that despite Genji's merits she could only acknowledge what suffering his lukewarm attentions had brought her, until she no longer knew why she had followed her youthful leanings and caused that dreadful scandal—one damaging not only to her name but to his. Such memories led her to rue the life that she had led.

The Heir Apparent's coming of age took place in the second month of the following year. Now eleven, he was tall and dignified for his age, and his face appeared to be traced from Genji's own. Both shone so dazzlingly that everyone sang their praises, but his mother was appalled and only wished fervently that it were not so. His Majesty looked on the boy with pleasure and gently let him know, among other things, that he meant soon to cede him the realm.

The abdication took place after the twentieth of the same month, suddenly enough to upset the Empress Mother. His

Majesty sought to calm her, saying, "I shall no longer have any importance, but I look forward to seeing you more at my ease." The Shōkyōden Prince was named the next Heir Apparent. The new reign began, for a change, amid many moments of novel brilliance. Genji rose from Grand Counselor to Palace Minister. His post had been added to the others, since no regular one of the kind was vacant.[1] Although expected now to take up the reins of government, he ceded the role of Regent to the former Minister of the Left, on the grounds that he was not up to its many responsibilities.

"Illness obliged me to resign my office," the former Minister said, declining to accept, "and now that I am also so much older, I doubt that I could actually manage." In the other realm,[2] too, though, the very men who vanished into the mountains in unstable, troubled times came forth, white hair and all, to serve in time of peace, which brought them acknowledgment as true sages;[3] and so all agreed in both public and private that there could be no objection to His Excellency taking up again, under the new reign, a post he had given up for reasons of poor health. It had been done before. For that reason he broke off his retirement and became Chancellor. He was then sixty-three.

He had shut himself away in part because he felt the world against him, but now he flourished as before, and all his sons who had languished in disfavor rose high. Tō no Chūjō, in particular, became an Acting Counselor. The girl he had had by the late Chancellor's fourth daughter was twelve, and he was bringing her up with care in order to present her to His Majesty. The son who had sung "Takasago" was now of age. Genji envied his old friend all the children he kept having by one mother or another, and the resulting liveliness of his household.

1. The posts provided for by the law codes were those of Minister of the Left and of the Right. The posts of Palace Minister (Naidaijin, Uchi no Otodo) and Chancellor (Daijōdaijin, Ōkiotodo) were therefore in a sense unofficial, although they were recognized by custom and normally filled. Genji is now expected to act as Regent for the young Emperor.
2. China.
3. The *Shiji* provides the example of four wise and ancient men who returned from retirement to serve Empress Lu of Han in her effort to secure her son's succession to the throne.

His own little son by Aoi was exceptionally handsome, and he frequented both His Majesty's and the Heir Apparent's privy chambers. His grandparents still felt their grief for their late daughter keenly, although even now, when she was gone, Genji's light alone so lifted the new Chancellor's spirits that his years of despair vanished into glory. Genji came to call on every occasion, for his goodwill had not changed, and his tactful kindness to his son's nurses, as well as to the other gentlewomen who had stayed on through the years, undoubtedly brought happiness to many.

His sympathy went to those who similarly awaited him at Nijō. Wishing to raise the long-despondent spirits of women like Chūjō and Nakatsukasa, he showed them such attentions, each according to her station, that he had no leisure even to call elsewhere. He ordered a magnificent rebuilding of the mansion—a legacy from his father—to the east of his Nijō residence, and he had its rooms done up with the idea of bringing there any lady whose plight concerned him.

Oh, yes—he never forgot his anxiety about the lady whom he had left in so delicate a condition at Akashi, and despite a press of affairs, both public and private, that kept him from giving her the attention he desired, he realized when the third month came that the day might soon be at hand, and in a rush of secret feeling sent off a messenger.

The messenger quickly returned. "The birth took place on the sixteenth," he reported. "The child is a girl, and all is well."

Genji was especially happy to gather that he had a daughter. He wondered bitterly why he had not brought her mother to have her child in the City.

An astrologer had foretold to Genji that he would have three children, of whom one would be Emperor and another Empress, while the third and least among them would reach the highest civil rank of Chancellor. To all appearances he had been right. Expert physiognomists had all agreed that Genji would rise to the highest rank and govern the realm, but years of unpleasantness had so dampened his hopes that the new Emperor's successful accession brought him pleasure and satisfaction. He agreed that his father had been right to remove him from the line of succession. His father had taken greater pleasure in him than in any other of his many sons, but on due consideration that decision to make him a commoner now confirmed that it was not he who had any such calling; no, it could never be told who the new Emperor really was, but the physiognomist had not been wrong. Looking to the future, Genji saw in all this the guiding influence of the God of Sumiyoshi. Yes, *hers*, too, was an extraordinary destiny, and her eccentric father had certainly entertained ambitions properly beyond him. What a shame it was, though, and what a waste, that one destined for such heights should have come into the world in a place so remote! He would have to bring her here, once everything was quiet again. He gave orders to hasten the rebuilding of his mansion to the east.

He could not imagine finding any worthy wet nurse in a place like Akashi, but meanwhile he heard of the daughter of a senior gentlewoman under his father, whose father at his death had been Lord of the Palace Bureau and a Consultant and who, blighted by the loss of her mother, had in these discouraging circumstances given birth to a child. Through the person who had told him about her he managed satisfactorily to obtain her consent. Still young and artless, and sadly depressed by a life spent grieving in a ruined house, she hardly paused to think; she liked the thought of being near him so well that she declared herself at his disposal. Genji, who felt quite sorry for her, sent her straight down to Akashi.

[. . .]

She left the City by carriage. Genji had her escorted by a close retainer whom he sent off with injunctions to strict secrecy. The baggage was bursting with the dagger[4] and other similarly suitable gifts, for he had left nothing undone. He showed exceptionally kind generosity to the nurse as well. The thought of the Novice doting on his granddaughter often made Genji smile, and the depth of his fond concern for her left no doubt about the strength of that karmic bond. He begged her mother in his letter never to neglect their daughter.

4. A girl of high rank received a dagger (*mihakashi*) at birth.

"O that soon these sleeves might touch her with their caress, that she long endure
like the rock the angel's wing brushes age after long age."[5]

The party traveled by boat as far as the province of Settsu, and from there they rode on quickly to their goal.

The Novice greeted the nurse with raptures of delighted respect. When he turned to bow in the direction of the City, the thought of Genji's most august concern made the little girl still more precious and prompted him even to feelings of dread.

She was so sweetly and so perfectly lovely that it was disconcerting: no wonder Genji in his wisdom intended to give her every advantage. The nurse had felt as though she were dreaming when she set out on her strange journey, but at this thought her distress melted away. She looked after her charge with the tenderest care.

The Akashi Lady, for months sunk in gloom, had felt herself weaken steadily until she doubted that she had much longer to live, but this new step by Genji made her feel a little better. She raised her eyes once more and gave Genji's messenger a very warm welcome. Since the messenger was eager to start back, she wrote down for Genji some of her thoughts:

"These poor sleeves of mine are too narrow: I cannot caress her alone,
and I look to the tall pine for his overspreading shade."[6]

Genji felt extraordinarily drawn and simply could not wait to see his daughter.

So far he had said little to Murasaki, but he did not want her to hear things from other people. "So that seems to be that," he remarked. "What a strange and awkward business it is! All my

5. Buddhist lore defines a "minor kalpa" (an aeon) as the time it takes a rock brushed once every three years by an angel's wing to wear away.
6. *Gosenshū* 64: "O for sleeves wide enough to cover the whole sky, that I might keep from the winds the blossoms of spring!" The poem also plays on *matsu*, "pine" and "wait."

concern is for someone else, whom I would gladly see similarly favored,[7] and the whole thing is a sad surprise, and a bore, too, since I hear the child is a girl. I really suppose I should ignore her, but I cannot very well do that. I shall send for her and let you see her. You must not feel resentful."

She reddened. "Don't, please!" she said, offended. "You are always making up feelings like that for me, when I myself detest them. And when do you suppose that I learned to have them?"

"Ah, yes," said Genji with a bright smile, "who can have taught you? I have never seen you like this! Here you are, angry with me over fantasies of yours that have never occurred to me. It is too hard!" By now he was nearly in tears.

Memories of their endless love for each other down the years, and of the letters they had so often exchanged, told her that all his affairs were simple amusements, and the matter passed from her mind.

"If I am this anxious about her," Genji said, "it is because I have my reasons. You would only go imagining things again if I were to tell you too soon what they are." He was silent a moment. "It must have been the place itself that made her appeal to me so. She was something new, I suppose." He went on to describe the smoke that sad evening, the words they had spoken, a hint of what he had seen in her face that night, the magic of her koto; and all this poured forth with such obvious feeling that his lady took it ill.

There I was, she thought, completely miserable, and he, simple pastime or not, was sharing his heart with another! Well, I am I! She turned away and sighed, as though to herself, "And we were once so happy together!

Not as fond lovers' languid plumes follow the wind toward reunion,
no, but as smoke myself I wish I were long since gone!"[8]

"What? Why, what a thing to say!

7. "I wish *you* had a child."
8. "I wish I were dead."

Just who is it, then, for whom I suffered so much, roaming hills and seas,

often enough near drowning in an endless stream of tears?

Oh, I wish I could show you how I really feel! I suppose that demands a lifetime, though, and one never knows . . . It is all for you, you see, that I so want to avoid having other women condemn me over nothing." He drew her *sō no koto* to him and went through the modal prelude idly, to tempt her, but she would not touch it, since she was perhaps piqued by what she gathered of that other's skill. For all her quiet innocence, sweetness, and grace, she still had a stubborn side to her, and, when she was offended, as now, her wrath had a quality so delicious that he only enjoyed her the more.

Genji calculated privately that the fifth of the fifth month would be his daughter's fiftieth day, and he thought of her with eager, affectionate curiosity. How much more satisfyingly he could have celebrated her birth here, and how much happier the occasion would have been! What a shame that she had entered the world in a place that hopeless! She would not have preoccupied him nearly so much if she had been a boy, but he regretted for her sake the affront of her birth, and he reflected that his own flawed destiny had all been for her.

He sent a messenger with urgent instructions to get there on the day, and the man did indeed arrive on the fifth. Genji's thoughtful gifts were magnificently generous, and he had included more practical items as well. He had written,

"How is she to know, the little sea pine whose life is all in shadow,

today's Sweet Flag Festival from her own fiftieth day?[9]

My heart has flown to her, you know. Do make up your mind to come, because I cannot go on living this way. I promise that

9. With wordplays made explicit here, Genji's poem laments his daughter's remote birth. "Sea pine" (*umimatsu*) is actually a kind of seaweed more often called *miru*.

you need not worry." As usual the Novice wept for joy. It will come as no surprise that at a time like this happiness all but drowned him in tears.

He, too, at Akashi had seen to everything magnificently, but without Genji's ambassador all would have seemed as though swallowed by darkness. Meanwhile the nurse was happy in the company of this most perfect and attractive of ladies, and she forgot her sorrows. Other gentlewomen, hardly less worthy, had been brought in as family connections allowed, but they, sadly fallen from service in the great houses of the City, had meant only to settle here quietly "among the rocks," while the nurse retained all her poise and pride. The tales she told were well worth hearing, and on the subject of Lord Genji she enlarged with a woman's enthusiasm on his looks and on the warm regard in which he was universally held, until her new mistress, who meant so much to him and to whom he had actually given a child, came to think more highly of herself. They read his letter together. Ah, the nurse said to herself, some have all the luck, while I have none! But Genji's thoughtful inquiry about her pleased her greatly, and she felt much better.

> "Yet again today, the fiftieth for the crane crying in the lea
> of this islet, all unseen, no one has asked after her,"[10]

the Akashi Lady gravely replied. "My fragile existence, you understand, hangs on the rare comfort of a letter from you, for everything draws me downward toward despair. I would indeed be glad of a reason to look forward to the future."

Genji read her letter again and again, and he sighed to himself loud and long. Murasaki gave him a sidelong look, then stared sorrowfully before her, murmuring under her breath, "The boat that rows seaward from the shore . . ."[11]

"You really mean to make an issue of it, don't you," Genji said irritably. "I feel sorry for her just now, that is all. Those

---

10. The "crane" is the little girl, the "islet" her mother.
11. *Kokin rokujō* 1888: "The boat that rows seaward from the shore at Kumano is leaving me and drawing ever farther away."

days come back to me when I think what the place is like, and I talk to myself a bit; and you do not miss it, do you!" He showed her only the letter's outer cover.[12] The writing had such character as to put the greatest lady to shame, and she understood why Genji felt about the sender as he did.

[. . .]

Even now Oborozukiyo could not give him up. Incorrigible as ever, he returned her feeling, but she had learned her lesson from bitter experience and no longer encouraged him as before. Despite his happy return he felt uncomfortably constrained, and he missed their affair.

Retired Emperor Suzaku, who now looked tolerantly on life, from time to time held very pleasant musical gatherings and so on. His Consorts and Intimates all continued to serve him; only the Heir Apparent's mother failed to enjoy any great favor, being eclipsed in his affections by Oborozukiyo. She therefore turned to reliance on her inalienable good fortune and moved away to attend His Highness.

Genji's lodging at the palace was the Kiritsubo, as of old. The Heir Apparent, who lived in the Nashitsubo,[13] conferred with him on every occasion, in a spirit of neighborly intimacy, and Genji lent him his assistance.

Since Fujitsubo could not properly assume a new rank, she was granted the emoluments of a Retired Emperor.[14] The officers of her household were correspondingly redesignated, and she lived in imposing style. Her constant occupation remained her religious devotions and the performance of acts of merit. Fear of appearing at court had prevented her from seeing her son during those years of intense worry and chagrin, but happily she could now come and go to him as she pleased, and it

12. This sort of letter would have been wrapped, first, in a formal envelope (*raishi*) and then in an outer cover (*uwazutsumi*) that bore the name of the person addressed.

13. Immediately south of the Kiritsubo.

14. Being a nun, Fujitsubo cannot assume the rank and title of Empress Mother. She had previously enjoyed income from the produce and labor of fifteen hundred households; this number has now risen to two thousand.

was the Empress Mother[15] who found life very bitter. On occasion Genji would treat her with embarrassing courtesy, and this only brought her new distress that would in its turn set off a buzz of gossip.

Prince Hyōbu had maintained an unfortunate attitude over the years, and Genji, who condemned his surrender to court opinion, no longer kept up with him the old close ties. Although generally well disposed toward everyone, he sometimes displayed toward His Highness an antipathy that Fujitsubo, the gentleman's sister, noted with sorrow and disappointment.

The Chancellor and Genji shared government evenly between them and wielded its powers as they thought best.

In the eighth month of that year Tō no Chūjō sent his daughter to serve His Majesty. Her grandfather put himself into it, and the ceremony was all anyone could have wished. Prince Hyōbu had carefully reared his well-regarded second daughter with the same ambition in mind, but Genji failed to see why she should be preferred over anyone else. What can he have been thinking of?

That autumn he went on a pilgrimage to Sumiyoshi. His retinue was grand, since he was to give thanks for many answered prayers, and the whole court, senior nobles and privy gentlemen alike, offered him their services on the journey.

It happened that the Akashi Lady, who made the pilgrimage every year, had decided to go, too, partly to atone for having failed to do so last year or so far this year because of her condition.[16] She traveled by sea. On reaching the shore she found the beach covered with a vast and noisy throng of pilgrims, while a procession bore magnificent treasures for the god. Ten musicians, plainly selected for their good looks, were dancing all in a single color. Her men must have asked what pilgrim had arrived, for a hopelessly low menial burst into laughter and cried, "Look! Here are people who don't even know that Lord Genji is here to give thanks!"

Ah, she thought, considering all the days there are, in all the

15. The former Kokiden Consort, the mother of Retired Emperor Suzaku.
16. Not only had her pregnancy made the journey too taxing for her, but in that state she was polluted and so unfit to approach the shrine.

months of the year, this really is too cruel! To see his glory this
way from a distance only makes me sorry to be who I am. Yes,
I have a fated tie to him, but what dire karma is mine, when
even so miserable an underling can blithely pride himself on being in his service, that I who yearn for him should have set out
in utter ignorance of this great day? This train of reflections
overwhelmed her with sorrow, and she secretly wept.

Formal cloaks light and dark drifted in untold numbers beneath the pines' deep green, as though the ground were strewn
with flowers or autumn leaves. The Chamberlains in leaf green
stood out among the young gentlemen of the sixth rank, and
that Palace Guards officer who had spoken so bitterly of the
Kamo palisade now belonged to the Gate Watch and was also a
Chamberlain, with his own imposing corps of attendants.
Yoshikiyo, likewise a Gate Watch officer, wore a particularly
carefree air, and in his red cloak[17] he looked very fine indeed.
Those whom she had seen at Akashi were all scattered about
here and there, transformed, brilliant and apparently without a
care, while young senior nobles and privy gentlemen vied eagerly with one another, their very horses and saddles glitteringly
adorned, and making a dazzling spectacle for the watchers from
the country.

It only upset her to notice Genji's carriage in the distance,
and she could not make out the figure she so longed to see. He
had been given an escort of young pages, following the example
of the Riverside Minister:[18] ten of them, handsome and of even
height, delightfully dressed, and with their hair in twin tresses
bound by white cords shading to deep purple ends. They had all
together an especially fresh appeal. Genji's son by Aoi, a young
man whose father gave him every advantage, had his grooms
and pages all dressed alike, so that there was no mistaking
them. The heaven of the imperial palace seemed so distant and
so glorious that she lamented her daughter's insignificance. She
could only turn toward the shrine and pray.

17. The color of the fifth rank, one higher than sixth-rank green.
18. The Riverside Minister (Kawara no Otodo), Minamoto no Tōru (822–895),
was the first imperial son to receive the Minamoto (or Genji) surname.

The Governor of the province arrived, and he no doubt prepared a magnificent reception for Genji, one far beyond any given an ordinary Minister. She felt agonizingly out of place. The god himself would neither notice her nor listen if she mixed with the throng to go through her own tedious little rite, and to start straight home again would be too disappointing. No, she would put in today at Naniwa, where she would at least undergo purification. With this in mind she rowed away.

Genji, who knew nothing of this, spent the night variously entertaining the god. He left out no touch that might give the god true pleasure and, quite beyond his thanks for blessings in the past, he kept the heavens ringing until dawn with beautiful music and dancing. Men of his like Koremitsu felt sincere gratitude for the divine aid they had received. When Genji emerged briefly,[19] Koremitsu presented himself and said,

> *"This great grove of pines here at Sumiyoshi brings many woes to mind*
> *when in thought I dwell upon those days under the god's care."[20]*

Indeed it does, thought Genji, who remembered, too.

> *"No such pounding waves as dashed themselves on that shore could shake me enough*
> *to drive from my memory Sumiyoshi and his boons.*

His blessings are very great," he justly replied.

Genji was very sorry to learn that all the commotion had driven a boat from Akashi away, and he wished he had known. He who knew the god's blessing so well thought of comforting her at least with a note, for she must be hurt. He set out from the shrine and went roaming far and wide to see the sights. At Naniwa he underwent the most solemn purification. A view of

19. From the pavilion where he sat to watch the dancing.
20. "Those days under the god's care" (*kamiyo*, literally, "the age of the gods") refers to Suma and Akashi and acknowledges the divine protection Genji enjoyed there.

the Horie Channel started him humming, "I have nothing left now but to try to meet her, at Naniwa . . ."[21] Koremitsu, who was near his carriage, must have heard him, because the next time the carriage stopped, he gave him a short-handled brush—one he kept in the front fold of his robe in case Genji should call for it. Genji was pleased, and he wrote on folding paper,

> "I who give my all for your love have my reward, for to find you here,
>   where so deep a channel runs, proves the power of our bond."[22]

He gave it to Koremitsu, who sent it on with a well-informed servant.

Her heart beat when she saw his retinue ride by all abreast, but his message, however brief, touched her deeply, and in her gratitude she wept.

> "Lacking any worth, I have no title to claim any happiness;
>   what can have possessed me, then, so to give my all for love?"[23]

She sent it tied to a sacred streamer from her purification on the Isle of Tamino.[24] Soon the sun would set. The scene's stirring mood, with the evening tide flooding in and the cranes along the inlet crying in full voice, must have been what made Genji long to be with her in defiance of prying eyes.

21. From *Gosenshū* 960, by Prince Motoyoshi: "Being so unhappy, nothing is left me now but to seek to meet her, at Naniwa, though it means giving my all." The poem plays on the syllables *mi-o-tsu-ku-shi* ("giving my all"), which also form the word for "channel marker" (a pole set in an estuary bottom to mark the channel). In poetry, *miotsukushi* was associated with the Horie Channel.
22. The poem's key play on *miotsukushi* is lost in translation. The "channel markers" of the Horie Channel have reminded Genji of "give my all."
23. The play on *miotsukushi* is repeated, and there is another on the syllables of the name Naniwa.
24. The Isle of Tamino that once stood near the mouth of the Yodo River vanished long ago.

"As wet now with dew as in those days we once knew, my traveling clothes find no shelter in the name of the Isle of Tamino."[25]

All along the way he enjoyed the pleasures of the journey, to ringing music, but his heart was still with her after all. Singing girls crowded to his procession, and all the young gallants with him, even senior nobles, seemed to look favorably on them; but not Genji, for he thought, Come now, all delight, all true feeling spring from the quality of one's partner, and a little frivolity, even playfully meant, is quite enough to put one off. Their airs and graces served only to turn him away.

She who filled his thoughts let his procession pass, and she made her offerings the following day,[26] since it was propitious. She had managed after all, as well as she was able, to put before the god prayers proper to her station. Then melancholy claimed her again, and she spent day and night lamenting the misery of her lot. A messenger from him reached her even before she imagined him reaching the City. I shall bring you here very soon, Genji had said, and yet she wavered, for although his words conveyed reassuring respect, she feared that troubling experiences might await her once she had rowed far away from the island.[27] She knew that her father must be very apprehensive about letting her go, although it was also true that the thought of wasting her life here now distressed her more than it had ever done in years past. She gave Genji a cautious, irresolute answer.

Oh, yes! After the Rokujō Haven returned to the City, the time having come for a new Ise Priestess,[28] Genji provided for her as generously as before and showed her such kindness that she was indeed grateful, although she did not encourage him;

---

25. "I weep with longing for you as I did at Akashi." The syllables *mino*, in the name Tamino, make the word for "(straw) raincoat"; hence, "Tamino Isle gives me no protection from the dew of my tears."
26. At the Sumiyoshi Shrine.
27. The "island" is Awaji, opposite Akashi; the phrase refers to a complex of poems involving departure from Akashi.
28. The Rokujō Haven had been at Ise for about six years. The accession of the new Emperor had brought her daughter's term as Ise Priestess to an end.

for she had no wish to test a devotion that had once proven doubtful and that, such as it might be by now, would only upset her again. For that reason he seldom actually called on her. He would never know how his own feelings might change, even if he were to go about winning her back, and besides, it seemed to him that clandestine expeditions no longer became him. What he longed to know was what her daughter Akikonomu was like, now that she had grown up.

The Haven led an elegant life once more in her old residence, for Genji still saw to having it done up and maintained. Her taste and flair had not deserted her, many distinguished gentlewomen and cultivated gentlemen gathered around her, and despite her apparent loneliness she was living very pleasantly when, all at once, she fell gravely ill and sank into such despair that alarm over her years in so sinful a place[29] decided her to become a nun.

This news brought the astonished Genji to her, for even if they were no longer lovers, she was still to him someone to talk to, and he wished that she had not done it. His expressions of sympathy and concern were extremely moving. She gave him a seat near her pillow and answered him leaning on an armrest, but even this much made it clear how weak she was, and Genji wept bitterly, fearing that it might be too late for him to assure her of his enduring devotion.

Deeply affected to find that he cared so much, she began to speak of her daughter. "Please think of her whenever she may need you," she said, "because she will now be left all alone. Hers is a perilous position, you see—she has no one else to turn to. I myself am no help, but I hope still to keep an eye on her, as long as I am able, until she can more or less look after herself." Her breath all but failed her, and she wept.

"I would never abandon her, even if I had not heard you talk this way, and now I am resolved to do for her all I possibly can. On that score please set your mind at rest."

"It is so very difficult," she went on. "Even if she had someone like a father to trust perfectly naturally, the loss of her mother

29. The Ise Shrine, where taboo had cut her off from any contact with Buddhist teaching or practice.

might well prove a great misfortune. And if her guardian were then to look on her with a lover's eyes, the consequences for her could sometimes be cruel, and for some she could become an object of dislike. I know it is unkind of me to imagine such things, but please, never allow yourself to think of her that way. My own life has taught me that a woman is born to endure many sorrows, and I should like somehow to spare her as many as I can."

Genji failed to see why she spoke as she did, but he replied, "Recent years have made me much wiser, and I am sorry to gather that you still believe I am given to the wanton ways of my past. Very well, all in good time . . ."

It was dark outside her curtains, but through them he caught the dim light of a lamp. I wonder . . . , he thought and peered stealthily in through a gap where the cloth failed to meet.[30] There she was, her short hair very handsome and striking, leaning on an armrest and looking piercingly beautiful, just like a painting; and yes, the girl lying beside her along the curtains to the east must be her daughter. With the standing curtain swept casually aside this way, he could see straight through to her. Chin in hand, she seemed very sad. By this faint light she looked extremely attractive. The way her hair fell across her shoulders and the shape of her head had great distinction, but she was still charmingly slight, and Genji felt a sharp surge of interest, although after her mother's speech he thought better of it.

"I am not feeling at all well," the Rokujō Haven said. "I hope that you will forgive me if I ask you to leave." She lay down with a gentlewoman's help.

"I am so sorry," Genji replied; "I would have been very glad if you had felt better with me near you. How *are* you feeling?"

She could tell he was watching. "I shudder to think what I must look like," she said. "It has been extremely good of you to call on me now when, as you will have gathered, my illness is unlikely to trouble me much longer. Now that I have told you a little of what has been on my mind, I can, I think, go in peace."

"I am moved and grateful that you should include me among

30. She seems to be lying in a curtained bed, at the entrance to which stands the curtain through which Genji is peering.

those worthy to receive your last wishes. My father had many other sons as well, but I have seldom felt close to them, and since he was pleased to count her as a daughter of his own, I shall look on her in the same spirit. Now that I am rather more grown-up, I am disappointed to have no one to look after."

Their conversation was soon over, and Genji left. His generous attentions now increased somewhat, and he wrote to her often.

Seven or eight days later she was gone. The blow left him acutely aware of life's uncertainty and so grief-stricken that instead of going to the palace he busied himself only with the inevitable arrangements. There was not really anyone else to do it. The trusted members of the Ise Priestess's former staff were left with few decisions to make.

Genji went there himself and sent in greetings to Akikonomu.

"I am afraid that I am in no condition . . ." she sent back through her Mistress of the Household.

"It would please me if you were to think of me as a friend," he replied, "because your mother and I reached an agreement." He called in her gentlewomen and instructed them on all there was to be done. His manner inspired complete confidence, and he seemed to have changed the attitude that had been his so long. He had the rite performed with the utmost solemnity, assisted by countless members of his own household.

He mourned, fasted, and practiced devotions behind lowered blinds and he wrote to Akikonomu often. Little by little she recovered her composure and began to answer him herself. Doing so made her shy, but her gentlewomen encouraged her with reminders that she must not disappoint him.

On a day of blowing snow and sleet he found himself imagining how sad and dispirited she must be, and he sent her a messenger. "How does our sky look to you just now, I wonder," he had written on paper the dull color of the sky.

"Now the skies are filled with such swirling flakes of snow, I mourn to imagine the departed roaming still the heavens above your home."

He had done up his letter with particular care, so as to catch a young woman's eye, and it was dazzling. Akikonomu could not think what to answer, but her women insisted that it would be rude of her to give the task to anyone else, and so she wrote on gray, intensely perfumed paper, in strokes light or dark as the ground required,

> *"Like unmelted snow I linger reluctantly, and in my darkness*
> *find that I cannot be sure who I am or where I go."*

Her cautious hand, innocent of pretense, was unremarkable, but he saw charm and dignity in it. Ever since she went down to Ise, he had felt that that was not to be all, and now it seemed to him that he might well decide to court her, although tact led him to restrain himself as before, since her mother had anxiously given him her last wishes on the subject, and people at large—understandably, alas—might entertain similar suspicions; no, he thought, he would on the contrary see chastely to her needs, and when the Emperor was old enough to understand a little more, he would install her in the palace, for this sort of thing was otherwise missing from his life, and he would enjoy having her under his care.

He sent her long, impeccably earnest messages and called on her whenever the opportunity arose. "If I may be permitted to say so, it would give me great pleasure if you were to allow me into your confidence, in memory of your mother," he would say; but she, by nature extremely reserved and shy, shrank from the thought of allowing him to hear her voice at all, however faintly, until her gentlewomen despaired of persuading her and could only deplore her disposition. Genji reflected, Some of them, for instance her Mistress of the Household, her Chief Lady in Waiting, and so on, are close relatives of hers in the imperial family, and most have a good deal of talent. If I do successfully place her as I hope, I see no reason why she should please His Majesty less well than any other. But if only I had had a better look at her face! His attitude may not have been wholly a devoted father's. Unable in the end to make up his mind, he told no one what future he planned for her. His special attentiveness to the funeral rites greatly surprised and pleased her staff.

Her loneliness increased as the months and days slipped by, a growing succession of miseries led those in her service to go their ways, and living near Kyōgoku in the lower district of the City meant deserted surroundings and a life often spent in tears amid the booming of the mountain temples' evening bells.[31] Not every mother, however devoted, would have remained so completely inseparable from her daughter or have gone down with her against all precedent to Ise, and her bitter regret that after so insisting on her mother's company she had not after all taken that last journey with her left her inconsolable.

Her large household staff included people of ranks both high and low, but once Genji, like a dutiful father, had forbidden even her nurses to take it on themselves to convey approaches to her, his daunting authority assured general assent that nothing improper must be brought to Princess Akikonomu's attention, and no breath of courtship ever reached her.

Retired Emperor Suzaku had never forgotten Akikonomu's almost disturbing beauty at that solemn farewell ceremony in the Great Hall of State. "Do enter my service, and join the Kamo Priestess and my other sisters," he had urged her, and he had mentioned the subject to her mother as well. The idea had not appealed to her mother, however, because while he was indeed surrounded by very great ladies, she doubted that her daughter had adequate support, and moreover she feared that his exceedingly fragile health might burden her in the end with added cares. Now, when her gentlewomen could not imagine who might be willing to assist her, His Eminence was still pressing her to come.

Genji shrank, when he learned this, from the thought of brazenly crossing Retired Emperor Suzaku and making off with her himself, but she *was* very attractive, and he was so reluctant to let her go that he broached the subject to Fujitsubo.

31. The lower district of the City (she lives near the intersection of Rokujō [east-west] and Kyōgoku [north-south]) was sparsely inhabited, and Kyōgoku was near the many temples built along the Eastern Hills.

"I hardly know what to do about it, you see," he said. "Her mother was a lady of great dignity and intelligence, and I deeply regret the way my self-indulgence earned me both an unfortunate name and her own rejection. While she lived, she never set aside her anger toward me, but since at the very end she talked about her daughter, she must have heard good things about me and decided she could be frank with me after all; and that is extremely sad. One could not ignore so distressing a matter even in the most commonplace circumstances, and I want to ensure that at least in death she can forget her bitterness; I wonder whether it might not be a good idea for His Majesty, who is still young although of course quite grown-up, to have in his service someone a little more mature. It is all up to you, you see."

"That is an excellent idea. The Retired Emperor's interest in her of course makes one hesitate to disappoint him, but you might simply invoke her mother's last wishes to bring her to the palace as though you knew nothing about it. By now this sort of thing preoccupies him less than his devotions, and I doubt that he really will be seriously put out when you tell him."

"Very well," Genji replied, "if you agree and are prepared to lend her your support, I shall have a few words with her and let her know. I have thought all this over very carefully, and I have been quite frank with you about my conclusion, but I am uneasy about what others may have to say."

He thereupon decided that he would indeed feign ignorance and move her to Nijō.[32] To Murasaki there he explained, "That, at any rate, is what I have planned. She is just the age to make you a good companion." She was pleased and began preparing to receive her.

Prince Hyōbu seemed to be grooming his daughter carefully in the hope of quickly achieving the same success, but Fujitsubo wondered unhappily how Genji would greet his ambition, in view of the rift between them. Tō no Chūjō's daughter was now known as the Kokiden Consort. The Chancellor had adopted her as his own daughter, and he maintained her in dazzling

32. In order to introduce her into the palace as his adopted daughter.

style.[33] She made a fine playmate for His Majesty.[34] Cloistered Empress Fujitsubo said to herself and others that her elder brother's middle daughter would only be joining a game of dolls, as it were, since she was the same age, whereas having someone older to look after him would be extremely welcome; and she told His Majesty what he had to anticipate. Meanwhile Genji, needless to say, missed nothing in the service of the realm, and he showed her such complete and tactful devotion at all times that she came to trust him implicitly. Fujitsubo could not easily attend His Majesty even when she went to the palace, since her health was poor, so that he urgently needed beside him a guardian somewhat older than himself.

33. The former Minister of the Left has adopted his own granddaughter in order to lend her the weight of his now supreme eminence.
34. The Emperor is eleven, she twelve.

17
(COMPLETE)

EAWASE
THE PICTURE CONTEST

The word *eawase* means a "picture contest," in which two competing sides submit paintings in pairs for judgment. No such contest is known to have taken place in the period before the tale was written, but the one in this chapter follows the established pattern for poetry contests (*utaawase*), and in particular for a fully documented example held at the palace in the third lunar month of 960.

Chapter 17 takes place from spring to autumn, a year or so after the time covered by chapter 14.

The former Ise Priestess Akikonomu's entry into palace service had Fujitsubo's willing support, but Genji worried that she had no one in particular to do for her all she would need to have done, and he therefore refrained from taking up the matter with Retired Emperor Suzaku; and since he had decided to bring her for the time being to Nijō, he pretended instead to know nothing about it. However, he generally honored his parental responsibility toward her.

Retired Emperor Suzaku was thoroughly disappointed, but for the sake of appearances he gave up writing to her. When the day came at last, however, he had her specially presented with the most beautiful sets of robes; with a comb box, a toiletry box, and a box for incense jars, all extraordinary in their way; and with such incenses and clothing perfumes as to fill the air far beyond a hundred paces.[1] The

---

1. The "hundred paces" are a proverbial measure of a perfume's excellence.

idea that Genji might be watching had no doubt put him on his mettle.

Genji was there at the time, and her Mistress of the Household showed him everything. He knew at first glance from the comb box just how marvelous they were in the exquisite refinement of their beauty.

On the gift knot that graced the box of ornamental combs he saw written,

"Did the gods decree, when the time of parting came and I, in your hair, set the comb of last farewell,[2] that we should not meet again?"

This gave him pause. He was very sorry, and his own heart's wayward fancies made it clear enough that Suzaku must have been smitten by her on that occasion when she left for Ise. How might he feel about having his hopes thwarted this way, now that she was back after all those years, and just when he could look forward to their being fulfilled? Was he bitter in retirement, after resigning the throne? I would be upset if I were he, Genji reflected. What can have moved me to force this through and make him so unhappy? He felt very bad. Yes, he had once been angry with His Eminence,[3] but he could only think fondly, too, of his gentle nature, and in his confusion he fell for a time into abstracted gloom.

"What sort of answer does she have in mind? And what about His Eminence's letter itself?" However, the Mistress of the Household was too nervously discreet to produce it. Genji heard the gentlewomen protesting vainly to their mistress, who was then unwell and in no mood to reply, that it would be rude and unkind of her not to, and he chimed in, "You really must, you know, if only for appearances"; and despite her confusion she remembered so vividly being touched as a girl by his graceful beauty and his many tears, and the memory brought with it such sad thoughts of her mother, that she managed after all,

2. The comb of parting that Suzaku gave Akikonomu when she left for Ise ("The Green Branch").

3. Because Suzaku (under his mother's influence) had forced Genji into exile.

> *"When I went away, you gave me that last command never to return,*
> *and now I am back again, the memory makes me sad."*[4]

That was probably all. The messenger received various gifts.
Genji, who wanted desperately to know what she had said,
could hardly ask.

Retired Emperor Suzaku's looks were such that one would
have gladly seen him as a woman, but Princess Akikonomu did
not seem unworthy of him, and they would have made a handsome pair. It even occurred to Genji to wonder indiscreetly
whether she might not privately regret his having been disappointed, since after all the Emperor was still very young. The
thought was torment, but there was no turning back. He explained what needed to be done,[5] told a retainer he favored to
see to his orders, and set off for the palace.

Out of deference to Suzaku, Genji refrained from any osten-
tatiously paternal gesture and only assured her well-being. Her
residence had long boasted many worthy gentlewomen, and
even the ones who were often at home gathered around her now,
so that she lived there in admirable style. Genji's old feeling for
her mother returned, and he thought, Ah, if only she were still
alive, how pleased she would be to have brought her daughter
this far herself! By any standard she was a wonder and a very
great loss. No, there will never be anyone like her! Such had
been her rare distinction that many things recalled her memory.

Fujitsubo was at the palace, too. The news that someone special
was coming caught His Majesty's interest in a charming way. He
was quite grown-up for his age. "Yes," his mother told him, "she
is a very fine lady, and you must mind your manners with her."

He was secretly worried that a grown-up might make forbidding company. She arrived very late that night. She was very
discreet and quiet, and so small and slight that he thought her
very pretty indeed. By now he was used to his Kokiden Consort,

4. Suzaku gave Akikonomu the comb together with the ritual injunction "Set
not your face toward the City again."
5. For Akikonomu's formal entry into the palace.

whose company he enjoyed and with whom he felt quite at ease, but this new one was so dauntingly self-possessed, and Genji treated her with such respectful formality, that he found it difficult to think ill of her, and he therefore divided his nights equally between them, although when he set off by day in search of youthful amusement, he usually went to the Kokiden. Tō no Chūjō had nursed a particular ambition when he presented his daughter to His Majesty, and it did not please him to find her now in competition with the new arrival.

Retired Emperor Suzaku considered the reply to his poem on the comb box and realized how difficult it was to give her up. Then Genji appeared, and the two began a conversation during which he happened to mention Akikonomu's departure for Ise as High Priestess, since he had touched on it before; though he concealed his interest in her. Genji pursued the matter so as to learn more about his feelings, without letting on that he already knew, and he felt sorry when he gathered how strong they were. He longed to know what feature of her beauty had so smitten him, and he chafed that he could not see her for himself. She was too profoundly deliberate in manner to allow any youthful liberty into her deportment, or he would have glimpsed her by now, and what hints he caught of her appearance were so unfailingly encouraging that he imagined her to be flawless.

Prince Hyōbu could not bring himself to make any move of his own, now that His Majesty was fully taken up by this pair of ladies, and he bided his time instead, confident that His Majesty would surely not turn his daughter away once he was older.

His Majesty loved painting above all, and perhaps because he liked it so much, he was also extremely good at it. Akikonomu painted very prettily, too, and so his interest shifted to her. The way they did paintings for each other meant that he went to see her often. He had been taking a pleased interest in the younger privy gentlemen who favored the same art, and he was charmed even more by this lovely lady whose paintings were not copybook exercises but entirely her own and who, reclining sweetly beside him, would pause gravely to consider the next stroke of her brush. He therefore visited her frequently and liked her far better than before.

This news spurred Tō no Chūjō, always so forward and quick to rise to a challenge, to gather his wits (Why, am I to be bested?), call in expert painters, swear them to silence, and have them turn out the most beautiful work on the finest papers. "Pictures of scenes from tales have the most charm and give the greatest pleasure," he said; and he chose the prettiest and most amusing tales and set the painters to work illustrating them. He also had his daughter show His Majesty paintings of the round of monthly festivals, done in a novel format with accompanying text. When His Majesty wanted to look at them with Akikonomu, the Kokiden side would not bring them out at all; instead they hid them and would not let His Majesty take them to the rival. "Tō no Chūjō is such a boy at heart!" Genji laughed when he heard. "He will never learn!"

"It is quite wrong of the Acting Counselor to upset you this way by deliberately hiding them and keeping them from you," he said. "Some of mine, though, are from early times, and you shall have them." At his residence he had cabinets full of paintings old and new thrown open, and with Murasaki he thoughtfully selected those most pleasing to modern taste. The ones on subjects like "The Song of Unending Sorrow" or the story of Ōshōkun were attractive and moving, but they were also ill omened, and he decided for now to leave them out.[6]

He removed the record of his travels from its box and took the opportunity to show it to Murasaki. It would have drawn willing tears from anyone in the least familiar with life's sorrows, even if the viewer was only barely acquainted with the circumstances, and for these two it brought back still more vividly the unforgettable nightmare that had engulfed them both. She let him know how unhappy she was that he had not shown it to her before.

"Rather than lament all alone, as I did then, I, too, should have gone
to see for myself this place where the seafolk spend their lives,"

6. Both stories concern tragically separated lovers and are therefore ill omened for any felicitously matched couple.

she said. "I would have worried a great deal less."

Touched, Genji replied,

"Still more vividly than in those sad days now past, when I suffered them,
those ordeals return to mind, bringing with them many tears."

He must at least show these pictures to Fujitsubo. Choosing
the scrolls least likely to be flawed and the most apt at the same
time to convey a clear picture of "those shores,"[7] he dwelled
in thought on the house at Akashi.

Tō no Chūjō redoubled his efforts when he learned that Genji
was assembling his own paintings, and he was more attentive
than ever to the excellence of rollers, covers, and cords. It was
the tenth or so of the third month, a delicious time of mild skies
and expansive moods, and since no festival was under way now
at the palace, both ladies spent their days absorbed in nothing
else, until Genji saw that he, too, might as well do what he
could to catch His Majesty's eye. He began marshaling paintings in earnest. Both sides had a great many. Since illustrations
of tales were the most attractive and engaging, Akikonomu's
Umetsubo[8] party had theirs done for all the great classics of the
past, while the Kokiden side favored tales that were the wonder
and delight of their own time, so that theirs were by far the
more brilliantly modern. Those of His Majesty's own gentlewomen who had anything to say for themselves spent their
time, too, rating this painting or that.

Fujitsubo, too, was then at the palace, and she neglected her
devotions to look through each side's paintings, since she could
not resist the desire to see them. When she heard His Majesty's
women discussing them that way, she divided the contestants
into two sides, Left and Right. On the Umetsubo side there were
Hei, Jijū, and Shōshō, while on the Right were Daini, Chūjō, and

7. Suma and Akashi. The expression *uraura* ("those shores") is from *Shūishū*
477, which names both.
8. "Plum Court," Akikonomu's residence at the palace. Red and white blossoming plum trees grew beside it.

Hyōe—in other words the quickest and most astute gentle-women of their time. Their lively debates delighted her. In the first round *The Old Bamboo Cutter*, the ancestor of all tales, was pitted against the "Toshikage" chapter of *The Hollow Tree*.[9]

"This tale about the bamboo is certainly hoary enough, and it lacks lively touches, but Princess Kaguya remains forever unsullied by this world, and she aspires to such noble heights that her story belongs to the age of the gods. It is far beyond any woman with a shallow mind!"[10] those of the Left declared.

The Right retorted that the heavens to which Princess Kaguya returned were really too lofty to be within anyone's ken, and that since her tie with earth involved bamboo, one gathered that she was in fact of contemptible birth. She lit up her own house, yes, but her light never shone beside the imperial radiance![11] Abe no Ōshi threw away thousands and thousands in gold, and all he wanted from the fire rat's pelt vanished in a silly puff of smoke;[12] Prince Kuramochi, who knew all about Hōrai, ruined his own counterfeit jeweled branch.[13] These things, they claimed, marred the tale.

The paintings were by Kose no Ōmi and the calligraphy by

9. *The Old Bamboo Cutter* (*Taketori monogatari*) is a short, fairy-tale-like work of uncertain date. Toshikage is the hero of the first chapter of the long tenth-century romance known as *The Hollow Tree* (*Utsubo monogatari*).

10. Kaguya-hime ("Princess Brightly Shining," the heroine) is found by the old bamboo cutter as a tiny baby, inside a joint of bamboo. She has been born onto earth from the palace in the moon, and at the end of the tale she returns to the heavens after refusing many suitors, including the Emperor. The original passage starts with a line filled with familiar puns on *yo* ("age" and "joint of bamboo") and *fushi* ("passage" and, again, "joint of bamboo").

11. She never married the Emperor and shed her light over all the land.

12. An incident in the tale. Kaguya is courted by five suitors, to all of whom she gives such impossible tasks that they fail comically. From Abe she requires the pelt of the "fire rat," which no fire can burn. At vast expense Abe buys an alleged fire-rat pelt that goes up in smoke when she tests it.

13. Kuramochi's task was to bring back from Hōrai, a paradise mountain far out in the sea, a branch from the jewel trees that grow there. He had craftsmen make one instead, and they turned up to demand their fee just as he was presenting it to Kaguya-hime.

Ki no Tsurayuki.[14] The whole was on utility paper backed by Chinese brocade, with a red-violet cover and a rosewood roller— a quite common mounting.[15]

"Now, Toshikage," the Right proclaimed, "was over- whelmed by mighty winds and waves that swept him off to un- known realms, but he still got where he wanted to go, spread knowledge of his wonderful mastery through foreign lands as well as our own, and achieved the fame to which he had so long aspired: that is the story the tale tells, and the way the paintings include both China and Japan, and all sorts of fascinating inci- dents, too, makes them incomparable."[16] The work was on white paper with a green cover and a yellow jade roller. It fairly sparkled with stylishness, since the paintings were by Tsunenori and the calligraphy by Michikaze.[17] The Left had no reply.

Next, *Tales of Ise* was matched against *Jōsanmi*,[18] and again the decision was hard to reach. This time, too, the Right's work was bright and amusing, and its scenes of a world familiar to them all, starting with pictures of the palace itself, made it the more pleasingly attractive.

> *"In rank ignorance of the great Sea of Ise's magnificent depths*
> *must the waves now wash away words thought merely old and dull?"[19]*

14. Kose no Ōmi, a painter active in the first two decades of the tenth century, was the son of the famous Kose no Kanaoka. Ki no Tsurayuki (died 946) was the most influential poet at the early-tenth-century court.

15. The mountings of the Left are in the red range, those of the Right in the range of green or blue. The same pattern appears in the poetry contest of 960 (see the chapter introduction) as well as in the colors of the two divisions (Left for "Chinese" pieces, Right for "Korean") of the *bugaku* dance repertoire.

16. During his wanderings, which took him as far as Persia, Toshikage gained ultimate mastery of the koto.

17. Both figures belong roughly to the present of this scene. The painter Tsunenori lived from 946 to 967 and the great calligrapher Ono no Michikaze from 894 to 966.

18. *Tales of Ise* (*Ise monogatari*) is a tenth-century classic, the influence of which is visible in *Genji* itself. *Jōsanmi* has been lost.

19. "Must those who champion the modern, and who know nothing of the ex- cellence of *Tales of Ise* [Ise is by the sea], now consign the work to oblivion?" Narihira (below) is the central figure of the work.

Hei objected lamely. "Is Narihira's name to be demeaned by tales of common licentiousness tricked out in pretty colors?"

Daini replied,

> "To the noble heart that aspires to soar aloft, high above the clouds,
> depths of a thousand fathoms appear very far below."[20]

"Whatever splendid ambitions the Guardsman's Daughter[21] may have entertained," Fujitsubo declared, "the name of Narihira is not to be despised.

> At first glance, indeed, all that may seem very old, but despite the years
> are we to heap scorn upon the fisherman of Ise?"[22]

The ladies' passionate arguments sustained an interminable debate over every scroll. Meanwhile the younger ones, who really had no idea what it was all about, were dying just for a look at them, but none of them, either Fujitsubo's or Akikonomu's, saw anything at all, because Fujitsubo kept them well hidden.

Genji joined them. "We may as well decide victory and defeat before the Emperor himself," he said, pleased by the spirit with which each speaker put her case. That had in fact been his idea all along, which is why he had kept some exceptional works in reserve; and among these, for reasons of his own, he had placed his two scrolls of Suma and Akashi.

Tō no Chūjō was no less keen. It was all the rage in those days to make up amusing paintings on paper,[23] and despite

20. "*Jōsanmi* is far superior in theme to *Tales of Ise*." The hero of *Jōsanmi* is apparently summoned to high station ("high above the clouds") by the Emperor, making Narihira's adventures seem contemptible in comparison.

21. Apparently the heroine of *Jōsanmi*.

22. On Narihira. Fujitsubo's poem plays on words associated with love and with the sea, and its defense of the exiled Narihira implies a defense of the recently exiled Genji.

23. *Kamie,* paintings to go into handscrolls, as opposed to paintings for screens or sliding partitions. "Make up" refers to mounting as well as to painting the work.

Genji's warning that it would not be in the spirit of things to do new ones now, and that they should keep to the ones they already had, Tō no Chūjō went to great lengths to prepare a secret room where he put his painters to work.

When Retired Emperor Suzaku heard of this, he gave paintings to Akikonomu. To scrolls by several old masters, showing delightful scenes from the round of annual festivals, on which the Engi Emperor had left comments in his own hand, and to others that he himself had had done of signal events of his own reign, he added one painted under his own close supervision by Kinmochi,[24] depicting the rite in the Great Hall of State that had so captivated him on the day when she went down to Ise as Priestess. They were dazzling works. Their lovely openwork aloeswood box, with its equally pretty gift knots, was in the height of fashion. The message with it was delivered orally by a Palace Guards officer in service with Suzaku. On the awesomely solemn scene that showed the High Priestess's palanquin beside the Great Hall of State, he had written simply,

> *"Yes, as I am now, the sacred rope keeps me out, but that does not mean*
> *I could one instant forget all I felt then in my heart."*[25]

It would have been unforgivable of her not to reply, and so she overcame her reluctance to do so. She broke off a bit of the comb she had had from him then, wrapped it in light blue Chinese paper, and sent with it:

> *"It now seems to me here within the sacred rope that all things have changed,*
> *and I think back longingly to the presence of the gods."*[26]

She rewarded the messenger very handsomely.

24. Kose no Kinmochi, a contemporary of Tsunenori.
25. The "sacred rope" (*shimenawa*) alludes first to Akikonomu's priestly duty at the Ise Shrine, which removed her from him, and second to the holy precincts of the imperial palace, where she is again inaccessible.
26. "To the days when I served the gods at Ise."

His Eminence Suzaku was greatly moved to receive this, and he wished that he really could bring back the old days. He surely held a grudge against Genji in the matter—one he no doubt owed to what he himself had done. His paintings had come to him from his mother, and the Kokiden Consort must have received many of hers in the same way.[27] Oborozukiyo was extremely fond of pictures, too, and she had had a great many made for her own collection.

The day was set, and with the arrangements prettily but still lightly made, impromptu as they were, the paintings of Left and Right were presented to His Majesty. His seat was prepared in the gentlewomen's sitting room, with the two sides before him to the north and the south. The privy gentlemen sat on the Kōrōden[28] veranda, each one across from the gentlewoman he favored. On the Left, the scrolls' rosewood boxes, covered by grape-colored Chinese silk, rested on sappanwood stands placed on purple Chinese brocade. Six page girls wore cherry blossom dress gowns over red, and wisteria layerings over scarlet.[29] They looked marvelous and seemed beautifully trained. The Right's scrolls, in aloeswood boxes, rested on stands of fragrant wood set out on green Koma brocade; the design of the stands as well as the cords with which the brocade was secured to their legs was wonderfully stylish. The page girls were in dress gowns of willow and of kerria rose over green.[30] They all went to place their stands and boxes before His Majesty. His Majesty's gentlewomen were divided into two sets, front and rear, each dressed accordingly.[31]

27. His mother, the Kokiden Consort of the early chapters, was the daughter of the Minister of the Right and the elder sister of the present Kokiden Consort's mother.

28. The building immediately west of the Seiryōden, across a narrow strip of garden.

29. "Cherry blossom" designates a layering of white over scarlet; a "wisteria" layering is violet over green.

30. "Willow" is a layering of white over green; "kerria rose" is ocher over yellow.

31. The front women are dressed in red tones, the rear ones in tones more in the range of green. "Left" (red, Akikonomu) is senior to "Right" (green, Kokiden).

Genji and Tō no Chūjō were present at His Majesty's invitation. Prince Hotaru, too, was there that day. Genji must have urged him privately to come, fond as he was of painting, because no general invitation had gone out, and he was at the palace when a word from His Majesty brought him to the gathering. He served as judge. Some of the paintings were truly magnificent, and he found it impossible to decide among them. Those scenes of the four seasons, painted by the old masters so fluently and with so keen an eye, were incomparable, but their scope was limited after all, and it could not convey the full richness of mountains and waters; so that the more ephemeral modern ones, works of human understanding and of the wiles of the brush, proved just as lively and entertaining as the legacy of the past and stood out in their way. What with the debate that raged around them, Left and Right today both gave great pleasure to all.

Fujitsubo sat within the doors of the breakfast room.[32] Genji was very pleased, considering how deeply versed she must be in such things, and when the judge wavered, she often put in a word or two of her own, exactly as it was proper for her to do. The contest remained undecided on into the night.

The Left had one more turn, and when the Suma scrolls appeared, Tō no Chūjō's heart beat fast. His side, too, had saved something special for last, but this, done at undisturbed leisure by a genius at the art, was beyond anything. Everyone wept, Prince Hotaru the first among them. Genji's paintings revealed with perfect immediacy, far more vividly than anything they had imagined during those years when they pitied and grieved for him, all that had passed through his mind, all that he had witnessed, and every detail of those shores that they themselves had never seen. He had added here and there lines in running script, Chinese or Japanese, and although these did not yet make it a true diary, there were such moving poems among them that one wanted very much to see more. No one thought

---

32. The *asagarei* adjoined the gentlewomen's sitting room to the north. There were sliding panels between the two rooms.

of anything else. Emotion and delight prevailed, now that all interest in the other paintings had shifted to these. The question answered itself: the Left had won.

Dawn was coming on, and the wine cups were going round, when in a rush of feeling Genji began to talk of the past. "From my earliest youth I put my heart into my studies, and perhaps His Late Eminence believed that I might really acquire some knowledge, because he gave me a warning. He said, 'What is recognized as learning commands weighty respect, and I expect that that is why those who pursue it to excess so rarely enjoy both good fortune and long life. One born to high station, or at least to an honorable position among his peers, ought not to carry it too far.' He instructed me in the extra-academic arts, but there I was neither particularly inept nor endowed with any special gift. Painting, though, was different, because I often longed to paint to my heart's content, however odd and idle a pastime it may be, and when all at once I found that I was now a mountain rustic and saw into the truth of the mighty oceans, I rose to heights I had not dreamed of before. However, I remained dissatisfied, since there is a limit to what the brush can convey, and I could not very well have shown you these at all without a suitable occasion. I suppose I may be called conceited for doing so."

"No art or learning is to be pursued halfheartedly," Prince Hotaru replied, "but each has its professional teachers, and any art worth learning will certainly reward more or less generously the effort made to study it. It is the art of the brush and the game of Go that most startlingly reveal natural talent, because there are otherwise quite tedious people who paint or play very well, almost without training. Still, among the well-born there are some exceptionally gifted people who seem to love every art and to do wonderfully well at them all. Who among His Late Eminence's Princes and Princesses did not learn several directly from him? And he used to speak of one who most truly repaid his special attention and who mastered every art, one after the other—letters, needless to say, but the *kin* as well, for which he had a magnificent gift, and the flute, the *biwa*, and the *sō no koto*, too. No one would disagree with this appraisal, and I had therefore assumed that you toyed also with the brush, as the spirit moved you, but it is extraordinary to find that you so utterly put to shame the finest artists of the past!" His words tripped over themselves, and perhaps it was the wine that now, at this mention of His Late Eminence, brought tears to every eye.

The moon rose. It was now past its twentieth day,[33] and while the room remained in shadow, the sky was so pretty that His Majesty sent for instruments from the Library. Tō no Chūjō received the *wagon* and played almost as well as Genji himself. His Highness played the *sō no koto*, Genji the *kin*, and Shōshō the *biwa*. His Majesty also called on the best of the privy gentlemen to mark the rhythm.[34] It was perfectly lovely. As dawn came on, to the caroling of birds, the colors of flowers and faces emerged from darkness into the light of a beautiful new day. Fujitsubo provided the gifts for the musicians. Prince Hotaru again received a robe.[35]

Genji was absorbed then in deciding what to do with these paintings of his. He asked that the scrolls of the shores be presented to Fujitsubo, and when she asked to see those that came before and after them, he let her know that she would have them later, one by one. He was delighted to see His Majesty, too, so pleased with them.

With Genji looking after Akikonomu this way, Tō no Chūjō must have trembled lest his own daughter's standing suffer. However, he did not really despair, because privately he could see quite well that the Emperor, who had always been fond of her, remained devoted to her even now.

This was an extraordinarily brilliant reign, for Genji aspired to add new touches to the festivals of the court—ones that would then pass on down the generations—and he carried off in grand style even little amusements of his own. Life still seemed treacherous to him, though, and his deepest wish was surely to renounce the world after all, once he had seen His Majesty

33. At this time of the lunar month the moon rises just before dawn.
34. Probably with their batons (*shaku*) or with their folded fans.
35. Having received one already for serving as judge.

mature a little more. All the past examples he knew suggested that those who rise to dizzying heights when young do not endure. In this reign his rank and fame had risen beyond his merit. Yes, he had outlived the annihilation of his painful fall, but he still doubted that his glory would last. His desire to shut himself away in peace, so as to prepare for the life to come and perhaps to prolong this one, moved him (one gathers) to secure a quiet plot in the hills and to have a temple built there and holy texts and icons consecrated; and yet his longing to bring his children up to be what he wished them to be dissuaded him from acting promptly. It is not easy to fathom what he really meant to do.

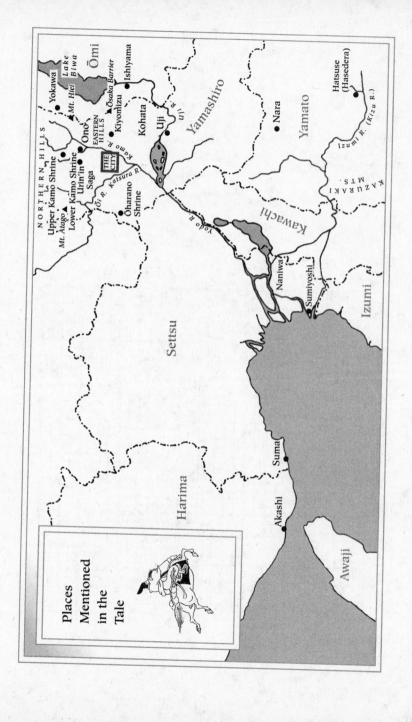

Places
Mentioned
in the
Tale

The City

1. Inner Palace
2. Eight Bureaus and Great Hall of State
3. Academy
4. Suzaku Palace
5. Reizei Palace
6. Kawara no In
7. Kōrokan

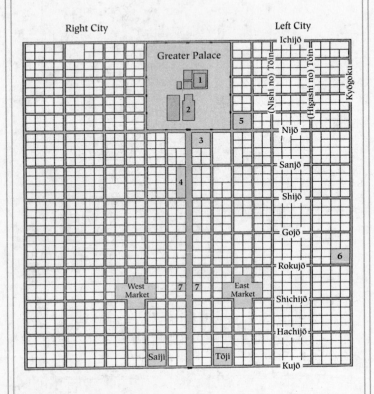

Right City   Left City

Greater Palace

1

2

5

Nijō

3

Sanjō

4

Shijō

Gojō

6

Rokujō

West Market   7   7   East Market

Shichijō

Hachijō

Saiji   Tōji

Kujō

Ichijō

(Nishi no) Tōin

(Higashi no) Tōin

Kyōgoku

The
Inner
Palace

1. Shishinden
2. Fujitsubo
3. Kokiden
4. Kiritsubo
5. Seiryōden
6. Jōneiden
7. Umetsubo
8. Tōkaden
9. Shōkyōden
10. Reikeiden
11. Kōrōden
12. Nashitsubo
13. Unmeiden and Hall
   of the Sacred Mirror
14. Crafts Workshop
15. Chamberlains' Office

north gate

orange
tree

cherry
tree

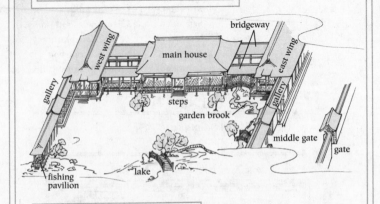

A Ranking Nobleman's House

west wing
main house
bridgeway
east wing
gallery
gallery
steps
garden brook
middle gate
gate
fishing pavilion
lake

Inside the Main House

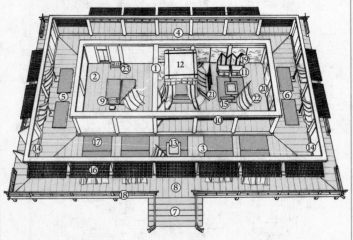

1. chamber	7. steps	13. cushion	19. screen
2. retreat	8. veranda	14. double doors	20. sliding panels
3. south aisle	9. armrest	15. *kin*	21. clothing frame
4. north aisle	10. blinds (rolled up)	16. lattice shutter	22. standing curtain
5. west aisle	11. cabinet	17. mat	23. two-tiered shelf
6. east aisle	12. curtained bed	18. railing	

Further Reading

Bowring, Richard. *Murasaki Shikibu: "The Tale of Genji."* Landmarks of World Literature. Cambridge: Cambridge University Press, 1988.

——, trans. *The Diary of Lady Murasaki.* New York: Penguin, 1999.

Field, Norma. *The Splendor of Longing in "The Tale of Genji."* Princeton: Princeton University Press, 1987.

Kamens, Edward, ed. *Approaches to Teaching Murasaki Shikibu's "The Tale of Genji."* New York: Modern Language Association, 1993.

McCullough, William H. "Japanese Marriage Institutions in the Heian Period." *Harvard Journal of Asiatic Studies* 27 (1967).

Morris, Ivan. *The World of the Shining Prince: Court Life in Ancient Japan.* Various editions.

Nickerson, Peter. "The Meaning of Matrilocality: Kinship, Property, and Politics in Mid-Heian." *Monumenta Nipponica* 48:4 (1993).

Shirane, Haruo. *The Bridge of Dreams: A Poetics of "The Tale of Genji."* Stanford: Stanford University Press, 1987.

Tyler, Royall. "'I Am I': Genji and Murasaki." *Monumenta Nipponica* 54:4 (1999).

FOR THE BEST IN PAPERBACKS, LOOK FOR THE

In every corner of the world, on every subject under the sun, Penguin represents quality and variety—the very best in publishing today.

For complete information about books available from Penguin—including Penguin Classics, Penguin Compass, and Puffins—and how to order them, write to us at the appropriate address below. Please note that for copyright reasons the selection of books varies from country to country.

In the United States: Please write to *Penguin Group (USA), P.O. Box 12289 Dept. B, Newark, New Jersey 07101-5289* or call 1-800-788-6262.

In the United Kingdom: Please write to *Dept. EP, Penguin Books Ltd, Bath Road, Harmondsworth, West Drayton, Middlesex UB7 0DA.*

In Canada: Please write to *Penguin Books Canada Ltd, 90 Eglinton Avenue East, Suite 700, Toronto, Ontario M4P 2Y3.*

In Australia: Please write to *Penguin Books Australia Ltd, P.O. Box 257, Ringwood, Victoria 3134.*

In New Zealand: Please write to *Penguin Books (NZ) Ltd, Private Bag 102902, North Shore Mail Centre, Auckland 10.*

In India: Please write to *Penguin Books India Pvt Ltd, 11 Panchsheel Shopping Centre, Panchsheel Park, New Delhi 110 017.*

In the Netherlands: Please write to *Penguin Books Netherlands bv, Postbus 3507, NL-1001 AH Amsterdam.*

In Germany: Please write to *Penguin Books Deutschland GmbH, Metzlerstrasse 26, 60594 Frankfurt am Main.*

In Spain: Please write to *Penguin Books S. A., Bravo Murillo 19, 1° B, 28015 Madrid.*

In Italy: Please write to *Penguin Italia s.r.l., Via Benedetto Croce 2, 20094 Corsico, Milano.*

In France: Please write to *Penguin France, Le Carré Wilson, 62 rue Benjamin Baillaud, 31500 Toulouse.*

In Japan: Please write to *Penguin Books Japan Ltd, Kaneko Building, 2-3-25 Koraku, Bunkyo-Ku, Tokyo 112.*

In South Africa: Please write to *Penguin Books South Africa (Pty) Ltd, Private Bag X14, Parkview, 2122 Johannesburg.*